the ASCENDANT FEW

BOOK FOUR *of* REVIVAL OF THE FALL

STELLA HOPE

Print ISBN: 979-8-9918400-6-4

Ebook ISBN: 979-8-9918400-7-1

Book Cover by MiblArt

Copy editing by Laura Josephsen

First edition.

Pronunciation Guide

Characters

Cerys: "Kehr-ihz"
Creiddylad: "Cree-thil-ahd"
Gwenddoleu ap Ceidio: "Gwen-tho-lay ap Key-dio"
Gwyn: "Gwen"
Llefelys: "Th-vel-as"
Nudd Llaw Eraint: "Nee-th"; the "th" sound is soft. "Thau-Errent"

Creatures

Afanc: "Avank"
Bukavac: "Boo-kah-vats"
Dullahan: "Dule-a-han"
Gwyllgi: "Gwith-gi"
Likho: "Leek-ho"
Púca: "Poo-ka"
Xolotl: "shuh·luht"

<u>Other</u>

Arawn: "Arr-own," close to saying "Our own," the king of the Otherworld in Welsh mythology

Annwn: "An-noon," the Otherworld in Welsh mythology

Sláinte: "Slawn-che," Irish way of saying "Cheers!"

CONTENT WARNINGS

This book contains material that some readers may find disturbing or triggering. Please review the following content warnings before proceeding:

- Fantasy violence typical of the genre

- Suicide

- Profanity

- Depictions of depression and mental health struggles

- Sexual content (spice level 1.5 out of 5)

- Dissociative episodes

- Death of characters

Please proceed with caution. Your mental health is incredibly important!

CONTENTS

Chapter One

Make it Make Sense

Seren

The smoke had already begun to clear by the time Seren emerged from the unmarked SUV.

To mundane emergency crews, it would appear to be a mundane explosion. The French authorities would conclude that a minor leak from the farm's propane tank had ignited into a devastating fire, claiming only one life. A few well-placed illusions would ensure that the news would spread the lie by morning.

Magic had to be hidden. Even when it cost a seated member of the French Assembly's life.

Seren stood at the edge of the Montsauche copse, her coat fluttering gently in the spring breeze. She was careful not to step on shards of scattered glass as her boots crunched over gravel and burned leaves. The countryside was no place for heels, but she had an image to maintain.

Thibaut Robail's corpse lay with limbs splayed at awkward angles, the scorch marks of his magic surrounding him in a perfect circle of destruction. Nearby were twenty more bodies, half-destroyed and burned to a crisp, their wings either folded beneath them or shattered. The fight must have been magnificent to witness; Thibaut had lasted until the final one fell.

Only after seeing the other casualties did the English expression Seren was searching for come back to her. *Two birds with one stone.*

Thibaut was a strong mage. That power had been his undoing. Yet he had died a warrior; he deserved her respect.

Again and again the International Assembly voted for their own destruction. They voted for the hard way of fixing the problem, which would tear civilization apart if something didn't change immediately. So Seren took it upon herself to make a solution.

As she leaned over to brush a lock of hair from Thibaut's eyes, she heard a soft footfall behind her. It was one of the field operatives from the Assembly's Paris Corded Brotherhood. The woman wore clothes more suited to the countryside, but her aura was all combat readiness and barely suppressed grief.

With arms tightly crossed, she accused, "You expected this." Though she stood perfectly still, there was a waver in her voice. "But you didn't stop him."

"He made a choice," Seren replied without turning. "His final one."

"You could have ordered him."

"I *could* have ordered him. But then we would be covering up the slaughter of an entire town instead of one corpse!" Seren did turn around then, raising an eyebrow. "*You* could have joined him in the fight!"

The woman's breath hitched, like she wanted to argue but couldn't find the fault in the logic. Seren shamelessly exploited the Corded Brother's guilt, ensuring her own insecurities prevented her from fully considering the predicament Thibaut had found himself in at his end.

Seren was cold because the world required it. The safety of the many over the lives of the few. It wasn't cruelty. It was balancing scales.

The woman's eyes flared, tear-bright and furious. "We didn't think it was this bad."

"None of you do until someone else dies!" Seren snapped.

"You're a monster."

"I've been called worse." Seren stepped forward, past the scorch circle that delineated one man's final stand against true monsters.

A quiet whimper startled them both. Seren turned sharply, hand half-raised in reflex before she saw the source.

A teenager—no, younger. Maybe eleven. She was hunched, trembling, holding a phone in her hand like it could ward off spirits. Thibaut's daughter. The girl had likely hidden as instructed when Thibaut had sounded the alarm. Smart. She had her father's stubbornness in the set of her face.

The girl studied Seren like *she* was the creature who'd killed her father.

The grieving child was only half-correct.

Seren stepped closer. "I'm sorry, darling. We did not know you were with him."

The girl didn't speak. Her red-rimmed eyes glared up at Seren.

Seren crouched, careful to keep her distance. "You'll be looked after. The Assembly will see to that."

"I don't want them," the girl whispered, voice hoarse from smoke or grief. "I want *him*."

Seren's face didn't change, but something in her chest pulled tight. She knew this pain. She'd lived it.

"I know," Seren said. She stood, unable to offer comfort, yet unwilling to be cruel. "Wishing doesn't stop the world from ending. Doing something does. He did *something* important."

With the arrival of another car on the gravel road, she left the girl with the Corded Brother and the Assembly's cleanup crew. By the time she was back in her SUV, Seren's phone was already blowing up with notifications. Assembly members were demanding answers she'd already given.

She was playing the long game. The game they were too scared to acknowledge even existed. The Assembly would argue over silly things like how best to bury Thibaut, how to eulogize him. Then they'd waste hours pretending this was a tragedy no one could have predicted.

But Seren understood the truth. This had been necessary. She wasn't finished doing things the hard way, exactly as they had voted for.

It was the cost of keeping the malevolents contained. Magic required balance, and his death wasn't enough.

Thibaut had made the right move.

Sometimes being a hero meant dying when the world needed you to. And sometimes being a villain meant letting them.

Esme

The past three months had been a nonstop flurry of malevolent sightings across the tristate area, leaving every Corded Brother and unaffiliated monster hunter in Seattle stretched thin.

Sightings were so relentless that even Colin and Will started commuting from Los Angeles every other weekend to help.

For the first time in what seemed like forever, Esme and Abby had a night to themselves—no monsters, no emergencies, only the luxury of asking "How was your day?" and actually listening to the answer.

Esme wandered back into the living room, wearing her fuzzy slippers and a hoodie that had mysteriously become hers despite technically belonging to Miles. Abby was curled sideways in the armchair, blanket half-draped, legs tucked like a drowsy cat, eyelids fluttering to the windows every time she heard a siren wail or boat's horn.

Esme announced, "We're breaking into the good stuff. So sit up. You remind me of Mr. Snuffles right now, and I miss that stinky critter so much!"

Even though moving into Miles' floating house hadn't been a huge adjustment, she still missed her childhood home that had burned down on New Year's Day. Mr. Snuffles, her neighbor's moody tabby, had sauntered into her heart like he owned it. She hadn't realized how comforting he'd been until he was gone. It had her thinking that maybe they should get a cat.

Miles and Gwyn had been gone for two hours, off chasing something eating dogs north of town. The insult was clearly personal, as they'd brought Lily and Cerys for the kill. Despite trusting them to handle it alone, Esme couldn't stop herself from checking the front door every few minutes like a golden retriever waiting anxiously for their person to arrive home after work.

Esme opened the cabinet above the sink. Doctor Healthy only had two bottles stashed there. One was a bottle of bourbon they'd sampled down to the last drops and the other was his favorite sloe gin that was difficult to get in the States. She reached for the familiar purple one.

"Sloe gin?" she called over her shoulder. "This one isn't as sweet as our American version, but it's tasty!"

Abby didn't even look up. "Miles will brood."

"Let him." Esme grinned. "I can guilt-trip his dad into sending us more."

James Goodwin had been kind from the start. Their meme-fueled bond had only grown over time. Esme was still working on getting Miles' mother to warm up to her, but that seemed to be on the upswing too.

Esme returned with two mismatched glasses and a pair of crinkly popcorn bags, balancing them like peace offerings. Their evening wasn't about putting on airs. It was about togetherness, free from any disturbances. Covering her legs, Esme tugged the blanket she'd attempted to knit while in her "coping via crafts" phase.

Abby took the drink without comment, eyeing it for a beat before taking a sip. "A bit sour." She made a face. "But it's growing on me. Who knew Miles had good taste in alcohol?"

Sipping, they fell into a familiar hush born of shared grief and the quiet strength carrying it required. As the city tucked in for the night, only the random bouts of hail created by the nearby mountains interrupted the hush as it tapped at the windows. It wasn't exactly awkward, but the silence was heavy with the unspoken emotions that bound them. A conversation hung in the air, yet both women hesitated to begin it.

Words can intimidate even the most fearless of monster hunters.

Esme leaned her head back and closed her eyes for a moment. "Remember that night after Leon?"

When she looked up, Abby's expression mirrored that of someone who'd bitten into a rotten apple. After a long pause, Abby said hesitantly, "Yeah."

"I keep replaying that night," Esme said. "We all sat there with our past lives hanging over our heads, and no one said a damn thing about it. And then... we just returned to life like we weren't suddenly new people. Like we weren't all suffering from a massive existential crisis."

Esme studied Abby. She was staring off into space, eyes, lips, jaw all tight.

"The trauma was fresh... and you can't exactly tell a therapist about reincarnation. Even a mage," Esme said quietly. "I think I'm ready to talk about it now. Are you?"

Abby let out a breath. "I don't even know where to start, bestie."

Being the more emotionally volatile of the two, Esme accepted her role as the initial unloader in their friendship. Sometimes that was necessary. Sometimes one person had to lay all of their cards out on the table so the other person felt comfortable doing the same thing.

"Sometimes I think it's all bullshit. It's trauma, magic, adrenaline, and a sprinkle of hallucination." Esme pulled her legs up and held the glass to her chest like a shield. "Then Miles wakes up talking about Elena and I'm like, 'Okay, but did they boink yet?'"

Abby snorted. A smile passed between them, but it was short-lived.

"I'm still too chicken to ask Gwyn if I can take a peek inside his head to see more of what Creiddylad was like," Abby admitted. "I know they got busy, but Gwyn gave the impression that

Elena and Nudd never sealed the deal. Star-crossed lovers and all that... Sad."

Esme couldn't respond right away–it was too real. She took another sip to bolster herself and said, "Elena and Nudd sounded so lonely. How can you be together for, what, twenty years, maybe more, and never give in to your feeling for each other? I've been thinking about that a lot lately."

"I get the impression that Gwyn was lonely, too." Abby took a long sip, then met Esme's gaze. "Can't blame him after watching Leon kill Creiddylad slash me, *whatever*."

"Do you ever wonder if it wasn't an accident? That we were meant to find each other again—now, in this time, in these bodies?" Esme leaned her head back on the couch to stare up at the ceiling. "I feel like we were."

A bit wobbly on her feet after her second pour, Abby moved over to sit next to Esme on the couch. "If it's a cosmic joke, it's an intricate one."

Relaxed now, Esme reached out and swung her arm over Abby's shoulder. "I've missed you... To emotionally responsible reincarnated girlfriends, version two-point-zero."

"I missed you, too." Abby clinked her glass against Esme's and downed the rest in one go. "Three-point-oh. The wisdom gained from two lifetimes elevates us beyond stage two."

"That Irish poet gene really kicks in when you drink, huh?"

"Don't tell Finn." Abby groaned. "If he knows, every time I see him, he'll try to get me drunk just for the thrill of it."

Their laughter wasn't carefree. It was the sound of two women desperately clinging to the remnants of normalcy with battered fingernails.

Gwyn

The creature stank of wet fur and dog's blood. It snarled once before Gwyn's blade opened its throat, thick black blood sizzling against the asphalt. By the time the body hit the ground, Miles was checking for any sign of survivors.

There weren't any.

Two hours later, Gwyn stood in Miles' living room, the kill already bagged and burned.

Months before, Gwyn had stood here, blade in hand, fighting beside a man whose magic was disturbingly like his father's. Back then, raw with betrayal and the fresh scar from the Dullahan's whip, he'd failed to see the man Miles really was.

Now, a new table, a new couch, and a new lamp replaced the ones that had broken. The state of Miles' living room wasn't far removed from the reality of the four people standing inside it. The room was patched together just like them. They were all broken, each in their own way, and all were each in the process of rebuilding themselves.

The malevolent they'd tracked had been an easy kill, one they probably could have put off. Yet the subtle decline in their partners' moods over the past few months had been harder to ignore. Miles had offered a solution by inviting him, and Gwyn had readily agreed to assist. Now, in the space of a few hours, Abby and Esme already seemed more like their old selves.

"And you lot have drunk up half my stash!" The forced scowl on Miles' face wavered, and his shoulders slumped as his anger proved unconvincing, even to himself.

Abby giggled before chugging a large glass of water, and Esmeralda grinned. They were sobering up. They'd clearly had a good time while he and Miles been out on business—exactly as they'd hoped.

Gwyn paused as he moved to sit on the couch. Over a year had passed since he'd awoken in this time, his past half a mystery, half a source of murderous frustration. Now, he knew the truth was possibly far worse.

Abby moved to sit on the floor in front of him, seeking comfort in her own way. She leaned into his touch as he lightly massaged her shoulders. Looking up, she said, "Babe, you look like you're about to stab someone."

He offered a mild, "Wouldn't be the first time."

She laughed, though he hadn't meant for it to be a joke. Lost in thought, in the past, in the present, he barely registered his own words.

His poetic side, the part of communication that modernity seemed to have forgotten, often came to the forefront in times like these—when something heavy was waiting in the wind. So Gwyn couldn't help but think of Esme's exhale as a burning ember drifting on the breeze, waiting to catch a piece of dry tender.

She reached for a bottle of water and took a long drink. "It's time to deal with our shared existential crisis out in the open."

As Elena, Esme had worn armor. Now, her primary defense was her words.

Miles rubbed his temples, as if trying to press Nudd's memories back into the recesses of his mind. He said lightly, "I'm gonna need a drink for this." He reached for the bottle and poured one for himself and another for Gwyn.

Gwyn's thumb traced the rim of his glass, a nervous habit left over from a time when avoiding poison was a prince's first lesson in politics. The tart sweetness of the berries, laced with the faint bitterness of herbs, evoked memories of another time, a time that had led them to this moment.

In truth, he was stalling. "Abigail, Esmeralda, I..."

His unfinished sentence hung in the air, heavy with unspoken truths and evasions. Noticing the subtle shift in his posture, Abby nudged him. "You're brooding."

"I'm considering," he corrected.

"Same thing," Esme added under her breath.

He intended to offer them an apology for not speaking the truth of their pasts sooner, but he couldn't because he wasn't sorry that he hadn't. And, of course, there was another part he hadn't told them—any of them. The part where a god had, in fact, assigned a leprechaun, of all people, to remind Gwyn of the deal he'd made with the king of the Otherworld for Elena's and Creiddylad's souls.

A deal he had no memory of. Not of the transaction, the stipulations, or, worst of all, the price.

Miles dragged a hand down his face. "Let's just... try to make sense of this."

More talk. As if words could put the pieces of who they were and who they'd just learned they used to be together. Gwyn was a born skeptic. This modern world was too soft, too loud, too full of things he still didn't understand.

And yet, he'd made a bargain to return to it.

Maybe he was being unreasonable, maybe words would help. And time.

Abby broke the silence. "I mean, I knew something was off. But this? That's a hell of a thing to drop on someone after nearly getting murdered, guys."

Esme snorted. "Tell me about it." Her gaze flicked to Miles.

His grip tightened around his glass at her words, but he said nothing, his jaw flexing with unspoken guilt. For a few weeks before their fight with Leon, Miles had known the secret of their pasts, but he had *also* kept it from both of them.

"So, neither of you are going to say anything?" The intensity of Esme's stare on both men was nearly lethal. She gestured between herself and Abby. "We're your dead exes in new bodies," Esme said flatly. "And you thought not telling us was the polite option?"

Miles raised a hand. "Technically, I'm sort of in that same category. So…"

How Nudd, now Miles, fit into all this was still a mystery. They weren't certain if Miles was Gwyn's father reincarnated or not. While Abby and Esme lacked all memory of their prior lives, Miles had nightly dreams about Nudd's life. On top of that, he seemed to have access to some of Nudd's powers. So… different.

The collective gaze swung to Gwyn.

He could tell them. He *should* tell them about what Finn had said.

But that terrible boiling-acid-in-the-gut feeling he got every time he thought about Arawn, the king of the Otherworld, held him back. Even now, Gwyn felt the phantom weight of that god's gaze on his back, a cold dread that lingered half a world away from his homeland.

Saying something prematurely would only add to their worries, and they had a mountain of them already. He wouldn't say anything until he understood more himself.

"I don't know how it happened!" Gwyn began, shifting forward and placing his arms on his knees. "None of you are the people you once were, not really. I'm not even the same man, and, as far as I know, I have not died. You all have years of *your* life, your choices, your experiences."

Gwyn shrugged. "That's why I wasn't certain about any of you. Nudd was far less relaxed than Miles. Elena was far more structured and quick to temper than Esmeralda. Creiddylad, greatly restrained and timid compared to Abigail. You *are* different. I apologize that I don't know how it happened, but we're here now."

He had to change the conversation to one more productive, to something that had been on his mind of late.

"Things are getting worse with the malevolents." Gwyn shifted again, uncomfortable with his intuition. "I feel like we're standing on a cliff edge, and none of us can see how far the drop is."

Abby frowned. "Are you saying you think we're in danger?"

"I think we don't know enough to say we aren't. Leon knew who we were. We all thought I was the only one to have been released by one of the malevolent prisons. But he was here *for years*. And he came searching *for us*."

That settled over them like a falling stone.

Esme scoffed. "Oh, fan-fucking-tastic. Love that for us."

"Now feels like the right time—yes, I mean that sarcastically—to bring up the fact that Leon's remains went missing," Miles said with a weary grimace.

"Like, gone-gone?" Esme asked.

Miles' shoulders raised, then lowered. "Without a trace."

Esme gave voice to everyone's thoughts. "What the fuck? Why?"

Miles shrugged again. "Strange." His truthful, one-word reply was troubling.

"That's not strange. That's terrifying," Abby muttered.

"Screw Leon, may he rot in... Wait, Gwyn is there a hell for ancient Welsh dudes?" Esme asked.

"No," Gwyn replied. "No eternal torment."

"Damn." Esme raised her glass. "Then, to not letting ancient drama ruin a good thing! All of this is bizarre, but I'm glad I'm going through it with you."

A genuine grin spread across Abby's face as she clinked glasses with her. "Hear, hear."

Miles followed, hesitant. Gwyn shook his head but raised his glass nonetheless.

Gwyn tried to exhale some of his worries and looked around the room at the three people who had fought beside him, bled beside him. At the two dogs cuddling in a corner. They weren't who they used to be. Neither was he. But that didn't mean they weren't something new.

What the future held was another matter entirely.

Tomorrow, maybe a god would come knocking. Maybe the past would catch up to them with fangs bared. Given the leprechaun's continued involvement, whether things would get better or worse was up in the air.

Chapter Two

The Inky Tendrils of Fate

Esme

At the Sanctuary of Spirits, regulars knew the seat in front of the garnish station was one of last resort. The cramped space, along with the lingering scent of bitter orange zest, muddled mint, and the cloying sweetness of maraschino cherries that clung to everything within a three-foot radius—it was a sensory assault and a logistical nightmare for both bartender and guest. So when Maureen Mitchell claimed that spot, Esme's internal alarm bells started ringing.

With a flick of her fingers, Esme summoned a sticky pint glass. It skidded across the bar top and into her hand. The sour tang of stale hops hit her nose as she caught it with a practiced motion. Nope, she decided, not tonight. She was not going to fight with Maureen. She'd let anything Maureen said go and move on.

Three months later, Esme was still reeling from it all. The emotional fallout, the fires, the betrayals—it all lingered like smoke in her lungs.

Revelations, as it turned out, came with consequences.

Her house had burned to the ground, forcing her to move in with Miles permanently, along with Lily, who had appointed herself Esme's furry emotional support system. It wasn't the fact that the paintings her mother had made were ruined or even the ashes leftover from her childhood stuffed animals that bothered her most. It was the betrayal.

Sylas, misunderstood and maligned, had tried to protect them, especially the most vulnerable in their community. While Leon, smiling, affable Leon, had orchestrated the whole murderous scheme.

And as if the ancient Welsh soap opera unfolding around them wasn't enough, Finn had decided to drop their shared mythological baggage straight into Jacob's lap. The information had sent him spiraling down a path of obsessive research. He barely slept, ordered every single piece of literature on the subject, from *The Mabinogion* to scholarly articles on the Welsh afterlife, and muttered constantly about "breaking the laws of magic."

Meanwhile, Abby and Gwyn were practically cohabiting, still debating whether to set up house in his cramped downtown apartment that was right next to her work or her cozy space with more room but a longer commute. Throughout this, there was one constant: Finn hadn't changed at all.

Esme took a deep breath, squared her shoulders, and plastered on a smile, ready to play nice with Maureen. She waved as she finished the cocktail she was working on. Recently, the powerful evocation mage and Esme had been getting along surprisingly well, a change from the past when Maureen's hateful bullying, because of Esme's demon blood, had made things unbearable between them. So maybe this interaction wouldn't be so bad.

Esme was psyching herself up to take Maureen's order next when a newcomer walked in and claimed the spot directly next to her former nemesis. Esme froze mid-step, then pivoted smoothly to polish a glass she'd already cleaned twice. Esme might have brushed it off as a friend dropping by because Maureen and the newcomer were about the same age, but Esme didn't miss the way Maureen's expression changed.

Maureen Mitchell, outwardly prim and proper but inwardly venomous and icy, stiffened in fear. As she clutched her glass, her knuckles whitened, and her face lost color. Even a tray of the world's best chocolates wouldn't have been able to distract Esme from eavesdropping on *that* conversation.

Maureen Mitchell was not afraid of people.

Maureen's companion was the picture of understated wealth with an edge, like old money dipped in danger. Her black cashmere cardigan, dress slacks, and impeccably styled light brown hair were traditionally professional in every way. But the tattoo of a detailed serpent, its scaled body wrapping around her neck like a living choker, and ears full of expensive-looking piercings gave her appearance an edge that Esme couldn't help but admire.

Hands now clasped too tightly in front of her, Maureen stood and greeted the other woman. Esme grabbed a rag and made her way down the bar, wiping surfaces that didn't need cleaning. She detected a subtle European accent in the stranger's voice, vaguely reminiscent of Gwyn but softer, perhaps from somewhere near France.

Esme missed the woman's name but caught onto the conversation mid-sentence thanks to her improved cambion hearing.

"—because it's my first visit," the woman was saying. "Though I see some people remain consistent."

"—hardly the most welcoming climate," Maureen muttered, her expression carefully neutral.

The other woman hummed, tipping her head as though amused. "That's a matter of perspective. Adaptation can be... messy."

Esme reached their section of the bar, noting how Maureen was fidgeting. Leaning against the bar, she flashed her usual work-friendly smirk. "Hello! I'm Esme. Can I get you ladies anything?"

With a cursory glance and a mumbled, "The usual," Maureen kept her attention wholly on the other woman. Catching herself, Maureen added, "Esme, this is Seren. She's... visiting."

"A pleasure," Seren said, studying the drink menu. When she looked up, Seren's gaze on Esme triggered an instinctive warning in her gut. "I'll try 'The Last Word.'"

"That's my favorite!" Esme said brightly, trying to shake off the strange sinking feeling. "Okay, I'll have those out in just a—"

Something about the way Seren looked at her as she said it made the hair on Esme's neck prickle. Or maybe that was—

The air shifted—sudden, nauseating, *wrong*.

The fine hairs on Esme's arms rose, a crawling sensation creeping down her spine. A sickening, wrong cold slithered from less than ten feet away, making the temperature plummet. Esme felt the distinctive magical signature that harbingered trouble of the tooth-and-claw variety.

Malevolent magic. In her bar. In front of *civilians.* If anything happened to the Sanctuary—her sanctuary—she'd never forgive herself.

She didn't know why she was surprised. Three months into the new year, they'd already endured more fights against malevolents than in all the preceding year.

Esme tensed, calculating the best way to act without drawing attention. She watched both women stiffen in recognition.

"Brr," Esme said loudly, shivering for effect. "Do you feel that? Must've left one of the refrigerators open in the back."

Fuck, fuck, fuck.

Maureen's gaze snapped to hers, sharp and knowing. Seren let out a sigh, not of fear or shock, but sounding like something close to resignation.

"Maureen." Seren's voice was barely above a whisper, but it carried the kind of authority that expected immediate compliance. "Weave an illusion of normalcy around the empty table to my left. Thank all the magic that it's not busy in here. Whatever is coming out is small. I'm slowing its emergence." Her violet eyes, starting to fill with shadows, locked onto Esme's. "I see that you know about our situation. Grab a towel and be ready to act if my aim is off."

Esme's mind reeled. The woman was aware of the malevolents. And she was slowing its emergence? *How?* Beyond that, she was clearly accustomed to unquestioning obedience.

Before Esme could decide if she should carry out the stranger's orders, she found herself moving.

She darted to the bar and grabbed the largest towel she could find, along with a mop bucket. By the time she reached the empty table, the feeling of Maureen's magic around her was strangely blunted, as if something or someone was cutting off everyone's perception of the magic being cast.

Who was this woman?

Esme had only witnessed a few malevolent emergences with her own eyes before that moment. They had been violent and fast. This was altogether different.

The same cold was there, chilling her feet through her shoes. The same wrong, nauseating feeling of malevolent magic was there too. But Seren's intervention had slowed its emergence and weakened it.

Sprawled beneath the table on the bar floor, the creature appeared dazed and immobile. It had skin that was more green than brown, needle-sharp fangs, a heavy brow, and sparse tufts of black hair sprouting from its head. Though small enough to be a child, it radiated malevolent magic and was damned mean.

Whatever magic Seren was working on it was powerful. The creature's feeble attempt to hiss and lunge at Esme resulted in a slow, awkward flop onto the floor. Esme averted her gaze. Staring would only make people more aware of the impossible event unfolding right before their eyes. *Double fuck.*

Esme nervously scanned the room, but the chattering, laughing patrons were oblivious. A selkie and a human man, the nearest couple, leaned in close to each other, blissfully unaware of the supernatural danger so near. Maureen's illusion was holding—for now.

Thank goodness it was after food service hours. Wexley, the Sanctuary of Spirit's púca chef, sensed malevolent magic even if he didn't know that monsters were a true possibility. He would have had a coronary event had he been serving somewhere nearby. Esme's immediate instinct was to squish the nasty goblin thing with her heel, but she held back, feeling a second surge of magic around the creature.

The shadows along the edges of the table moved as she pretended to be cleaning up a mess with the broom. Tentacles of inky blackness, stinking with the scent of brimstone, slithered up from the floor.

Esme barely stifled a gasp. The tentacles—they looked exactly like her infernal creations. Like her conjured blades, like her summoned shadowcat, but most of all like her eldritch abomination. Seeing her most private magic, perfected by a stranger's hands, chilled her in a way that went deeper than mere recognition.

Three strikes of the tentacles were all it took, flawlessly executed: one down the creature's throat to silence it, two through its nostrils to end it, one wrapped across its arms and legs to bind it. It thrashed weakly, trying to claw and bite down on the tentacles. Within seconds, its struggles weakened and finally ceased.

Snapping back to reality, Esme felt the sweat beading on her back and her rapid heartbeat.

That was... holy hell. What had she just witnessed?

Esme forced herself to move, to act like everything was normal. Fighting the urge to stand there, she wrapped the goblin in the towel, making it appear like she was soaking up a mess. Esme glanced at Maureen, whose hands trembled slightly as sweat beaded along her hairline, her eyes slightly narrowed in concentration. While Seren examined her nails as if waiting for Maureen to finish her thought, not the least bit ruffled. Esme tossed the body into the mop bucket, its wheels squeaking in protest as she shouldered her way through the swinging kitchen doors.

The corpse was a problem for later. Figuring out who the hell Seren was had become Esme's immediate priority.

As she exited the kitchen, Seren was waiting, already smoothing her elegant coat and leaving money on the table.

"Enough bullshit for what was supposed to be a relaxing night," Seren muttered to Maureen, then added with a slight nod to Esme, "Passable. Let's see if you survive."

Esme scowled. The door's magic hadn't finished buzzing with Seren's exit before Esme was back at Maureen's side. "What the hell was that? Who is she? *Passable*?" With each question, her voice climbed an octave higher.

"That," Maureen said, gesturing with her glass, "was some sort of test for both of us. You passed." She pushed away from the bar. "Barely."

Maureen exhaled, draining the last of her drink while standing. "Could've been worse, Charity Case. She's... not someone you want to cross," Maureen said tightly. The glance she cast at the door wasn't fearful; it was reverent in the way one might show a vengeful god.

And, for once, her words contained no venom; only a weary sigh hinted that Seren hadn't finished with any of them.

Gwyn

Across town, a very different scene was unfolding.

Exasperated, Gwyn was nearly ready to give up trying to pry information from the uncooperative leprechaun. He decided to make a final attempt.

"Four months ago, you stood on the deck of the ferry and said that we had 'work to do.' Three months ago, you told me that I made a bargain with Arawn. But you haven't said anything more about that agreement since. Precisely *how* does your inaction fulfill your duty to remind me of the cost of Arawn's favor?"

A strange dread overcame him whenever he heard the god's name. Although his memories of his time as a demigod had been erased, unsettling emotions tied to the king of the Otherworld remained. Arawn was one of the most powerful of the Welsh gods. So he told himself that it was wise to be afraid.

Finn threw his arms up in the air. "It's not like I can communicate with him, lad!"

"No, you've just waited around for however many hundred years doing whatever pleased you!"

The leprechaun had the audacity to grin! An answering, simmering violence pulsed beneath Gwyn's skin.

"Because I can tell you're fit to burstin' with rage," Finn spat. "Here's some truth: I popped outta one of those prisons the same as you. Just a long time ago."

Of course, Gwyn had suspected that Finn was like him, that Finn had also been dumped from a magical prison to more than a millennium into the future. So this truly wasn't news, but it was a start. Gwyn ground his teeth. "Keep talking."

"Lad... I don't even know about the bargain yet! The big man is still hangin' around on the other side of that threshold—yes, the one between life and death. So I also gotta see how this is gonna play out. We need to be focusin' on gettin' everyone trained up, stronger, instead of worryin' on your deal with the dead king!"

Finn couldn't lie. Gwyn's mood plummeted, leaving him feeling deflated and empty. He couldn't dismiss the idea that Arawn might be selectively leaking information to the leprechaun. "You sincerely can't tell me anything?"

"I can tell you what I suspect. I can't help but think that Abigail bein' your girl was a trap to get me to find you."

"Or an incentive for you to do your job. Arawn would know a leprechaun's nature well enough," Gwyn mused. "Your people are very family-oriented."

"Too right!" Finn's cane cracked against the floor like a gunshot, the sound echoing through the apartment. It was too early for Gwyn's neighbors to be in bed, but still. "The second I knew about 'em, I was here! Don't you even *think* about sayin' anything bad about my choices!"

"By all the magic... I just complimented your species and you react like this," Gwyn scoffed. "Something else is bothering you, isn't it, imp?"

Finn still hadn't thought it was the right time to tell Abby, her mother, or brother that he was her grandfather several generations removed.

Generally speaking, Finn was cheerful and amiable. Something was going on with him. His fidgeting, shifting, and clothes-picking hinted that he was hiding something.

"Yes, something else is most grandly feckin' botherin' me," Finn ground out. "Let it slide for now, lad. Just... trust me on this."

From that statement, Gwyn made one inescapable conclusion: disaster was looming on the horizon. So what exactly was coming their way that they needed to train and get stronger for?

Miles

Every death added to the weight Miles carried, a quiet burden he bore alone to shield the others from the human cost of the malevolent problem. They knew people died, of course, but actually being there for it was something else entirely.

Gasping for breath, the tween boy before him lay in a spreading pool of his own blood. His abdomen was shredded, a gruesome mess of torn tissue and oozing body fluids. Miles would never know his name, but he'd always remember his eyes pleading with him for help—for anything.

The boy was past saving. Perhaps Nudd could have managed it, but it was doubtful. The regeneration of so many organs and so much lost blood seemed impossible, even with a demigod's power.

So Miles did what he could with a heavy heart. He allowed the warmth of his magic to stream over the boy, not a flood, but a trickle, offering only a fleeting comfort in the face of his inevitable fate. The pleasant warmth it provided was all Miles could think to do to ease his passing.

The boy's pleading eyes softened into resignation as his chest stilled, and the pulse beneath Miles' fingers faded.

A pair of claws had snuffed out a future, one bright with whatever kind of life the boy had hoped to live. This was why Miles had joined the Corded Brotherhood—to stop *this* from happening.

Gwyn had been right: the malevolent problem had shown undeniable signs of worsening since the new year had begun.

The relentless march of death through the Evergreen City cast a shadow over what should have been the season of renewal. This was the second death Miles had personally observed in the past week.

Something, somewhere, somehow, had to give. And Miles feared it would be them.

A moment to mourn, to grieve a life that could never be, to wipe away a tear that never should have fallen, was all Miles could give himself. With the boy's body in his arms, he stood and prepared to stage a more natural death scene.

Chapter Three

THE NEW BOSS

Jacob

Jacob put on his most reassuring expression. Given his inability to maintain a convincing charade for long with Seren, it might help to start their meeting pleasantly to avoid immediate conflict, even if it was inevitable. "Ms. Lewis, wonderful to see you again."

"Mr. Spencer." She paused to smile coolly at him—seeing right through his gambit, no doubt. "I am happy to visit Seattle for the first time. The city is beautiful."

"Wait until summer. There's nothing like it." Was he overdoing it? Seren was among the select few who had the power to make Jacob feel ill at ease.

The bland, impersonal environment of the Seattle Assembly headquarters, where Jacob had worked for forty-plus years, offered little comfort. He was meeting with arguably the world's most powerful person, human or otherwise. She could make his life inconvenient—at his age, inconvenience could be worse than death.

"It's already better than New York." Mischief flickered in Seren's previously cool smile. "If summer is as wonderful as you say, I might be tempted to stay."

A deep, genuine laugh rumbled up from Jacob's chest. "Let's not get ahead of ourselves, Ms. Lewis. I know as well as you do that we'll drive each other mad."

She looked him dead in the eyes and said, accent thick, "I think I can handle it."

"Ms. Lewis, I fully expect you to make that same face as you gloat over my still-warm corpse." Jacob shook his head and barely restrained himself from rolling his eyes. He didn't fear death, but he did fear leaving his people to fend for themselves before they were ready.

He sensed his blood pressure spiking. He was sure he was turning an unappealing shade of red. But he'd had enough of this farce. "I recognize my current predicament and accept the responsibility. But I draw the line at you messing with my people. Shall we get on with it, then?"

A pout almost formed on Seren's lips. "You're quite skilled at dashing a woman's hopes of engaging in a bit of verbal sparring, aren't you?"

All at once, he could feel the heat draining from his face. "Ten years of experience dealing with a forceful personality equal to yours has prepared me for this moment."

Seren Lewis relaxed in her chair. Her winter-honey-colored hair, smattering of freckles, high cheekbones, and plump lips made her an undeniably attractive woman. Jacob wasn't sure how old she was. He estimated anywhere between her early fifties and seventies or even eighties—cambions were hard to read after their thirties.

He didn't know anything about Seren until twenty years ago, when she'd suddenly appeared front and center of the international mage community. In this, he suspected political machinations were involved, similar to how a mundane political party might carefully develop a candidate over years to win a key election down the road.

His and her political ideologies were fundamentally opposed when it came to the malevolents, yet Jacob couldn't deny her effectiveness as a leader. Or her ruthlessness in protecting other mages, especially demon-blooded ones.

"Tell me about the deaths," she said, the pleasant facade crumbling, replaced by an unyielding seriousness. "Everything you've kept out of the official reports."

Seren had said she could tolerate the wait to meet the "hired help," but the notion of giving him an entire day to rehearse his answers for this meeting was simply too much. He had to be very quick-witted for his people's sake.

Jacob's lips pressed together, the corners turning down in a subtle expression of displeasure he couldn't quite mask. "The reports are comprehensive."

"Are they?" For a fleeting instant, shadows flickered in Seren's eyes as she leaned toward him. "Philip Luis, Juniper, Sylas, Leon Chan, recently David Abington—all dead. Guillermo Cruz and Maureen Mitchell nearly killed by a pishacha. Our top neuromancer in the area stripped completely of her magic. Six Dullahan corpses complete with dead stallions. A dire boar, nøkk, and a ghoul killed in this very building. Not to mention, four low-powered human mages dead within months of each other from 'increasing malevolent activity.' All with your little band of troublemakers constantly in the thick of it."

Her information was, as expected, impeccable—unfortunately.

Seren paused, a vicious smirk playing at her lips. "Not a single report mentions the leprechaun mist walking or where the hell the 'Welsh' mage who came out of nowhere leading a blasted gwyllgi is actually from, Jacob. *Do not* play these games with me."

He smiled, holding her gaze. "Those details are not pertinent to the reports, Seren."

"Fine. Then help me understand why you're choosing to keep our people blind." Her voice hardened even further. "The prisons are failing, Jacob. And Seattle seems to be the hardest hit. How many have to die before you admit you can't handle this alone?"

His actions had little to do with pride or arrogance. Everything he'd done was to keep his people's secrets safe. "And what would you have me do? Announce to every magic user who can levitate a feather that the monsters of legend are returning? How are they to fight back? You would have me create panic."

He was getting worked up now. "You would have me create monsters out of the powerful and strong-willed as they race to protect themselves and those they love. Fear clouds judgment, Seren. When magic meets poor judgment, the result is a very dangerous person!"

Seren laughed as she stood, but there was no humor in it. "More dangerous than a basilisk in downtown Portland? Good thing the O'Malley boy chose not to return to Los Angeles yet, or else you'd have had no bodies on the ground there. How long before something appears that your pet teams can't handle?"

"They're not pets," Jacob snapped. "They're the future."

"They're practically children," Seren countered, but there was something like respect in her voice. "Talented children, I'll grant you, but children nonetheless."

Weighed down by age, Jacob let out a heavy sigh. "The physically demanding nature of hunting malevolents limits the work to the young. Maureen had to give it up. That's precisely why we brought in Dr. Goodwin. He's thirty-six. Even he has only ten, maybe fifteen years left at it."

With the hunters coupling up, the increased likelihood of babies amongst them in the next decade further reduced the chances he'd have them at the Corded Brotherhood's beck and call for even that long. Parents were less likely to volunteer for dangerous assignments, and it wasn't the Brotherhood's way to force them to hurt their relationships or *day jobs.*

For a man of one hundred and six, this experience, subtle intimidation from a middle-aged woman, should have been profoundly demeaning. But Jacob was not a petty man. In the larger context, this was a small price to pay to ensure the safety of his people.

He respected Seren despite her sometimes-abrasive nature and her opposing political ideology. She had a track record of solving problems. She might even be able to help his people in ways he couldn't. So he chose cooperation instead of confrontation.

But before he could say something conciliatory, she pivoted on her heels and considered him like the viper she was. Jacob knew what was coming before she said it. "I'm very interested in your cambion conjurer. Though I have a feeling that you're keeping the true extent of her abilities back from me."

Jacob's fingers curled around the edge of his desk. He had expected this, but the reality of it still set him on edge. He needed to subtly, yet firmly, delineate the line in the sand. "Esmeralda's under my care. That's not going to change."

Seren's lips curved into a faint smile. "Perhaps, with the right guidance, her potential could blossom into something truly extraordinary."

Jacob stiffened, his protective instincts flaring. "She already is extraordinary."

He knew Seren meant no harm, not in the traditional sense, but her interest in Esme worried him. "She's exactly where she needs to be," he added carefully.

"Is she? Or are you holding her back out of fear?"

"Seren, this is becoming too personal. Are we having a professional meeting or a personal one?"

"I only want to guide her," Seren said smoothly. "With or without your cooperation."

Jacob gave her a pointed look. "Your idea of guidance is not the same as mine."

"She should be empowered."

Jacob forced himself to breathe evenly. "Esmeralda is not a weapon to be forged or a pawn to be moved. She's a young woman with a future. I won't have you turning her into a newer version of yourself."

Seren tilted her head, the predatory glint returning to her eyes. "Would that be so terrible?"

"Yes." *Let the truth land like a gavel.*

Seren walked sedately to the other side of the desk and placed a hand on his arm. The gentleness of the gesture surprised him. "I get it. I can see that you're trying to hold things together during a difficult situation. You're trying to protect your people. That's why you're still sitting in that chair."

Seren's hand dropped from his arm. "And I'll be staying for a while," she added, settling back into the seat across the desk. "Overseeing, et cetera. You understand the situation. Again, this happens with or without your cooperation."

"You have my cooperation, Seren." Jacob let out a grunt of displeasure but nodded. He had little choice. "Just be nice to my staff, please."

A slow, feline smile stretched across her face, and he could almost imagine horns sprouting from her forehead. "Oh, I will be. I'll also be testing them immediately."

Chapter Four

Necromancer

Gwyn

Gwyn felt himself floating, weightless, untethered from the weight of mortality, but saw nothing for a long, terrifying moment. The sensation was familiar, though it had been centuries since he'd last experienced it. He was transported back, not in a dream, but in the grip of a memory—one he'd thought locked away forever.

One from his ascension.

Gwyn was a passenger, watching the scene that had occurred long ago unfold for the second time through his own eyes. Such a lengthy absence had not dulled the familiarity of the immense power he knew he could wield, a sensation at once alien and yet deeply resonant with who he was. It was a freshly opened wound, a phantom reminder of everything he'd lost.

The haze of recollection cleared, allowing him to see again. It revealed a landscape recognizable and yet somehow foreign. New leaves adorned the trees, the heather was yet to bloom, and the grass below him was a vibrant fresh green of renewed life. Spring.

The sound of clashing steel and shield snapped Gwyn's attention downward. Spectral figures stalked unseen between the fighting men. Though still massive, powerful hounds, these gwyllgi, unlike their living counterparts, were as pale as death, wraithlike and silent.

The battleground beneath their spectral feet was a gruesome slurry of mud, blood, and human refuse. The combatants were mud caked, clashing with sword and shield. Their cries of fury mixed with cries of pain and grief. A familiar river ran nearby, its water turning brown with churned-up soil, blood, and a few unlucky men whose families wouldn't have a body to burn.

Gwyn recognized it. This was not his homeland of Wales. This was the River Clyde. This was Scotland.

The Battle of Arfderydd.

The memories of that time rushed back to him, terrible, unbidden. He remembered the bleakness, the despair that had consumed him in those days. As he watched the men slaughter one another, driven by more bad reasons than good, a crushing sense of futility fell on him like a leaden weight.

He had been so tired then. So very tired, weary of the fighting, of the senseless death and destruction.

His gwyllgi weaved between the combatants, untouched by blade or armor, and where they paused, the warrior fell. He felt every death as it happened.

Each life snuffed out was a pain in his chest. Frustration welled in him—at the folly of men, the senseless, wasteful cycle of slaughter. Too much grief, too much loss.

Yet each death also sent a shuddering wave through him, filling him with power even as it filled his soul with sorrow.

Gwyn had forgotten this part of himself, buried so deep beneath the layers of his humanity that it might as well have been erased.

It was cold, but not the numbing cold of infernal magic. This was aloof, detached, as if the magic itself regarded the living with a kind of aversion. With every death, he absorbed more power, becoming a reservoir of magic fed by the fallen.

The terrible truth struck him like a thunderclap: he was a necromancer.

How had he forgotten? The realization reverberated through his very soul. He had always known he could feel death when he was ascended, could guide souls, but this—what he was witnessing was different.

This was not the work of a psychopomp. This was twisting the natural order, bending it to his will.

A living dread coiled in his gut. Necromancy was not merely feared—it was the domain of those who dared to defy the gods themselves. A violation.

It was the magic of the damned. And he had wielded it.

He wanted to turn away, to deny it, but he was trapped, forced to watch as his past self gather the death magic. Gwyn ap Nudd's gaze fell upon a man surrounded by layer after layer of protective spells, placed there by mages in service to his crown.

Even with all their magical preparations, a demigod breaking the rules rendered the mortal mages' protections moot. Gwenddoleu ap Ceidio, King of the North, crumpled as the death bolt Gwyn released tore every scrap of life from his body. His guards, all those closest to him, were, to the last one, snuffed out like candles in a storm. The spectral hounds appeared instantly, sweeping away their souls in the wake of Gwyn's overwhelming power.

To stop the killing, he killed them. The logic was flawed in its most basic form.

This must be when Gwyn had taken the first step in sealing his fate to be locked away in a malevolent prison—one he was paying for nearly two thousand years later. This had to be the moment Gwyn had intervened in mortal affairs beyond his remit.

As the shock of the king's death rippled through the ranks, it broke some men and forged others in the fires of determination. The demigod's eyes turned to Myrddin Wyllt, frozen amidst the carnage, eyes wide, filled with something deeper than horror.

It was Gwyn's revelation of his true form, the well of power within his demigod body, that caused Myrddin's madness.

Gwyn remembered—remembered the hope he had placed in the prophet. He had hoped that Myrddin could shape the future, that he could guide them toward a path that might spare others from continuing the endless cycle of bloodshed.

Myrddin fled the battlefield into the forest, his mind shattered by what he had seen. This would break him. He'd seen how vulnerable, how delicately balanced between prophecy and insanity his mind was. Yet the demigod version of himself still staked everything on a hopeful vision: that Myrddin's shattered remains could be the foundation for rebuilding a better future. That his prophecies could convince the people to lay down their arms—to end the suffering.

In the present, Gwyn Newman knew the truth. All of his hope had been tragically misplaced. Myrddin's prophecies had shaped the kings of Wales for centuries, but the wars had never ended.

Because war was eternal and even demigods could be hopeless romantics.

As the dream faded, the battlefield dissolved into darkness. Gwyn awoke with a gasp, his heart hammering. He had been a *necromancer*. And somehow he had forgotten.

He should have known. There had been signs. He recalled the first incident, when the ponaturi shaman had almost ended his and Cerys' lives on the beach. A strange energy had surged through him before he'd lost consciousness. Then, to his shame, when Llefelys, when *Leon*, had died, it was the same. Five, ten, fifteen times over the past few months, it had happened again and again. And every time he'd shrugged off the energy, denying—no, *repressing*—its very existence.

Gwyn's room was dark, the only light coming from Cerys' eyes beside him. Abby had the night shift that week, so his gwyllgi could sleep in her favorite spot. Those glowing red eyes slowly turned, fixing on the foot of his bed. Gwyn followed her gaze and froze the blood in his veins.

A ghost.

Not a dream or memory. Not an illusion. The real thing. He knew it all the way down into the marrow of his bones. Although he ought to have been panicking, a strange, instinctive calm settled over him.

Its figure was unmistakably male. An eerie, perfectly white glow was all that defined its form, which was only faintly visible in the perfect darkness of his bedroom. Gwyn recognized the clothing he wore; it was the style worn by men for feasts and celebrations during his time.

He sensed he recognized the man but couldn't quite place his name.

The ghost didn't move to harm him. It showed no reaction to his waking whatsoever. When it spoke, its voice was a whisper that somehow echoed in the room. "It is time to remember more of who you are, Fair Son of the Mists."

The words were in Brythonic, the language of Gwyn's youth. Beside him, Cerys did not react at all. She simply watched the ghostly figure with mild interest, like there was nothing to be alarmed about at the foot of the bed.

Was this simply another dream? This couldn't be real. Ghosts did not walk freely among the living. They were bound to Annwn. Bound to…

Arawn.

Then the fear came—unbidden and as cold as the grave. A deep-seated dread, heavy as a tombstone, settled in his gut at the thought. This fear was personal, a memory his body couldn't quite shake even if the reason for it had been removed from his mind.

The deal. Finn had said Gwyn's fate was tied to that deal, though he couldn't yet share the details.

Gwyn pushed himself upright. "Are you from Arawn?"

The ghost inclined his head. "I am."

"Will you tell me of my deal with your king?" All those years of bluffing his way through terrifying court situations were now paying off handsomely. Gwyn's voice didn't shake. "What does the leprechaun have to do with it?"

"No." The ghost's tone sharpened. "Be easy on the Fae. He too suffered imprisonment for his audacity and is still paying for it now."

Gwyn frowned. What had Finn done? What had *he* done?

Why was Arawn being so cryptic? Gwyn exhaled, frustration bleeding into his tone. "Arawn must have sent you for more than riddles. What am I meant to do? How do I remember?"

"Your questions have been answered," the ghost said without inflection. With a slow, deliberate movement, the ghost raised one hand, palm up. A luminous orb of swirling white and burgundy light formed in his ghostly hand. "I am here as a messenger and courier."

With inhuman speed, the ghost slammed the orb into Gwyn's chest… and disappeared.

Gwyn's heart strained, a final, futile attempt to beat, before surrendering to the darkness that swallowed him whole. Thousands of miles and years from his old life, Gwyn Newman died with only Cerys as witness.

CHAPTER FIVE

PARALYSIS

Miles

"It's no problem at all, Dr. Novak. I'll be right down."

Miles sighed, returning his work phone to its holder. He stared at his untouched lunch. His stomach growled, but he slipped on his coat anyway. He hadn't exactly been excited about eating *another* salad, but skipping it entirely hadn't been part of the plan. Maybe today would be a fasting day after all.

One of his patients, Cristiano Nakamura, had presented with sudden paralysis of an arm and leg—an unusual complication, considering the man had undergone a lumbar fusion. Upper body symptoms shouldn't happen for him without significant trauma. But there'd been no accident. No fall. No clear reason.

He tapped the hand sanitizer dispenser. The familiar alcohol scent hit his nose—along with something else: the distinct reek of malevolent magic. It clung to the edges of the room, completely invisible, but unmistakable to someone trained to sense it.

He turned away for a moment, composing himself before greeting Dr. Novak, who stood by the closed curtain surrounding Nakamura's bed. It was improbable—but not impossible—that a malevolent entity was in the bed with the patient, unseen by either Novak or Nakamura. More likely, it was lingering energy, residual from a brief encounter.

But Miles doubted it was over.

"Dr. Goodwin, nice to see you," Dr. Novak greeted. "MRI's clean. No stroke, infection, or tumors, no obvious spinal impingement other than the preexisting issues that look unchanged to the radiologist."

Miles frowned. "Just to verify—no recent trauma?"

"Nothing he can recall. Happened overnight. Thought you might want to take a peek."

Miles announced himself, then opened the curtain. Cristiano was one of his regulars—a former fighter in his fifties who still looked like he could go a few rounds in the ring, despite his ongoing issues. Miles had been helping him manage the pain and maintain mobility since he'd started practicing in Seattle.

On the hospital bed, his patient attempted to hide his bad mood. Cristiano was the kind of man who hated showing weakness but was too good-natured to get angry. Miles offered a reassuring smile as he approached the bedside. "Let's see what we're dealing with."

A neurological assessment had already been done, so Miles concentrated on testing the limbs. The paralysis was real, but the usual culprits were absent. While the potential for useful information was a factor in his assessment, his primary motivation was to locate the source of the malevolent magic. If Cristiano had been a mage, his own magic would've masked the poisonous residue Miles now sensed in his shoulder and hip—small mercies.

"I'd like to do some more testing at the clinic," Miles said smoothly. "To be thorough."

Miles had Cristiano transferred to his clinic, where he prepared two syringes. "You're a pro at this, so I don't need to explain anything to you. First shot will help your muscles relax since this is a unique situation." A lie. "The second is your standard steroid."

He helped Cristiano lay on his stomach with arms folded under his head. The first injection went into the muscle near his shoulder. Within seconds, Cristiano's breathing slowed and his body fully relaxed as the sedative took effect. Miles waited a moment, then administered the second shot for appearances' sake. Once he was sure Cristiano was out, he closed the door and locked it.

With the door locked, Miles pulled out the daggers he had stashed in his briefcase, just in case. This could be like the pishacha that had separated from Maureen after it had possessed her. In which case, he would be utterly screwed trying to fight it in this tiny office, but at least he'd be doing something to end his patient's suffering.

He placed his hands on Cristiano's back, and a golden glow emanated from his palms. Almost immediately, he felt the malevolent magic—a dark, writhing presence coiled around Cristiano's shoulder and hip joints.

Miles let out a sigh of relief—there would be no fight today.

The magical residue he sensed there was the mark of several types of monsters. Each fed on the pain and vital energy they drained from their victims, even if they were separated by great distances. With time ticking before his nurse would drop by to remind him of another patient, Miles pushed all speculation of which type it could be to the side.

They'd discovered his healing repelled malevolent magic when an alp had attacked Esme. He poured a steady stream of it into the spots within Cristiano where he felt it most. It resisted, but his insistent pressure caused the golden light to flare before the intrusive malevolent working lost the battle and dissipated into the air.

Sweat beaded on his brow as he slumped against the exam table, now doubly regretting skipping lunch. He shook his head, amazed at where life had taken him. The number of felonies he committed on a regular basis would have him in jail for several lifetimes. This was yet another one of them to add to his list.

He put the unneeded daggers away and gave Cristiano a third injection—a stimulant this time—and waited. It didn't take long. With a groan, the patient woke, only to find he could move once more.

"Son of a..." Cristiano lifted his arm, then his leg, blinking in disbelief. "Sorry, doc. Must have fallen asleep."

"Muscle relaxers can do that sometimes." *Lies upon lies.*

"Seriously, though, doc, you're a miracle worker." He wiggled his once-paralyzed leg and lowered his chin, considering Miles with one raised eyebrow. "That wasn't a simple steroid shot, was it?"

"Just good medicine." Miles smirked.

"I'm gonna square with you." Cristiano raised his chin and laughed. "You've never given me completely straight-laced vibes, so I'm guessing you aren't gonna talk. But, fuck... I don't care if you used 'unconventional methods.' You get a five-star rating and my silence. I thought I was wheelchair bound."

Miles smiled gently, his eyebrows raised. "Listen, if this ever happens again, call me directly. We need to catch it sooner next time."

Cristiano looked years younger than he had when he'd still been lying in that hospital bed.

The emergency had cost Miles time, but it was worth it. He rushed out, practically jogging, so he could salvage his night to cook dinner at home.

Dim lighting and the smell of exhaust filled the underground garage. He was halfway to his car, tapping through his phone to call Esme, when he sensed the foul magic for the second time that day.

Bloody fucking hell. It was never-ending lately.

He swapped his phone for the daggers in his briefcase and walked toward his car. While he needed to protect himself, a public altercation outside his office wasn't ideal. He might have to avoid it and hunt whatever it was later.

The creature was by his car, probably drawn there by lingering residual magic within. The single faintly glowing eye and long gaunt legs and arms that made it look like an underfed gray goblin stretched too thin made it easy to recognize on sight.

It was a Likho.

The Slavic creatures were associated with multiple ailments. They were said to cause symptoms of smallpox, tuberculosis, lockjaw, and rabies. Other types left their victims paralyzed or growing tumors from their style of feeding.

Miles should have predicted this. He *had* deprived it of nourishment when he'd removed its magic from Cristiano. It was likely that it trailed its victim and had sensed the only magic in the area on his car.

Miles dropped his briefcase and lunged.

Mid-step, he summoned a shield around himself. Though invisible, his protective shields could reflect light at certain angles. He hoped his movements and the dim lighting would obscure any visible hints of magic.

He needed to pin it between the cars to hide his actions from the garage's cameras. The Likho's unnatural speed allowed it to dodge, but it wasn't the type of malevolent built for physical combat.

Instead of attacking, the creature spoke in a surprisingly deep voice as it evaded each of Miles' blows. "I will serve you," it rasped, showing the first signs of fatigue.

This wasn't the first time a malevolent had offered to serve him, but it was the first time it had done it without getting a hit in first. A Likho's "special diet" enabled them to speak their victims' language and exploit their memories for whatever nefarious purposes they desired.

Not caring what it had to say, Miles lunged again.

Again, it dodged.

"The man of death has himself died," it whined. "I cannot find the changing woman... but she is close."

Miles' pulse slammed in his ears. That phrase. It meant something. It had to—

Gwyn.

Miles froze, despite his twenty years of training to the contrary.

Gwyn

Only Gwyn and Cerys had been there when his heart stopped. But only Cerys had stayed awake through death.

Five minutes passed—an eternity for a hound. She licked his face, threw her weight across his chest, and wailed to wake him.

Then a flash of burgundy light tore across the ceiling.

Gwyn gasped back to life.

His eyes snapped open. Pain bloomed across his ribs under the weight of Cerys, claws raking through his shirt and into skin. But he didn't push her off. Her warmth, her noise, the simple act of *being there* was enough to anchor him in the present. Still in the dark, with blood soaking into his clothes, he whispered to her, calming her trembling body with soft words and steadier hands than he felt.

He remembered the dream—but there was something he was missing, like a task forgotten the moment you walked through a doorway. Finally, after nearly two thousand years of torment, Gwyn understood why his father had treated him with such distrust. His father's constant suspicion, the watching eyes, the harsh silences—they all made sense now. The scrutiny had never been punishment. It had been fear. Of *this*.

Though he accepted it, he still mourned the truth. He was a *necromancer*.

Gwyn closed his eyes and breathed that truth in like the poison it was. And behind him, Cerys stayed close. Still shaken and silent, she was alone in knowing what her master could not remember.

Miles

Without warning, the Likho's claws raked at his shield. He'd been too distracted to react appropriately to the danger.

With a quick slash of his dagger, Miles stepped closer, pushing the Likho farther behind his car. He countered the creature's strike with one of his own that sliced clean through its thin arm.

It hissed and tried to crawl away, but Miles grabbed its retreating form with his prosthesis and slammed its gaunt body onto the concrete.

Holding it down with magic-enhanced strength, he slammed his dagger into its spine with his left hand. The creature let out a final, gurgling sob.

Miles didn't waste time. He lifted the body and shoved it into the trunk before speeding out of the garage. His hands trembled on the wheel as he drove, his mind racing.

Gwyn. He had to get to Gwyn. He'd been an enemy for so long but now... They were... Something.

In spite of his reservations, in spite of the past, Miles had to concede that there was more than reluctant respect between them now. Damn it all, they were *friends*. And he might already be dead if what the creature had said was true.

Blessedly, Gwyn's apartment was only a few minutes away. Miles, a man who paid for parking meters on holidays, stopped his car in a reserved spot, not caring about the consequences. He took the stairs two at a time. He pounded on the door, breath ragged, body trembling with exertion.

When Gwyn opened the door, what Miles saw did not immediately dismiss his worries.

Gwyn looked like he'd been to hell and back and hadn't slept the entire journey. He was shirtless, his chest covered in bruises. Deep scratches marred his shoulders and chest. Dried blood crusted at the edges of the fresh bandages, showing he'd been cleaning his wounds. His face was far too pale, his eyes deep-set and purple-rimmed.

Gwyn barely glanced at Miles before turning back inside. "Come in," he muttered, dragging himself to his pull-down bed and collapsing onto it.

Miles followed, eyes scanning Gwyn's battered body. Cerys lay in the corner, her red eyes watching him warily.

"She did this?" Miles' voice was sharp. For a terrible moment, he thought he'd have to put her down for Gwyn. Cerys was technically a malevolent, after all, even if she was "domesticated."

Gwyn pushed up on one elbow, suddenly much more alert. "She was trying to help."

Miles narrowed his eyes but didn't ask. That wasn't how their relationship worked. Gwyn had to choose to be forthcoming, or they would only fight instead.

So he sat next to Gwyn and sent a quick text to Esme: *Helping Gwyn. Be home soon. I'm sorry about dinner.*

She immediately texted back. *Gives me an excuse to try that new sushi place. XOXO.*

Putting the phone away with a shake of his head, Miles asked, "Were you attacked?"

Gwyn barely shook his head, his eyes fixed on nothing at all.

Then, quieter, Miles asked, "Can I take a look?"

Gwyn hesitated but eventually nodded, stripping off his bandages.

Miles carefully controlled his expression. The wounds were deep, the bruising extensive. "Tell me what happened."

Gwyn sat perfectly still, his gaze unwavering as he scrutinized Miles. It was as if he was weighing a crucial decision instead of answering a simple question.

"I don't know. I had a dream, really a memory... of when I was ascended."

Miles froze. "Again?"

Gwyn's expression was one of exasperated dread. "Yes."

"Let me heal you," Miles offered, his tone leaving no room for argument. "Then tell me how a memory could possibly be connected to having your chest mangled by a two-hundred-pound gwyllgi."

It no longer mattered how exhausted he was. Something told him he needed to have a deeper inside look while he healed Gwyn's surface wounds.

Golden light shone as warmth blossomed beneath his hands for the second time that day. Miles focused, knitting the tissue back together, the gashes closing as if they'd never been there.

While he healed, he probed, searching for anything unresolved deep beneath the surface.

There. Subtle but unmistakable. An unnatural weakness in Gwyn's heart. It looked like a myocardial injury that had a circular pattern of damage. It was too damned perfect. There were also signs that his blood... His blood had *stopped moving.*

Fucking hell. Gwyn hadn't suffered a simple injury. He had *died.*

The day just kept getting weirder.

Fortunately, the damage to his heart wasn't severe. If it had been much worse, Miles would have had to wait another day to heal the strange injury to his heart.

When he was done, Miles sat back, unable to prevent his expression from turning grim. "Alright, I did you a favor. Now do me one. Tell me what about your dream gave you a bloody *heart attack*."

"What even is a heart attack?" Gwyn muttered, looking anywhere but at Miles.

"Mate, *not today*," Miles growled. Gwyn was trying to deflect by asking questions. "Unless I'm mistaken—and my multiple degrees and, frankly, magic suggest otherwise—you were briefly *deceased*. Get to explaining."

"Fine." Defiance briefly flashed in Gwyn's cold blue eyes, but a tired exhale snuffed it out. "The memory..." Gwyn's voice cracked like ice under pressure. "It was of me... killing Gwenddoleu ap Ceidio. And not by sword or fire."

"...Okay," was all he could dredge up. Gwenddoleu ap Ceidio had been a king in sub-Roman Britain. Miles remembered that much due to his fondness for his name.

Gwyn met Miles' eyes. "I used necromancy."

Miles blinked once. The word echoed in his mind like a church bell before a funeral. His hands, still warm from healing, went suddenly cold. That particular magic had never been accepted in society.

"I have no idea why that memory would nearly cost me my life."

"You said the memory was of your time while ascended. Does that mean you can still use the power, or...?"

Gwyn gave a weak shrug. "If my recent history is something to go by, the worst must be true."

Miles wasn't certain if "the worst" meant Gwyn having necromantic power was a good thing or a bad thing. Sure, its practice was illegal, but Abby's magic was also banned, and she wasn't a monster—even if what she'd done to Leon was terrifying.

Gwyn shifted uncomfortably, so Miles dropped it. He told him about the Likho and its cryptic statement instead. "That's why I ran up here sweating through my shirt."

"I..." Gwyn glanced away, then settled his gaze directly on Miles'. "I'm grateful."

"Mate, things are... getting out of hand with the malevolents. I'm working double-time to stage deaths and go on hunts. But now this..."

"This is like the Dullahan." With a heavy sigh, Gwyn ran a trembling hand through his hair. "I almost wonder now if Llefelys' repulsive presence was deterring malevolents from the area. Allow me to recover for a day and I will help with your tasks."

"I just..." Miles hesitated, searching for the right words to avoid sounding callous. "Esme hasn't been there when a victim dies. I want to keep it that way."

Miles wasn't worried about her ability to cope. What troubled him was the pain he couldn't protect her from. He had only managed to shield her from it thanks to her evening shifts at the Sanctuary of Spirits a few days each week. But recently, she'd mentioned cutting back on weekdays so they could spend more time together. He wanted that too—just not if it meant bringing her closer to death on a regular basis.

Gwyn nodded, understanding. "This *changing woman*. What do you think?"

Miles didn't like the implication. A chill ran down his spine as his sweat cooled at the thought of another powerful, unknown entity potent enough that malevolents would seek her out.

"Don't say anything to Abigail or Esmeralda yet." Gwyn cleared his throat roughly. "I... need to work up to it myself."

"Because *that* has a history of going well." Miles slapped Gwyn's back, hard.

Gwyn snorted. "Thank you. *Now get out.* I need to sleep."

Miles shook his head and gave Cerys a few reassuring pats before doing exactly that.

CHAPTER SIX

PAST MEETS PRESENT

Gwyn

The indoor mall reminded Gwyn of the days when caravans rolled into the keep, clustered together for protection from bandits and monsters. Less shouting and a nicer smell improved this version, yet the underlying threat remained consistent across eras. Gwyn's nose guided him to a little bakery, where the sweet bread rolls lived up to the delicious scent.

Between bites, he mused with Esme about his many foibles in adjusting to modern life. "Do you know I almost didn't get Abigail a Christmas gift?"

She caught the edge of remorse in his voice and grimaced.

He added, "I wanted to avoid making that same error with her birthday coming up."

"And that's why you called in the expert." A knowing, approving smile played on Esme's lips. "Good boy."

He sighed, exasperated. "Can we please forestall the canine metaphors already?"

"Absolutely not." She smirked. "So, what were you thinking of getting her?"

The designer clothing and handbags caught his eye only
momentarily. He didn't understand the appeal at all. "Esmeralda, I have no clue. From my perspective, she possesses
all the necessaries for a fulfilling life. But I still lack the knowledge of what a modern woman like her could possibly want."

"The sentiment is what matters, not the price. But, yeah,
you're right, you gotta find *something*."

He gave a nod, but inside he was nothing but uncertainty.
"What did Miles get you for your birthday?"

She gave him a look.

"Right. You were unconscious."

Esme's smile softened. "He told me he loved me for the first
time."

Gwyn nodded, speechless to say anything against the gesture. That was... an action probably long overdue for him.
His feelings for Abby were more than simple fondness. Ever
since he'd admitted the truth of who she and Esmeralda
might be, his relationship with her had deepened. Somewhere between their quiet moments sharing coffee and her
laughter at his confusion over technology, he'd fallen in love
with her—again.

He opened his mouth, but Esme's sudden shift in subject
threw him off.

"Miles and I talk about Elena sometimes," she mused,
wiping the frosting from her fingers, "but it's all secondhand
memories from your father. Miles can tell how much he
cared, how much he regretted about their lives together. But
that's not the same as actually knowing her." She gave Gwyn
a sidelong glance. "You did."

A ghost of a smile flickered across Gwyn's face. He saw where the conversation was headed but was surprised it had taken so long to start. "I did."

"I'm willing to beg, Gwynnyboy. What was she like?"

Gwyn's mind journeyed back a millennium. "Elena was... remarkable," he said at last. "She was my older sister in so many ways. I was probably in my early twenties when she joined the household guard."

"Older sister? So she was younger than Nudd?"

"Why are you so surprised? Things were almost always that way in the past. I would have been married off to a woman who was little more than a teenager had I not ascended."

Esme made a face like she'd bitten into a lemon.

"Yes, now you see why I was so happy to have escaped that life." Gwyn didn't suppress his amusement. "At first, my father rejected her when she came looking for a position in his service. He cited her bloodline as one that would cause too many problems in the court. But then she saved him and his retinue from a pack of gwyllgi when the Wild Hunt was without a helmsman."

Esme listened quietly, enjoying her snack. But her eyes, the same eyes as Elena's, urged him on.

"Elena was... a memorable character. Not only for her battle prowess, not because she was a friend and ally, but in everything. Her loyalty, her love, were both fierce. She was my champion with Nudd. Contrary to the violent disposition that ran in her blood, she was unfailingly compassionate and forgiving. Much like you, Esmeralda. Among the Nergalian cambions I've known, you share that unique quality with her. The others I'd met in the past were more like raging berserkers than men."

That same grimace showed on her face again.

"Esmeralda, you're also very different from her in a few ways. I mentioned her gentler nature already. Yet, this was countered by a noticeably... *harsher* side, one that shouldn't be ignored. My father had a lethal weapon in Elena, one he was reluctant to use, yet she pushed him toward it. I saw her mow through packs of malevolents—and men—with her sword on countless occasions. Make no mistake, she was a relentless killer."

The remnants of their snack lay scattered on the table as they cleaned and gathered their things. "Except there was always something there about her past, about her family, that hung between us. We trained together; we even fought in battles together, and yet she never spoke a single word about her life before meeting my father. I wish—"

Before he could voice the rest, the air shifted. A ripple, barely perceptible at first, like the sensation of a spider crawling along his skin. The vile sensation sharpened, slithering through the mall's dry recirculated air, a tingling wrongness that made his arm hairs stand on end.

Beside him, Esme stiffened.

Casually stepping closer, she whispered, "You feel that?" as her eyes scanned the mall.

Gwyn offered a tiny inclination of his head.

Their casual browsing ceased as they instinctively fell into step, their focus shifting to the hunt. The shoppers around them continued their day, blissfully unaware of the threat lurking in their midst.

Esme groaned. "We can't exactly go full magic here. Too many mundanes. What the hell is a malevolent doing out in public?"

"By that, I assume you mean we require subtlety." Gwyn's eyes tracked movement on the escalator. "Your trolls are out of the question."

"And most of your fighting techniques would cause a panic." Esme pretended to window shop while they talked. "We need to draw it somewhere quiet." Her fingers twitched at her sides, the demoness within her itching for the fight. "You can use this." As inconspicuously as possible, she handed her new dagger to him. She'd been reluctant to use the siphoning dagger again after it had ended Leon's life. "I can conjure an inconspicuous pair of daggers—they're small, at least."

As the revolting magic curled around them, Gwyn's stomach churned in reaction. He was beginning to regret that sweet roll.

Esme spotted it first. Her chin tilted slightly toward a door marked "Employees Only" as a squat figure that passed for human at a glance slipped through it.

"Perfect," Esme muttered. "No witnesses—hopefully."

Gwyn didn't hesitate, following silently.

As Esme summoned a pair of daggers, they stepped into the dimly lit back corridors that connected the storefronts to loading bays. Gwyn listened for movement as the door shut behind them with a click. Having lost sight of the creature, only two paths remained: left and right. The malevolent magic pressed down on him from all sides, rendering his sixth sense useless in deciding. The malevolent must have done something, or worse, cast something to make the magic so abundant in the narrow corridor.

Gwyn instantly forgot all his directional anxieties as reaching claws burst from the darkness—headed straight for his throat.

Three blades blocked it.

The formless shape of their attacker darted to the left and bounced off the wall with unnatural fluidity.

"Watch your neck," Gwyn murmured, shifting to track the creature. His ribs ached with the persistent stiffness from Cerys' attempts to wake him.

As it moved, its shape morphed, twisting in midair. A boggart. No one knew its true form, as it changed so frequently. Some claimed it was nothing more than an ooze, others a spirit. As he watched its body lose corporeality in the act of shifting, Gwyn's opinion leaned toward the latter.

The boggart ricocheted off the opposite wall. He braced himself as its shape settled into something resembling a raccoon. Except this raccoon's limbs were elongated, its fangs jagged, and its claws oversized—enough to shred flesh with a single swipe.

"Murder trash panda," Esme breathed, eyes alight with adrenaline. Of course she was enjoying this. *Cambions.*

Too fast for their blades, the creature darted between the narrow walls, trying to take swipes at them on every pass. Gwyn slashed with his borrowed dagger. It sliced through the air, always a hair too slow. Esme's conjured weapons proved equally ineffective.

It blurred faster, more erratic, more desperate—until its motions snapped into precision, zeroing in on Gwyn's exposed throat with outstretched claws.

In a flash, Esme's daggers vanished, replaced by a single elongated sword in her right hand. Gwyn turned toward the creature. As the conjured blade moved in an achingly familiar arc, Gwyn experienced a double vision of his past and present.

He turned—and saw Esme's blade cut through the boggart midair in a perfect arc. It was Elena's strike, cleaving it into two pieces. Soundlessly, it vanished, leaving only the lingering miasma of its foul magic in its wake.

Gwyn stared at the empty space where the creature had been, memory overlapping reality. He knew that strike from a battle a millennium ago in rain-soaked Welsh hills.

Unlike in the past, there was no corpse. No mess. No evidence of the battle that had just taken place.

The sudden silence was heavy. Gwyn let out a slow breath, relaxing his tense muscles. He was certain he would have caught the creature in time, but it would have been a very near thing. His student was certainly improving at her swordplay.

"Well, that killed the shopping mood." Esme shook her head, grinning with battle frenzy. "I need to walk this adrenaline off. Let's get out of here."

They made their way to the nearest exit, stepping into the refreshing afternoon air. As they walked toward Esme's car, Gwyn cleared his throat.

He started the conversation awkwardly. "We spoke of Elena earlier, about her compassion, about her brutality..."

This wasn't like performing his promised scribing duty with Abigail. He was always prepared with something to say for those. This was personal and emotional in a way that was difficult to contextualize. He addressed the person who carried the soul of his deceased friend, the very friend he was about to discuss. This was also a new memory, one he'd only just recalled when the boggart had been inches from his throat.

As she read him, Esme's face took on a graver cast. "Yeah?"

"What you did back there. It reminded me of the first time I truly understood Elena's harder side. I think you are right. I think it is time we spoke more about our past."

He gave himself over to the memory and used his words to paint a picture of the scene.

"It was an autumn of endless rain. A constant downpour that turned roads into mud, soaking through your shoes no matter how well-oiled they were. Father dispatched Elena, me, and two other soldiers on patrol duty. In truth, it was little more than a thinly veiled punishment."

"What did you do to piss Nudd off?" Esme asked.

"You would call what she did 'wing manning.' And me, well, given that information, you can guess exactly what I did and with whom." Gwyn grinned, a slow, sly smile that crinkled the corners of his eyes. "We traveled light. We slept rough under crude tents, suffering all the while, exactly as Nudd desired. No one dared attack four armed fighters, one clearly a mage since we dressed according to our stations back then. This meant we could afford a fire at night. Elena always wore her helmet when we went out. It hid her features enough to disguise her gender."

Esme said nothing, listening intently as they reached her car. She leaned against the driver's side door, waiting.

"Perhaps it's best that I finish the story in the car." With a meaningful glance, he reached for the door handle and got in.

In the driver's seat, Esme sat with folded hands, waiting anxiously. "What? I'm practically vibrating with anticipation here. I can't drive like this!"

He wanted to join in her simple delight at sharing the tale, but the emotions evoked by the memory held him captive, and Gwyn could only nod. "His name escapes me, but I vividly recall the face of the youngest soldier. Elena had taken him under her wing. He was a kind and respectful young man, especially to women. He treated her as his equal, superior really, from the start.

"One night, while he was on watch duty, he dozed off. That was when the brigands came. The other guard and I woke to the sound of his death cry." The words tasted like the ash of that night's campfire, of sweat, adrenaline, and blood in Gwyn's mouth.

"As was appropriate back then, Elena kept her camp at a respectable distance."

Esme waggled her eyebrows. She was spending excessive time with that cursed leprechaun. "Didn't want the lads thinking she was out there pitching tents while pitching a tent." She mimed holding a broadsword with two hands.

"Essentially." The old memory was so heavy that Gwyn could only manage a weak laugh. Though he understood: Esme was perceptive; she was using humor to lighten his load.

He continued the story. "The brigands struck separately, not all at once. There were so many of them. I was forced to go without a shield. All I could grab in time was my sword. My attention was split between using bursts of fire to defend the other guard and fighting off the direct attacks that came my way with my weapon. I worried they'd already taken Elena in the darkness."

"But they hadn't," Esme guessed.

"No." Gwyn smiled grimly. "She had magic. Only once did she ever use it in my presence. I never learned why.

"When I cast a great mage light to illuminate the area, I saw her." His voice dropped lower. "She wasn't missing. She was busy slaughtering the cowardly rest of their band who had been hiding in the trees, waiting to attack once I had exhausted my magic enough."

Gwyn shook his head. "In a later conversation, she revealed that she had earlier left the camp to discreetly relieve herself.

Bladeless, she'd summoned a sword, exactly like yours, and was cutting through our attackers like barley. Only after the fighting did we realize that these weren't untrained thieves. Most carried proper shields and swords. But Elena… She ripped through them with a savagery that I had never witnessed the likes of before. I'm willing to say now, in her absence, that her fury wasn't human.

"Her black blade danced like a phantom, finding openings in their defenses that defied logic. One tried to flank me. I never saw him coming. But Elena did. She intercepted his strike and"—Gwyn gestured across his head diagonally—"split his skull clean in two. I did not realize the extent of her strength until that moment."

Esme's eyes widened in surprise. "If she never used her magic, did Nudd know what she could do?"

Gwyn said, a little too pointedly, "Naturally, he knew she was capable of magic, like all cambions are." Then he softened. "But he was never the type to push her. Much like our Miles."

Noticing the way Esme's eyes darted away in silent agreement, he continued, "Elena made us swear on our life-price never to tell him. I never did. Though I suspect the surviving guard eventually did under pressure from Nudd. I later heard him and Elena discussing her choice never to use her magic. Now I wonder why she was so careful with it."

Esme's voice started out strong, then trailed off. "Maybe the allure of the infernal became too much for her…"

"I doubt it, Esmeralda. I often saw her eyes darken in battle. She must have been using some infernal magic. Yet she never lost control of it. I've heard of other cambions mistaking friends for enemies during berserker rages—I know Llefelys did it more than once—but Elena never did. No… looking back, I realize it must have been something else. She was always so careful about keeping her past hidden. I knew nothing of her life before she came to the keep. There was something in her past. Unless Miles dreams a buried memory, it may stay lost forever."

Esme started the car and asked, "Think we're going to get in trouble for this? Jacob is already breathing down our necks about all the malevolents popping up lately, and we probably just killed one on camera. That was weird, right? It was walking through the frigging mall in broad daylight!"

Unlike so many other fights he'd been a part of recently, he'd also felt no strange energy fill him upon the creature's death. That strange, inexplicable phenomenon continued to puzzle him.

"Quite bold of it, truly." Gwyn shook his whole body, trying to release the lingering tension from the fight and the memory. "And I still don't have a birthday present for Abigail."

"Oh." Esme's playful attitude returned. "I have an idea about that..."

Esme

Since Jacob was now the only one with a backyard in town, they headed straight to his place to pick up Lily and Cerys from their arranged playdate. Cerys was back to her full size, so allowing her to play at dog parks, even with a glamour on, was less than ideal. As soon as they entered, both dogs sprinted out of the library and down the hallway, their paws scrambling on the hardwood. A soft, exasperated yelp from that direction told Esme that Jacob was frantically searching for his hearing aids.

Esme's old mentor had time to compose himself thanks to the dogs' slobbery welcome. His usual confident demeanor was on display by the time they entered the library. He stood. "Welcome back." He gave them all a thorough appraisal. Then harrumphed. "You had another fight, I take it?"

Esme threw her hands up, clearly implying *of course we did.*

"Well, I see no blood on your clothing, so buck up. Everyone is alive to fight another day."

"We need breaks sometimes, Jacob," Esme snapped, her hunger and tiredness getting the better of her. "Something is seriously wrong if they're showing up in the middle of the mall!"

Jacob raised one bushy eyebrow, and Esme felt a small surge of magic come from him.

"I've ordered a repast." Seattle's top mage spoke more gently and eased his rigid stance fractionally. "Tell me all about it. Then we have other important business."

That didn't sound ominous at all.

His generosity provided a feast of sandwiches, crudités, and dips for her and Gwyn as they talked about the events of the past two days.

When they finished, Jacob straightened up and set his napkin aside. "I should probably tell you all this when your counterparts are present, but... I regret to inform you that our Assembly, and by extension myself, are coming under review from the International Board—immediately."

Gwyn arched an eyebrow, and Esme groaned. They were the main reason for Jacob being in hot water.

"Our assigned overseer has summoned all five of you—yes, including the leprechaun—to a meeting tomorrow. She tried to push it through today, but I told her about your plans, and she backed down. While not unreasonable, Seren Lewis is known for her firmness. We will have our hands full in attempting to keep... certain matters under wraps in dealing with her."

"What marks her as especially dangerous?" Gwyn asked, always looking for the political bent of a situation.

Esme noticed how at ease the fallen demigod now seemed with Jacob. The covert scheming to handle Leon had transformed their relationship to a more relaxed, natural one.

"For starters, she's the most powerful mage in existence." Jacob raised one hand to emphasize his point. "That I know of, at least. Miles put the point quite elegantly when I called him about it this morning. He described her as a less friendly, older Esmeralda."

"Uh, what exactly is *that* supposed to mean?" Esme refused to believe that Miles was talking badly about her to Jacob.

"It means that she's incredibly intelligent but can be... terse, at times. She's easily underestimated and uses that to bend others to her will. Her magical specialization is also a type of conjuration."

Esme made a face, then clarified her reaction. "I think I met her briefly at the bar last night. She choked a goblin thing to death with tentacles made of infernal magic. The malevolent emerged under the *table,* Jacob!"

Both men were stunned into silence by this.

Gwyn straightened, curious. "What does she expect to learn from us? You mentioned keeping certain information concealed. That means you must think she has knowledge of something specific related to one or all of us."

While he talked, Esme wasn't exactly subtle in her efforts to feed Cerys meat from her sandwich under the table. Luckily,

Gwyn ignored the not-so-covert snacks his gwyllgi was receiving, focusing instead on the brewing trouble.

"She's aware of Miles' gifts," Jacob said immediately. "She's also aware of most of the details surrounding Leon's and Sylas' deaths."

Probably everything other than the fact that Leon was actually Llefelys, Gwyn's uncle and Nudd's half-brother.

Jacob tapped the table with his knuckles. "Gwyn is correct. I am more concerned with keeping Gwyn's identity concealed. She also has a keen interest in you, Esmeralda."

"Why me? The cambion slash conjuration thing?"

"That," he said, picking imaginary lint off his sweater, clearly reluctant to elaborate, "and she wants to be more involved with your training."

"Just when I figure out what I am, my people keep popping up, creating problems. Well"—Esme made a weighing motion with her head—"other than Katia. She's a gem."

A demon-blooded conjuration mage, exactly like her. Who also sat on the International Assembly? *Damn.* Jacob said Seren wasn't unreasonable, at least.

Esme was already composing a list of questions she wanted to ask the older mage. Questions she'd hoped Leon would answer when she'd thought they were becoming friends...

"Old-fashioned beheadings on the menu?"

Jacob sighed. "Probably just one."

His.

Chapter Seven

INTERVIEWS

Seren

The office Seren waited in smelled faintly of laser printer ink and burned coffee. The stark, unwelcoming gleam from the fluorescent ceiling lights illuminated the desk and chair. There wasn't even a window in the room assigned to her. Knowing Jacob Spencer, this arrangement was an intentional middle finger to her and to the International Assembly at large.

Before even looking up to meet her first interviewee, Seren sensed a subtle shift in the magic surrounding her. "Abigail O'Malley," Seren said, standing to greet her. The shimmering magic surrounding Abby's head in a halo pulsed with a soft, ethereal glow that seemed to vibrate on the edge of visibility. "Please, sit."

The petite blonde woman sat, her stillness forced. Every muscle in her small body was taut, and a silent tension radiated outward from her rigid posture. Voice carefully controlled, Abby said, "Ms. Lewis, it's nice to meet you. I asked my mother about you after finding out you were here, and I have to say, I'm impressed."

Seren fought the urge to smirk. Flattery was not what she'd expected out of the Enchantress, who, by all accounts, had no problems speaking exactly what was on her mind. It wasn't yet clear to Seren if Abby's approach was calculated or if she was being genuine. To the older woman, one thing was clear—Abigail O'Malley had received a divine blessing.

Seren glanced at her notes. "You're a neuromancer, first rate from the looks of it. Why have you *not* taken your mother's seat?"

Still stick-straight, voice clear, Abby answered. "Not interested."

With an understanding nod, Seren shook her head. "It certainly isn't for everyone. But you've been a Brother for a decade now, why not elevate yourself? Haven't you ever felt like you were meant for something greater?"

To Seren, Abigail appeared younger than her age, which was nearly thirty-two. Seren had to stop herself from grinning. Her official file had made no mention of Fae ancestry, yet Seren had known the truth of her lineage the moment she'd set eyes upon her.

Abby's brows furrowed slightly. Seren could tell she'd upset her first interviewee; the slightest movement of her left hand betrayed her. "I'm fine with where I am right now. I'm busy enough with my work and helping the Brotherhood."

Seren gave a slow, deliberate nod while examining Abby's halo. With a casual air, she diverted the discussion. "And yet, you've been present at almost every single catastrophe over the past ten months. How do you explain that?"

Abby's reply was without emotion, completely deadpan. "Bad luck."

"Perhaps." Deciding she had the right of it, Seren chuckled, honestly amused. She leaned in, her voice low but with a distinct edge. "Buy a shamrock necklace, lassie. Might help that luck problem out. You're dismissed."

"That's it?" Abby appeared unconvinced.

"Shoo." Seren waved her hand, chiding her.

As she closed the door, Seren heard Abby grumble to Gwyn, who was hovering protectively on the other side of the door—like Seren hadn't known exactly what he was doing, "Gods, Jacob wasn't freaking kidding about her being just like Esme."

Seren smiled broadly at that.

***

Her next interview of the day was less pleasant, but highly informative.

"Gwyn." She made a show of studying his features. "You claim to be... from Wales." Her lip curled in a display of disgust. Her eyes, disdainful, lingered on his worn jacket. "But we both know that is only half the truth," she finished, the words smooth as silk but carrying the weight of cold steel.

His stare back was unwavering. "Shall I bare my teeth next? Perhaps you'd also like to examine my hooves?" A smooth veneer covered his words, yet the subtle rasp betrayed a sharp edge to his tone.

Some things hadn't changed.

"Did you know you share the name of a fallen warlord? A psychopomp with connections to Annwn? By all accounts, he was a great man. But you, you… what? You hunt weakened malevolents and follow a half-organized Assembly of mages?" She tilted her head, the move purposefully canine. "I would have expected something… grander from a man with a name such as yours."

Trying to seem unbothered, he answered, "Disappointed?"

"Surprised." Seren offered up a bit of bait. "I imagine you must have opinions on how this territory is managed."

He leaned back, watching her carefully. "I have many thoughts. But I doubt you brought me here for that."

Seren gave an approving nod and then gestured toward the exit. "No, I didn't."

Gwyn departed wordlessly, leaving Seren to watch him go with a mix of wonder and hope.

***

"Dr. Goodwin, it's nice to see you again. Please, take a seat." The god-touched man's handshake was perfectly measured, even with his prosthesis, his gaze steady and respectful in a silent acknowledgment of her position.

Seated at the desk again, she pretended to flip through his file, though she'd memorized its contents long ago. "Miles Goodwin. Combat medic slash doctor. Field-trained agent. Ex-military. Went to the London Academy. You're nothing but stars all around on paper." Her eyes met his, ready to plunge in the knife. "And yet, here you are, still answering to an aging bureaucrat who, by all accounts, has been struggling to maintain control."

Seren watched as his jaw tighten. Unfortunately, Miles still hadn't shaken his first impression of her. They'd met years before when she'd first been let in on a few of the Assembly's little secrets—Miles' magic being one of them. Although their previous encounter hadn't been strictly antagonistic, meeting a young man with *his* power had left her on edge. Her comments during that meeting had been unnecessarily sharp and sarcastic.

But Seren knew all too well that there was nothing that could be done about the past.

She wanted to be impressed. Miles was competent, charming, disciplined, and carried himself like a man used to being obeyed. But a part of her bristled at how contained he was. His potential was always present, but never unleashed—like a weapon forever sheathed.

Miles' response cut through her musings. "Jacob has kept this city from falling apart, has kept the secret from getting out time and again. He's doing fine."

Seren replied, "But at what cost? The number of malevolent attacks in this area is unprecedented. Given that, do you honestly think he has the situation in hand?"

"Do you blame yourself for catching cold?" Miles replied flatly. "No. This is no different than that. He isn't weakening the prisons."

He isn't doing it alone, at least.

Seren pulled her trap's string taut. "Loyalty is an admirable trait." She offered him a subtle, knowing smile. "If not always a useful one. Are you loyal to your team?"

He answered without hesitation. "Yes."

She sprang it. "Who holds more of your loyalty? Your team or your Bastion?"

Expression guarded, Miles answered, "Whichever one needs saving first."

"Not a very helpful answer, Dr. Goodwin." Seren smirked.

Shrugging, he replied, "But it was an honest one."

Seren shook her head. He wasn't wrong. "You're dismissed."

He walked out without another word.

***

Seren realized very quickly that she'd been wrong in expecting the leprechaun to take his interview seriously. He did not, nor would he ever.

She started, "Fionn, with no last name—" but he cut her off.

"You can call me Finn, *Madam*." He waggled his eyebrows at her. Then he rudely placed his feet atop the desk.

Raising one eyebrow, Seren said, "Jacob signed you on as a reporting agent. All of your reports have lacked detail."

"Not my fault the Assembly's got a few unimaginative readers on it." Completely unfazed by her authoritative tone, he grinned. "The whole lot of ya have gone mad with power if you think you're gonna get a coherent report from a leprechaun." He chuckled.

"That's... fair. Your saving grace has been your insightful contributions."

"I think we both know I don't give a rat's arse about givin' insightful contributions."

Seren studied him for a moment. Finding what she was looking for, she leaned forward slightly, pitching her voice low. "You play the fool very well. I wonder—are you actually one, or do you just find it convenient?"

"Oh, sweetheart, I find a lot of things convenient." Finn leaned back, stretching leisurely. Then he met her eyes with something almost too knowing, too measured for his usual easygoing demeanor. "Like knowing when to keep my mouth shut. And when to remind someone that they should be askin' better questions. Are we done with this farce yet, Seren? You know good and well that Jacob isn't watchin' right now."

Seren exhaled slowly through her nose, a bad habit she'd never broken, even after so many years. It was either that or let the irritation spill over into her tone. He was playing with her, and worse, he was enjoying it. "Snacks, then? I can already tell this... conversation is a lost cause. I ordered a pizza, and I think there were cookies in the staff cafeteria. Interested?"

A feline smile spread over his face. "Now yer talkin' my language, ladyboss!"

***

Though Esme had clearly been aiming for charm, Seren's final interviewee of the day only managed resigned reluctance in her showing. The woman she'd been waiting to meet leaned against the back of her chair with her arms crossed and an unreadable expression on her face.

"Esmeralda Morgana Turner. Nice name. You've done well for yourself, considering the circumstances..."

Esme forced her body and tone to make the conversation seem casual. "Circumstances?"

"Two dead parents and"—Seren flipped through the file in front of her—"what looks like a complete lack of formal magical education."

The strike was calculated; its purpose was to assess Esme's reaction, not to cause harm. Only a twitching knee betrayed Esme's facade of composure as she smoothed her hands against her thigh.

"Few of our kind ever get this high in the Assembly," Seren added. "We're on shaky ground once they know about us. People are eager to find a reason to get rid of cambion."

Seren thought Esme was affecting a light tone when she replied. "The last person who talked to me like that was trying to steal my magic."

"Trust me," Seren said, sending her a meaningful stare. "I don't need your magic. I take it you've adjusted well to your cambion nature in a short time. That's commendable."

"It's been an... adjustment," Esme replied.

"But you've accepted it. Embraced it even." Damn it all. Seren couldn't keep how proud she was from showing on her face. If Seren was correct, as she usually was, Esme had lost control at least once and been on the brink several more times. Each time she'd come back unchanged.

Esme's eyes narrowed. "What are you *really* here for, Ms. Lewis?"

"Classic." Esme chuckled. "Switching topics trying to catch me off guard and make me forget that you never answered my question. What's next, more compliments?"

Seren blinked, surprised.

Esme grinned, realizing she'd won a point in a game Seren had set out for the two of them. Then Esme appeared to choose her words carefully. "Jacob has been a stabilizing force for quite some time."

Staying in the game meant an escalation. Seren added a bit of sarcastic punch to her next truth. "And yet, from what I've observed, things seem to be... unraveling."

Without heat, Esme fired back, "Handling crises is part of his position. Do you believe you could do a better job?"

"No, you misunderstand," Seren said, her voice sharp with correction.

Esme's eyes narrowed slightly at that.

Seren laughed softly and shook her head. "I'm simply asking if you think *he* could."

Voice neutral once more, Esme answered, "I think leadership is complicated."

Seren looked her straight in the eyes, steepled her fingers on the desk, and suggested, "True. Maybe Jacob's problem is setting too many boundaries."

Both of Esme's eyebrows rose in surprise at that.

"Do you think you've had sufficient autonomy in making judgment calls during your fieldwork? You've probably had to make more difficult decisions than the average enforcer."

"Am I really an enforcer anymore, though?" Esme shrugged. "Honestly, I usually act on instinct and fill Jacob in afterward."

"It sounds like you have a good relationship with him." Seren leaned back in her chair, making a show of nonchalance. She had her own facade to maintain.

Esme didn't hesitate in her reply. "We're up and down. But he's always there for me in the end."

"Your responses already show your ingenuity in crafting politically savvy answers. You bring a unique and valuable skill set to the Assembly. But tell me. Does Jacob, or any of the other seated members of the Seattle Assembly—including your boyfriend—know what you're really capable of? Or do you keep that to yourself?"

Esme flinched, just a fraction of an inch, but Seren didn't miss it. "Didn't know your beau was technically a seated member?"

Esme shook her head. "I don't see how that's relevant to this discussion."

"Of course you do. But you play nice. You follow their rules."

Thoughtful, Esme smirked. "Only when it makes sense."

Perfect answer. Every detail, from Esme's eyes to the way she carried herself, confirmed to Seren that she'd found the woman she'd been searching for.

CHAPTER EIGHT

MAKE IT OFFICIAL

Miles

The unusually high turnout of non-humans at the spring quarter meeting said it all. Things weren't right in Seattle—and everyone knew it.

With a faint *click-click,* Miles tapped his prosthetic fingers against his knee. Non-human mages had fewer options for blending in. Unlike humans, who were able to disappear into mundane life, they needed protective wards or constant glamours. This demand drove them to find safe places where they could truly be themselves—the Assembly filled this need for them.

But that wasn't the only reason for tonight's high turnout at the spring quarter meeting. The whispers and excited chatter had made that clear enough. They all pointed to the same person. The celebrity. The enigma. Seren.

He'd watched a brownie hold out a notebook with the reverence of a churchgoer offering scripture, as if Seren's signature might bless the page.

Ridiculous, Miles thought, maintaining his professional composure despite his internal disapproval. He'd met Seren years before he'd accepted the Brotherhood's tattoo. As far as he could tell, the only thing special about her was a deep well of power and a flair for the dramatic. Underneath it all, she seemed just another bureaucrat.

The quarterly meeting started as expected, the occasional cough reminding everyone that cold and flu season wasn't quite over. Miles shifted in his uncomfortable hotel chair, watching as Jon Doe droned through some dates of note.

Across from him, Abby was nearly asleep in her seat, her head bobbing. The only thing stopping her from nodding off entirely was Gwyn's discreet squeezes of her knee. Having lived through medical school and the military, Miles was used to forcing himself to stay attentive through tedious administrative meetings.

As the business portion concluded, the room's atmosphere shifted, expectant. All eyes returned to the stage the moment Jacob stepped forward. "I'd like to introduce you to our guest, a representative sent by the International Assembly. Please welcome Seren Lewis."

Applause rippled through the room, louder among the non-human attendees. Seren took the microphone, radiating the self-assurance of someone completely comfortable commanding an audience. She surveyed the adoring eyes surrounding her with a dazzling smile.

"Thank you all for the warm welcome," she began, her voice carrying effortlessly. "As some of you already know, I've been sent to audit the Seattle chapter."

A disturbed murmur ran through the crowd.

She held up a hand. "Let me be clear: your leadership is not at fault for recent events. I trust the seated members."

A sharp, derisive scoff sliced through the air. "That isn't true!" someone called. "Come out with it!"

Miles couldn't identify if the voice belonged to a human or non-human, but he instinctively scanned for potential trouble, a lifetime of training kicking in. An anxiety crowded the space, an atmosphere that had become far too frequent these past few months.

The veil of secrecy around the malevolents was wearing thin, too thin.

Seren's smile didn't falter. "Instead of assumptions, let me tell you what is true." Her gaze flickered, briefly catching Miles' eyes before moving on. "We unknowingly had a siphon in our ranks. He came to your noble city pretending to be a friend, but he was not. He left several of your members halfway to death, and others he allowed to die by his inaction."

A fresh wave of shocked murmurs rippled through the audience. Miles kept his expression neutral. Years of delivering bad news had trained him to mask his emotions. Seren's game was clear now—reveal *just enough* to build trust without threatening the leadership. But how long would her playing nice last?

Miles didn't need to look to know Esme had tensed beside him. He could still remember the expression on Leon's face when Leon had made his choice to kill them. The cold certainty and loathing.

"The siphon is no longer among the living," Seren continued flatly, "but we must take the necessary steps to ensure that someone like him can never threaten your community again."

The phantom pain of Leon's sword sliced across Miles' collarbone. His prosthetic fingers curled into a fist as he pushed the memory away, focusing instead on Esme sitting beside him. Her presence, as usual, grounded him.

Seren pressed on, her voice smooth as she unearthed their traumas in front of more than a hundred souls. "Members of your community brought that magic-stealer to justice. I will not publicly acknowledge them, but know that you have people ensuring your safety. Some in secret, in the shadows. Not all of them human. We are stronger together."

She let the words hang, then grinned. "Yet I also realize that no one in this room is stupid."

A few surprised laughs met her bluntness.

"Yes, I said that word in a public forum," she continued, amused. "But I hope my frankness only underlines my sincerity. No one here is blind. You've all noticed the vacancies on the closed board. I am here to help Seattle have the bright future it deserves. Changes will be made. There will be some winners and some losers."

Her gaze settled briefly on Jacob. "However," she said, "you all deserve the truth. I am making a promise before you now: there will be more of that particular commodity from the top moving forward."

Miles watched Jacob's expressionless face. The Bastion seemed calm and composed, but Miles detected underlying tension in his shoulders.

So, her playing nice had only lasted about sixty seconds.

As Seren returned to her seat amid another round of applause, Miles considered the implications. *More truth from the top*? Which truths? So many of them were dangerous. He glanced at Esme, wondering if she was having the same thoughts.

Seeing her frown, Miles gave in to follow suit and exhaled slowly to relieve some of the apprehension. Seren was laying the groundwork for something... something he probably wasn't going to like.

Finn leaned over, scaring Esme enough with the sudden movement that she nearly jumped out of her seat. That was an outcome the imp was probably thrilled with, even if that hadn't been his intention.

He whispered, "We've got a golden boy, a golden girl, and a woman with golden horns. Who's next, you or the ancient crybaby?"

Esme elbowed him hard in the ribs. "Do not call Gwyn a crybaby again, troublemaker," she hissed. "He's sensitive, and that's adorable, damn it. Wait, who's the golden girl?"

"Haha, pretty tellin' that you knew exactly who the crybaby was..." Then, lowering his voice even further, he added, "What the boy needs is to be on some antidepressants."

Another elbow to the ribs. "Abby is working on it. Shut your mouth."

The sound of their banter was enough to ease the tension in Miles' jaw. Esme's fiery nature was one of the many things he loved about her.

There was only one speaker after Seren finished her speech—Josiah. The powerful mage was almost universally beloved by all the nature-related beings like the dryads and nymphs because he was always the first to offer help to the non-humans.

Josiah cleared his throat and put on his usual display of casual swagger. "I hear a lot of talk about change, about power shifting hands, about who wins and who loses. But I want to remind you all—this city, this community, was built with the calloused hands of its people reaching out in times of need. On trust. Should a dryad's grove be threatened, a selkie pup lost, or a mage's magic uncontrolled, a helping hand can be found here. Not because they were ordered to, not because the helpers wanted something in return, but because that is who we are. That is what we fight to protect."

This was blatant political maneuvering. He'd seen enough power plays to recognize one when it unfolded before him. Josiah was positioning himself as standing behind Jacob, the necessity of which yet remained to be seen.

The meeting wrapped up, and Miles barely had a moment before Sorcha peeled away from the stage and grabbed his arm. By now, he was used to the selkie's relentless pestering. She always had a pretext—his Corded Brotherhood seat in the Assembly, a request, a question. But that day, she seemed particularly intent on his attention.

"Dr. Goodwin," she greeted, her voice carrying that musical quality unique to selkies. "Might I have a moment of your time?"

"Of course," Miles replied politely. He sent Esme a small, apologetic smile before turning his attention to Sorcha.

"Your attendance at these meetings has become more regular," Sorcha observed, leading him slightly away from the dispersing crowd. "The Brotherhood appreciates your dedication, especially given your... other commitments." Her eyes flickered briefly in Esme's direction.

"The clinic keeps me busy," Miles admitted, "but my responsibilities here are important, too."

Sorcha nodded, her expression growing more serious. "There's been talk amongst the selkies about the sort of changes Seren might be interested in implementing. We're... concerned."

"Understandably so," Miles replied diplomatically, though he shared those concerns.

"We value having allies like you," Sorcha continued, touching his arm lightly. The gesture, while innocent enough, made Miles uncomfortably aware of how this might look to Esme. "Someone who understands the responsibilities invested in the seated members."

"I appreciate that," Miles said, gently creating some distance between them. "Was there something specific you needed?"

Sorcha's eyes sparkled with mischief. "Just checking in"—she leaned in slightly—"and reminding you that you have a reserved seat that would greatly benefit from actually having you in it."

He made his way back to the group, where Esme, Abby, Gwyn, and Finn were waiting.

"Sorry. I think us getting married might be the only way to get rid of Sorcha at this point," he said, deliberately keeping his tone light.

Esme nodded. Abby's comically intense reaction, a face so loaded with meaning, already had Miles expecting a tough interrogation. He shrugged and grinned, saying only, "Selkies," to defuse the moment.

The small box hidden in the false back of his gun safe had waited there for months now. He'd nearly given it to her on Valentine's Day, thinking Esme would laugh at the cliché. But then she'd gotten hurt on a hunt. He'd healed her. Then an argument had flared, fueled by his protective instincts and her simmering resentment at his occasionally overbearing nature.

Carving out a future for them amid such uncertainty felt like a cruel lie, a fragile hope built on shifting sands. And yet, wasn't that the point of it? A defiance of love in the face of it all?

His prosthetic fingers tapped against his knee again, this time slower. Was it selfish to want something real and grounding when their lives kept skimming the edge of catastrophe? Or was it more cowardly not to ask?

The box would need to wait a little longer—until this latest crisis had passed and he could be certain they could have a future worth planning for.

While they fought their way out through the throngs of people around Seren, she stopped them. "Mr. Newman, Ms. Turner, a word."

Miles battled a twinge of apprehension at her tone. Something about that tone, her tattoo, tugged at his memory, but he couldn't quite place it.

Seren stared meaningfully at Miles, Abby, and Finn. "I'm certain you all are quite busy, so you don't have to stay."

Miles hesitated, reluctant to leave Esme alone with Seren.

Something about her triggered a strange sense of déjà vu that Miles couldn't quite place. Her power signature was oddly familiar to the part of him that was Nudd. But what did that mean? A whisper in the back of his mind—was it his own thought, or something from Nudd Llaw Eraint's memories? The ancient soul whose power he'd inherited usually left warnings in his dreams. He'd learned that lesson the hard way with Leon. But his dreams had been either absent or repeats of past dreams over the last few months—nothing about them seemed like a warning.

Also unlike with Leon, he didn't have the same intense instinctual distrust toward her. Nudd had left Miles with a sense of overt threat about the siphon, a warning that lingered even when he was awake. With Seren, he got none of that.

Perhaps she simply reminded Nudd of someone from the distant past? The ancient Welsh king had encountered countless beings in his long life before his soul, his essence, his *whatever* had become part of Miles.

Miles reasoned it away. Seren had been around for twenty years. The only people to escape the malevolent prisons were Gwyn and Leon, and that had happened within the last five. It wasn't possible that Nudd actually *knew* her.

Still debating, he left what he did next up to Esme. A glance silently asked if she wanted him to stay. A small nod made his decision to stay.

With perfect timing, Finn snorted in derision. So low that Miles barely caught it, he said, "I hope this meddlin' has a good point, Queenie." A fractional acknowledgment, nothing more than a flick of the eyes so quick that Miles almost missed it, was all that the leprechaun received from their new boss.

Despite Seren's dismissal, Miles and Abby made no move to leave. If Seren took issue with that, she didn't show it.

The five of them waited together in an abandoned room until Seren had finished greeting her fans. Explaining what a "fan" was to Gwyn took up part of that time—a good five minutes, in fact.

With privacy secured, Seren let her public mask drop, her expression hardening. "I've been reviewing your files. Again. And again. I hoped I missed something, but no. The problems keep mounting."

"Problems?" Gwyn asked, arms stiff, ready for a verbal spar.

"Gross misuse of magic." Seren's voice was ice. Miles swore he saw her snake tattoo move—a trick of the light, surely? "Conjurations sighted by mundanes. Property damage that required extensive cover-ups. The list goes on." Her eyes flickered between Esme and Gwyn. "You two have caused more incidents than your other three companions combined."

A protective instinct rose within him. While he understood the need for protocol and discretion, the situations Esme and Gwyn had faced were extraordinary. Context mattered.

"Mistakes have consequences. You are both under scrutiny." Seren let that hang before adding, "Don't give me any reason to bring this up again."

Esme said, more curious than offended by Seren's attitude, "I thought you were from the International Mage Assembly. Why are you looking into Corded Brotherhood records too?"

Gwyn folded his arms, showcasing the bravado he fell back on whenever he was uncertain.

Miles started to speak, ready to mention her Brotherhood credentials, but Seren silenced him with a gesture of her hand. And that same nagging feeling intensified, like an itch he couldn't scratch.

Seren pulled up the sleeve of her loose black sweater to reveal a wispy green tattoo wrapped around her arm. Then, to Miles' shock, the snake tattoo unmistakably moved. It coiled around Scren's neck, and the Corded Brotherhood band shifted like wisps of green shadows around her arm.

"No need for titles," Seren said with a smug tone. "However, I am indeed a member."

Everyone stared, momentarily stunned. Miles' own Brotherhood tattoo had never demonstrated such abilities. Was this a higher-level perk he wasn't aware of, or was it something unique to Seren's magic?

Staring pointedly at the tattoos, Esme tried, fidgeting all the while, but failed at containing herself. "I want that. Like... badly."

Miles shifted his attention to Esme, fondness tempering his concern. Only she would be fascinated by the magical application rather than threatened by what it represented.

Gwyn shot Esme a face of utter betrayal, but Abby looked like she was considering the same thing.

Finn unsuccessfully tried to smother a laugh. "Ya thinkin' about gettin' tatted, lassie?"

"Damn if I'm not tempted," she said honestly. "Especially a magic one."

Seren, to Miles' surprise, let out a short, quiet laugh.

It softened her, if only for a moment. "For what it's worth, I genuinely want you all to succeed. But stop screwing up, *damn it*! Consider this your warning. I won't deny your methods get results, but the exposure risks..." She shook her head. "Do better. Next time, I won't have the luxury of being so understanding."

As they left the meeting room, Miles found himself turning Seren's warning over in his mind. He didn't like the implications for Esme or Gwyn. Maybe it was time to take up his seat, if only to ensure that the people he cared about had a voice speaking for them. The only problem was that, thanks to Nudd, he understood how heavy a title could be.

Yet even as he strolled alongside Esme, his hand holding hers, he couldn't shake the impression that they were missing something important about their new overseer. For now, though, he pushed those thoughts aside.

CHAPTER NINE

LUNCH BREAK WITCH

Abby

The hospital cafeteria hummed with urgency as families scooped up food between visits and nurses stole a few minutes to breathe. Miles skewered a piece of lettuce with his fork, glaring at it like it had personally offended him. He wasn't happy with his diet. Esme's therapeutic baking had been a trial for everyone—especially Miles' waistline now that they lived together.

"Esme and Gwyn ran into a boggart at the mall," Miles muttered, stabbing the lettuce like it owed him money. "Disguised as a human. Strutting like it owned the damn place, then snuck into a staff-only hallway."

"Wait." Abby swallowed her fries. "What were they even doing there? Gwyn *hates* malls. The noise and halogen lights bother him."

"Uh... no idea." Miles hesitated, his fork hovering in midair. He opened his mouth, then closed it.

"Miles, you're a terrible liar." Abby smirked, one brow arched. "She's already complained to me about you playing pretty-pretty-princess with her."

He coughed and took a long sip of water. "What does *that* mean? Is this some Americanism I should be aware of?"

"It means you're going a little overboard on the whole 'provide' thing." Abby stared at him for a beat and grinned with a realization. "Oh my gods, my birthday!"

"Not another word," he warned, pointing his fork at her, but he looked defeated more than anything. "And now I've ruined the surprise. Hell."

Abby snorted but let him suffer in silence, focusing instead on her food. Their peaceful lunch was cut short when they both stiffened, sensing a mage approaching. A strong one.

Moments later, Seren Lewis glided into the cafeteria. Her gaze carved through the jumble of tables, locking directly onto them. A slow, tight smile spread across her face. As she approached, the glossy black of her nails clicked softly against the leather of her bag.

Miles set his fork down with a quiet clink, expression darkening.

"What could she want? Here?" Abby whispered, eyes tracking her approach.

"I haven't the foggiest," he murmured, clearly unhappy. "But let's keep this short."

Seren's style was what Abby privately dubbed "mid-life goth chic"—all black, from tailored pantsuit to chunky loafers.

"I can't believe I'm getting a two-for-one deal," Seren said, settling into a chair across from them without asking for permission. "What luck!"

Miles leaned back in his seat, arms crossing over his chest. "I had a boss disrupt my workday recently. It was as irritating then as it is now."

"And yet, you seem to be on your lunch break." She tilted her head, her expression mock-innocent. "So no harm done."

Abby, less openly hostile, cut in before Miles could respond, her tone polite but firm. "Hello, Ms. Lewis. What brings you here?"

"I'll be brief." Seren paused for effect. "I'm here to apply pressure. The selkie has already spoken with Dr. Goodwin about this, but it wouldn't hurt to reiterate. Ms. O'Malley, it's time you took up your seat in the Assembly."

Abby blinked. "Excuse me?" Seren was really doing this here and now?

Seren folded her hands on the table. "You and Dr. Goodwin would be excellent representatives for humanity." She side-eyed Abby. "Well. *Mostly* human."

Abby narrowed her eyes. "What is that supposed to mean?"

Seren ignored the question, turning instead to Miles. "Any thoughts?"

Miles shrugged. "No need to pressure me anymore. I'm in."

"Oh, good," she said breezily. "But I still need Ms. O'Malley."

Abby frowned. "Why do you need me?"

Seren sighed, as if the answer should be obvious. "Other than the fact that your mother can no longer hold her position?" She ticked off the answers on her fingers. "You're qualified. Everyone likes you. And we need you to do some dirty work. *The end.*"

Abby gave her a skeptical once-over. "Are you trying to get to Gwyn through me or something?"

Seren let out a hearty guffaw, the sound loud enough that it echoed through the cafeteria. "That one? No. He's a bit of an idiot, but I do like him."

Miles and Abby exchanged a confused glance. Gwyn was many things—arrogant, moody, occasionally infuriating—but an idiot? Hardly.

Seren leaned in slightly. "That said, I suspect he'd do just about anything you asked him to. Am I wrong?"

"If I say yes?" Abby already felt her hackles rising.

Seren's smile turned feline, her eyes glinting with amusement. "You get a pat on the back, dearest." Her expression shifted, turning nearly feral. "And maybe I'll look the other way at all of your little team's recent transgressions. You'll all be of better use to me with your asses firmly planted in the proper seats."

"Alright." Abby tossed the fry she'd been nibbling back onto her tray, her eyes narrowing. "What do *you* get out of this?"

"I gain two promising people involved in decision-making in a place I am eager to see prosper. And... Admittedly, it's also very satisfying to move the pieces on the game board."

Frustration tightened Miles' voice. "Game pieces?"

"I don't play pretend with people I respect." Seren's half smile held no warmth or amusement. "I'm offering Ms. O'Malley a chance to step into her rightful role. I offer the same to you. And if that happens to benefit me as well, so be it."

Abby crossed her arms. "And what if I say no?"

All traces of joviality faded from Seren's face, her expression turning deadly serious. "Then you'll leave yourself—and your friends—vulnerable. The malevolents are a bigger problem than ever, and rogue mages... Well, you know about that problem intimately. I'm here to fix things, not break them. I don't want Seattle like David Abington did."

Miles flinched at the name. He hadn't gone to his funeral, so the wound was still fresh.

Abby hesitated. Seren was manipulative, sure, but she wasn't wrong. The fight with Leon had been close—too close.

Abby's mind raced. The last time someone had talked like this, it had ended in blood and regret. This was power... and a chance to wield it on her terms.

"Fine," Abby said at last, her voice steady. "I'll take the seat. But on one condition."

Seren raised one perfectly sculpted eyebrow. "Do tell."

"You keep being *that* honest with us."

Seren appeared almost impressed for a moment. Then her knowing smirk returned. "Agreed. But don't expect me to hold your hand. Things will get messy before they get better." Seren stood, smoothing the front of her coat. "Good. This will be good."

Seren's expression sharpened into something that made Abby's danger sense prickle. With a gesture encompassing the trio, she said, "We can even work through your recent development together, Ms. O'Malley. Dr. Goodwin has had much more time to adjust to his halo... Just me, offering some of that *honesty* we agreed upon."

Seren's smile had fangs.

Across the table, Miles stared at Abby like she'd sprouted wings. She wanted to melt into the table.

"Halo?" he repeated as Seren walked away, his voice tinged with disbelief.

Abby dropped her head onto the tabletop with a quiet groan. She stayed like that for a long moment before mumbling, "Gods *damn* it."

So far, no one had been able to explain how one acquired a halo. But there were some undeniable benefits to the "blessing." Finn was convinced that it made your magic stronger and even granted additional abilities, like Miles' healing.

But she wasn't like Miles. She didn't have a demigod king living rent free in her head. If Gwyn was right, she was Creiddylad reincarnated, but that was the extent of her connection to the past. Creiddylad and Abby's essence were the same, but they would never be the same person.

She was simply... Abby.

Miles, patient Miles, sat with her, not saying a word as she straightened up with a snap. "Well," Abby said, lifting her head, "that seals it. I'm officially a magical mess."

"Abby?" he asked, subtly persistent.

She rubbed her temple. "I didn't understand it, okay? I noticed it after the fight with Leon."

Miles ran a hand through his hair, his expression a mix of shock and concern. "Bloody hell, Abby."

She shook her head. "Ugh, gods, I know."

"Why didn't you say anything?" Miles' voice was quiet but firm. "We've seen what secrets can do."

Crap. He was disappointed in her. Miles was the stable, dependable one. Abby did not like the expression now on his face when it was directed at her at all.

"It wasn't priority number one. I figured I'd deal with it when something came of it."

"Right, because unexplained magical phenomena tend to work themselves out." Miles scoffed good-naturedly.

Abby flicked a fry at him, which he caught without looking—and ate it. That diet really was getting to him.

"Have there been any other changes, anything at all?" Miles drummed his prosthesis on the table. "I have no idea if there should be with how long mine has been there. But the fact that Seren knows about it means mine must have been around for a while. Which, uh, thanks for telling me, Seren." A rare flash of genuine anger narrowed his eyes.

"It's mostly just... there," she admitted, voice tight. "But my magic is stronger. I don't know how useful it will be."

"Yet. You don't know how useful it will be *yet*. Think this has anything to do with... she who shall not be named?"

He was clearly trying to avoid upsetting her. Gwyn calling her Creiddylad in his confusion after he and Cerys had been electrocuted by a ponaturi shaman had been the instigating factor in their brief breakup a few months before. But they were over that now, so Miles needn't worry.

"Maybe. Probably. Gods, I'm clueless."

A tense silence stretched between them before Miles finally leaned forward, eyes locked onto hers. "We need to figure out what it means."

They glanced around the hospital cafeteria. It was bright, sterile, and full of people unaware of the magical world brushing against their own. She asked, "Okay... how?"

Miles grinned, finally giving up on his salad. "First, we torture you by making you tell the others. Then we torture you some more with good old-fashioned magical testing."

"Lose-lose for Abigail O'Malley." Abby gave a tired smirk. "I guess that saves me the trouble of deciding whether to tell Esme or Gwyn first."

Miles shrugged. "Do what you always do."

Abby pressed her lips into a thin line, pretending anger. "And what is that, *Doctor* Goodwin?"

"My official diagnosis is stress-induced loquacity. To put it in layman's terms, Nurse O'Malley, you experience 'word vomit'—unfiltered speech—when under duress."

She threw another fry at him. He ate it, too.

"Consider yourself, Cerys, and the imp invited for dinner at my place. The leprechaun will push his way into testing you anyway. Might as well cut some time before that happens."

Abby gave him a flat stare.

Looking for all the world like it completely put him out, Miles said, "Fine, Gwyn can come."

***

The sun was dipping below the Seattle skyline, reflecting the orange and lavender hues of the March sunset on Lake Union. The dock creaked beneath their steps as Abby and Gwyn walked down it toward Miles' floating house.

Gwyn shoved his hands into his coat pockets, grumbling to keep his voice low for their ears only. "I feel like I've spent more time with Miles these past few weeks than is strictly healthy."

Abby elbowed him lightly, a smirk tugging at her lips. "Stop pretending like you two aren't friends."

"Friends is going a bit far, Abigail," he countered, nose wrinkling. "More like comrades-in-arms. Occasional allies. Reluctant meal companions at best."

Abby rolled her eyes. He could protest, but a bromance was brewing. They bickered like an old married couple, but there was a mutual respect there, even if neither of them would ever admit it out loud. They'd even had a few recent conversations that didn't involve weapons or magic. *Progress*, Abby thought.

Before either of them could knock, the door to the floating house swung open, revealing Esme in an apron, holding a wooden spoon like it was a weapon. She threw her hands up dramatically. "I swear, I have baked nothing! Mr. Grumpypants even hid the flour!"

Abby bit back a laugh. "You look like a proper homemaker."

Esme gasped in mock horror. "Take that back."

"Nope," Abby said, stepping forward to pull her into a hug. "And thanks for understanding. I didn't have the energy to go out tonight."

Esme waved a dismissive hand. "Please, you're doing me a favor. I need one night off from him complaining about heart disease."

Esme had the benefit of a cambion's defenses against diet-related health problems—unlike the rest of them.

Finn was already inside, making himself at home hunched over a bowl of chips and salsa. He took one look at Abby's expression and groaned dramatically, sensing what was coming. "Bajesus, we're at it again already. Uff, can't a man take a break? I'm too old for this."

Abby flopped beside him, stealing a chip. "I thought sowing chaos was your natural state."

"True..." He handed her another chip.

They tucked into dinner, a spicy affair Esme had apparently learned to make from Will's abuela. The conversation was easy at first. Then Miles gave Abby "the look."

Abby started by sharing that she had agreed to be on the closed board. Miles backed her up by saying he'd agreed to do the same. That was the easy part. The truth about her halo was far more difficult to explain, especially after everything they'd been through together. She'd deliberately omitted the truth, which was basically the same thing as lying in her book.

Finn was the only one who didn't seem surprised in the slightest.

Abby pointed accusingly. "You knew, didn't you? Just like you didn't tell Miles about his halo earlier. You didn't say any-thing—*again*."

All eyes turned to Finn, who shifted uncomfortably under the sudden scrutiny. Esme, always the inquisitor, accused him with a single finger and a fierce glare. "What else are you keeping from us, leprechaun?"

For some reason, Finn's gaze flickered to Gwyn.

Abby caught the suspicious glance instantly, as did Esme. They exchanged a glance of their own, and Esme took Abby's unspoken cue to go after it.

"Time to tell us exactly why you're being cagey, Finn," Esme said, her tone leaving no room for argument. "Start talking, Pipsqueak!"

"You're all a buncha magpies!" Finn sighed, throwing his hands up in defeat. He stood up from his seat at the table and walked around the living room while everyone stared after him.

With Finn in a state of panic, Abby, not knowing how else to help, stood to start cleaning the table. "Abigail, dove."

She jumped and dropped the plate she was holding. Miles' swift telekinetic intervention prevented it from smashing into a million tiny pieces on the floor. *Good catch.*

Finn drummed his fingers against the back of a chair as his gaze shifted between them, obviously debating something. "You're my granddaughter, Abby. Gods help me. It's... compli-cated."

The spell keeping the plate aloft failed, and the plate completed its original descent to the floor. Its momentum gone, it gave only a slight bounce before rolling away.

Esme also nearly dropped the spoon she'd been holding. "She's *what*?!"

Finn muttered, "Oh, for feck's sake," as he stepped backward—straight into a side table. A fork clattered to the floor. Esme made a strangled noise somewhere between a gasp and a laugh.

Finn waved off the shock. "Oh, don't look at a man like that for no good reason. Had a bit of fun about one hundred fifty years ago, didn't find out about the results of it 'til two years back." He shrugged. "Sure, it's uncommon, but not unheard of for Fae to have a child with a human. I was a much younger man back then."

A feeble "what?" was all Abby could manage at first.

"Now the word vomit makes sense." Miles groaned, pinching the bridge of his nose. "But how did you 'find out' two years ago, Finn?"

"A little birdie chattered it in my ear. That's not important." Finn turned back to Abby, his expression softer. "What *is* important is how she feels about it."

Silence.

Abby could feel all their eyes on her. Her cheeks burned. She opened her mouth, then shut it again. Her mind whirled. A halo. A board seat. A grandfather who was literally a trickster Fae. What else hadn't she known about herself? What was she becoming?

Finn reached over, placing a tentative hand on her shoulder. "I wanted to get to know you before I said anything, dove. I was tryin' to take your, your mother's, and your brother's feelings into consideration."

When she finally regained the ability to speak, the first words that came out of her mouth proved Miles right. "Gods damn it, Finn!" Abby rounded on Gwyn. "You knew?"

Gwyn lifted his hands in surrender, expression sheepish. "He let it slip in Irish. I merely understood his words. It wasn't my place to tell."

Abby groaned and walked into the living room. She slumped back against the couch, muttering, "Unbelievable."

Finn cleared his throat. "So... do you still love your dear ol' great-however-many-grandpa?"

"Wonderful," she muttered. "I'm a magical smorgasbord. Do I at least get a pot of gold out of it?" But her voice wobbled on the last word.

"Doesn't matter if you're half-leprechaun or half-dragon," Esme said without missing a step. "You're ours."

Raising her eyes, Abby met Finn's earnest gaze. Despite the chaos, a curious sort of warmth spread through her.

Finn, for all his bluster and secrets, had become family in his own way. She sighed, leaning back. "You're lucky you're family, or I'd be way madder!"

The tension in the room broke as Esme burst out laughing. "Oh my gods, she and Colin have your hair! How did we never see it?"

With her characteristic unrestrained joy, Esme did a little dance and clapped. Beaming, she declared, "This is the strangest family reunion I've ever attended. If anyone else has a secret lineage they're hiding, now's the time to speak up."

Miles raised a hand. "I'm good, thanks."

Gwyn moved to the living room and slid an arm around Abby's shoulders, pulling her close. He didn't say anything, letting her lean into his warmth. And Abby found herself relaxing.

She'd deal with this by taking it one step at a time, the same way she dealt with everything else: the weight of her job, her parent's crumbling marriage, and the ever-present threat of monsters.

For now, though, she let herself enjoy the moment. What being part Fae meant, what having a halo meant, were both huge things. But now she had these people to share all of it with.

Chapter Ten

GRANDPA LEPRECHAUN

Abby

"Why, exactly, am I the rodent in this scenario?" Gwyn asked, legs folding like a broken marionette as he tried to settle onto a cushion clearly designed for someone much shorter.

Something about Gwyn's bewildered expression, so at odds with his usual grace, made Abby's heart flutter. She wanted to kiss him, but the revelation that Finn was her grandfather made showing affection in front of him seem inappropriate.

It was her first time being in Finn's house, and it was exactly as Esme had described it. He had recently moved the whole thing closer to town, a feat she hoped he would partially explain the mechanics of to her.

Gold trinkets littered every flat surface, weighing down the undersized, hand-hewn furniture like a dragon had raided a fancy thrift shop and never left. The white-washed cob walls and exposed support beams made Abby feel like she was sitting in a medieval Irish house instead of a fairy one in the trunk of a tree on the outskirts of Seattle. A crackling fire burned steadily in the fireplace, and Finn had even served them pie.

It had been a pleasant afternoon, even if Gwyn was becoming nervous at what came next.

She answered Gwyn's innocent question. "It's a science thing. They test medicine on guinea pigs so humans don't die. So yeah, you're my guinea pig. But I like you too much to let you explode or something."

Gwyn gave her the look that meant he was questioning his sanity in agreeing to this scheme.

Finn made a rare attempt at comforting him. "Relax, mate, it's gonna be fine!"

"Abigail, I think we should have brought this up with Jacob. He certainly would have helped." A slight frown creased Gwyn's face as he sniffed disdainfully at Finn. "Do you have an actual plan for this session, or will we be improvising the entire time?"

Two voices tried to answer at once. Abby said, "Jacob has enough on his plate right now. I don't want to add to it."

And, "I have a plan, ya narkey hole!" from Finn.

Gwyn sat back, giving his head a slight shake. His continued patience with both of them was worth acknowledging aloud.

"Be nice to my guinea pig!" Abby scolded, hands on hips, trying to sound stern through her grin.

"How can I not rile him up when his face looks like he's been suckin' on a fresh turd?" Finn dramatically rolled his eyes. "Fine! Dove, see that door? Go through it. I'm gonna have Gwyn try to scry ya. Your job is to block him, got it?"

She opened the door wide, expecting a closet or guest room. Instead, she stepped into a hidden conservatory lit by a warm, enchanted sun. Apple trees bowed under the weight of fruit, wheat shimmered like spun gold, and roses tangled with wild lavender, flooding the air with perfume. Herbs filled the final corner—basil, rosemary, thyme, and sage.

Finn hadn't simply blended magic and nature—he'd married them, growing a secret world inside a hollow tree. How it all fit inside a tree trunk was anyone's guess, but the sheer skill behind it left Abby awestruck. Esme hadn't told her about this! Seeing it made Abby momentarily forget what she was there for in the first place.

"I'm ready!" she shouted, hoping the sound would make it to the other room.

Settling before the herbs, she picked a thyme leaf, enjoying its scent as she rubbed it between her fingers. The subtle *ping* that resonated at the edge of her awareness was the only sign that Gwyn had done anything. Not wanting to leave the garden yet, she shouted, "Was that it?"

A blend of weary defeat and unmasked pride resonated in Gwyn's voice as it reached her. "Yes. I failed."

When Abby returned to the other room, Finn's cheeks were flushed a bright red, and a wide, beaming smile stretched across his face. "He couldn't even ding yer defenses, lassie!"

Abby was confused. "I didn't actually do anything."

"It's no matter. You're like Miles—can't be scried. Another test!" Finn was already up and bustling around the room.

He yanked open a drawer and pulled out a chef's knife that looked like it had seen battle. "We've got the perfect guinea pig for stabbin'."

Gwyn took a hasty step back.

"Stop!" It was Abby's turn to shake her head in wonder at what was wrong with Finn. "I can't heal like Miles. Already tried it."

Finn's shoulders slumped as he realized he wouldn't be stabbing Gwyn that day. "Alright, let's try somethin' you're shite at. How about conjurin' a bit of fire?"

"My hot hands spell is much hotter than before, but I still can't manage a real flame."

Gwyn was either bored or uncomfortable from sitting on the floor, fidgeting and staring at the ceiling, before an idea animated him. "How about an illusion? I don't think I've ever seen you cast one."

"A candle, right here on the table," Finn suggested, "Sounds simple, but gettin' the wax to melt and an illusory flame to look real, well, that's something' different altogether."

"Too simple. No illusions." Abby dismissed the idea with a wave. "Can we go to your conservatory instead? I have something different in mind."

Abby was actually excited for her family's annual Spring Equinox feast. Her parents had halted their divorce, and it seemed like they might even reconcile. Her brother and Will would be home for the weekend. She had Gwyn—really had him now. And Finn, well, he was a troublesome but welcome addition.

Finn blinked, then shrugged. "Sure. Just don't charm the tomatoes to sing or somethin' like that. I like it quiet at night."

They crossed into the sun-washed conservatory, warm with the scent of rosemary and loamy earth. Abby's eyes swept over the neat rows, the dwarf fruit trees, the riotous rose trellises, and finally landed on the tidy herb garden.

She kneeled before a modest patch of basil, the stems soft and the leaves branching out for every scrap of sunlight they could grab. "My dad always said basil was the hardest to grow in Washington. He's not even a plant mage, but somehow, he can coax anything green to thrive."

Hesitantly, she reached out, her fingers brushing the cool, smooth surface of the leaves. "I want to try something like that."

"You're thinkin' sentimental thoughts at the dirt now?" Finn asked, though his tone was more curious than mocking.

"Maybe." Abby smiled faintly and inhaled, closing her eyes. She remembered summers in the garden with her father, the dry warmth of the soil, the sound of him humming while pruning vines. He never used spells that she knew of, but his plants always leaned toward his magic.

With her hand resting against the basil, she reached for her magic. Abby already possessed a small amount of green magic, enough to coax a few flowers to bloom or make leaves sprout if she put a lot of effort into it. Her education with Josiah had guaranteed that.

Now, she closed her eyes, letting the warmth of happy memories and bright hopes for the future fill her before opening her eyes and channeling that energy into the plant.

At first, nothing happened. Then the leaves shifted under her fingertips. Tiny white flowers burst along a new stem, fragrant with sweet licorice and summer sunlight. The scent was stronger than it should've been—like it had been distilled from memory.

That scent intensified now. It grew sweeter, fresher, more intense.

For a breathless moment, the plant wasn't the only thing blooming. Something inside her unfurled at the sight.

"Hells..." Finn stepped forward warily, rubbing the back of his neck. "Abby, what exactly were you tryin' to do?"

Gwyn inhaled deeply. "That scent..." He kneeled beside her, eyes wide. "Reminds me of my mother's garden in the keep. I haven't experienced it since I was a small boy..." He trailed off.

Gwyn tore his gaze from the plant and turned to Abby, studying her carefully. "Abigail... Did you pull a memory from my mind?" His voice was quiet, almost hesitant. His face held no anger at her supposed intrusion; instead, he wore a strangely calm, vulnerable expression, his eyes soft and warm.

Did he truly trust her so completely, even after witnessing her destruction of his uncle's mind? Had this new magic twisted things without her realizing?

"I don't think she entered your peanut-sized brain, ya oaf," Finn answered for them both. "That prison really did a number on you." Though his brow furrowed, Finn spoke with pride. "I swear I can smell Wicklow... Dove, did ya mean to cast two magics at once?"

Two magics at once?

"I wanted it to grow a little. Flower," she said quietly. Abby was puzzled by their strange reactions. "I was thinking about my dad, how our family is growing."

"Cariad"—the grin Gwyn reserved only for her creased his cheeks—"I feel as though I've enjoyed the most pleasant day outdoors as a child."

Finn agreed. "You didn't just make it grow. You fed it feelin'." Finn huffed, waving a hand at the plant. "Well, that's a fine thing. You're sneakin' magic into our hearts. I take it this is the first time you've done somethin' like this?"

Abby nodded, nervously tucking an errant curl behind her ear.

Naturally, the next thing that happened was more arguing. Gwyn and Finn went at it for a few minutes while she was standing right there, confused.

Gwyn stood, hypothesizing, "Might this simply be an empathic extension of her neuromancy?"

"Maybe... she stretched her aura?"

"Only certain Fae can do that."

"She's part Fae."

"Barely. Leprechauns can't."

"Uff, true, but perhaps this is just the begin—"

"I'm right here!" Abby interrupted.

A chorus of apologies followed.

"I was feeling all nostalgic and hopeful about the upcoming equinox dinner with the family. Some of that likely influenced the magic. I didn't mean to do anything strange."

"Possibly," Finn replied, his scrunched expression hinting at uncertainty. "Or maybe somethin' about that emotion allowed you to tap into the magic. That's how it went down for Esme. To use infernal power, she had to focus on her anger."

Abby's eyes widened. Was that what this was? Her magic didn't feel dark, demanding like Esme's. It was... warm. Familiar.

"But Miles said his powers unexpectedly appeared."

"He's also possessed by a feckin' dead king!" Finn's patience held, though he was a little exasperated. "Count your blessings, dove."

Gwyn's earlier warmth vanished, replaced by the intense focus of a scholar. "If you didn't intend to do that, what could you do deliberately?" His hand twitched at his side, like he wanted to reach for her but held himself back.

"Aye," Finn added, crossing his arms. "This is a bit terri-fyin'. If you change your intentions, you might be able to do somethin' more than grow a tiny plant. You could torture a man with feelings of guilt or despair."

Gods, that made her power sound like something she needed to handle carefully. Well, it was fortunate that she'd spent her whole life knowing that she could make a brain melt inside someone's head if they pissed her off enough. She had excellent self-control—she hoped.

"Let's try again!" Finn suggested. "I know you said illu-sions were too simple, but try puttin' emotion into it—a pleasant one, please. Then we can move on to losin' the il-lusion altogether and focus on projectin' just the emotion." Finn made an excited sound that was somewhere between a *yip* and a *squee*. "I'm so proud of ya!"

***

"I thought my soul was being pulled from my body." Gwyn was panting, curled up in her sheets. "We cannot do this frequently, cariad, or I might actually die."

Gwyn's grumbling was at odds with the satisfied, smugly content expression on his face.

"Can't have that," Abby purred, her smile suggestive as she lightly ran her finger along the hard contours of his chest. "Thanks for allowing me to experiment some more."

He'd put up with her practicing magic on him all day. While mostly positive, some emotions she'd projected onto him earlier hadn't been pleasant. At the end of a long, productive day, he deserved a reward. It was all the better that she could share it with him.

Gwyn pulled her in to nestle in the hollow of his shoulder. "Abigail, given what happened today, we should speak of Creiddylad," he said, his voice heavy with regret.

Abby raised to meet his eyes. "Please, tell me."

"She didn't cast fire or storms." He gestured in an arc with his free hand. "That wasn't her way. But she could... change a room by walking into it. She could bring peace to men too angry to see straight. Make warriors stop fighting long enough to remember they had children." He spoke into her hair, ruffling the strands with his breath. "There was something in her magic, your magic, that didn't work like everyone else's. What you did earlier... it resembled her work."

Abby swallowed, unsure whether it was fear or wonder rising in her chest.

"We already know you have the power to control minds," he said gently. "I think this addition is the other side of it. I think this power is meant to move hearts as well. You're exactly the right kind of person who deserves to wield that strength, cariad."

They sat in silence for a moment, the kind that didn't need filling. She reached up, fingers brushing his hair as he leaned into her hand without hesitation. He kissed her palm once and closed his eyes.

His gentle kiss was like the perfect punctuation mark at the end of a pleasant conversation. While that was nice, it still wasn't enough for her. So she pulled him into another kiss. Never before had she been so happy that he'd chosen to let her in, to tell her everything.

Chapter Eleven

FAMILY FEAST

Abby

Abby leaned on the granite countertop, absently spinning her wineglass as the scent of rosemary and thyme curled through the air. Her mother placed the steaming lamb roast on a trivet like she was presenting her triumph to a televised food competition host.

"Need any help?" It wasn't the first time Abby had asked. "I think this is the first time we've ever done lamb. Why the change?"

Her mother, Christi to most people, shot her a glare that would shrink the ovaries of a lesser woman. "Abigail Grace, if you keep asking me if I need help, I'm going to walk out of this kitchen in protest. Drink your wine and let a woman work!"

"See? I knew you needed a break." Abby grinned, sipping her wine. "Still doesn't explain the lamb, though."

"We have three guests this year! The lamb is to make Gwyn and Finn feel at home. Will doesn't care so long as it contains protein, so I'm not worried about him. Now, go get the door."

Except the doorbell hadn't rung yet.

A wave of relief and hope washed over Abby as her mother's prediction came true. She must have regained enough of her magic to "listen" to the house's wards.

"I'll get it," her father called from the living room, where he'd been watching some historical documentary with Gwyn. It turned out their shared bond was a mutual love of pointing out inaccuracies on television shows. Plus, Sean O'Malley had grown up in County Mayo, so his Irish was good enough that Gwyn could practice (and update) his own while they did it.

Abby followed her father to the door, wine in hand, to see that Finn had shown up looking like an Irish mobster flanked by his two toughs, her brother and his boyfriend, Will. Beige details and gleaming gold buttons punctuated the leprechaun's blindingly white suit. Naturally, he'd overdone it with a large golden shamrock on his lapel and another on the side of his fedora.

Colin and Will wore the same casual attire as everyone else, fitting for a family get-together. Her brother and Will were similar and yet still opposites. Will was a tall, broadly muscular, heavily tattooed Hispanic man with enough innate sass to make anyone blush. Colin was fairly short, like Abby, with blond hair and blue eyes. He was also quite fit, but his strength was in dexterity and agility rather than brute strength.

Before either Abby or her father could get a word in, Finn boomed, "Happy Equinox!" and shoved a beautifully wrapped box into her father's hands.

"I brought the eighteen-year. Only the best whiskey for a family dinner!"

Her father blinked down at the box as Finn shoved past him. By the time he looked back up, Colin and Will engulfed him in a hug. Once her father could finally breathe freely, Colin asked, "How are you managing, old man?"

"Colin, you were here two weeks ago," Abby snapped. "Lay off the mother hen crap."

Colin had been overbearing since New Year's when Leon had shattered her father's body and nearly stolen their mother's magical gifts. Colin was still guilty about not being at their house that night since he'd been staying with them for the holidays.

Secretly though, Abby was relieved Colin had been out. She was sure Leon would have killed him; Colin wouldn't have quit until he couldn't move or cast magic.

Their mother appeared, wiping her hands on her apron. "Are you all going to stand in the doorway all night, or can we eat?" She'd already enlisted Gwyn and Finn to carry trays of food and wine to the dining table.

An hour later, Abby leaned back in her chair and surveyed the scene with a second glass of red wine in hand. The whole family was there *and* getting along. Such moments were uncommon, even if monsters weren't constantly trying to kill them, so she refused to let it slip by unappreciated.

As Colin and Finn traded barbs, her father rested a hand atop her mother's on the tabletop. Through all the fighting, the divorce papers, and months of therapy, they'd found their way back to each other. Abby wanted a return to their past, to the deep love they'd shared before her mother's magic and the Corded Brotherhood's secrets had driven them apart.

Across the table, Colin had his arm draped casually over Will's chair. Will, ever the sass master, was mid-story, his hands animated as he recounted some ridiculous encounter with a drunk customer at his new bar in L.A. Beside her, Gwyn sat quietly amused, his sharp features softened with a rare smile. And then there was Finn, who was currently doing his best to charm the entire table.

"So," Colin said, stabbing a roasted carrot, "how's civilian life treating you, Mom?"

Their mother's smile tightened. "Fine. I do my nine-to-five, then my day ends. Honestly, it's a pleasant change of pace. Perhaps I'll finally get around to pursuing some hobbies. Getting nearly killed really puts things in perspective."

"Oh, honey," Will drawled, grinning as he tipped his wine glass toward their father, "nothing says romance like a near-death experience."

Colin snorted, nudging his boyfriend. "And you call me dramatic."

"Yeah, don't pretend that you didn't fall for me when you saw me tackle that nasty fish Fae thing."

"It was a nøkk." Abby rolled her eyes but grinned. The conversation flowed easily, laughter punctuating every few sentences. Still, she still had one more bombshell to drop.

Abby cleared her throat, fingers tightening on her glass. "So... I've accepted the offer to take Mom's seat in the Assembly."

The table went silent.

A moment of wide-eyed shock from her mother made Abby think she might cry. But then her mother smiled, her eyes glistening. "Oh, Abby. That's... that's wonderful. You'll be better than I ever was."

Abby still didn't quite understand why she was being strong-armed into the position, so she kept quiet on the details. Seren had already admitted that she wanted to use her mental manipulation abilities. Abby could only discover how she planned on doing that by playing along.

"To Abby," Colin said. "Seattle's newest power player. Gods help the Assembly."

"And to new beginnings!" Finn added, eyes suspiciously bright. "Sláinte!"

As everyone raised a toast, Abby felt a lump in her throat as her glass touched Gwyn's. So what if she was being a bit melodramatic about the whole thing? Her entire life, even her identity, had been upended in the past year. For once, everything was perfect.

Until Finn ruined the perfectly serene moment like a dropped glass. He clapped once, far too cheerfully. "Well, if we're makin' confessions, might as well get on with it."

Abby glanced at him warily. "Finn..."

Instead of jumping straight into the confession like she'd thought he would, he told a story about waking up in a whiskey storehouse in the middle of Dublin, piss-on-himself drunk.

"So there I was," Finn said, leaning forward with a grin, "with flames licking at my boots, and I thought, 'Well, Finn, you've really done it this time!'"

Abby snorted into her wine. "Let me guess. You accidentally set the whole place on fire?"

"Ah, dove, you know me too well." Finn winked.

Finn's story had held her father's attention for several minutes, his expression unreadable, until he finally asked, with an expression of awe on his face, "Is this *the* infamous Dublin Whiskey Fire of 1875?"

Finn froze, his mug of ale halfway to his lips. "Ah... well..."

"Aye, the streets ran with whiskey," her father said, eyes gleaming with academic enthusiasm. "Thirteen dead. Poisoned from scooping it straight from the gutter."

"Not my fault they had low standards! They didn't perish to my flames." Finn scoffed, a hint of shame showing on his face for the first time. "But, aye, that might've been the fire."

The table erupted into laughter. Even Gwyn, who usually remained stoic, cracked a smile.

"In my defense, it was an accident!" Finn shrugged, his cheeks reddening. Then he pointed at Colin. "Besides, it led to me meetin' their great-great-great-grandma, so I'd say it all worked out in the end."

Silence descended upon them like a leaden weight. Christi O'Malley blinked, started to ask a question, but then decided against it. Colin opened and closed his mouth. Sean O'Malley's expression suggested he'd swallowed a fish whole.

"No way." Will was the first to recover.

"Maggie..." Finn said reverentially. "Lovely woman. Fiery red hair. Great pair of—"

"Finn!" Abby interrupted him.

At this, the leprechaun didn't appear the least bit shame-faced. "I was wanderin' through the streets, most of my clothes burnt off, tryin' not to attract attention, when a beautiful mage saw right through my glamor. She was a widow at that point, mind. Childless and still in the mournin' blacks. She invited me in, one thing led to another, and nine months later—well, turns out I left somethin' behind."

"Gods above and below," her mother muttered into her white wine.

"How long have you known?" Her father's tone suggested he was uncharacteristically upset.

"Not until two years ago," Finn admitted. "When I found out, I wanted to get to know my family before dumpin' this all on ya."

Her father sat back, sufficiently mollified by the statement, but he rubbed their mother's back, trying to comfort her or keep her from lashing out, or both.

Will was laughing silently, shoulders shaking. "Only in this family," he managed between breaths.

"So we're part leprechaun?" Colin asked, examining his hands as if expecting them to turn green.

"Part Fae," Gwyn corrected. "It should explain a few inherited traits."

Her father leaned back in his chair, a smirk tugging at his lips. "Like why Christi's always been too honest for her own good."

"Oh, hush." Abby's mother swatted his arm, but she was laughing. "If anything, it explains our height deficit."

Finn's eyes softened as he looked at Abby's mother, an expression of warmth and affection that was far more familiar than any he'd ever revealed before. "She's got the same fire Maggie had."

Her mother was shaking her head, but she was smiling. "This is... a lot to process."

"Why tell us now?" her father asked.

Finn shrugged. "Seemed like the right time. Family coming back together and all that." He nodded at her parents. "New beginnin's, like I said."

Even after all that, everything felt... right.

"Well," Abby said, raising her glass, "to family and new beginnings. However weird and complicated."

"To family," they echoed, rolling with the punches just like they always had.

CHAPTER TWELVE

OLD FRIENDS

Seren

Seren sat rigidly, frozen mid-keystroke at her desk in Assembly headquarters, her fingers hovering over the keys as she resisted the very real urge to strangle her visitor. Finn sprawled across the visitor's chair, his boots up on the edge of Seren's formerly immaculate desk. His presence felt like a candle flickering too close to dry parchment, comforting in the light it provided, but always on the verge of catching fire.

The serpent, agitated and coiled tight, shifted around her neck. She didn't need to ask what had stirred it. More than the leprechaun's presence was affecting it that morning. The open windows behind her desk offered a view of the city slowly awakening, unaware of the approaching disaster.

Finn eyed the tattoo moving on her shoulders and asked, with that trademark half-smirk of his, "What's the message, oh legless one?"

Seren's gaze remained fixed out the window. "Everything I've done still isn't enough," she said quietly, trying to control the twitching of her fingers. "You already know what that means."

The storm she'd seen forming on the horizon wasn't clouds. It was a list of names, inscribed for death, and Finn's was near the top.

There was a beat of silence as she turned to face him. Finn tensed, his grin faltering. He sat up properly, the well-made soles of his shoes making a soft thudding sound on the floor. Too casually, he said, "I still don't think this is right. He couldn't wait until I got one more grandbaby out of it?"

She almost forgot why she put up with his antics until he said something like that.

"That's pretty much guaranteed with how those two look at each other when they think no one is watching." Seren shuddered theatrically to conceal how close she came to smiling.

The snake moved, slow and thoughtful, curling up along the curve of her neck to whisper in her ear. Its message transcended words; its impact went far beyond mere speech to form as pressure behind her eyes. The cold, ancient brush of Arawn's presence seeped into her mind.

"You'll get that grandbaby," she said with a flicker of amusement that couldn't quite reach her eyes. Hope was a dangerous thing for people like them—people caught up in a millennium of plans made by gods.

Finn's grin returned quickly, too quickly, brighter and more brittle than before. "Have the big man give the little one a fightin' spirit and we've got a deal."

Seren laughed, rich from its unexpectedness. "I'm surprised you didn't ask for your own second chance."

She folded her hands together and leaned back. The snake settled again, its body cool under her skin, but its mind was far away, listening to another voice. She studied Finn, noting the weathered hands, the grin that didn't quite reach his eyes anymore.

"Could it be me?" Finn asked softly. Hope flickered in his eyes and died just as fast.

"The world needs another millennium before it's ready for another one of *you*." She added more gently, "You may not want that. We don't yet know what Gwyn's deal with Arawn was. Though Arawn likes the idea of you being on solid ground, if you get my meaning."

She watched the message land. A fleeting, frozen smile flickered across his face, but she saw the underlying pain threaded with a string of hope.

He was coming to terms with the necessity of what needed to happen next.

"Ha!" Chuckling, Finn rubbed the back of his neck. "Doesn't think he can put up with me for too long, does he?"

"You're still quite good at pretending this doesn't bother you."

"I shoulda been dead a long time ago." Rising from his seat, Finn stretched in a way that seemed less like a simple action and more like a theatrical display. "Guess we'd better get to work, then. Before we start countin' out graves."

Seren said nothing. She'd been counting out graves for so long that the years blurred together. The viper's tail flicked once on her collarbone in approval. "It's hard for your kind to notice, but time is passing much more quickly than you think. This is where the ending begins."

She didn't need to say the rest because Fionn already knew what they were working against: catastrophe.

And maybe, just maybe, she had one more idea that might keep him out of a hole in the ground...

The moment he left, the names on the list filed one by one across her thoughts.

One of them... one of them had started it all. When she dreamed that night, it was a memory.

She'd been there so long that time folded in on itself, devouring its own tail like a serpent. Even her anticipation of what came next had long since dissolved into silence. One moment, the void was all there was. The next, the crush of gravity brought her to her senses.

The air was too warm.

It pressed against her like wet wool set too close to the hearth fire. Eyes closed, she breathed in. The scent of crushed grape leaves, blooming elderflower, and something unfamiliar. It was a burning, acrid stench, like rotten oil and smoke, thick and suffocating. The very air reeked of strange magic.

She had known to expect over a thousand years of change, but she hadn't expected to first experience it in the way the world smelled.

She opened her eyes. She was on her knees in a patch of wild earth, breath shallow and sharp in her chest. Her hands sank into the cool moss. Her woolen gown clung to her, heavy and far too hot. It was once fine wool dyed the deepest black of her magic. Now it hung in tattered strips off her body. It, like she, belonged to a world that no longer existed.

Her heart surged with panic. Her body with magic. One fought to disappear, the other to destroy. Magic thrummed beneath her skin, coiled tightly, barely contained. She did not know the names of the trees around her, did not recognize the sun's position in the sky, and the sounds of this place—a constant growling sound in the distance—felt utterly alien.

A twig snapped.

Before she could think, a whip-crack of magic exploded from her. It was an instinctual surge of power, older than the towering oaks that surrounded her. A figure yelped in surprise as the invisible force slammed into the tree trunk beside him. "Feckin' shite!"

The sharp snap echoed through the silent woods as the bark splintered.

The figure moved between two narrow trees at the edge of the clearing and leaned leisurely against a trunk. He was too bright—sun-blond hair, clever blue eyes, clothes made of fabric so fine they must have been crafted from magic. He held a bottle of dark red liquid outstretched in one hand like it might save him from her wrath.

"Bonjour." He grinned. "Or... feck, what do I even say to a wrathful goddess with murder- hungry eyes?"

She stood so fast the frozen ground cracked beneath her feet. Her magic coiled again, a violent eruption of shadows ready to snap his spine like kindling. She didn't recognize his language. Didn't care.

The man didn't flinch, only held up a hand. "Dhuit!"
Irish... Hello.

A tentacle of her wrath erupted from behind him like a striking viper.

She saw his pointed ears a moment before he mist walked away. A leprechaun. He was so tall she'd simply thought he was a short man.

He appeared some twenty feet away, wheezing, still holding the bottle of sloshing liquid.

"Arawn sent me a piece of work," he grumbled, though she couldn't understand a word. "I only came for the sauvignon, not a smiting!"

He held the bottle high in the air like a white flag.

Arawn. She immediately leashed her magic.

He spoke in Irish. "S'pose I should've led with that."

She sniffed the air again, a puzzled frown furrowing her brow as she tried to decipher that strong, unfamiliar scent.

"Yeah, that smell?" he added, sniffing the air dramatically. "Not brimstone. That's gasoline. Cars. Machines. Humans figured out some wild things in the past fifteen-hundred years, Queenie."

She stared. His accent was strange, the vowels too round, the consonants softened by time. But finally, he'd said a few words she could understand.

She stepped toward him, magic crackling at her fingertips.

"I said—I'm not here to fight, lady! Arawn sent me. You know, Lord of the Dead, Lord of Shadows, King of Scary Shit?"

"You lie," she rasped.

"Do I look like I lie for free?" he asked, tossing back a bit of the red liquid in his bottle.

She blinked, and her brow furrowed in confusion. For a moment, she forgot to kill him.

"Name's Fionn. Former prisoner like yourself, currently on magical parole, and sent here to collect you before you accidentally implode the entire feckin' Bordeaux region."

While she didn't understand everything, his tone, the way he said her name, and his posture conveyed genuine sincerity, albeit in a ridiculous sort of way.

"Fionn," she said slowly, tasting the name. "Leprechaun."

The leprechaun watched her face, then raised the wine bottle in a toast. "I actually go by Finn now. You'll need a new name too. And you, my terrifying lady, look like you could use a drink."

She nearly shattered the bottle out of spite. But then the scent caught her. It was dark, spiced, alive. All the things she hadn't been for far too long.

Finn's grin widened. "That's a yes, then."

She tilted her head, regarding him. He appeared utterly re-laxed, almost unbothered by the fact that she had tried to reduce him to a pile of gore. It was rare that her aim was off. It probably had something to do with her emergence from the prison. Lucky.

She could still kill him. The urge prickled under her skin. But she let her hands fall to her sides. Her magic sizzled down to an ember.

She took the bottle and drank deeply. Let the searing alcohol, a ridiculous Fae, and the smell of a foreign land bind her to her strange new reality.

Finn plopped onto the moss beside her, heedless of the danger, and pulled a second bottle from his coat. "Grand," he said. "Now that we've survived the traditional Fae greeting, explosions and death threats included, how about we work on the not-murder-ing-each-other part of this arrangement?"

She let out a measured breath, trying to rid her body of doubts, of the lingering chill of the prison. She drank from the offered bottle as she stared at him, assessing.

He grinned again.

For the first time since waking, something tugged at her mouth. Only a ghost of a smile flickered across her face.

Finn's eyes twinkled. "There it is. I knew you had a sense of humor in there, deep under all the divine wrath."

She glanced meaningfully at the shattered tree behind him. "That was me being merciful."

"Oh, believe me," he said, brushing bark off his shirt, "I noticed. Welcome back," he added, clinking his wine against hers.

She remembered thinking, So this is where it begins. With wine and a ridiculous leprechaun.

Chapter Thirteen

A Spring Wedding

Esme

The thin layer of snow reflected the light of a thousand polished surfaces, making the crisp spring mountain air shimmer and dance with it. Esme pulled her jacket tighter, warding off both the cold and the feeling of being underdressed. Much to her dismay, she'd learned too late that the dress code for a Sasquatch wedding involved being draped in precious metals and cabochon gems—preferably in excess.

Unfortunately, none of the humans in attendance were billionaires or covered in fur, and they had hiked six hours through snowmelt to get to the ceremony. So they stood in waterproof boots and insulated layers, painfully practical amid their hosts' resplendence.

A few months back, the groom, Sitkum, had playfully teased Finn regarding the golden bridal crown he was crafting for Matika, his soon-to-be wife. Esme had suspected playful exaggeration, but the wedding left no doubt about the People's passion for going all out.

The hike to get to the wedding's location was long enough that returning home immediately after wasn't an option. The Sasquatches had directed them to a location among the towering trees a short way past the ceremonial grounds, where the tents they'd brought along would be shielded from the wind. They'd left Lily and Cerys at home once again with Jacob. Esme thought privately that he seemed to enjoy the dogs' rowdy company.

A vein throbbed in Finn's temple. He had been twitchy ever since they'd arrived, eyes darting among the mountains of gold adorning the People's furred bodies. He was acting like a drug addict in dire need of his next hit.

Gold cuffs encircled thick wrists, pendants the size of dinner plates swung against shaggy chests, and gemstones—some uncut, others polished to a high gleam—were woven into their fur. The People put on a display that should have had Finn gleeful, but instead, he was nearly feral, hands clenched at his sides as if resisting the urge to start cataloging the value of everything in sight.

"Breathe, Finn," Esme muttered. "Gods, if we'd known, I'd have asked Miles to bring some strong anti-anxiety meds for you."

"I am breathin'," he snapped through gritted teeth. "Ya don't understand. They're wasting it. That ruby—" He pointed a trembling finger at one particularly ostentatious Sasquatch. "It's raw. It hasn't even been cut properly. And the gold? Sittin' there, barely worked—"

"Not our culture; our opinions don't matter," Esme reminded him with a bit of bite in her words. Though Finn was likely too deep in his personal crisis to actually hear her.

At least everyone else had adjusted. Abby and Gwyn stood nearby, their hiking gear slightly softened by the flower crowns Abby had woven from the first brave blooms of spring. Delicate white petals sat against Abby's bright hair and Gwyn's dark, a small nod to the wild opulence around them. Esme lifted a hand to her own crown, fingering the petals. She felt slightly less like an intruder wearing it.

Miles, however, remained stubbornly bareheaded.

"You could just wear the damn thing," Esme whispered.

Miles didn't even glance at her. "No."

"You're the only one not wearing one."

"I'm aware."

Gwyn, standing beside them, sighed in exaggerated disappointment. "It's a symbolic gesture, Miles. A way to honor the occasion."

Miles folded his arms. "I don't need a flower crown to show respect."

Tension showed in his jaw and shoulders. The real reason he refused. Ever since Nudd Llaw Eraint had decided to make his presence undeniable during the fight with his half-brother, Llefelys in disguise as "Leon," Miles had been wrestling with what that meant for his future. No matter how simple the crown was, Miles undoubtedly saw it as another symbol of a fate he hadn't asked for.

Gwyn must have sensed the true reason behind Miles' hesitation, because he let out another sigh. This one softer, less exasperated. "Ridiculous," he murmured, though the sharp edge had dulled.

The ceremony began before Esme could needle Miles about the crown any further. A deep, resonant hum emanated from the Sasquatch officiant. The weight of his gold chains seemed to amplify the sound, vibrating through Esme's bones. The gathered People joined in, their deep voices a powerful counterpoint to the wind whispering through the trees. Not a song, not quite speech. It was something older, something primal, that seemed to make the mountains feel closer.

With their fur meticulously groomed, Sitkum and Matika stepped forward. Directly in front of them, a thick, heavy log lay on the ground. When the officiant signaled them, they simultaneously took hold of the opposing handles of an impressively large, hand-hewn saw.

Esme leaned toward Abby. "So, do they—"

"They cut it together," Abby whispered back. "Symbolizing how they'll overcome hardships as one."

Esme nodded, watching as the couple began sawing in unison. Their pace was deliberate, not from weakness, but from a careful, coordinated movement. The sound of metal on wood punctuated the low hum of the waiting guests. As the log split with a satisfying crack, the humming reached a crescendo. And the sky above them ignited with light.

Illusory shooting stars, created by the audience, blazed across the clearing in fiery arcs. Golden streaks reflected on the snow, highlighting the glittering gemstones and precious metals woven into fur, creating a stunning spectacle of light and color. It was utterly breathtaking.

As the stars faded and the crowd broke into cheers, Esme turned to Miles, hoping to see the same awe she felt written on his face. Instead, she caught something softer in his expression—he seemed genuinely peaceful.

Or maybe, just maybe, he was reconsidering the flower crown.

She smirked, holding it up. "Last chance, babe."

Miles growled quietly, shaking his head. "Fine."

Victory.

The newlywed couple, now covered in flecks of wood, navigated the throng of well-wishers. Sitkum absorbed back slaps that would have felled a human while Matika held hands with countless matriarchs as they wished her well.

The wedding reception was also a study in vegetarian excess. Fire-roasted root vegetables glistening with honey, massive platters of nuts and dried fruits, and bread so dense it felt like a meal on its own more than made up for the lack of meat. Sweet blackberry mead flowed abundantly, loosening everyone's tongues and encouraging laughter. Torches lining the rough-hewn wooden tables kept the darkness at bay.

Finn, to no one's surprise, had taken to the blackberry mead like a dying man to water. "For feck's sake," he slurred at one point, gesturing wildly with a half-empty wooden mug. "Ye lot are proper artisans, each one sittin' on a king's ransom. I might never leave."

Sitkum chuckled, patting Finn's shoulder with a heavy, furred hand. "From you, leprechaun, that is high praise. I get it; this is a lot, so here's a little something as an apology and a thanks for coming to my special day."

Sitkum produced a small ring, its top fashioned into the shape of a shamrock.

Finn groaned dramatically and took another swig, eyes never leaving the glinting gold. "I can't accept a gift on yer weddin' day." The trickster instantly sobered. "Because I have a few presents for you lot! Haha!"

The humans had already given the newlyweds their presents, mainly hard-to-obtain human goods that could be easily packed in. Esme had given them a starter of special yeast for baking.

Miles had handed over a tray of Sasquatch-friendly med-ications, some of which were likely prescription drugs he wasn't exactly allowed to distribute that way. But that was him, morally gray if it helped someone. Gwyn had brought a pair of finely honed knives for daily use. Abby had gifted the happy couple a bag of freshly dug alpine-friendly fruit and vegetable roots, promising a garden unlike any other.

Of course, Finn relished being the center of attention during this dramatic moment. He was likely pretending to be intoxicated. His magic act continued as he conjured a large gold coin out of nothing. He held it out before the couple and announced, "All couples get into a fuss at some point. I put a wee bit of Fae magic into this stunnin' coin. It only lasts about ten uses, but it'll be enough to get your relationship started. If you can't agree, flip the coin to settle it."

He showed the crowd now watching both sides of the coin. One side was clearly Sitkum, with a heavier brow and broader face. The other side was Matika's face, with more delicate features. "Ya both imbue a bit of magic into it, flip it, and whichever side lands face up has a bit more of the truth in it. Doesn't mean it's right, mind. Just means it's true." He straightened up, holding the coin aloft and announced, "Many happy years and fat furry babies to you!"

The cheers he'd hoped for came his way.

By the time the festivities had wound down, even Esme found herself pleasantly dazed by the heady mix of warmth, mead, and the lingering magic in the air. The Sasquatches bid them goodnight, disappearing into their mountainside homes.

Miles was already unlacing his boots when Esme crawled into their shared tent. "Tired?" she murmured.

"Wishing I hadn't had that third helping of bread," he admitted, rubbing his stomach.

She snorted. "You and Finn both."

Through the thin material, they could hear Gwyn and Abby whispering in the next tent, their voices low in the night's stillness. Finn, by contrast, was sitting fireside, audibly grumbling to himself about his full stomach.

A smirk played on Esme's lips as she nestled into their sleeping bag, lulled by the quiet mountain night.

For a while, only the wind whispering through the branches broke the silence. Sleep came easily.

Until the scream.

A sharp, startled yell cut through the night, followed by a thump and a flurry of curses in Irish.

"What the hell—" Esme was upright in an instant, pulling magic to the ready.

Miles was already on the move, yanking on his boots and grabbing the camp lantern he'd wisely brought.

A gust of wind slammed into the tents, billowing the fabric and rattling the stakes. Somewhere outside, Finn was cursing, his voice pitched high with peevishness and a bit of panic.

Then came a flapping sound—massive wings.

Esme knew another fight was brewing the moment she heard Miles' muttered "fuck" as she trailed him from the tent. Gwyn and Abby, sleep-rumpled but alert, emerged as Miles shined the lantern on the disturbance.

Finn's evasive maneuvers were aimed at a creature that looked like it was stuck somewhere in the evolutionary timeline between a T. rex and a modern-day harpy eagle. Despite the bright flash, it relentlessly chased what it considered its prey—Finn. It was easily twice Gwyn's height. How had something so enormous maneuvered through the branches to reach the forest floor?

Finn let loose thin ropes of fire at the bird, keeping it at bay. He shouted, "It's tryin' to feckin' eat me!"

Abby muttered to Gwyn, "Inconvenient time for you to leave Foxkiller at home," as they all started cautiously moving in Finn's direction.

Gwyn didn't have his crossbow, but he had brought his short sword, which he brandished then with a shout, trying to take some of the attention away from Finn.

It failed.

It was one of the rare occasions when Esme was sad that Miles hadn't brought his gun. She despised guns but knew they were sometimes the best tool for this job. Out of respect for the People's beliefs, he'd left it behind. European settlers had slaughtered thousands of Sasquatch as they'd traversed the continent. As a long-lived species, their population still hadn't rebounded in the centuries since.

A shimmering shield of magic burst into existence around Finn as he dodged the bird. Miles' aegis spell was world class. Even a hastily cast shield from him could withstand at least one blow from the enormous bird.

"It's a roc," Miles said, sneaking up on the bird, his daggers woefully inept for the task at slaying the huge animal. "Once they choose a target, they hyper-focus on it."

"Hear that, tasty Fae morsel? Keep dodging!" Esme shouted, already drawing power. Abby hung back, keeping pace with her.

The power Esme pulled from was all her own. Since Leon's death, she'd consciously reduced her reliance on infernal magic. Though they'd all been surprised with this fight, she wasn't going to risk attracting more trouble after everything they'd endured, particularly since they'd learned that having multiple god-touched people in one place had lured every malevolent for a hundred miles over the past few months.

"Trolls incoming!" she called out. "They'll hold it down!"

Miles and Gwyn took up positions on either side of the massive bird, waiting for their moment. A surge of power from Miles briefly solidified Finn's flickering shield.

Standing guard over Abby, Esme watched as Tom and George ripped through the fabric of reality near the roc's tail. The nine-foot trolls were hideous, their yellowish-gray skin stretched taut over bulging muscles with patchy gray hair. They were usually a trio, but Bert had been ripped apart last week by a horde of bloodthirsty rats the size of cats, and even if he was only a conjuration, Esme figured he deserved a break.

The trolls lunged for the roc's legs. But Esme had underestimated its feathers. Instead of a solid grip on flesh, the trolls came away with fistfuls of black plumage. Oops.

The roc screeched, furious.

They were all shocked by a second answering piercing screech.

The roc on the ground swung its head back with terrifying speed, its beak snapping inches from Tom's face. Its talons lashed out, gouging deep furrows in George's shoulder. But the conjurations held. Tom lunged again, this time managing to seize the roc's leg. George followed suit, their combined weight slowing it down, though not stopping it entirely.

The bird's head whipped around again with terrifying speed, wings snapping out to keep its balance. Its massive beak struck at George while its talons raked Tom's stomach, trying to disembowel him. The conjurations flickered, having lost some stability, but held firm.

The rustling of wings, a whistling of air, and a *thud* announced the second, even larger roc landing in the nearby clearing where the wedding had been held.

Finn used the distraction to catch his breath, though his hands smoldered with fire.

Abby stood slightly behind Esme, seemingly doing nothing.

Except she was. Abby's eyes were unfocused because her concentration was directed beyond the physical realm.

"Its mind is too slippery," she gritted out. "It's too—too stupid. Can't control it."

"Great," Esme muttered. "Plan B?"

All the while, the second roc approached on clawed feet, slowly squeezing its way through the trees.

Esme considered briefly using her infernal magic on the approaching malevolent creature, trying to control it like she controlled her conjurations. But the memory of Leon's desperate hunger for such power—the absolute worst person she had ever met—and Jacob's and Maureen's warnings against it made her wary.

"I'm going to confuse both," Abby decided, saving Esme from the impending mental debate.

After all the thrashing, the trolls finally got proper holds on the roc's legs in time for Abby's magic to hit it like a thunderclap.

Instead of bumbling around in confusion like Abby had aimed for, it went berserk.

Wings spread wide, the one focused on Finn thrashed violently, its beak snapping and claws raking at anything and everything. The trolls' grips slipped as they struggled to maintain control. The creature lunged, forcing Miles and Gwyn to leap away to safety.

Esme saw the strike coming before Abby did. "Shit—"

She shoved Abby aside as the roc's wing clipped their position. Abby hit the ground hard, but she didn't break her concentration.

Finn sent careful streams of fire at the roc, precise enough to avoid setting the forest ablaze. The creature was so crazed it barely seemed to notice.

The second roc bit at the trunk of a tree, slicing gouges so deep with its claws that Esme thought the tree would fall down soon.

"Not working," Abby hissed. She'd grown considerably more powerful after her halo had appeared, but they were working out the kinks in what kind of creatures her newly enhanced magic worked on. Humans, it did, reliably... too reliably.

The moment the confusion spell lifted, the first roc's primitive brain refocused on Finn. The second roc, well, it decided that its food of choice was the next smallest target: Abby.

The Enchantress became the sole focus of its attention.

Miles and Gwyn moved as one as Esme renewed her trolls with more magic. She and Abby crept slowly backward, not turning from staring down the larger roc.

Gods, it wasn't going to be enough. The only thing keeping the newcomer at bay was the mass of limbs it had to maneuver its massive feathered body through.

Miles dove in low at the smaller roc, his daggers finding the tendon in one leg with surgical precision. The beast shrieked, staggering. Miles had beat Gwyn to the punch, his blade striking first, making the bird round on him. Its movement deflected Gwyn's short sword at an awkward angle, only grazing it when his aim had been to skewer the beast.

As the roc's top half went for Miles in retribution, its claws lashed out at Gwyn. Abby sent a telekinetic burst to knock Gwyn off his feet—just in time. Esme was already summoning Bert and Oatmeal to join the fray.

From the ground, Gwyn sounded like he was cursing. Gwyn glanced up at Miles, gauging whether his distance from the group was sufficient for safety, and a burst of fulminomancy streaked from his fingertips, lighting up the night. It struck the roc as it turned to refocus on Finn. It shrieked but shook off the lightning magic like it was nothing.

"Enough!" Abby's voice rang with power as she unleashed a calming spell so strong it nearly knocked Esme off her feet. The valve allowing adrenaline to pump through her veins closed, and her heart rate slowed. She wanted to curl up for a nap right there in the leaves. Miles, mid-step, blinked and nearly sat down but smiled instead.

The trolls and shadowcat only stood there, awaiting orders from their puppeteer, who was far too relaxed to give any. Finn, Abby's primary magic instructor, gave Abby two thumbs up and collapsed in the leaf litter from physical exhaustion.

Both rocs swayed. Dazed. Drowsy. The larger one was now so near that Esme could almost feel its breath.

But Gwyn had been practicing with Abby since her powers had grown. He shook off the effect first, exhaling powerfully to rid his lungs of all air.

He sucked in a huge breath and surged forward, sword in hand. With all the force of his body and a bit of magic, he thrust the blade home into the first beast's ribcage.

With the sound of a falling tree, the massive bird collapsed.

Miles was so quiet in his sprint that she barely noticed his movement until he was at the larger roc's throat, slicing.

Silence returned to their supposedly sheltered campsite.

The rising sun was starting to peek through the branches overhead. Esme groaned and let herself fall back onto the dirt. Some help she'd been.

"So," she said after a moment. "Early breakfast?" She couldn't wait to pester Abby about that intense burst of calming magic. Her best friend had become a living, breathing weapon of crowd control.

CHAPTER FOURTEEN

UNSEELIE VISITOR

Jacob

Jacob steepled his fingers and exhaled slowly. He had endured countless meetings with Seren, each one a game of verbal chess, but tonight, exhaustion gnawed at his patience. He was too old and too tired for this.

"Enough," he said flatly, cutting through the pretense. "Then say it, Seren. Just say it."

A silence fell between them, yet Seren's face remained unchanged. If anything, she looked pleased that she had finally gotten a reaction out of him. The viper around Seren's shoulders shifted restlessly as her expression turned blade-sharp. The serpent flicked its tongue, as if tasting the air for prey.

A cold, heavy dread settled in Jacob's gut. He knew what came next. If he was lucky, a political move was about to be made. If he wasn't...

"Knowledge is preparation," Seren said smoothly. "Not threat. Unless it needs to be." She reached into her briefcase and slid a single photograph across the desk.

Jacob didn't want to look but forced himself. The price of ignorance could be worse. He sensed the trap close around him. He had walked right into it with eyes wide open.

Despite the poor quality, the picture unmistakably depicted David Abington, drool on his lapel, boarding the private jet Jacob had hired for their trip to London three months previous.

"And? I was taking him back to his wife."

"Ha!" Seren pantomimed a laugh. "You had him erased by a certain Enchantress in your employ. No trial. No justice. Only a vanishing act. *Poof.*" She tapped the photo. "Christi's magic isn't what it used to be, but the Assembly would still burn her for this. And Irene?" A soft chuckle. "Her soft heart... I think a trial by the Assembly would be too much for her."

Jacob's voice trembled more than he had hoped. "You wouldn't."

"Wouldn't I?" Seren leaned forward, her smile widening. "Your guided tour through Assembly politics all those years ago? Very educational."

Jacob's countless sins were steadily and surely sealing his fate, each one a shovelful toward his freshly dug grave.

"What do you want?" he whispered.

A slow lift at the corners of her mouth. "We've come to the part where I no longer give you a choice but to step aside, Jacob."

"You want Esmeralda." Jacob closed his eyes a moment to temper the rising frustration. If this were only about him, he could have accepted the risk. But Irene and Christi? No. He wouldn't let them suffer for his choices.

An insistent voice, like a long-forgotten conscience, reminded him of his repeated failures to shield Esmeralda. Jacob should have learned his lesson by now. Esmeralda was thirty-two years old. He'd been overprotective for far too long, and she'd continually called him out for it.

She'd been justified in her anger at his behavior each time. Maybe it *was* time he took a step back.

"Damn you," he muttered — not to her, but to himself, for failing again. But the decision was made. He pushed away from her desk, standing so abruptly his chair scraped against the floor. "I'm taking a vacation before I start acting rashly."

In his mind, he was already packing his and Irene's bags. If he had to accept this deal, he could at least enjoy sunshine and good food while doing so.

Seren smirked. "I was just about to suggest that."

"If any harm—*any* at all—comes to her. I will die to make you regret it."

"I would expect nothing less." She clapped enthusiastically in celebration.

Jacob fought an overwhelming urge to burn down her office.

Esme

The People were upset about the attack on their guests, but their relationship with the Corded Brothers allowed diplomacy to mitigate the blow to their pride. But, being a practical group, they were thrilled by the sheer volume of feathers now at their disposal. Plans were already underway to supplement the newlyweds' gifts with soft bedding and pillows. Sitkum suggested that some mountain lions, facing the last stretch of winter's lean times, might discover an unexpected abundance of poultry in their territory that day.

The hike and drive back to civilization took most of the next day. Arriving at Jacob's to collect the dogs, they were exhausted and slightly smelly from the lack of showers after battling two rhinoceros-sized birds.

Jacob, courteously (and suspiciously) silent about their disheveled states, surprised everyone by making a startling announcement. "I'm going on a vacation."

Jacob did *not* do vacations. Something was definitely going on.

Esme narrowed her eyes. "Where and why?"

Cerys and Lily were sitting at his feet, doggy faces smiling adoringly up at him. "Excuse me, young lady. I am not beholden to answer your questions."

Despite his serious demeanor, Jacob's eyes crinkled slightly, suggesting a smile was barely held back.

"Jacob, the last time you traveled, you were planning a murder!"

"Very well." Then a smile tugged at the corners of his mouth, the movement surprisingly strong, pulling at his wrinkled skin and making him appear almost youthful for a moment. "I'm going to Barbados with Irene. Happy?"

He was... *Holy shit.* Jacob was sleeping with David Abington's widow. Her brain stalled. Esme's mouth was not the only one hanging open.

"You're serious," she said finally. "Jacob. In flip-flops. On a beach." Esme shook her head and sniggered. "Okay... uh, we thought we'd also report to you on another malevolent attack at the wedding."

"No!" He held up a hand. "Absolutely not. Stop right there. I am officially on vacation. Take your problem to Ms. Lewis. I need this break. That woman drives me mad!"

Miles

They all headed home, resettled the dogs, and cleaned up. It was Sunday evening by this point, so Miles contacted Seren to meet them at the Assembly headquarters for a quick report. Finn politely declined, reminding them his prior agreement to assist *only when he felt like it* still stood. Miles couldn't blame him one jot.

The hallway to Seren's office was quiet. Miles walked beside Esme, Abby, and Gwyn, his mind already preparing a concise report. Jacob had a valid reason for his absence, but the resentment simmered as he prepared to face Seren's judgmental gaze instead.

He didn't trust her and doubted he ever would.

As they approached the door to Seren's office, Miles heard voices—low, urgent, and unmistakably tense. He held up a hand to stop the others, instincts kicking in. Something wasn't right. Esme tilted her head, her cambion hearing catching the muffled conversation. She mouthed, *Fae.*

He sensed the Fae magic, but the smallest taint of malevolence corrupted it. He gestured for them to stay back, and he approached Seren's office door on silent feet. Esme's eyebrows shot up in surprise.

He hadn't deliberately hidden his ability to silence his movements with magic; it simply hadn't come up in conversation before. He hoped Seren and whoever or whatever was in that room wouldn't detect his minor magical burst amid the magic that constantly soaked the Assembly offices.

He peeked through the slight opening. Inside, a hunched figure bowed before Seren's desk. Closer, he saw that it was actually prostrating itself before her. Its single arm was outstretched in supplication. The creature's voice was raspy, almost reverent. Miles, however, didn't understand a word. It wasn't speaking Brythonic, English, or Welsh.

And Seren was smiling at it. She was watching the creature like it was the neighborhood cat she was about to feed a snack to. *Fuck.*

A cold spike lanced through Miles' gut. Fachans were dangerous, unpredictable, and notoriously difficult to subdue. This unseelie Fae was intelligent and could work magic.

He crept back to the group and whispered, "It's a fachan. I'll silence our approach. Gwyn, if you can, tell us what they're talking about. She must be using some translation magic—who knows with what she's capable of. Abby, can you *subtly* cast a ward of silence on us?"

He eyed Abby. Her halo explained her recent incredibly powerful bursts of magic. They couldn't take the chance of her accidentally using too much magic and giving them away.

Stuffing down his rising anger at seeing what looked like one of their own consorting with a malevolent, Miles gritted out, "It's on the ground, unbound. If Seren is... It doesn't matter; we can't win against her."

He couldn't believe what he was about to say to the people who had become like family to him. "So keep a cool head and pretend like it's not a concern if she's working with it."

He was telling them to give up, to not fight. He couldn't see any way around it.

With a nod, he and Abby cast their concealment spells. Gwyn listened in for a moment, then dictated.

"He... it wants to serve her." Everyone heard Seren's lack of response. The silence stretched, and Miles peeked through the crack again.

Seren nodded her head. Her expression shifted into a cruel one. Seren raised one hand. The light drained from the room as her eyes blackened, a cambion storm brewing behind them.

A chill crept up Miles' spine as inky-black tentacles erupted from the floor, coiling around the fachan like spectral serpents. The creature moved its mouth to scream. But one tendril shot through its mouth and out the back of its head with a sickening crunch.

A small splash of dark purple blood sprayed on the office's rear wall.

A gurgling sound escaped the creature as the tendrils crushed its ribs. All at once, the tentacles disappeared and the remains of the creature thumped down on the floor in front of the desk, lifeless.

Miles flinched. Not from the violence, but from how clean it was. Like she'd done it a thousand times before.

Esme's minions were a testament to the art, but this was something else entirely. The sheer power, the precision, the cold efficiency of it... Seren was a force of nature. Miles' exhale was shaky, his heart beating rapidly as he pulled away from the door.

"I see what you mean about her," he murmured to Esme, just as he noticed that she'd seen the whole thing too.

With an unreadable expression, she nodded. Something flickered briefly in her eyes. Admiration? Fear? Miles couldn't tell.

"Think it wanted an internship? Brutal screening process," Esme whispered.

Miles grimaced. "Aye, bit of a rough exit interview."

Seren appeared in the doorway, completely unruffled. "*Bonjour*," Seren greeted them, her tone light, as if they'd walked in on her doing paperwork rather than disposing of an unseelie Fae. "Come in."

Esme stepped forward, her gaze flicking between Seren and the body. She was the first to enter. Miles exchanged a glance with Abby, who looked equally uneasy. They slowly filed into the office, following Esme. Gwyn was the only one who lingered near the door, his eyes scanning the room.

Seren's new office was bright and airy, boasting a stunning view of the Puget Sound. Miles was familiar with Seren's complaints about the original office Jacob had given her. Considering Jacob's nature, the action had been deliberate. And the upgrade, a concession.

The fachan's corpse sprawled on the floor and the blood sprayed on the back wall was jarring. Somehow the blood hadn't touched the four chairs Seren had already arranged for this meeting.

"Seren," Miles acknowledged her. "Care to share what *that* was about?"

Seren waved a hand dismissively. "It was hiding in my office. Nasty creatures. Best dealt with quickly."

Miles frowned. So she wasn't planning on explaining why it had been begging to serve her. Still, there was a strange comfort in knowing she'd killed the fachan rather than recruited it. *Small mercies.*

"Now," Seren said, settling into her chair, "what brings you to my office? I am here at your beck and call."

A flick of her wrist propelled the fachan's body backward to the rear of the room, a streak of dark blood following its path.

Esme's face scrunched up in horrified surprise. "Why are we all pretending like this is fucking normal?"

Seren laughed, the same hearty laugh they'd heard from her the day she'd shown up at the hospital cafeteria. "It isn't, but such is our life."

As Seren leaned back in her chair, her gaze lingered on Esme a moment too long. "I forgot to mention earlier. Congratulations on the boggart." Seren's expression was open, welcoming, but her eyes held a calculating coldness as she gestured for them to be seated. "Impressive work. Especially you, Esme. Took charge. Led well." Her gaze slid to Gwyn, narrowing, and her voice turned icy. "Unlike you. Acting like aristocracy, doing *fuck all* to lead."

Gwyn met her stare evenly. "I defer to those who understand the terrain better than I do."

Seren leaned forward. "Understand the terrain? Wales has malls." She let the comment hang before adding, "It's almost like you've been lying the entire time about where you're from."

Gwyn's past was a secret they'd all agreed to keep, but Seren wasn't one to let things go. They'd have to be careful.

Esme interjected, "How did you learn about the boggart fight?"

Seren shrugged. "I have spies everywhere."

Miles watched Esme's brow furrow as she clearly wrestled with whether to say what was on her mind. Avoiding eye contact, she itched her ear and pressed her lips together. Exactly as he predicted, she gave in to what was troubling her. "That, or that boggart was a conjuration."

"*Bon boulot*! It was." Seren's eyes returned to Gwyn as she restated her earlier words. "Fuck all, Mr. Newman. I expect better of you moving forward."

Miles interrupted, trying to get them back on track, his tone clipped but professional. "We've come to report on a malevolent attack."

As he detailed their encounter, Seren went from bored to interested. "And you say the People are handling disposal? *Mon Dieu*, there were two of them. Did no one think to check for eggs?"

"No." Miles drummed his prosthetic fingers on the edge of her desk, a nervous habit he couldn't quite shake. "It was an oversight."

Seren's lips twitched downward. "Too right. And I know you two"—she pointed at Miles and Abby—"have work tomorrow. So, Esmeralda, Gwyn, you're on the hook."

"For?" Esme asked.

"Fixing this error. Make an omelet for all I care. We cannot abide a brood of rocs."

Esme mumbled something under her breath. Miles suspected it was something about at least knowing where Seren's allegiances lay. Seren's gaze flicked to her, and for a moment, Miles was certain she understood every word.

The older mage only smiled in return. "Actually," Seren said, her tone shifting, "I think I'll join you, Ms. Turner. Mr. Newman can stay behind and catch up on his overdue paperwork.

No fun for him out in the field." She shot Gwyn a look that could curdle milk.

"You?" Esme blinked.

"Yes, me," Seren replied, her expression sharp. "I may be older, but I'm still quite fit. And I'd like to see why those mountains are such a magnet for malevolents."

Jacob's warning echoed in Miles' head: *Seren will try to influence Esmeralda. For good or bad, I do not know, but she will successfully sink her fangs into her one way or another.*

Except when Miles glanced at Esme, he saw the barely contained excitement in her eyes. Seren wasn't just another conjuration specialist. Of all the cambions Esme knew, she was the only one who could teach her something about her magical specialization.

Miles clenched his fists, his prosthetic fingers whirring softly. He hated this. Esme was his anchor, and the idea of someone else trying to control her—like David had warned, like Leon had done—made his skin crawl.

But what could he do? Esme wasn't his to control, no matter how much he wanted to protect her.

He wanted to scream. Not at her. At the world. At fate. At the slow, steady pattern of people seeing Esme as something to harness rather than someone to know. And worst of all? She was hopeful. He'd seen that look before. The last time, it had almost broken them all.

With effort, Miles let it go. She was her own person. Always had been. But knowing that didn't stop the fear. "Okay," he said, his voice tight.

Seren's expression toward him softened. "She'll be safe. You have my word on it. I value potential."

Yet Miles couldn't shake his apprehension, no matter how much he reasoned it away. Jacob didn't think she was a danger to Esme, but he didn't trust Seren. Trusting in Esme would have to be enough.

As they left the office, Miles turned to Esme, his voice barely above a whisper. "Be careful with her. Please."

Esme's earnest expression showed that she understood his torment. "I will. But this could be it. She could be the one person who can actually teach me what I need to know. I have to see where it leads, babe."

He gave a nod, but a knot of worry constricted his chest.

CHAPTER FIFTEEN

A PIECE OF THE ROMANTIC PAST

Miles

*"Without you, we would have met a different fate today."
The king—Nudd, Miles now remembered—gestured to the
sprawled corpses of gwyllgi, their fur matted with blood. "I
apologize for my errors and thank you for coming to our aid,
lady. We are in your debt."*

*Miles remembered this moment. He was back in the dream
he'd had the first night he'd met Esme, more than a year
before.*

*Nudd bowed deeply. After a puzzled moment, his retinue
followed suit. The action seemed to have struck Elena like an
arrow to the chest, silent but devastating in its impact. For a
single moment, her steel-clad composure cracked.*

*Regathering her wits, Elena looked around her as if expecting
another attack. "King, this place is not safe. I can feel evil about us.
What is the path forward?" she asked, her tone slightly less acerbic*

than it had been moments before when she'd called him out for wrongly rejecting her employ.

She was so much like Esme. How had Miles ever been confused about their connection?

Nudd replied, "I hope your sword will remain as sharp as your tongue. If you will stand with us, the way forward is together. We shall face whatever awaits us."

Previously, the dream had ended abruptly here, but this time, it continued.

"Lady, do you have a horse?"

Gore still clinging to her, Elena shook her head, sending her braid tumbling forward.

Something in her eyes, a sharp, clear intensity, laid bare the fragility Nudd had suppressed within himself.

This moment struck Miles as a pivotal turning point, as the precise moment when Nudd's perception of Elena and himself shifted. Her presence uncovered a fragment of softness he had thought long buried beneath years of duty. His defenses, built up over years as a son of Beli Mawr, as a king, crumbled before the remarkable beauty of this stranger.

For the first time, Miles understood why Gwyn had fallen so fast for Abby. When someone cracked open the walls you didn't know you'd built and gave you the things you lacked, it was impossible not to fall. Nudd ordered the fallen soldier's horse to be given to her while the rest of his men gathered the body of their comrade. "Ride beside me, Lady Elena. I would know more of you."

"Yes, my king."

Miles experienced Nudd's subtle discomfort at those words. His rank always kept him at a distance from everyone, regardless of his wishes. Elena swung easily into the saddle, but their pace was slow. Exhaustion clung to the men and horses alike, and each step was a laborious effort.

"Your fighting style is unique. Where did you learn it?" Nudd questioned, his gaze fixed ahead while he surreptitiously watched her out of the corner of his eye.

"From my father, lord. He was in service to one of your vassals."

Nudd ruminated on that, then asked, "I did not know that I had a… one such as you as a warrior I could call upon." He avoided using the word "cambion."

Elena was quick to answer as she stroked her horse's neck. "My father was not like me."

Nudd made the same decision Miles would have in that situation and stepped away from that line of questioning. "Your magic, lady. What strength can you call upon to help me defend our people?"

Here she hesitated. "I pledged to wield my magic only in defense of the righteous. I will use it to strengthen my body to fight, but I will not use it in other ways, except for emergencies." Elena shifted her gaze from the road to Nudd, a hint of challenge returning to her eyes. "If that is insufficient, King, I will depart once your party is secure."

Nudd raised his silver hand, his reins in the other, and said, "You have proven your merit, Lady Elena. I shall never ask you to break your vow."

A small smile touched her lips. Even dust-covered and blood-streaked, she held a kind of untouchable grace. Distracted, Nudd couldn't help but notice every delicate mark of her features, the way her lips moved when she spoke.

Miles felt a bit giddy. A lightness buoyed his chest, and a silly grin spread across his mental face. Men may deny it, but as a whole, they secretly loved a good romance. He was no exception—especially when watching the beginnings of his own love story take root.

"And with that allowance," Elena said, "you have proven the righteousness that initially led me to seek an audience with you. Before my father died, he spoke of your ways. He claimed you were a benevolent king who used your magical and military might for the people's benefit."

"Your father sounds like he was a great man. Has he passed to Annwn?"

"Yes... I was too late. Too late to save my family from—" Her voice faltered, the pain too fresh, too raw to finish.

Nudd gave a solemn nod. "There is no need to speak of it. I am grateful for your presence in my company. I would not press you, lady, but I sense there is more behind your grief. You say your father was not like you—your mother, then?"

Miles felt the words settle heavy in his own chest. He wondered if Elena had ever been free at all. Nudd had never been.

Elena flinched, visibly caught off guard by the question. Miles noticed a momentary hesitation, a visible surge of intense emotion in her eyes that he had seen in Esme's so many times before. Still, he thought Nudd hadn't noticed. He didn't know Elena yet at this point in their story, not like Miles knew Esme.

Elena straightened up, her voice quiet and sincere when she spoke. "My parents never told me I was adopted," she said, her tone hinting at feelings of betrayal that she buried deep. "After they died, a woman came to me. My... birth mother." The pause was thick with conflicted emotion. "She was cloaked in power, so much of it that I was suffocating simply being near her."

Nudd kept his face carefully still, yet Miles sensed a strong, poignant sympathy beneath Nudd's surface. Nudd saw not *the warrior under his command, but a woman grieving two lives—the one she'd lost and the one thrust upon her.*

"And now you bear a truth they never meant for you to carry. Do you know your birth mother's family?"

"Yes." Elena gave a single nod. "I fear I must tell you, lord. Should you, upon learning the truth, elect to keep me in your service, I trust you will maintain discretion. My mother is a...powerful figure."

Even Nudd's composure wavered. Despite his steady voice, he looked ahead once more. "You speak the word 'powerful' like it's both blessing and curse. Which is it when it comes to your mother?"

"I do not know her well enough to answer your question easily. But my gut tells me that the answer is 'fear.' She claimed a prophecy bound us both. That my birth, my blood, would set something in motion she feared to face. She said keeping me would have harmed many, so she gave me up." Beside him, Elena scrutinized Nudd's face. "I turned down her invitation to learn under her tutelage. My choice might have been folly, but I refused to allow the fury my blood ignited within me to be spent on anything other than a righteous cause. That is why I sought you out."

"Is she an enemy, then?" Nudd had to know, even if he wanted to keep this woman close.

"She said I had a choice. So, no, lord. I did not sense any ill will from her on my departure. I have not heard word from her or seen her since that day." Elena's fingers tightened on the reins. "She told me I could not ignore what I am forever," she added, her voice barely more than breath. "If there's even a narrow path where I can shape my own fate, I will find it. Or make one. I refuse to simply walk in the shadow of the woman who bore me."

"You are more than blood, Lady Elena. And your future is not hers to claim." Nudd was silent for a long moment. "Do you carry this burden alone? Is there no husband waiting for you?"

Both Miles and Nudd cringed internally. Was Nudd, always regal in manner and speech, so overtly trying to glean information about her lover?

Elena laughed, the sound unexpectedly bright. It was a musical ripple in Nudd's weariness, startling in its softness and strength. "Apologies, my king, no. There is no husband waiting for me. I fear I am condemned to maidenhood, to spinsterhood. My father's land has already gone to his brother. I seek purpose, not a husband from amongst your ranks."

She had taken his question to mean that Nudd worried that she was husband hunting among his men. Miles sensed Nudd's instinct to apologize, to correct the misstep, but he remained unable to speak it aloud. A king was never supposed to be wrong, and he had already admitted folly once that day.

Miles watched through Nudd's eyes as he glanced at Elena once more. She sat on her borrowed horse in silence, awaiting his judgment.

"I fear a mother will not let a child as bright as you go so easily," Nudd replied simply.

Was Nudd already flirting with her?

Elena glanced over at him, and for just a moment, she was Esme. "Then she'll see I can make the same hard choices she made in giving me away," she whispered.

Then, without warning, the dream world distorted, and time slipped.

Miles found himself still in the dream, but now surrounded by dark stone walls. Firelight and shadow filled the rooms of Nudd's private chambers within his fortress. But it was far too silent, unnaturally so. Nudd's gaze was drawn, without knowing why, to the center of the room.

There, atop the worn, battle-stained cloak, lay a scrap of parchment sealed with the emblem of a coiled serpent. It reeked of magic.

Nudd stepped forward, every motion deliberate as he watched for danger. He broke the seal with a whisper of thought and unfolded the page.

The ink shimmered faintly, as though alive. The message was in an unfamiliar hand.

"She is precious to me, son of Beli Mawr. Her fate is braided with yours. I will not see it severed before her time."

A threat.

A sudden gust of wind swept through the chamber, scattering embers and leaving only one torch burning. As Nudd turned, defensive shield blazing, his sword halfway out of its sheath, he glimpsed a fleeting reflection in the polished metal mirror across the room.

Two blazing points of amethyst fury locked with his through the mirror. They vanished in a puff of brimstone smoke. But the mark they left behind burned. Miles felt Nudd stiffen—not from fear like Miles had expected, but from dawning recognition.

Miles awoke suddenly, his mouth dry and his heart pounding in his chest. Esme's alarm clock was blaring in *his* ear even though she wasn't in the bed any longer.

She ran back into the bedroom. "Sorry, sorry, babe. I woke up early."

"Nervous about today?"

Wrapped in the fuzzy robe he'd bought her for chilly mornings, she leaned over to give him a kiss. "Of course." She chuckled. "I'm always a bundle of nerves beforehand, but then I'm fine once I'm in it."

"You'll be brilliant, lovely." He smoothed his palm up and down her arm, enjoying the warmth of her skin beneath his fingertips. "Just be careful."

He felt a powerful urge to protect her, spurred by the memory of the intense, watchful gaze in the mirror from his dream. He clamped down on the compulsion to drone on about being wary around Seren. His overprotective nature had already frustrated Esme countless times. Neither of them needed the added irritation of a random dream fueling his anxieties.

His dreams of Llefelys had taught him to always take Nudd's subtle warnings seriously. But unlike the last time he'd stepped back into a dream, in this one there was no lingering feeling of foreboding, no unsettling premonition that stayed with him after waking. So maybe he was worrying over nothing.

"I had a new dream." Now that everything was out in the open, his discovery would interest Esme. "Learned Elena was adopted."

Esme sat down heavily on the bed. "*Huh*. Gwyn did say she never talked about her past."

He pulled her hips closer, wanting to feel more of her warmth in the wake of those unsettling violet eyes, even if he had dismissed them as not an active threat. "Elena asked Nudd to keep it a secret. Her mum was a mage who gave Nudd the creeps. Didn't get a name, though. Woke up before the dream got to that part."

"Damn alarm clock," Esme said as she untied her robe. "Can't have things the easy way, can we?"

"Seems not... Nudd started flirting with Elena immediately. Poor chap was smitten from the first."

Esme's voice turned husky. "I seem to remember a certain man who said, 'I see you're a wanted woman,' winked at me, then dramatically exited the bar the first time I met him."

The memory brought a hearty chuckle from Miles. "Smooth as sandpaper, but look where it got me."

Dropping her robe, she presented a breathtaking sight that banished all thoughts of the disturbing eyes from his dream, all thoughts of anything else.

As she leaned over him, her hair brushing his cheek, Miles was struck by the symmetry. Two women who could level kings with a single glance.

"I only have thirty minutes," Esme said as gooseflesh erupted on her skin. "Make me warm."

"Yes, ma'am." Miles did not have to be told twice. "I guess waking me up early is worth it if this is the reward."

He kissed her fingertips before drawing her close, silently promising every past life version of himself that he'd do better this time around.

The warmth of her body against his was a balm. The feel of her skin beneath his hand was smooth, warm, and yielding. As he trailed it down her back, one last thought echoed through him—not Nudd's, but inspired by the dream: *She is precious to me.*

It made him feel bad for Nudd. Miles had *everything* Nudd had ever wanted.

CHAPTER SIXTEEN

EGG HUNT

Esme

The helicopter's rotors sliced through the air, their violent hum rattling Esme's bones. She clutched her harness and peered out the open side door. Bright spring morning sunlight illuminated the Cascade Mountains. Part of her reveled in the thrill of soaring above the trees; the other was nauseous.

"Always travel in style?" Esme yelled over the roar. "I could get used to this. Way better than slogging through snow for hours."

Seren raised an amused eyebrow. Her high-end hiking gear, blood-red from head to toe, was a stark contrast to her usual black. "Money exists to be spent, Esmeralda. I'm fit, but not as young as you."

Esme could feel Seren's gaze on her, sharp and assessing, even behind the expensive sunglasses.

Seren said, "And before you go thinking that I'm embezzling Brotherhood finances, the helicopter is privately funded. It was worth it to get above the gloomy clouds in the city."

Damn, Seren was *rich* rich.

Stomach fluttering, Esme asked, "We're seriously going to just... climb out of this thing?"

"You'll be hooked up to a tension cable that we'll release on the ground. When I say run, get at least thirty feet away from the helicopter."

"I take it you've done this before."

Wind tossed her hair, but Seren sat calmly, utterly composed. "When the need is great enough, I am called to the hunt."

An odd turn of phrase—maybe because English wasn't her first language. Earlier during the flight, Esme had learned that Seren split her time between Paris, Rome, and Warsaw.

The radio crackled as the pilot's voice cut in. "Dropping you off in sixty seconds, ma'am. Hold tight."

"Ready for the fun part?" Seren asked.

Esme managed a nod. "And flippin' terrified."

The helicopter hovered over a low peak, the downdraft whipping up a small storm of pine needles and dirt. The rope ladder dropped down, swaying in the wind.

Esme's pulse was thundering in her ears. Reaching solid ground seemed to take forever and yet no time at all, but she was soon unclipped and sprinting away from the whirling helicopter blades as fast as her feet could carry her. Seren followed five steps behind.

With the helicopter gone, the hush of the wilderness seemed like they'd stepped into an entirely different world. Esme spun in a slow circle, taking in the view. She loved everything about being in the mountains. "Okay, I'll admit it," Esme said, grinning like a madwoman. "That was awesome."

"Consider it a perk of working with me," Seren replied smoothly and started walking.

They hiked down the peak, the rocky terrain giving way to the cool shade of a dense forest. The air grew noticeably damper with every step.

Seren wasted no time. "Can you track malevolents with your conjurations?" she asked, her tone casual but probing.

"To an extent," Esme admitted, the shame stomping around in her gut. Being on display in front of calm, capable Seren made Esme feel even more inadequate. "Mostly.... vibes."

Seren tsked. "Vibes aren't enough. You should be able to see it."

Ugh, gods, it was a record. This unexpectedly pleasant trip seemed to be already taking a turn for the worse thanks to Esme's lifelong record of magical incompetence.

Esme frowned. "How?"

Seren extended a hand. "Magic lingers. Use an infernal conduit on your conjuration, but line it up to be in the center of all the strings you normally pull on to order the conjuration around. That conduit needs contact with your control. You'll see the malevolent magic—wispy red streaks of light. Let that be our little secret, yes?"

Only a conjuration specialist would understand Seren's explanation. A light bulb went off in Esme's mind. But one thing bugged her. She cleared her throat. "We already have a few people, all non-cambions, who can see magic."

Seren sent her a look that could cut glass. "Yet another thing Jacob has failed to report."

Shit. She was really fumbling this. Jaw clenched, she shut her stupid mouth.

Seeing Esme's expression, Seren fluidly shifted moods. "If they're using their talents to help others, it's not a problem."

"They are!" Esme quickly added. "I'd love to learn."

"You can train your conjuration to supplement your sixth sense." Seren guided Esme through the process, her instructions clear and concise.

Esme summoned Irritella, her pixie conjuration, infusing her with infernal energy. Usually a six-inch pastel puff trailing sparkles, Irritella now emerged wreathed in shadows, black thorns across her skin, a jagged crown of bone rising from her skull thanks to the demonic influence.

"Observe," Seren said as she flicked a stone with a telekinetic burst.

At first, there was nothing but the usual hum of energy. Then, near the end of the stone's arc, Esme saw a faint streak of blue trailing behind it—exactly as Will had described telekinetic magic looking.

"Holy smokes." Esme sucked in a breath. "I think I did it."

Seren's lips quirked in approval.

Esme stared, awestruck. "Six months of practice, and you taught me in less than an hour."

And just like that, despite her best efforts to the contrary, Esme felt herself folding. She already liked Seren. Unlike Leon, who had been all talk, Seren was there, boots literally on the ground, helping to clean up a mess Esme hadn't been wise enough to see at the time.

Was it foolish of her to succumb to another cambion's charm so soon? Maybe Esme was a sucker, but it felt damn good to make some progress with her magic after beating her head against a wall for months.

"Let's do this the easy way." Esme sent Irritella soaring above the canopy. Through her pixie's eyes, she scanned the forest for traces of red.

"Impressive," Seren remarked as they walked on. "Flying conjurations are tricky."

"It's taken me a while to get her to this point," Esme replied, her cheeks heated from the compliment.

For an hour as they hiked on, Irritella sensed nothing. Then faint ribbons of red, like smoke, drifted between the trees. Esme pointed. "That way!"

Eventually, they found the roc eggs, hidden in a shallow depression beneath a fallen tree. Esme dismissed Irritella as Seren kneeled and carefully packed them into a padded bag.

"Hopefully they didn't grow too cold," Seren said.

Esme had to say something. "So you're not going to smash the eggs before they become a problem?"

"*Petit-déjeuner,*" Seren replied with a toothy grin. Her hand brushed her pack briefly, fingertips tapping a silver serpent charm near the zipper.

Okay, that meant breakfast. *What is it with people suggesting eating malevolents?*

Seeing Esme's horrified expression, Seren said, "These will be used for training. No worries. There will be no torture, but my Brothers do require test subjects. We'll put them out of their misery before they become a genuine threat... Speaking of my Brothers, why have you not taken the oath?"

Esme shrugged. "At first I didn't think it mattered because I was committed to doing the work regardless of a title. But then I realized that the bureaucracy Miles and Abby have to go through is, pardon my frankness, bullshit."

"Ha! That's why I'm at the top." Seren cocked her head, considering. "A privileged statement, I know. Sadly, though, not everyone is as conscientious as your friends. Magekind must be reined in, even if they deserve to know the truth about the malevolents."

Esme's ears perked up at that. The exact opposite of Jacob's position.

Before she could dig into Seren's contention with Jacob, a familiar, unwelcome wave of nausea, but so powerful it nearly forced Esme to her knees, crashed over her.

Seren somehow managed to stay on her feet beside her. "*Merde*." Seren's accent became thicker than usual, her voice low. "I have my answer to what is making this area such a magnet for malevolents."

The creature burst from the trees so fast Esme didn't have time to question her about it.

It stood impossibly tall, emaciated. Gray skin stretched taut over angular bones. Noxious yellow eyes, blazing with magic, glared above a jagged gash that revealed a multitude of sharp teeth. The air chilled sharply around them as filthy, dagger-like claws extended from its hands.

The wendigo lunged.

Esme was already working on conjuring her trolls when she sensed a surge of magic building around Seren. Seren's hand extended—

A pointed gust of freezing wind, as sharp as a knife, slammed Seren into a tree trunk.

The older mage lay motionless where she'd fallen.

This was it. This was how Esme died, not old and content in Miles' arms—alone but for an unconscious woman.

She and Miles had talked about wendigo before. The slightest whisper of a sighting—a mere *inkling*—forced the mobiliza-tion of a full team of Brothers and powerful representatives of the Assembly together for the fight. The malevolent spirit had supernatural strength, speed, dexterity, rejuvenation, and could even use wind magic.

Its sole desire was to consume human flesh.

But Esme wasn't going out without putting up a fight. Bert, Tom, and George appeared around her in a circle.

At first it started toward Seren's prone form. Then it turned its gaze to her, the slits of its nostrils flaring as it sniffed the air.

With guttural roars, her conjured minions rushed forward. All three trolls met the wendigo's claws with brute strength. Esme's recent practice had made it so that they were smarter, using a bit of her connection with them to gain a type of borrowed intelligence.

But the wendigo was relentless, tearing at them with unnatural speed.

Panic seized Esme. This wasn't enough. It was pushing toward her.

Esme reached for her infernal magic. Darkness bled into her vision, eager to meet her fear with its rage.

With her next breath, the familiar, dangerous internal battle began. A cold numbness took hold of her heart, filling in the cracks left open by her human fear with something old, something as bestial as the man-eater staring her down.

For a quarter heartbeat, Esme was lost in it.

Then anger broke through, violent and vengeful for a death not yet suffered. Miles. Abby. Jacob. Gwyn. Finn. Countless faces flashed before her eclipsed eyes.

She'd never cast faster in her life. Her trolls, their forms now grotesque and hulking, sprouted tentacles of wrath. Three sets of tentacles twisted around the wendigo's body tightly.

The malevolent shrieked as the spiked claws at the ends of the trolls' tentacles tore into it. Something that looked like black

smoke curled where infernal power bit through the malevolent's flesh. Was that how it bled?

Strengthened by her infernal magic, she thought she'd
turned the tide. Except now, Esme was fighting on two
fronts.

All three conjurations pulled at her, demanding she merge
with them—to ride with them into the kill, to lose herself in
the ripping and tearing, in the death. Overwhelmed by the
intoxicating rush of unrestrained magic, Esme's sense of self
became less important.

Three pulls. It was *too much*.

Even as her conjurations strengthened, Esme was slipping
away, piece by piece, disappearing into the void created by
the infernal influence.

Like grasping at a lifeline for survival, her magic instinc-
tually reached for the nearest thing.

A string caught.

Esme grabbed on and pulled with every ounce of fight she
had left.

Rising above the infernal magic that had threatened to
drown her and taking a breath of fresh air, Esme realized two
things at once: the wendigo was still alive, but her conjurations were no longer fighting it.

A new cold, crawling hunger slithered through her mind.
It was insatiable, ancient, and utterly foreign to her senses.
Barely in check, the desire to consume struggled against the
few restraints she had on it.

She tasted blood on her tongue, but it wasn't hers. She, it,
they together wanted to gnaw. To tear. To feed.

The slithering hunger had been pulled into her mind by
the lifeline she'd connected to it.

Compared to the truth of what Esme was experiencing, the lure of damnation she'd felt only moments before seemed almost appealing. The string she'd grasped onto, the lifeline that led back to her sanity, *was the wendigo.*

She'd pulled it under control, but holding it was another matter. It was *so strong.*

Her lungs seized as she stumbled, too afraid to hold on but terrified to let go of the control she had claimed in her desperation. Esme fell to her knees, trembling uncontrollably as she hit the dirt.

Cornered and enraged, the wendigo unleashed its fury inside her mind, slashing and gnashing in desperation.

With one mental hand, Esme held on to the rope tying her to the malevolent. With the other, she directed her conjurations.

Three sets of tentacles squeezed. Three sets of fists beat.

Then, like it was nothing, Seren stood, brushing the hair away from her face. She disappeared from Esme's sight.

A blur of inky-black scales whipped past, filling Esme's vision. Then came the hiss, susurrant but final for all its lack of force. Before she lost consciousness, the image seared into her mind was of a huge hooded viper, its fangs extended, ready to strike.

***

Esme felt gentle hands shaking her. "Esmeralda, darling, wake up."

Her limbs were heavy and unresponsive, while her thoughts were sluggish and muffled. For a moment, she wasn't sure if she'd won or lost. Her nostrils burned and her heartbeat stuttered like a skipping record.

A groan. Was that her voice?

That snake. Surely she'd been hallucinating it.

Esme had never passed out from magic exhaustion. She'd thought that, due to being a cambion, she was immune to the affliction common to all mages. Apparently, that wasn't true...

Energy flooded her body. It was an overwhelming rush of power, a searing, molten core of energy that seemed to burn within her. Then, in an instant, it shut off completely.

"What?" Esme mumbled.

In a single, instantaneous shift, the blurry world around her crystallized into perfect focus. The sudden clarity was a gift from Seren, Esme realized, feeling the lingering effects of her donated magic. Afternoon sunlight streamed through the canopy above, warming her as her head rested on an inflatable pillow.

Esme shot upright, almost hitting Seren in the face with the movement. "The—"

"It's dead." Seren pointed at the fire burning some twenty feet away. Only then did Esme realize she smelled acrid smoke.

"What...?" Since waking, the statement had become a monotonous refrain, laced with growing anxiety.

"I'm impressed," Seren said, her tone wry, her expression sardonic. "Even with shit training, you exceeded my expectations. You went too far, but we can fix that. I'm only being brutally honest because I promised your best friend I would be."

"Abby?" What the hell was Seren talking about?

The look on Seren's face, her cryptic comment about *exceeding her expectations*... The obvious finally dawned on Esme: Seren hadn't been unconscious at all. She had *let* this happen.

Esme had trusted Seren. *So naïve, so stupid—again.*

Any prudent caution Esme possessed scattered in the gale of her fresh outrage. Fueled by fatigue and burning betrayal, Esme ground out, "Why?"

Seren shrugged. "I needed to assess your capabilities. Infernal magic is more than just power. It has always been a *test*. If you lose yourself to it, you'll become as dangerous as the malevolents you hunt."

"Testing me *again*? With a gods-damned Wendigo? Are you flipping *crazy*?"

Seren quipped, "Careful, that eye might never stop twitching if you keep it all bottled up."

"Bullshit." Esme's vision blurred with the shadows of her anger. "That's not the whole truth. Miles, Jacob, they said we were two of a kind. So I know the whole 'if you lose yourself to it' crap is the sort of thing I'd say to distract from the *real* answer."

Seren's eyes bounced off Esme, then resettled onto her pack as she returned to what looked like preparations to leave. The infuriating woman was completely unfazed by Esme's outburst. More to herself than to Esme, she mumbled, "I knew something was attracting malevolents here, but a wendigo... I didn't expect that."

"Seren!" Esme screeched. "I've only been that close to death once before, and I *ripped apart* the person who caused it. Tell. Me. Why."

Seren slowly rose from her crouch and faced Esme. The older woman huffed out a breath through her nostrils and squared her shoulders. "I needed to see what you were made of, Esmeralda. To know if you'd break or fight back. Even if it meant pushing you to the edge. Even if it broke you, you have to be *worth it*." Her voice became a growl. "The world doesn't care about your limits, child. It will push you, break you, and leave you for dead. I needed to see you push back until you couldn't."

Esme didn't stop to think before she responded with far too much honesty. "In the last twelve months, the world has hit me so many times in my face, heart, and freaking soul that I'm beginning to feel more comfortable being down than up!"

She'd made it far too personal, but how could Seren judge her without knowing about the ghosts she carried *from two lives*? Seren knew nothing more than things she'd read in a file. She hadn't seen the blood, sweat, and far too many tears over the years.

"I've been trying to get back on my feet for the past three months. Then you come along and pull the rug out from under me again! I *will* do what I need to do to improve, but I have people I care about! I refuse to put them through another death for a... a bloody mystery wrapped in the guise of a teacher."

When the tension mounted, her tendency to find humor in everything kicked in. "Bloody mystery." She was starting to sound like Miles. It could be worse, though. She could sound like Finn. Humor was her crutch, and the floor had just collapsed beneath her feet.

Now that the words were out, the mirth subsided, leaving only a quiet seriousness, heavy with gravity, in its wake. Only then did Esme realize how desperately she needed to say them.

Still seeking the hidden truth, Esme softly pressed, "Why? Please tell me."

Seren inhaled slowly, paused, clenched her fists, and then spoke. "Because I need to get this right. I can't fail again. The cost... too high..."

Either the acrid smoke had finally affected Seren, or the world's most powerful mage had unshed tears in her eyes.

Chapter Seventeen

DISAGREEMENTS

Esme

Esme's desperate plea for honesty, coupled with Seren's visible tense struggle to maintain composure, made the wait for the helicopter excruciatingly uncomfortable. Seren hadn't looked back once, her silence more suffocating than the lingering scent of smoke. The minutes dragged by in uncomfortable silence as they hiked back toward the peak they'd originally descended.

Esme was hopeless with awkward lulls. She reached instinctively for words to bury the tension, to fill the fraught space between them—anything to forget the wendigo's hunger. Yet it seemed like a very bad idea to broach the topic of what Seren had meant by "I can't fail again."

The path stretched ahead, silent and still. The whole way, Esme couldn't shake the image of the hooded snake, its obsidian scales gleaming in the dappled sunlight seeming to slither in her memory. Had Seren conjured that? A fleeting glance was all it had taken for Esme to appreciate the exquisite detail she'd somehow worked into the creature. It had too much presence to be a mere hallucination.

Instead of the confident tone Esme had aimed for, her voice emerged as a series of uncertain, halting sounds. "Seren... back there, when I passed out. I saw a snake go after the wendigo."

Seren didn't pause her stride, only tilted her head slightly, as if considering. "Magic-induced exhaustion can play tricks on the mind, especially with infernal influences involved. Maybe your subconscious was inspired by my tattoo."

Maybe, though that didn't feel like the truth. That was another dangerous topic to wander into. So Esme went for something innocuous instead.

"What was your day job before you started working with the Assembly?" Esme asked, knowing that modern-day mages still had to have a mundane job to pay the bills.

A brief falter in Seren's step betrayed that she'd had to think about her answer to that question, a detail Esme couldn't overlook. The question had landed harder than she'd meant. *Interesting*.

"I... come from a wealthy family, so I was doing whatever pleased me, pleased them."

That sounded nice. Esme wanted to know what life was like when you didn't have to worry about earning a paycheck. Still, there was something else nagging her. She was fresh out of ideas on what else she could say to fill the space. "Anyone with eyes can see there's tension between you and Jacob. He claims it's about the malevolent secret, but I'm not buying that's the whole story."

Seren finally looked over, frowning. "We have known each other for a long time, Esmeralda. Our social circles have always overlapped to a certain extent. I suspect Jacob views me as something close to an interloper, or maybe even a political pawn."

Esme countered, a mix of admiration and exasperation in her tone, "You don't strike me as someone easily manipulated."

Esme didn't know what Seren had done to earn her position at the top, but she had a feeling it hadn't all been clean—it rarely was.

Kicking a rock out of their path back up the slope to where the helicopter would pick them up, Seren huffed out a small laugh and slowed her pace to walk alongside Esme. "I think he knows that, too. But it's only natural that he's suspicious of me. Twenty years ago, I emerged from complete obscurity and started making a name for myself."

"What made you decide to start being more active in the Assembly?"

"I got bored," Seren said with a half-smirk, one shoulder lifting. "Didn't like the direction things were headed. So I did what I do best: stepped in and took control."

Esme could feel herself being studied sidelong. Seren abruptly changed the topic. "My turn. Same topic. How long have you known Jacob? Since you were a girl?"

Esme couldn't stifle the half-amused, half-weary laugh that bubbled up in her chest. "No, not at all. I thought I was mundane until I was seventeen. I figured Jacob was some old guy my parents occasionally met with for boring adult reasons. Like the guy you call when you mess up your taxes or need a will drawn up."

"You didn't know until you were *seventeen*?" Now a few steps behind, Seren mumbled something under her breath that sounded like, "...Some things never change..." When she caught back up, she asked, "How? And I cannot wait to tell Jacob you thought him a tax accountant. Ha!"

It was Esme's turn to shrug, but the memory was still a persistent ache. "My parents hid everything about magic from me until it was undeniable."

"By all the... *why*?" Seren's accent thickened.

"They didn't want me to be judged for being a cambion. Didn't want me to shoulder that bias until I was an adult. I... guess I get it. But I've already decided I won't be hiding what I, well, 'we' are from my children. Ya know, *if* I'm lucky enough to have them."

"I think your Miles will be a good father." Seren had a slight smile on her face when she said it.

And, damn it, the anger Esme felt at Seren for testing her again had already begun to subside. That small smile, her honesty, and even that compliment about Miles had forced a grudging shift in Esme's emotions. It would be easier to write Seren off. To let anger keep things simple. But that wasn't who Esme was. And maybe that was why this hurt more.

Esme's own lips quirked up. "With the way he babies Lily—that's his dog, by the way—I don't doubt it. *Anyway*, to answer your earlier question, Jacob became my mentor after my parents died. He helped me learn all the mundane things I needed to know to be an independent adult, gave me a job, and mentored me a bit on magic stuff. He's always been there for me, so I try to do the same for him."

"It sounds like you've grown quite close."

"Eh." Esme waved it away, trying to play it off. "He's my substitute grumpy grandpa."

When they reached the top of the peak where the helicopter was supposed to pick them up, Seren looked at her watch. "We still have forty-five minutes. Enough time for a snack."

Then Seren unzipped her pack, set the roc eggs aside, and produced an entire cheeseboard and a half bottle of wine like it was a *normal* trail snack.

"Good grief," Esme said, "the jokes about the French only doing food 'right' are correct."

"I am not French," Seren stated, her lips pursed.

"Oh. Sorry. I thought with your cursing in it so often…"

"Does 'Lewis' sound French to you? I am English and Welsh like Jacob and your Miles. I've spent far too many years away from home."

Esme felt her eyes widen at that admission. "Really? Is that the real reason why you and Jacob don't get along? Different football teams?"

Seren's face went completely expressionless. It was the exact look Abby wore before telling Esme she was being an idiot.

"Fine." Esme deflated. "Is it not obvious at this point that I'm angling to find out what drama exists between you two? You changed the topic earlier for a reason, and I want to know the dirt."

Seren handed her a plate holding a gooey wedge of brie that she'd drizzled with honey and some pre-sliced apple and baguette on the side.

"Alright, you win, Seren," Esme admitted. "This is way fancier than the homemade soup and hot chocolate Miles surprised me with on a hike. I won't tell him though because he'll try to one-up you."

"So glad to see that I've won in some small way."

Esme raised one eyebrow in an expression that asked *"seriously, Seren?"*

Giving her a "why would you ever question me" look back, Seren daintily placed her cheese and bread back on the plate. "I'll talk. Jacob used to be my mentor too."

"Like, *magical* mentor?"

"No." Seren scoffed in a very French way, no matter what her nationality was. "He was assigned to guide me through the Assembly's political labyrinth. For a time, we made a good team... but."

"He can be prickly," Esme answered for her.

"Something like that," Seren said, her voice growing quieter as her gaze drifted toward the trees below. She stared a moment too long, as if watching someone or something that wasn't there.

Then a fleeting glimpse of intense sorrow, or maybe even guilt, flickered behind Seren's carefully composed mask. "For many years, Jacob was the one person in the Assembly who looked past my bloodline. Everyone else saw me as a threat, but he saw me as a person."

That was easy to believe. Esme felt the same about Jacob's unconditional acceptance of her. The warm, fuzzy feeling thinking about it brought a wide smile to Esme's face. The wine after a long hike certainly helped in relaxing her completely.

"Jacob saw my imperfections, my many faults, and wasn't afraid." Seren sighed, hands palm up in the air. "When everyone else tried to smooth out my jagged edges, Jacob put on leather gloves and respected the serrated shape of who I was."

She gave a small, almost rueful chuckle. "I learned the art of reading a room and wielding presence like a weapon from him. He taught me how to outmaneuver people double my age without ever raising my voice. Our relationship wasn't nearly as close as yours appears to be. But it was... steady.

"I remember that first day when he showed me the International Assembly headquarters. He joked about the seemingly infinite labyrinthine corridors of bureaucracy that one must traverse before even considering a trip into the main meeting space. With him, I felt like I could implicitly trust someone for the first time in many, many years."

"So when did things go south between you two?" Esme asked, but gently.

"When I started making choices he wouldn't. I stopped being his student." Seren's nostalgic expression faded. "This is off the record, so don't bother looking for it. About a decade or so into my career, Jacob and I led an operation to remove a group of malevolents that were causing outbreaks of diseases in a remote village. The problem was that the malevolents were nezhit."

Esme remained silent, though her puzzled expression spoke volumes.

"The diseases nezhit spread allow them to feed on the vitality drained from the victim," Seren clarified. "We don't know how it works exactly, but even after the nezhit dies, the disease is bolstered and spreads more rapidly. This particular group had become infected with rabies."

Esme sucked in an involuntary breath.

Seren shook her head sadly. "If rabies is not caught immediately, it is a guaranteed death sentence. By the time we got there, even the babies in cribs were infected."

Esme took a gulp of wine. She had a feeling she'd need it for the rest of the tale.

"I ordered a, let's call it... a remote strike," Seren continued. "There was no time for sentiment or second opinions. The people were not only suffering, but they were also a danger to everyone if their contagion spread. Jacob argued for quarantine, for a chance to hope that the curse might wane on its own."

"We were equals back then. I overrode him." Her fingers tightened around the stem of her wine glass. "I handled it myself. Afterward, it was like I revolted him, like I had become a monster. Sometimes, I still see his expression when I close my eyes. Like I was the thing he came to fight."

Jacob had never looked at Esme like that. He'd never judged her so harshly. Maybe he had softened with time. Or maybe she hadn't truly disappointed him yet.

Might she someday face such a horrible choice? Pull the trigger or hesitate? Gods, she hoped not. She'd already learned that this life didn't leave room for soft hearts forever.

It was Seren's turn to take her own fortifying sip. "The Assembly called me 'decisive.' Not long after, my position was elevated."

"And Jacob?" Esme asked.

"He never said a word about it. I suspect he's resented me for ignoring his orders ever since."

With a whirring sound growing steadily closer, Seren looked toward the skyline. "He always said, 'Temper your fire, or it'll burn you from the inside out,' even as I continued to throw myself into one calamitous circumstance after another. I sometimes worry that I should have listened to that advice."

For a long moment, Esme wasn't certain they were still talking about the same Jacob. "Temper your fire" didn't sound like something Jacob would typically say, but his relationship with Seren differed greatly from Esme's, so she couldn't truly know.

With Seren at the top of the Corded Brotherhood, she likely knew everything there was to know about Jacob, so offering a bit of comfort through a vague truth didn't feel like a betrayal to Esme.

"Or maybe," Esme shrugged, "maybe Jacob saw his own past choices come to life and didn't like it."

Jacob's past, especially his actions during the Second World War, haunted him more than seventy years on.

A sad, almost pained smile touched Seren's lips as the helicopter descended. The deafening roar of its propellers cut off any further communication.

With a decisive click of the safety carabiner, Esme began her climb. The ladder swayed precariously with her weight, but with magic, Seren blocked the wind from whipping at her face or from making its movement worse.

When Esme glanced back down at the flawed woman who wanted to be her teacher, Esme realized she didn't trust her, but she *would* be giving her a second chance.

Chapter Eighteen

DARK TRADES

Seren

The blackness of that evening—the moonless sky pressing down like a weight—still haunted Seren. That night had carved its lesson deep into her: do whatever it takes. In sleep, the memory returned, dragging her down like quicksand, back to the moment her heart turned the color of her magic.

Even in sleep, Seren could almost feel the tingling warmth spreading through her chilled feet as the magic worked, melting the icy mud around her toes. The bonfire crackled fiercely, and the heavy wool robes weighed heavily on her, but still, the biting cold of the night seeped into her bones.

Seren stood at the edge of the sacred forest, there to perform a ritual with her mentor to beseech the gods for an easy winter. It was Samhain when the veil between this world and the Other was thinnest. The night was alive with the murmur of unseen things. It was said that night was the perfect time for the mages' desperate pleas to reach the gods in the Otherworld or for a helpful ancestor to relay the living's message to the king beyond.

Her people, sensing the potent magic thrumming within her, had elected Seren for the task. She'd said she would perform the ritual, but Seren had stopped believing in the sanctity of their gods long ago. Unaware of her beliefs, her people deemed her the closest to the gods of them all. On this, they were wrong.

She was the closest of them all to becoming one.

Her mentor, Dresta, approached the forest line where Seren still stood. The older mage was wrapped in the woolen folds of her ceremonial garb, face lined with wisdom but slowed in its aging by the power she wielded. Dresta's eyes fell to Seren's bare feet first. Her expression tightened, forming a silent rebuke before words were ever spoken.

"Child, you must have contact with the mother if we are to complete the ritual correctly. You are a full woman grown. You should know that your magic will weaken the connection to the earth. This momentary hardship we face is a small price to pay to prevent immense suffering for our people."

Seren begrudgingly halted the warming magic flowing to her numb feet. The least she could do was give in to the woman's simple request born of piety. Back then she'd been barely twenty but, in many ways, had remained very much a girl. Dresta had been as much a mother to her then as her own.

They performed the ritual, Seren beseeching the gods only half-heartedly. Her mind wandered throughout the ceremony, preoccupied with what she must do and with her agent's concealment amongst the trees.

Once the final chants ended, a sacred silence descended on the clearing, so profound that it seemed even the wind dared not trespass. The bonfire crackled, casting long shadows across the ritual stones, across her bare feet, raw and red against the frozen soil. Her breath came slow and steady, but her heart pounded like a war drum.

The time had come.

Seren looked across the circle to Dresta. She was kneeling in quiet reverence; her eyes remained closed in devotion. It struck her then how old the woman appeared, how fragile. A surge of guilt choked her like the curse she wanted so badly to avoid.

Slowly, deliberately, Seren raised her hands to the knotted ties at her shoulder and began to loosen them. The significance of her upcoming act made a simple gesture feel as strenuous as lifting a heavy rock.

The necromancer had insisted her skin must be bared for the magic to take. Though her doubts remained about that, she could no longer take chances.

Her fingers quivered. It didn't matter. This was not for him. Not even for herself. This was for her.

Seren let her robes fall. As the fabric pooled at her ankles, the firelight shone brightly on her shoulders, uncovering the viper that magic had gifted her. The light exposed her secret: the rounded belly given to her by a man. Dresta gasped, causing the serpent's twin emerald eyes to snap open and fix unblinkingly on her.

The older mage staggered back as horror and something like reverence filled her voice. "The bastard of scales and flesh."

The old prophecy. The doom of magic. Seren knew it well.

Seren's response was ice. "Will not be loved by me. This is to ensure the prophecy does not come to pass for my child."

Back then, she was still new to wielding so much power. Her fists trembled as shadows slithered up from the half-frozen ground to surround her mentor in a living cage of brimstone. At once they *surged upward and curled around the older woman's arms, legs, and mouth.*

"I will not bring about magic's downfall. But what kind of mother would I be if I left my child with nothing?"

A figure emerged from the shadows. The necromancer stepped from the shadows, eyes hollow, soul already half-consumed by what he had done—and what he was still bound to do. The geis Seren had placed upon his son ensured that he would do this. He had no choice if he wanted the curse lifted.

Her arms stretched wide, the aging woman struggled, her eyes betraying her pain. Dresta rasped Seren's true name, but there was no plea in it. Her voice carried a deep current of understanding. It resonated with a sorrow that nearly tore Seren in two.

The necromancer's magic, coupled with Seren's control, rendered Dresta unable to fight back.

Magic surged between the mages, wrapping around the dying woman's form. Dresta let out a shuddering breath as Seren's magic drained the life from her body. The necromancer channeled the dark energy, guiding streams of it toward Seren. She gasped as icy tendrils enveloped her unborn child. Death, a shadowy serpent, coiled around the vibrant, unborn life, protecting instead of harming. Anything to stop the inevitable hand of Fate.

Tears streaked down Seren's face as she whispered, "Your sacrifice will ensure that none know of her true nature, that none can scry her, that magic cannot touch her until she is a woman grown. If I cannot give her love, I must give her a chance."

The tentacles of Seren's darkness tightened around Dresta. The old woman's bones were hollowed out by the sacrifice of her magic, her essence. Her breath ceased as her body gave out. As the tentacles uncoiled, her body fell, silent and final, to the sacred earth.

No one expects physical danger from a heavily pregnant woman. Her form, the perfect picture of vulnerability, had lulled her agent into a false sense of security. Seren unsheathed the dagger from her belt and turned. The necromancer barely had time to react before the blade sliced across his throat.

A gurgling breath escaped his lips as he crumpled, knees hitting the earth with a thud; the crimson stain of his blood spread at Seren's feet.

She rubbed at the babe now kicking in her belly. Even if she had to force the emotion, this had to be an exchange—a simple transaction that ensured her daughter's safety. Anything more would be too much.

Hunters would have come for the necromancer soon enough. This was a mercy compared to the burning he would have suffered. His family had received from her a generous purse for his service, enough to ensure their comfort for years to come.

Seren refastened her robe and leaned over the body of the woman she loved most of anyone in the world. Three tears were her entire allowance of grief. Three tears blessed the corpse of the woman who had been more mother than her own. Three tears stood as the only apology Dresta would ever receive. Her regrets couldn't matter now, because she could feel the magic solidify into a ward around her baby.

Seren woke with the lingering ghost of a sob clinging to the back of her throat. She was drenched in sweat, the silk sheets heavy with her perspiration and too hot against her skin.

Through the floor-to-ceiling windows, Seattle sprawled beneath her feet, the city lights streaking like tendrils of the necromancer's magic through the dark. The penthouse was utterly silent save for a low, persistent drone of traffic below. With a trembling hand, she touched her forehead, the cool, polished surface of her nails a stark contrast to the still-feverish heat of her skin.

Love for the bastard of scales and flesh will bind magic beyond all reach.

She had failed her daughter. Despite her best efforts to the contrary, Seren had loved her.

She'd been so naïve, imagining only a mother's love could hold the power to alter the balance of magic. Now, so many years after her daughter had died, the question lingered: Was it her love or another's that had been magic's undoing?

Seren did everything she could to relax, to break the memory's hold on her. It was overwhelming and ultimately pointless to worry over who was at fault. Revisiting the issue only caused her more pain. Especially when she had immediate tasks at hand that could make a difference.

To the empty room, to the unseen listener, she murmured, "Arawn, you had better make things comfortable for me."

Even as she fought the shaking that tried to overtake her, Seren remained upright. Nothing remained buried forever. Death came for everyone. Some thought she had earned it more than most. Occasionally, she agreed with her detractors. But more often than not, they failed to understand that truth, righteousness, and justice were each nothing more than a matter of perspective.

When the sun rose, Seren had a second chance to take. She had magic to practice and, later, a few malevolents that needed to be freed from their captivity.

Chapter Nineteen

Masculine Recalibration

Miles

The gym was empty this late at night. Harsh fluorescents buzzed overhead, their glare bouncing off padded mats and mirrored walls that reflected nothing but shadows and tension.

Barefoot in the center of the training area, Miles tightened the wraps around his knuckles, eyes locked on Gwyn. Gwyn was already there, as silent as ever, warming up his muscles for the match. His bruises had faded, thanks to Miles' magic. Gwyn's eyes still carried that hollow gleam Miles had seen that day he'd healed his heart—not quite broken, but damaged enough to let his past seep through.

"You sure you're good for this?" Miles asked, now jogging in place.

Gwyn's lips curved into a hint of a smirk. "You healed me, remember? If I drop dead now, that's down to... malpractice?"

Miles rolled his eyes. He was definitely picking up on Esme's habits. "Yes, malpractice is the right word. Try not to die, then."

Wrapped fists bumped. And then they exploded into motion.

Gwyn didn't hold back, not that Miles had expected him to. Elbow, feint, low kick. Miles absorbed the blows, redirected, and countered. Their movements were fluid and controlled, like experienced warriors who knew violence but preferred to avoid it.

Miles wiped sweat from his brow, rolling his shoulders as he circled Gwyn. Gwyn lunged, a controlled burst of speed, and Miles barely sidestepped the sweep aimed at his legs. He countered with a sharp jab. But Gwyn twisted, catching his wrist and redirecting the momentum. They broke apart, breathing hard.

"You're holding back," Gwyn said, voice low.

Miles snorted in derision. "You're still recovering."

Gwyn's eyes darkened. "I am not a babe that needs coddling."

Then they crashed into each other again. As they wrestled for leverage, Miles grunted, breathing heavily. "So. Necromancy?" The word hit harder than his last jab. "You told Abby yet?"

Gwyn shoved him off with a growl and climbed to his feet. For a second, Miles thought he'd snap, but instead, he huffed in frustration and stepped back. "No." Gwyn wiped his face with his sleeve.

Miles stood too, shaking out his limbs.

Miles considered his words carefully. This wasn't only about Gwyn. It was about the malevolents, about Esme's and Abby's safety, about the fact that Miles knew that Gwyn's heart had stopped. "I don't get it. If it's something you can do, why are you avoiding it?"

Gwyn's expression shuttered. "It's death magic. What more do you need me to explain?"

"Plenty." Miles dodged another half-hearted strike. "Esme's magic is infernal. Abby's is banned. Mine is a secret. Hell, even Finn has malevolent magic!"

Gwyn's next punch connected hard and fast. Miles blocked, but the impact rattled up his arm.

"Because it is different," Gwyn snapped. "This is *harvesting* death. My power feeds on it. I take what's left." His voice cracked slightly. "That is... vile."

Miles pressed. "Says who? Nudd?"

Miles had seen enough of Nudd's memories to know that there was something about his son he'd kept hidden, even from Miles.

"Yes," Gwyn said flatly.

They closed in again. Jab, hook, slip. Gwyn landed a sharp knee to Miles' ribs. Miles grunted and retaliated with a body shot that forced Gwyn back.

"But do you hate it?" Miles pressed.

It was in Gwyn's footwork—a half-second hesitation, a subtle shift in weight before he stepped back in, that gave him away. "I don't know. I was raised to. My father—"

"The same man you said feared you for it?" Miles interrupted, sidestepping a vicious knee strike that came closer than expected.

Gwyn breathed out through his teeth, visibly reining himself in. "You don't understand."

"I understand a lot," Miles said, tapping his head with one glove.

"Maybe you do know him better than I did," Gwyn continued, voice tight. "He watched me like I was a sword he regretted forging."

Miles studied him. "And now?"

"Now I don't know if he was right." Gwyn's hands flexed and his jaw worked. "I don't feel corrupted. But that doesn't mean I'm not."

Miles mulled over that as he circled Gwyn. Abruptly, he dropped his guard. "Hit me. Do it."

Gwyn's stare said he thought Miles had lost his mind. "What?"

"You heard me." Miles spread his arms. "Hit me. Right now."

"Why?"

"Because *you're* holding back. Because you're afraid of your own strength." Miles met his gaze, challenging. "And if you can't trust yourself, how the hell are we supposed to trust you?"

Gwyn's face showed anger, frustration, and a deeper hurt beneath. Then, with the speed of a viper, he struck.

Miles saw it coming. He could've dodged. But he didn't.

The punch landed squarely on his ribs with a heavy thud that echoed through the empty gym. The air rushed from his lungs. Wheezing, Miles staggered, but he didn't fall.

Gwyn's eyes widened in horror. "You fool—"

Miles coughed, grinning through the pain. "See? *Control.*" He straightened, rubbing his side. "You pulled the shot."

Gwyn's hands clenched. "That's *not* the same."

"It is." Miles stepped closer. "Most of my dreams are about your father's regrets. The only conclusion I can draw from that is he doesn't want me to repeat his mistakes. The way he treated you was one of his missteps."

Miles was unsure if Gwyn's sudden intake of breath stemmed from anger or emotion. For a moment, Miles thought he'd walk away.

"I'm not done yet," Miles said, voice low. "If he was afraid, maybe it wasn't about you. Maybe it was about what others would do if they knew. Maybe he was terrified of *losing you*."

That landed harder than any punch. Miles' words had the effect of instantly paralyzing Gwyn.

Gwyn frowned. "He called necromancy reviled. Forbidden."

"Reviled doesn't mean evil."

Gwyn let out a bitter laugh. "You make it sound so... academic."

"Science helps me sleep at night," Miles said, shrugging. "So does order. But this isn't about me."

He stepped forward, raised his hands again. "You remember killing a king with this power. But that doesn't mean you're a monster now. You're not your past," Miles continued, his voice quieter now, more deliberate. "Like you said when we finally sat down and talked about this reincarnation nonsense. You're not the leader of the Wild Hunt anymore; you're not even *ap Nudd* anymore. You're the man who stood between the Dullahan and Esme and Abby without flinching."

"I didn't ask for this power... I don't want it."

"No one asks to be what they are," Miles said. "And"—he elongated the word for effect—"we've circled back to *choice*, mate."

Gwyn finally came forward again. He shot out a jab, slower this time. But it wasn't a challenge; it was a way of continuing the conversation with their hands. "I don't remember enough about it. What if the magic is dangerous? What if I lose control?"

"Then we'll deal with it," Miles said, deflecting the blow easily. "But you have to tell Abby sooner rather than later. At the very least come to terms with it. Practice it."

"You sound like him too often," Gwyn said in a tone that, for once, wasn't accusatory, only observant.

"Nudd was drowning in his responsibilities. Constantly making choices he couldn't apologize for. You weren't a failure to him."

Gwyn turned away, running a hand through his sweat-damp hair. "Then why did he never say that?"

A hollow ache, a subtle echo of Nudd's voice, resonated faintly in Miles' mind. Miles realized it was his guilt, buried so deep it had grown cold.

"Because kings don't get to be vulnerable," Miles answered. "They get to suffer in silence."

Gwyn didn't answer. But when he turned back, his shoulders were straighter. "Again?" he asked, raising his hands to a loose guard.

Miles grinned faintly and raised his own.

They collided again, but something had shifted. It wasn't just sparring now. It was trust, recalibrating itself, one strike at a time.

Maybe, just maybe, they were moving forward together.

Chapter Twenty

BONES

Gwyn

Gwyn moved soundlessly through the underbrush with practiced ease, his crossbow ready in one hand and his sword strapped to his back, eyes flicking from shadow to shadow. Every rustle of wind through the foliage made his muscles tense. Every shadow held a threat; every sound hissed *malevolent*.

The crisp April air carried the scent of damp earth and hemlock, but he barely noticed. Every fiber of his being was tuned to the hunt. Every time he hunted, a surge of energy, a bit of the strength and confidence of his old self, invigorated him.

In contrast, Finn lagged, looking like he had not a single care in the world. The imp was even whistling softly—a habit that had already earned him more than one scolding from Gwyn that day.

The third or fourth time Gwyn was tempted to set Finn's ridiculous suspenders on fire, he knew. He knew that agreeing to do this job with a leprechaun was a gross miscalculation.

A snapped branch. Was it the malevolent? Or the leprechaun? Gwyn's fingers tightened around his weapon.

Then, breaking the silence with all the grace of an ox, Finn cupped his hands to his mouth and bellowed, "Oi, beasties! Come out, come out, wherever ya are! Ya waitin' for an invitation?"

Frozen in place by shock, Gwyn ignited into fury as he turned a scathing glare on his companion. "Are you out of your mind?"

The leprechaun stood atop a moss-covered log, grinning like a fool, arms spread wide as if inviting an ambush. For a heartbeat, Gwyn considered shooting him on principle.

Noticing Finn's smug, triumphant, frankly *insufferable* expression, Gwyn suddenly understood. He'd been played.

"There is no malevolent," Gwyn said flatly, lowering his crossbow.

Finn grinned, far too smugly. "Uff, don't look at me like that. You'll still be gettin' paid for a whatever-ya-call-it gettin' slain. We'll make up a story." He hopped down and dusted his hands off. "I called in a little favor, and a malevolent story was hatched."

Gwyn's fingers flexed against Foxkiller. "What is this about, leprechaun?"

"I told ya we had work ta do."

"That was months ago."

"Well, the time has come." With a flourish, Finn pulled a shovel from thin air and jabbed it with a thud into the ground nearby. "Start diggin'."

Gwyn didn't so much as twitch. "Order me again and I'll bury *you* instead."

Finn sighed theatrically. "I have ta do everythin' myself, don't I?" He snatched up the shovel, muttering, "Haven't I been punished enough?"

"Dramatics!" Gwyn smirked. "You clearly enjoy all the drama surrounding us. Stop pretending otherwise."

Finn giggled. "True." Then, stamping his foot, the leprechaun whined, "Ya really won't dig? You've got two feet of height on me and ya won't move a single inch of it to help yer old great-great-grandad-in-law out?"

"You've yet to describe your purpose. Also, Abigail and I aren't wed."

"Ya aren't *yet*." Finn waggled his eyebrows. "You're curious about what's down there. I'll trade ya one truth for the task done. Plus, what's down there is to help you, lad. Not me." Finn leaned on the shovel. "What'll the truth be, then? One I can answer, mind."

Gwyn considered. Finn's past, Gwyn's ties to Arawn, and their interconnected history were all topics Finn consistently avoided. But there was one question he'd never asked outright.

"You only mentioned that you couldn't tell me what the bargain I made was," Gwyn said slowly. "But that statement never included yourself. How did you get involved with Arawn in the first place?"

"Clever lad." Finn's grin widened. "I've been waitin' for you to ask that question." He sprawled onto a fallen log, lacing his fingers behind his head. His smile faltered for the first time. "Yer father happened."

Gwyn squinted up at the midday sun, exhaling sharply before he picked up the shovel. "Why am I not surprised?"

As he drove the blade into the soft earth, Finn began his tale. "Thanks to that piece of human refuse Leon, you and I met when I was a child. Stuck around the keep for years after. Nudd took a likin' to me—inevitably ended up doin' a bit o' spying for the big man. I was quite good at bein' sneaky in those days."

"Far less so now," Gwyn muttered.

"Off with ya!" Finn made a scandalized noise. "You're not good enough for my Abby. I swear." He clicked his tongue before pressing on. "I was spying even when the two of you were flittin' around doin' demigod stuff. Nudd asked me to follow you the day you two got into a snit. The one after Elena passed... Think he wanted to know if you were goin' to do somethin' stupid so he could stop ya."

Ancient resentment at never being trusted welled up within Gwyn anew.

Finn, oblivious to Gwyn's thoughts, snorted. "Turns out yer father had somethin' mightily stupid planned all on his own!"

A shadow fell across Finn's features, and his demeanor grew more solemn. "I trailed you far beyond where I was supposed to be able to go. All the way to the threshold. That's where I got caught. And... Where I earned my punishment."

Gwyn paused, dirt clinging to his sleeves. "You made it all the way to the threshold between life and death. *How*?"

"The magical equivalent of holdin' onto your coattails."

Gwyn's brows drew together. "And I didn't notice?"

"I'd been at it for so long ya probably thought the sensation was normal."

Gwyn dropped the shovel, hands on his hips. "Marvelous."

"Aye. Yer father had some questionable morals underneath all that sanctimoniousness. Probably why we got along so well."

Gwyn threw his hands up. "I shouldn't be surprised."

Finn nodded sagely. "Ya shouldn't be surprised."

With a grumble, Gwyn resumed digging. The soil felt loose and unsettled, as though recently disturbed.

Finn let out a yawn and stretched luxuriously before closing his eyes, not unlike a cat basking in the sun. "Arawn caught me," he said lazily. "Tossed me into one of the malevolent prisons, gave me a job to do. So here I am. Thanks to your father—and *you*—for bein' lovesick fools."

"So how did you get your ifrit powers?"

"Didn't bargain ya another question." Finn cracked an eye open and yawned outrageously.

Silence stretched, and Finn's eyes drifted shut while Gwyn kept digging until he could stand in the pit and just barely see out over the edge.

Then—*thud*. His shovel struck something solid. Gwyn had first assumed it was an ordinary stone, but the dull sound of his shovel changed his mind. He crouched down, brushing away the loose dirt. The object was oblong and brownish-black in color.

"I think I found something," Gwyn said, voice low.

Finn didn't open his eyes. "Took ya long enough."

"You could have helped!" Gwyn hissed. He cleared more earth, his fingers tingling with the pulse of lingering magic. The deeper he dug, the stronger it grew—a familiar but still new to him resonance.

His fingers brushed something too rough and pitted to be stone. The stench of old smoke flooded his nostrils. Charred. He knew all too well what fire did to—

It was a human bone.

His head snapped up. "What is this?" Gwyn demanded.

Finn sat up, grinning with malevolent glee. "Practice."

No one had said anything to the leprechaun, Gwyn was sure of it. "You *knew*," Gwyn said in a growling whisper. It was an accusation and demand for answers all wrapped up in one.

"'Course I did." Finn hopped down, peering into the hole. "Might be easier to get those bones to dance out than to dig 'em all up yourself."

Gwyn's vision blurred with fury. "Who is this?"

Finn's smile faded. "I think ya know."

Llefelys. Leon. One and the same.

Finn continued jabbering on as if he weren't asking Gwyn to desecrate his uncle's grave. "He doesn't need the bones anymore. And it might be good for him to be of some use for once, don't ya think?"

Gwyn recoiled. "Is this some kind of perverted revenge on my kin for *your failure* to recognize him?"

"No, lad, this is practicality." Finn shook his head sadly. "His bones are still thrummin' with magic. Can feel it from over here."

"This is wrong."

"No!" Finn barked, uncharacteristically grave. "This is what ya need to do. This is who *you are*. This is how you save her!"

Gwyn's breath stilled. "Abigail?"

"That's as much of the truth as I've been given." Finn jabbed a finger at the grave. "So bury your squabbles and unbury that skeleton."

Gwyn stared at the bones, his grip tightening around the shovel. What other choice did he have? Then it hit him. "You stole his remains from the house."

"'Course I did."

His answer was so offhand, so infuriatingly cavalier. Gwyn removed more of the loose dirt and shouted, "So you've known for months of my power. Yet again!"

Without concern for the leprechaun's safety, Gwyn heaved the shovel clear of the hole and pulled himself out. "I believe you are correct. Further practice *is* warranted."

He was so furious that he abandoned his attempt to speak English. "Your nonsense and half-truths have been tolerated for *far* too long. Everyone dismisses them casually, as if they're insignificant, a mere trifle."

The loose dirt around the bones shifted. "But I am *weary* of it. I understand that trickery is your way, but if you had only told the truth *months* ago, we could have had far fewer misunderstandings."

Something otherworldly, shimmering with an ethereal red-purple glow, flitted across Gwyn's vision as he stared Finn down. From behind him, a sound like the scraping of a sword being dragged through dirt slowly and stealthily crept upward.

Gwyn hadn't finished his tirade because he was also shaping the magic. "You failing to mention the truth is *not* insignificant; it is *not* trivial. You are playing with our lives—often when we are at our most vulnerable. So, yes, I think I should practice my necromancy. Let's see what happens when the one being manipulated stops playing nice." He practically hissed his last word.

A complete skeleton, its bones not the ivory white of a clean specimen but the charred black and brown remnants of a body consumed by an inferno, crawled out of the hole. Once on the surface, it gained its footing and barreled toward Finn with frightening speed, trailing the lingering smell of smoke and ash in its wake.

Panic constricted Finn's face. Gwyn had seen him stare down malevolents without wavering, but this... Finn's reaction was something else.

Finn's face went corpse-pale. No smirk, no quip—only raw, unfiltered terror. For a heartbeat, he wasn't the man who'd caused so many difficulties for them. He was a tiny creature who'd seen the dark behind Arawn's smile.

Then he was gone, mist walking so fast Gwyn barely felt the magic before he disappeared.

Finn appeared some twenty feet away, hands blazing with ifrit fire, expression ready for war. The skeleton crumpled mid-stride, scattering ash and cracked joints as it collapsed into stillness. Externally, Gwyn was hunched over, shaking with laughter.

Internally, however, a maelstrom of feelings and realizations rampaged. First, he realized that he'd gone too far. The fear on Finn's face was unmistakable and singular. Despite previous brushes with death, he'd never looked so afraid. Something in his history, recent or ancient, likely connected to Arawn, must have triggered Finn's reaction. And Gwyn had done it to him.

By all the magic, he was an unthinking, uncaring idiot.

Gwyn's second realization was equally disturbing. Practicing necromancy felt... incredible. A sense of congruity washed over him, of vindication, a feeling deeper and more profound than any thrill the hunt could ever provide. A torrent of fresh power roared through his veins, right and wrong, entwined like lovers.

For one glorious moment, Gwyn was a god again.

Then the shame hit. *This* was what his birthright had become: not kingship but *corruption*.

The intoxicating rush of power he wanted to hold on to was a despicable desecration of the dead.

The leprechaun allowed the magic to slip from his hands, but his face remained grim. His usual bright, ringing laughter was absent. In its place, a quiet resentment filled Finn's silence.

When Gwyn met his eyes, Finn said, "I see that you've remembered more than I thought…"

"Fionn… Finn…" Gwyn breathed out his regrets with every syllable. He'd demonstrated nothing short of poor judgment in practicing necromancy while enraged. "I am ashamed. I regret terrorizing you in such a manner. I went too far."

Finn nodded once, expression unchanged. But then, with a sigh, he sat down heavily, the damp earth and decaying leaves squelching beneath him.

"Can we speak in English, lad? My old tongue's rusty, and that apology deserves proper talk from me."

What could Gwyn do but join him on the sodden ground? He was already filthy anyway.

"Gwyn, lad… you're right. Everything you've said is correct. I deserve your ire. But I need you to understand that if I had said anythin', it wouldn't have done a *single* bit of good. Y'all didn't trust each other. You and Miles were practically drawin' out where to cut first every time ya saw one another. The girls bein' nice has been yer savin' grace the entire time. Like I said, *heh*, too good for you."

Gwyn nodded. "Too good by far."

With a sharp jab of his index finger, Finn rose. He shouted, his voice echoing, the loudest Gwyn had ever heard it, "And don't you forget that!". The leprechaun reseated himself heavily.

He had been… touchy about his family of late.

Quieter, he explained, "I needed to have you get to where you are now for Arawn's, for *your* damned plan, to work! The one ya carved into your own soul when ya begged for her life. I'm just the poor bastard makin' sure ya remember it. And no, before ya ask, I still don't know exactly what that entails. You will need this"—he pointed at the heap of bones—"to get it to work."

"The bones?"

"No, ya id-jet, the *power*."

Gwyn cleared his throat of the second apology lodged within it and said, "I will do all in my power to care for Abigail, Christi, and even Colin. I hope you know that."

With a piercing glare, Finn looked directly into his eyes. "You'd better," Finn growled, low and lethal. Leprechauns didn't make idle threats about kin.

Gwyn started, "Abigail still doesn't know about this—"

Finn cut him off. "There's no rush in tellin' her—yet. I *can* keep a secret."

Then, in the blink of an eye, Finn's jovial expression returned, his posture relaxing. "Now, I'm gonna enjoy my well-earned nap in that sunny spot. You? You've got what's left of a corpse to make dance."

Reluctantly, and with an ominous tone, Finn cleared his throat and added, "And later we're gonna have to kill somethin' for you to practice usin' the power released at death…"

CHAPTER TWENTY-ONE

UNDER THE STREETS

Miles

With a slow, reverent touch, Miles trailed his fingers down Esme's back. He'd spent more time than he'd care to admit aloud perfecting the exact temperature his hands needed to be to massage her. The trick was balancing the magic between his prosthetic and his natural hand. The prosthetic heated more easily, but it also lost the magic more readily than his own flesh.

His ministrations coaxed a soft sigh from her lips as she arched beneath his touch. This was not the kind of work he minded. At all. Not even a little bit.

She was so impossibly beautiful. How had he gotten so lucky? *Thanks, Nudd.*

There were still times when he half expected to wake up alone in his old flat, only to find that she had been a dream his lonely heart had conjured.

Yet she was there, undeniably real, and by his side.

Miles basked in the moment. The subtle sweetness of her skin, the gentle gasp of her breath against his ear, and the quiet confidence in her eyes as she continued to trust him, inviting him back into her life again and again. It was *her*; she was everything.

Years of slinging drinks and breaking up bar fights had left knots in her shoulders, stubborn reminders of her trade. So he traced the ridge of her scapula with his thumb, feeling the smooth skin and the subtle tension in the muscles as he followed the curve of her spine down to the small of her back. A shiver ran down her body.

He smiled against her neck, his lips brushing the skin below her ear.

"Tease," she murmured, but her voice was thick with pleasure.

"Absolutely nothing teasing about it," he whispered back. "A promise."

He nearly said more. The words had risen in his throat, unspoken but burning hot: *Marry me.*

But Miles swallowed them down. Timing mattered. She deserved the perfect moment, not one interrupted by a shoulder knot and a back rub, no matter how intimate. That little velvet box in his gun safe might as well have been a landmine. It ticked louder every day.

Then his bloody phone shrilled the high-pitched wail he'd reserved for magical emergencies. He wanted to launch it with a burst of telekinesis to smash against the wall into a million tiny pieces. He shut his eyes for a half-second, trying to hold on to the moment for a single second longer.

The mood died instantly, and Miles let out a groan, the sound thick with frustration and laced with a hint of that special type of despair. He reached for it, but Esme snagged it off the nightstand and gave the blaring phone a glare.

"Just one damn night off," she grumbled.

Another groan, this one quieter. He gave her the "gimmie" sign with his hands, and she tossed it over with a devilish grin on her face.

That grin. When he did get down on one knee, he hoped that would be the face she gave him.

He knew exactly what she was thinking: *They interrupted us; they can wait.*

He silently agreed. Expecting yet another false sighting, Miles lifted the phone to his ear only to hear frantic, gasping breaths on the other end. His eyes met Esme's, and she instantly understood that this was a serious situation unfolding.

Miles sat up straighter. "Miles Goodwin."

Words came tumbling out of the unfamiliar voice on the other end of the line. "Dr. Goodwin, it's Otto Krum. A... thing came through the flooded tunnels. We're holding it back with ice, but—"

Miles cut in, already reaching for his gear. "Describe it."

"It's huge. A frog with six legs, horns, and glowing blue eyes."

To a Nisse barely two and a half feet tall, everything loomed large, rendering "huge" an inadequate descriptor for his fight planning.

Esme was already typing quickly into her phone. With a grim set to her jaw, she said, "Bukavac," the name heavy with unspoken threat. "It can paralyze with its booming croak. What the..."

Otto must have heard her. "Ms. Esmeralda? Yes! It's done that twice already. We've got layers of ice blocking the sound, but it already took one of our... It took..."

Miles met Esme's gaze. She was already changing into what she had dubbed her "monster hunting" clothes—black leggings with a black long-sleeved shirt and black hoodie on top. He wanted to tell her to stay back, to let him handle it. But that argument was futile.

Damn woman always won.

"We're coming," Miles said.

Otto's voice, though still trembling, held a palpable relief. "She can bring those terrible trolls."

Esme's grin had a bit of an edge to it.

Miles leaned in, capturing Esme's mouth in a deep kiss, letting his hands linger for a breath longer than necessary. It was a promise, a plea, and a silent *be careful* all at once. Then he pulled away, reluctantly strapping on his daggers and tying his boots.

They had a monster to kill.

Esme

The human-sized entrance to the Seattle Underground was unmarked—a rusted maintenance door, nearly invisible between two buildings, unless you knew exactly where to look. Flashlight at the ready, Esme hesitated at the doorway until Miles nudged her forward.

"You're worrying about the dark *now*?" he muttered.

She scowled. "I'm worrying about *tripping* in the dark."

As they crawled inside, her fears dissolved. This section of the tunnels, supposedly condemned and unsafe, was lit overhead, crisscrossing every corridor.

A tiny, ghost-pale Nisse woman waited near the entrance, her silver-streaked hair framing wide, fearful eyes. "Jessica," she introduced herself quickly. "Otto's reinforcing the ice. He—he said you'd come." She was shaking. "What is that thing? I—I've never seen anything like it."

Esme exchanged a glance with Miles. If even the younger Nisse were being pulled into this, things were worse than they'd thought. Only the elders were supposed to know that malevolents periodically returned to the world.

They followed Jessica deeper into the tunnels. As they descended, the air grew colder until the walls were slick with frost. They found Otto knee-deep in water, hands outstretched, as another Nisse used a bucket to splash more of it onto the wall so he could freeze it in place. Nauseating malevolent magic filled the space.

Beyond it, something massive shifted, its movement creating waves through the water flooding the area. A deep, resonant *twope* rolled through the tunnel, a bass-heavy croak that vibrated in her ribs even through the wall. The ice shuddered, fractures spreading like spiderwebs.

Esme didn't hesitate. "I'll scout." She summoned Thursday, a cream-colored ferret with red eyes. She sent the agile conjuration slipping through a tiny gap in the ice.

The image flickered in her mind: darkness, then—

Six legs. Gnarled horns. A gaping maw.

The ice groaned under the force of another brutal blow as the creature leaped forward. Esme went rigid, unconsciously bracing for the danger to burst through. Her instinctive reaction to threats had been reshaped by the constant fighting against malevolents over the past few months.

Esme split her mind between watching through the conjuration's eyes and speaking with Miles. "It's bigger than the ogre," she whispered. "Ten, eleven feet long, takes up most of the tunnel. I think it's stuck in the corridor; it's narrower behind the ice wall." She stopped, swallowing hard.

Her ferret's eyes caught on a plastic toy boat that was bobbing gently in the water. In her own body, Esme froze in shock and sickening understanding.

The realization forced a sudden surge of infernal magic to blaze up inside her, fierce and all-consuming. On the phone, Mr. Krum hadn't been stammering out of fear. He'd been trying to say something. He'd been trying to say it had already killed one of their children.

The bukavac shifted, oblivious to the conjuration beneath it, and in an instant, Thursday was gone. Her ferret had been crushed, cutting off Esme's view of the malevolent. It didn't matter; she had what information she needed. And anger. Lots of it.

When Esme turned around to look at Miles, Otto stumbled back a half step. "By all the..." he muttered, struggling to maintain composure.

Her eyes were fully eclipsed. Miles alone deciphered the silent language of her expression.

Miles barked orders. "Everyone out."

With no further comment, the Nisse fled, leaving Esme to wrestle with her rising temper. Only three months earlier, she'd given a toddler Nisse a quick ride aloft using Irritella. If it had...

Her rage flared to heights that nearly choked her. Instead of dwelling on the what-ifs, she needed to shift her attention to action—as soon as possible.

They donned the earplugs and industrial-grade earmuffs they'd picked up from the hardware store on the drive over. "We're signing," he reminded her, and she nodded.

Her heightened emotions made summoning Oatmeal, her infernal shadowcat, as easy as thought. Miles, in the same way, readied his weapons.

Their preparations ended just in time for the ice wall—nay, dam—to shatter outward in a flood. In a flash, Miles detonated a protective shield around them both.

The sound that the bukavac made was less like a croak, as the references had called it, and more like a soul-deafening roar. Even Oatmeal's form, outside the aegis, flickered in response to the sound. The entire tunnel, and all the way down to the marrow in Esme's bones, vibrated violently. It was like standing atop an industrial subwoofer turned up to eleven. How had the Nisse tolerated it? Dust and loose pieces of the crumbling ceiling rained down on them, but the shield held.

The water now pooling around their legs was freezing cold. The surge of sound vibrated through the water, causing waves to wash over Esme's legs. The hot infernal magic brewing within wasn't shield enough to keep goosebumps from erupting across her skin.

Even with heavy-duty hearing protection, a dull, throbbing pain pulsed behind Esme's eyes. Thinking the water had splashed on her face from the flood, she was surprised to find blood when she wiped at her nose. When she looked over at Miles, his was bleeding too. The awful smell made matters worse. Now that the ice wall was gone, it reeked like a sewer or a stagnant swamp.

The bukavac convulsed with grotesque urgency, its slime-slick limbs wrenching against the stone confines. Each movement sent wet, echoing cracks down the flooded corridor. Its bright blue eyes darted frantically between the two humans and the conjuration, as if choosing its next meal.

It must have emerged from its prison in the spot to have gotten there. Or there was a way in through the dark waters beyond they couldn't see. The monster's predicament had granted them a lucky (and rare) moment to strategize.

Esme sent Oatmeal racing forward, feeding her shadowcat a slow drip of infernal power like gasoline to a flame. She watched as the cat steadily grew in size until she pounced, claws raking against the creature's thick hide, but it barely flinched in pain. The enormous toad-like malevolent snapped at the conjuration with its toothless mouth. The tight quarters meant it had little room to maneuver, so it only won a glancing blow against the nimble shadowcat.

Given his characteristic blend of bravery and recklessness, Esme could tell from a single glimpse that Miles was preparing something daring and dangerous. She made an emphatic "X" with her hands and mimed throwing something.

His reply insinuated that he hadn't brought his gun.

Yeah... that was her fault. She hated guns.

It was fortunate that she could fight effectively both up close and at a distance.

The bukavac had one and a half mucus-covered webbed paws free of the confines of the tunnel. Up to this point, Esme had danced Oatmeal beyond the monster's grasp and away from its horns. But now a distraction and possibly a sacrifice were in order.

A ten-foot-long, wickedly sharp spear of shadow, smoking with brimstone, materialized in Esme's hands.

Miles motioned for her to throw it, but she couldn't throw it hard enough to pierce the monster's hide, much less keep it conjured exactly right during the flight. Esme mimed at herself then did the running man to communicate her plan.

Turning his handsome, scarred face up at the ceiling, Miles seemed to implore some higher power for the strength to continue dealing with her. His eyes returned to hers, and he seemed like he was about to agree to her plan when the decision was made for them.

The bukavac's hunger and rage had finally reached a breaking point. With a mighty heave, it strained and wriggled against the tight corridor, the rough stone and wood holding up the walls scraping against its scaled hide. Three legs were the first to break free; two lashed out at Oatmeal.

One wrong move would send the entire tunnel crashing down on them.

Do or die.

Using the magic from her own body, Esme increased the strength and speed of the muscles in her legs to propel herself through the shallow water, spear held at the ready. She remained hesitant to use much infernal magic after her run-in with the wendigo.

Luckily for them, the creature wasn't the brightest. With Oatmeal positioned on the far side of the monster, the monster's loose paws and horns repeatedly swiped at the cat. Too much more of this and Esme's conjuration would disintegrate altogether. Oatmeal only needed to survive until the distraction was no longer necessary.

When Esme reached the halfway point, a powerful magical shield erupted around her. For a heartbeat, her stomach dropped. *Don't you dare, Miles.*

She remembered the bats. The nandibear. Finn screaming through flames. The situation had been so dire that Finn had resorted to detonating his ifrit fire magic around himself like a bomb. Then Miles' rescue had only made things worse by causing another malevolent prison to fail.

But Miles didn't arrive through the mists of magic. Not this time.

Just as she thrust the spear in, a surge of force slammed into the butt of her weapon—Miles' telekinesis. His force drove it far deeper than she could have otherwise on her own. Gods, she loved him.

They'd never practiced that move, but his timing was perfect. Oatmeal gave one last soundless snarl, leaping beyond the reach of a paw.

Then the spear struck true.

The shadowcat froze mid-swipe—then unraveled into ribbons of black smoke, dissolving into the air.

She was immediately grateful for the protection of his shield. Esme staggered back, panting. Those three steps saved her as a massive antler plummeted down right where she had just been standing. The antler glanced off the shield Miles had erected around her.

Miles' rapid approach caught her eye. *No.*

They both needed to stay away from the huge demon toad. It was thrashing wildly now, almost completely unstuck. Its enormous jaws could easily crush either of them before it swallowed them whole.

She backed away, fast. If she didn't do something now, Miles was going to go all superhero and put himself at risk.

Not today. Because through it all, Esme had managed to keep her conjured spear active. Progress.

She snapped her arms out wide. *Stay back.* The message was unmistakable. No more heroics. Not today.

He *knew.* He gave the slightest nod. *Stay alive,* it said.

She didn't plan to hold the bukavac under her control like she had with the wendigo. Even a week later, the desperate, disastrous experiment continued to haunt her dreams. She planned something different.

If Abby had reshaped a wrought-iron chair into a charging horse in under ten seconds, Esme could reshape her spear on the fly. A slight mental adjustment to the valve she imagined controlled the flow of magic unleashed the infernal conduit into Esme's conjured spear.

With power surging between her and the weapon, she changed it. The spear, buried in the bukavac, pulsed, shadow warping its edges in her mind. It gently unfolded like a blooming steel flower. Then snapped violently outward into a razor-sharp disk.

A guillotine, born of hellfire and hate, tore outward from the monster's throat.

The bukavac's head dropped forward with a heavy thud, splashing into the water—a silent event, thankfully without Miles nearby, she noted with relief. For one terrible second, the world froze. No more roaring. No magic. No frantic movement.

Then the bukavac collapsed. Fresh gore sprayed weakly from its neck and shoulders as its body sloshed into the water with a final groan.

Holy shit.

Her hands were still clenched around air, mental fingers locked in a spell that no longer existed. Her chest rose and fell in stunned gasps.

It worked. It actually worked. The infernal magic had obeyed her, and she hadn't had to fight it tooth and nail for control. For once, she didn't feel like she was one breath away from breaking.

Her triumph evaporated when she saw Miles, motionless by the water's edge, in a state of shock. He turned toward her slowly, water dripping from his coat, eyes wide in stunned disbelief.

With the adrenaline fading, Esme drooped. Miles was instantly at her side, his hands gripping her arms as his eyes scanned for injuries. He removed his bulky hearing protectors and pulled her into a tight hug. His hands reached up and pulled the ear muffs from her head.

The sounds of the underground world rushed back in all at once—dripping water, distant echoes, and their heavy breathing mingled. Miles crushed her into his chest before she could say a word.

When he leaned back, his face no longer showed her the shock and disbelief she'd expected to see there again. Wonder shone through his loving gaze. "You're a one-woman army, lovely."

Esme sagged in relief. She should know by now that he wasn't easy to scare away.

They found Otto in a separate corridor, sitting down against the tunnel wall, completely exhausted. Tears gathered in the older Nisse's eyes on their approach. The others present grouped together, staring at Miles and Esme in bewildered astonishment.

Miles kneeled beside Otto. "However you want to handle this, it's your call. What do you want me to do with the body?"

All Esme could manage in the face of those tears was, "Otto, I'm... I'm sorry about the..." She trailed off, unable to mention their lost child aloud.

The Nisse man let out a weak, broken laugh, wiping his face. "The body... that's usually our job, anyway."

Esme blinked. "Wait..."

Otto only nodded, his expression tired and grim.

It clicked like puzzle pieces meant to be together in her mind. The quiet, unassuming Nisse had been cleaning up Brotherhood messes all along. How many messes had they quietly swept under the magical rug? And now they'd lost one of their own to the monsters that weren't supposed to exist.

Half an hour later in the car, Esme rubbed her temples and turned to Miles. "That was... This is bad. All of them know about the malevolents now."

He gripped the wheel tighter. "Yeah."

"So what do we do?"

He exhaled slowly. "We tell Jacob. And we hope he has a plan."

"If he'll even do anything at this point! He practically shooed us out the door to go on his vacation. Something is going on. I've never seen him like this before."

The silence between them said it all. The secret wasn't a secret anymore. And they were standing right in the middle of the fallout.

CHAPTER TWENTY-TWO

SERPENTINE LESSONS

Esme

Esme tugged her beanie lower, grudgingly grateful she'd followed Seren's specific packing list. The wind tore across the beach, biting through her clothes. At least the scenery made the cold bearable. Even with cloud cover, the beach was stunning. The wind whipped up choppy waves that crashed against the rocky shore. High above, seagulls wheeled in the sky, their raucous cries cutting through the crashing surf.

The boat that sidled up to the dock wasn't what she'd expected. Nothing about it matched Seren's mythos—no sleek lines, no ominous presence. Instead, it was a practical, weatherworn vessel, the kind more suited to a fisherman or smuggler. As it drew close, the man at the helm gave her a curt nod and eased in for her to board.

Miles had begged her to put safety first. But stepping onto that boat, with its peeling paint and oil-slick scent, seemed anything but safe. Esme took the damp life vest, the deck perilously slick beneath her boots.

As they pulled away from shore, Esme watched the coastline recede, the familiar shapes of buildings and docks softening into the mist. They passed a few sea lions lounging on buoys like bored sentinels. Bit by bit, the skyline gave way to the dense, brooding greens of Maury Island's southern forests.

The helmsman's silence unsettled her more than she wanted to admit. Esme usually filled awkward silences with chatter, but the man gave her nothing, not even eye contact. Maybe he was being paid to keep quiet and not ask questions. That sounded exactly like something Seren would arrange.

The breathtaking scenery, with the salty air rushing past her face, was a welcome distraction. It was easier than thinking about the surreal choice she'd made a day after the bukavac fight. Too soon, maybe. But that look in Seren's eyes when she'd asked if Esme would train with her again… It hadn't been a calculated plea. It had been honest grief.

And Esme had always been weak for grief. It wasn't logic that brought her here. And against her better judgment, she decided to give Seren a second chance. She just hoped she wouldn't regret it.

After the eerily silent boat ride, Esme was relieved to find Seren waiting for her on the dock as promised. Seren greeted her with a cheerful hello and led her toward a bland and forgettable midsize sedan. It was obviously a rental car. After Esme's comments about the helicopter, was Seren trying to assure her she was "normal"?

"No limo," Esme quipped. "A sensible boat first, then a car that doesn't scream 'I'm rich and powerful.'"

"I *occasionally* have a sense of restraint," Seren said with a smirk. "It just doesn't come naturally to me."

The gesture made Esme feel marginally better. She climbed into the passenger seat, buckling in as Seren pulled onto the winding road. Their drive took them farther inland, through dense evergreens and with occasional glimpses of rocky beaches through the trees.

The knot in her stomach tightened when the forgettable warehouse appeared at the end of the gravel road. Though it resembled an old barn more than a warehouse, with its aged wood and heavy metal sliding door, an undeniable malevolent aura emanated all the way down the street from it. The prickling wrongness on her skin wasn't the only thing that gave Esme pause. It reminded her too much of where her parents had died.

Seren gave her a sidelong look before she stepped out of the car and waved Esme to follow. Chiding herself, Esme pushed down her embarrassment and stepped out. The building pulsed with malevolent magic, a suffocating pressure that threatened to crush her with the weight of another nightmare.

Even mundanes would feel this much malevolent magic and instinctively avoid the place. This "warehouse" probably needed little security.

What the hell had she gotten herself into?

Inside, fluorescent tube lighting buzzed overhead, illuminating metal cages that hummed with the wards placed upon them. Something moved inside one, and Esme's breath hitched in surprise.

A hissing púca, a shapeshifting trickster with eyes of molten gold, flickered behind the bars. Its appearance wavered between its true form—a black rabbit-like creature—and a stretched humanoid one.

The sight of it—caged, twitching frantically—sparked a gut-deep fury. Driven by impulse and instinct, Esme lunged forward, her hand grasping the padlock before she consciously realized what she was doing.

"What the hell?" Her hand was already on the padlock when Seren's voice stopped her.

"*That* is not your chef friend or his mate, or even one of his kits. *That* is a púca 'gone to the dark side,' as they say." As if on cue, the púca hissed again and launched itself at Esme's hand on the padlock.

Esme flinched back as its sharp, talon-like claws encountered the ward spell that was helping to keep it contained. Seren was right; Wexley's true form was far tamer than this creature. This púca had an elongated mouth with fangs. Its ears were shorter and the claws on its paws longer.

While Esme stared at what the chef at the Sanctuary of Spirits might have become, had he not changed paths when they'd met, Seren spoke. "I thought it was a shame that Jacob didn't know about the phenomenon before Sylas succumbed to it."

The phenomenon that had pushed Sylas over the edge. For beings whose existence was interwoven with magic, succumbing too long to dark intentions twisted their bodies alongside their hearts.

"It wasn't Sylas' fault!" Esme snapped. "Leon pushed him to it."

She didn't care if Seren was trying to be diplomatic. Sylas had been forced. There was a difference between falling and being pushed.

"You're right, of course," Seren said, sounding more like she used the words as a calming gesture rather than actually meaning it.

With Sylas gone and Leon dead, Esme realized it was pointless to argue with Seren and dropped the subject. Sylas remained a hero in the eyes of those who knew him best.

In another enclosure, a furless dog-like animal gnashed its teeth as spit dripped onto the straw-covered floor of its cage. A shapeless, limb-heavy creature pressed against the bars in the far corner, its body shifting like smoke. Having no clue what that thing was, she decided she'd rather not find out.

Esme took a slow step back. "Okay. What the hell is this place?"

"Training facility." Seren shut the door behind them. "One of a handful of training sites. There aren't many, but they're necessary."

Esme's mouth pressed into a thin line. "And you just happen to have malevolents stored here?"

Seren shrugged. "They're contained and well-fed. We have staff that makes sure of it."

Holy gods, had Miles helped capture these things? *Why are you surprised, Esme? You're the one who fell in love with a thoroughly morally gray man.*

Seren didn't look at Esme as she moved toward a nest containing large, mottled eggs. They were the roc's eggs, Esme realized, recognizing them from their last trip together.

"We *are* here for training," Seren said. "We'll return to the topic of the malevolents after we run a few tests."

Seren put Esme through her paces. Her trio of trolls lumbered into being, filling up the warehouse, followed by Oatmeal, her shadowcat, whom she made flop onto her back and beg for belly rubs. Following Seren's instructions, she showed off her conjured arsenal, each weapon a perfect example of her growing mastery over the magic.

"Good," Seren said. "Now show me something outside your specialty."

Esme grimaced, then focused. Weak telekinesis lifted a clipboard that contained notes on the captive creatures' feeding schedule. It wobbled in the air before dropping back down. She followed it with a facial glamor, subtly shifting her features into the teenaged boy she'd used when trying to blend in for her old work for the Assembly.

"I don't use disguises anymore," Esme admitted, dismissing the spell. "Not since I stopped doing enforcer work."

Seren hummed. "Useful skills, but not what I want you working on today...."

Seren lapsed into contemplation, the rhythmic tap-tap-tap of her nails on the table a counterpoint to the squawks, hisses, and snarls otherwise filling the room. With a faraway look in her eyes, she stared at the wall, seemingly oblivious to the fact that Esme was standing there, waiting to hear what she *did* want her to work on.

Finally, she said, "I want you to practice harnessing your connection to a malevolent using an infernal conduit."

Every muscle in Esme's body went taut. "No."

Seren's steady gaze met hers, firm like the oldest tree in the forest standing tall against the wind. "You used it before."

The memory of all that Leon had been willing to do to get that power flooded back. In a moment of desperation, she'd used it; the result had been horrific. The wendigo's hunger had slithered into her mind—and part of her had *understood* it.

"I'm not doing that again." Esme was firm in her conviction. "The connection I had to form with it... That's not something I want to repeat unless I have no other choice."

Seren's tone remained gentle, but Esme recognized the push anyway. "That disgust you feel? That's good. It means you're resisting the pull." Her voice was too calm, too practiced. Like she'd rehearsed this speech. "But if you can control it, it could save your life. It could save your friends' lives. Imagine if you could turn a malevolent against itself to save a bystander."

Esme's fists clenched. The memory of the tiny plastic boat floating in the water near the bukavac flashed in her mind. If they had shown up earlier, if she had controlled the malevolent that day, maybe that tiny life would not have been cut so short.

Seren would have let the wendigo eat her, or would have done the deed herself, if she had truly wanted Esme to be harmed. Esme exhaled sharply, decision made. "Fine."

Seren gestured at the púca's cage with a tense expression. "Try it."

Esme ignored that one. It reminded her too much of her friend. She focused on the dog-like creature instead. "What is it?"

"That's a malevolent xolotl. I specify because, like your púca friend, these too can turn malevolent. The neutral ones are quite wonderful creatures, and there is a mundane version of them too, the Xolo dog."

As Esme approached its cage, the xolotl snarled, its claws and teeth scraping and snapping at the magically reinforced bars. The hairless dark hound's eyes shone like Cerys', yet unlike her warm gaze, this one was cold and empty.

Esme forced her fear and rage down into a tight coil inside her chest. She let that hidden part of her that wasn't strictly human rise to the surface. It was like peeling away her skin and letting something older, darker, crawl forward in her place. When she couldn't hold it anymore, she let go. It felt like releasing a scream held too long into the void.

She released it in one great push out at the rabid dog creature. A strange quiet fell over the room as the magic lanced out of Esme.

"Sit!" It wasn't the most inventive test to use on a dog, but it worked.

The xolotl trembled, its body going rigid before slowly, reluctantly, crouching. Its snarling and snapping stopped. Held captive by her, it returned her look with burning resentment.

Unlike the wendigo, with its endless hunger and intelligence, she sensed a different kind of malevolence in this being.

This xolotl was more... sadistically playful. It wanted nothing more than to see blood spurting as it tore her apart with its teeth. While it would most certainly eat her, the twisted amusement it would derive from the game of it was more alluring than simple hunger.

Esme kept her control in place for only a second before retreating into herself.

A thrill shot through her. The thrill wasn't infernal in nature, but something close. She had done it.

With her connection to the infernal cut off, Esme was suddenly light-headed. This was heavy-duty magic the likes of which she'd only experienced once before. She'd found magic relatively simple up to this point because for years she'd been inadvertently drawing on her cambion powers. This was stressing her abilities in entirely new ways.

Bracing herself for Seren's criticism at the simple display, she turned to the older mage.

Seren was smiling. With a warm, approving expression, she gently rested her hand on Esme's shoulder. The touch felt like a silent blessing. "Well done."

Esme grinned, buoyed by the rare praise.

Maybe with a bit more practice, she could do exactly as Seren had described. She could save someone.

For a moment, Esme let herself believe this could work. That Seren might actually be the mentor she'd once hoped Leon would be. But behind that approving smile, something else flickered—something biting. Something... hungry.

CHAPTER TWENTY-THREE

CRACKS IN THE FOUNDATION

Abby

Abby tugged at her blazer sleeves for the third time in as many minutes, fingers unable to stay still as her stomach tied itself into knots. She'd arrived early, too early, hoping the quiet would settle her nerves. The hastily called Saturday board meeting was Jacob's first act after returning home. It also marked Abby's official debut in her new role. Though she had once spied on such a meeting from an adjacent room, the rushed scheduling left her worried about what surprises might be dropped.

Miles slid into the seat beside her before anyone else could, offering a quick, reassuring grin. Maybe she wasn't alone in her nervousness. He was a relative newcomer himself—sort of. A moment later, Josiah, a tall Native man who was going more silver every day, took the chair on her other side.

"Abby girl," he murmured, voice warm. "Nervous?"

"A little," she admitted.

"Don't be. You belong here."

She forced a smile, but the tension in her gut didn't ease. She wasn't sure she wanted to get used to it. Did she really belong here? She knew that Josiah, who had been like a second father to her and Colin growing up, had shown up early to help her get settled.

The other members arrived in a slow trickle. Next came Maureen, then Sorcha the selkie, and Winnie the aziza. As usual, Ved, the Garudas' leader, arrived last. No one blamed him, given the powerful glamour he needed to conceal his avian form just to enter the building. Jon Doe, a human mage whose specialization was in alteration of materials, was conspicuously absent. He was probably off getting richer somewhere.

The room fell silent the second Jacob walked in. Abby did a double take.

He actually went on vacation.

Jacob was vacation tan. Not "weekend-in-the-yard" tan; he was *Caribbean-cruise, cocktail-in-hand* tan. When he'd disappeared under the guise of a business trip, he'd been in London, orchestrating David Abington's institutionalization. She'd half expected this to be another lie.

But here he was, looking relaxed in a way she hadn't seen in years—maybe ever.

"Welcome back, Jacob," Maureen greeted him with a wide grin.

Jacob nodded, then gestured to Seren, who had somehow slipped in unnoticed. She now stood near the head of the table like she owned it, which she kind of did. "We all know Seren Lewis. She's here to assist with our recent... *escalations.*"

His tone made it clear he'd rather she wasn't.

Next to her, Jacob launched into addressing the surge in malevolent activity. Then he turned to Seren, his voice spiking with enough power to send shivers down Abby's spine.

"Less than a month in the city, Ms. Lewis, and the attacks have *doubled*. I fear to say this, but I think that your contribution to a city already overflowing with too many powerful magic users has tipped malevolent activity into unprecedented territory. It's a powder keg waiting to blow!"

A ripple of tension passed through the room. Several members went completely still. Even Ved's feathers bristled.

"A bukavac has killed a Nisse child in clear view of a whole host of their children!" Jacob leaned forward. "Or do you *want* this? You've made your stance on secrecy clear enough. Maybe all these incidents are exactly the kind of excuse you need to force our hand."

But Seren didn't flinch. A slight smirk played at her lips as she folded her hands, waiting. "You give me far too much credit, Jacob. The Brotherhood's secrecy has caused generations of ignorance and suffering. The magical community should be informed, prepared—not kept in the dark like children waiting to be devoured by the very things they don't know exist."

Seren's gaze swept the table. "Ignorance doesn't protect people. It gets them killed."

Abby's fingers tightened around her pen. She agreed, in theory. But something about Seren's certainty, the way she spoke like she had all the answers, set her teeth on edge.

Jacob's smile was thin. "And yet, your 'transparency' hasn't stopped the bodies from piling up."

Jacob had hinted at these old battle lines, and they'd seen their feud partially play out in the quarterly meeting. But seeing it unfold behind closed doors with heat behind the words was something else. Other members joined in the argument. Unsurprisingly, Maureen was on Jacob's side. Ved joined Maureen. Sorcha voiced her firm support for Seren, and Winnie made a buzz of her agreement as well.

Only Abby and Miles sat quiet, unsure.

The debate spiraled from there, but Abby barely heard it. The divide was clear: Jacob's fortress of secrets or Seren's ruthless transparency—two forms of power, neither offering safety.

And for the first time, Abby had no idea whom to trust.

After the meeting adjourned, though harsh words still echoed in the room, Abby waited patiently, hoping for a brief, private moment with Seren. A sheen of sweat covered her palms.

The leather of Seren's briefcase creaked softly as she snapped it shut. Abby wiped her palms on her pants for the third time. Her heartbeat thudded in her ears. Still, she stepped forward. "Can I ask you something?"

Seren didn't turn but said, "You already are, Ms. O'Malley."

Abby rolled her eyes but stepped closer, though she wanted to stay back. She cast a weak ward of silence around them both. "It's about my halo."

That got Seren's attention. She glanced over her shoulder with one eyebrow raised. "I'm listening."

"Thanks for that," Abby snapped as her voice threatened to waver. "How does it work? It's already making spells easier. Since you knew about it before anyone else, I just want to know what I'm walking around with."

Seren studied her. "Some call it a blessing. A divine gift. But I'm not convinced it's either of those things."

"Of course it's not." Abby folded her arms, trying to make herself believe it. The timing of its arrival so soon after her dawning realization of her connection to Creiddylad felt too coincidental. "Then what is it?"

"I think of it like... a reaction," Seren said at last. "I can't help but think that it manifests when your magic becomes *loud enough*. When your conviction or need punches through the divide between this world and whatever else is out there. Think of it like... feedback from the universe. You pushed magic *so hard* that it left an indelible mark on your aura."

Abby recoiled slightly in surprise. "You're saying I screamed loud enough into the void that it *screamed back*?"

"That's not a bad way of putting it." Seren's lips curved into a smile that was half amused, half something else. "It changes you. Not only your magic, but also the way people look at you. I've learned that a halo will attract people in the same way malevolent magic repels them. Mundane humans included."

"Perfect," Abby muttered. "Another thing I didn't ask for."

"Life isn't fair," Seren said softly. "But I think it means you've already chosen something. I hope I'm around to find out what that is..."

A chill that had nothing to do with the breeze snaked its way over her skin. She'd been curious since Seren had arrived, but now seemed like the time to finally *look* with her magical sight at the older woman.

Abby blinked, gasping. Looking at Seren was like standing in front of a three-thousand-watt lighthouse after days of blindness. Her presence was overwhelmingly bright. So bright, so tangled together and vast, that her aura blurred together into white. There were too many pieces of light for Abby to take it all in.

"Gods be-fucking-low—" she gasped, staggering back. Her ward shattered with a soft pop. She grabbed the edge of a chair to stay upright.

"Abigail?" Seren's voice cut through the static. "Is everything alright?"

"Yep..." Abby clamped both hands over her face. Her eyes were *burning*. "Just... seriously regretting some of those choices we were just talking about."

Her vision swam with afterimages that she couldn't blink away. Her eyes teared up underneath the press of her palms. Flashes still pulsed behind her eyelids.

"Okay..." Seren's voice was wary. "Come to me if you need anything."

Abby peeked through her fingers with only mundane vision. The woman standing there was exactly as she had been before. But Abby wasn't sure she'd just looked at a person at all.

Go to her?

Abby wasn't sure anymore that Seren was even *human*.

***

The afternoon sun was pleasantly warm, the air thick with the scent of blooming fruit trees and pollen. So. Much. Pollen.

Abby sneezed for the third time in five minutes as she stood near the water's edge at Green Lake Park. Why did she agree to this? Her allergies were bad enough without the added torture of exercise. She knew her eyes would be burning without her sunglasses to shield them while they ran.

Cerys sat obediently at her heels, glamoured to look like a muscular Cane Corso, her glowing eyes only occasionally breaking the illusion. They had been glamouring her to look like a more common Rottweiler, but her recent weight gain now made that impossible.

At least that was something she could be thankful to her halo for. Getting the illusion to stick to the gwyllgi was easier than ever. Gwyn had wanted to come, but Abby had sworn off exercising with him long ago. His legs were too damned long. Plus, she missed having time alone with Esme.

Esme jogged up a moment later, Lily's leash in hand. The massive Irish wolfhound trotted beside Esme like an oversized shadow. Watching Lily and Cerys sniff at each other in a doggy greeting, glamoured and harmless-looking, Abby wondered how many monsters wore friendly faces now.

"Ready?" Esme grinned, already bouncing on the balls of her feet.

"Not really," Abby muttered. At least running with Esme wouldn't be as terrible as it was with Gwyn. Maybe. Being vertically challenged had many drawbacks, and being slow was one of them. Her friends were all far too athletic for her liking. Esme hadn't chosen to have a genetic one-up on them all with her demonic heritage, but it still made a difference.

"Everything okay?" Esme asked, noticing Abby's hesitation.

"Yeah." Abby rubbed at her eyes. "Let's go before I suffocate in my own sinuses."

They started out at a leisurely pace with the gravel crunching beneath their feet. Esme, damn her, barely broke a sweat, while Abby was already regretting her life choices. She hadn't eaten enough that morning—nerves from the meeting still lingered.

"So," Esme said between breaths, "I'm thinking of quitting the Sanctuary."

"No!" Abby stumbled mid-step, catching herself. "You're kidding—why?"

"I don't do any Assembly work anymore. Since I moved in with Miles, I'm basically freeloading until I *insist* on doing the grocery shopping. You said something about it to him for me, right?"

Abby only nodded. She was avoiding the effort it took to speak until it was absolutely necessary. The dogs weren't even breathing hard!

"Miles took what the sasquatches said to him far too seriously." Esme shot her a sideways glance. "I barely see you guys anymore. While I'm working, they're out hunting, or you're buried in the ER. Plus, I'm basically just a manager now. The new staff we hired does all the work! Might as well free up my schedule."

"You and Gwyn do tons of stuff during the day we can't get to," Abby huffed. "You could just... cut back? Work weekends. Jacob won't care."

"I thought of that." Esme made a noncommittal noise. "Gods, Miles makes me feel like we're a different species sometimes."

"Uh... you sort of are?" Abby had to stifle a laugh.

"She says, not being fully human herself!" Esme whispered, then rolled her eyes. "It's just that he never stops. He works two jobs and still insists on cooking for us both half the time. That's probably why I've been baking so damn much. I want to look like I'm doing *something* special."

"You know he's dieting at work, right?"

Esme groaned. "See, I even screw that up."

"Stop it, Morgana. At least you have a boyfriend who knows how to do things. I spend half my time explaining stuff to Gwyn."

Esme waggled her eyebrows. "I bet you do."

"Pervert."

"I know I'm right, though." Esme somehow managed a shrug and a wink while running—*without* tripping. Then, after a beat, she asked, "How was the meeting?"

Abby didn't even try to soften it. She laid it all out as they slowed to a jog. Beginning with Jacob's accusations and Seren's counterargument, and concluding by highlighting the worsening tension among the members.

"It's like... Jacob hides the monsters, and Seren wants to parade them in the Assembly meetings," Esme said.

"Yeah. Either way, someone's going to get hurt." Abby hesitated before adding, "And then there's what she did to you with the wendigo."

Abby jogged ahead before realizing Esme was no longer beside her. She turned back, breathing hard, to see Esme stopped dead, Lily's leash taut in her grip. "What? What's wrong?"

Esme got to it before Abby could. "Abby, at this point, I don't know who to trust. Jacob has lied to me half a million times. And Seren—she says she's trying to help me. Objectively, she has. But her methods... And something about her just doesn't feel right."

Abby's fingers dug into Cerys' fur, seeking an anchor. Esme had reached the same conclusion she had. She didn't know what to do. "I talked to her after the meeting about my halo."

Esme's head snapped toward her. "Wait—seriously?"

"She already knew about it, so what's the big deal?"

Esme's expression turned sour with worry. "And?"

"A cosmic side effect," Abby said, trying to explain. "She said it happened because my magic got too loud, so now I'm stuck with the echo. Weird, right?"

Esme frowned. "That's not comforting."

"Nope." Abby let out a dry laugh. "I used my sight on her. Esme... Her magic is... it's like staring into the sun."

"Gods," Esme muttered. "I always knew there was something off about her. That's—"

"—not human, not anymore," Abby finished quietly.

They kept walking in silence for a stretch, dogs close. Abby was preoccupied with thoughts of how insane their lives had become in the past year, and she knew Esme well enough that she was probably thinking the same thing.

Abby grimaced. "And I feel like the fallout from the bukavac has just started."

"Fuck..." Esme grumbled. "That too..."

Cerys whined, nudging Abby's hand. Lily leaned against Esme's leg, sensing the shift in mood.

Regardless of their worries, the sun still shone. The lake still glittered. Rude bikers still refused to share the path. The world turned, uncaring.

Abby had always trusted her eyes, her instincts. For the first time, she wasn't sure she saw clearly at all. She had never seen such deep divisions within the magical community. Now? She didn't know who was lying, who was hiding things—or who would get them all killed.

Chapter Twenty-Four

True Power

Miles

Miles leaned back, watching Esme command the room with effortless charm. His mouth twitched upward. Her energy was infectious, and her laughter drew the others in like moths to flame. She was successfully transforming Abby's birthday from a small gathering into an event.

"I was smart and pre-mixed Abby's favorite drinks so we can avoid Grandpa Leprechaun exhausting us all by running a marathon back and forth from the bar."

Finn's face crumpled in dismay, as if robbed of his purpose. Yet a nudge from Katia quickly got the leprechaun back on track. Anything the succubus did pleased him. His smitten expression was a small price for peace.

Ignoring the leprechaun, Esme grinned. "Wexley is also here, and he's cooked all of Abby's favorite dishes for us to share."

"Brilliant, lovely," Miles said, genuinely meaning it. Finn approached his rounds with the utmost seriousness, and Esme wasn't exaggerating when she said that even just watching him try to keep the party lively was utterly exhausting. When it came to booze and food, he was a boundless source of party energy.

Abby mouthed, "Thank you," to Esme as she headed to the bar to grab a tray of drinks for everyone.

Gwyn shot Finn a murderous look before asking, "How have things been in California, Colin, Will?"

Since Colin and Will were back in Seattle for the weekend, they'd pushed several tables together in the Sanctuary of Spirits to make room for everyone.

"Sunny, unlike here," Colin answered with a grin of his own. "Speaking of exhausting, Will, you should tell them about your brief foray into hunting last weekend."

"I am so done with all of you." Will groaned. "One time! I get worried about him and decide to help one time, and suddenly I'm covered in filthy sewage!"

Colin corrected him dryly, "It was compost."

"The thing had *boobs*! Giant, swinging ones! Right in my face!" Will shuddered dramatically, hands graphically showing for all the world how large said "boobs" were. Poor sod looked completely horrified at the discovery that malevolents could have mammary glands.

Laughter rippled through the group as Colin patted his boyfriend's shoulder. "You're a natural."

Will took a sip and scowled over the rim of his glass. "Not the word I'd use."

Colin lowered his voice. "It was a Roggenmuhme. And, obviously, we're fine. L.A. is the wrong city for an agricultural minor demon type to show up in."

Finn, ever the instigator, attempted to launch another round of drinks, much to Gwyn's visible dismay. Miles noticed more than a few glances flickering toward the corner where Seren sat with Carloff and Ivar. She and Ivar were locked in an intense game of chess. Though unspoken and unacknowledged, Seren's presence loomed in the corner, impossible to ignore.

True to form, Finn raised his glass in a toast. Honestly, Miles found it surprising that he hadn't had to join in on three or four toasts by that point. "To Abigail. She's only terrifyin' if ya know 'er!"

He laughed uproariously, but heads nodded along. They all knew what she'd done to Leon.

Abby rolled her eyes but still clinked her glass. "I regret inviting you already."

The party wound down. Abby and Gwyn left first, followed by Colin, Will, and a theatrically mournful Finn supported by Katia. Finn was brooding about not being able to run himself ragged for his granddaughter's birthday.

Esme lingered to help tidy up, and by the time she and Miles stepped into the parking lot, the night had settled into a damp Seattle chill.

Esme tossed her keys his way. "I saw you barely touching your drink all night."

Damned diet.

Esme's car sputtered uselessly when he turned the key.

Miles let out a sigh, biting his tongue against what he really wanted to say. "Lovely, I'm begging you. Buy a new car."

She narrowed her eyes. "It just needs a jump."

"This car is old enough to buy a pint inside without showing identification! I'll buy one; please just..."

She looked as though she was about to retort but changed her mind at the last second. Esme huffed, "I'll see if anyone inside can give us a jump."

Miles pulled out his phone with a resigned sigh. "I'll find a tow while you work your magic inside."

Watching Esme disappear around the corner, Miles felt the familiar, odd mix of exasperation and affection that always seemed to be with him these days. Her insistence on keeping that death trap of a car was both frustrating and oddly sweet. He knew what it was about. She was desperately clinging onto every material possession that was left from her life before the fire, but the car was too unreliable, too dangerous for her to keep using.

But that was only half of it. The woman who could summon guillotines and rage with demonic fury feared car payments more than facing down a hungry malevolent. The thought made him smile, despite everything.

He opened two tabs on his phone. One to search for a towing company's number, the other a search for used cars she might actually agree to. As he scanned listings, a prickling sensation crawled up his left arm. His years of training had instilled in him a deep sense of paranoia, yet the still shadows of the parking lot and low ambient levels of magic in the air failed to trigger real alarm.

Ignoring the feeling, he continued his search. The tow company's number was half-entered when the silence pressed in, holding its breath.

The world around Miles shattered.

Glass shattered beside his head as something heavy slammed into the car window. Pain exploded across his skull. His ears rang as his training still propelled him forward.

He rolled out of the car a split second before another blow came. Two push daggers slid into his palms as he put space between himself and his attacker.

The fachan lurched from the shadows on its single leg. Its distorted face filled with teeth twisted toward the driver's side door. Miles feinted to his left. But his go-to grappling moves were ineffective against its asymmetrical limbs.

He ducked the next swing and drove a hidden dagger into its side. A kick sent him reeling, and his vision swam.

Pain flared, sudden and all-consuming. He blinked blood out of his eyes. His own blood. The world around him tilted, and the fachan saw the opening. A single, powerful jump sent it barreling into him, and he landed hard in the driver's seat through the open door.

He was losing con—

Light flickered behind his eyes like dying stars.

Healing energy flitted in his palms as a third kick prevented him from rising. He'd been a bloody fool for ignoring the chill creeping up his arm, the silence too complete.

Darkness fell as he heard his name called.

Esme

Esme sighed, scanning the thinning crowd inside the bar. "Jumper cables?"

A few heads shook; others remained blank. She wiggled her fingers in mock spellcasting. "No one can just... zap it for me?"

Seren stayed focused on the chessboard. "After I crush this svartálfar. Three moves, that's all."

A mournful groan emerged from the dusky-skinned dwarf. This at least was something the powerful mage could be helpful with in a straightforward way—hopefully.

With a muttered curse, Esme headed for the bar's concealed exit. As she stepped into the dimly lit parking lot, her eyes adjusted slowly to the night. She thought she saw Miles waiting by the car.

Until the figure standing by it shifted.

The fachan pivoted on its single leg, blood-slick from a wound on its side, its misshapen body twisted toward her.

Then she saw Miles slumped in the driver's seat. Her world narrowed to the crimson streams trailing down his temple. Terror rooted her in place, unable to breathe or move. For one awful second, the possibility of losing him completely overwhelmed her.

Then rage ignited. This time it was hot and living, not numbing coldness like usual. This was like a second heartbeat pounding through her veins *for him*. It whispered promises, seductive and sadistic: *Cut it down. Make it suffer.*

It swept away her paralysis with the numbing sense of purpose. The infernal power coiled around her bones, whispering all the things she wanted to hear. *Damn the Assembly. Damn the edict.*

Then she saw Miles stir. He was trying to get up to—

A warped sword materialized in her grip as the darkness within her roared.

Without a thought from her, Oatmeal exploded from the shadows. Fangs first, a streak of molten silver and shadows slicing through the night to take the malevolent from behind.

The fachan went down, and Esme's blade followed. She gritted her teeth, her jaw aching from the pressure, as her sword arced up and chopped down in rhythm with her pounding heart. Conjured steel and teeth bit into its flesh, over and over, until the thing was pulp beneath her feet.

Footsteps. Magic. These things she barely registered.

Esme whirled toward the sound, breath heaving, vision dark with fury. "Enough!" Seren sighed, her gaze flicking between the pile of mangled flesh and the car. "Where is Miles? Did he leave you?"

The sound of his name shattered Esme's demonic haze. She allowed the sword's magic to dissipate and gave the corpse one last contemptuous kick before she moved to open her car.

Miles hadn't moved. Esme scrambled into the passenger seat, her hands finding him before her mind could process the horror of what she was seeing. Blood soaked his face, his scalp, everything.

Her stomach did a somersault. She could see his skull. *Cracked*.

Seren appeared at his side.

Esme's hands shook as she fumbled for her phone. She had to call...

"Stop." Seren's voice was a command.

Esme's fingers froze, even as she fought the compulsion.

"Say nothing of this, little demoness."

Then Seren placed her hands gently on Miles' head, and a dark light tinged with a touch of silver spread from her palms.

The magic felt achingly familiar—but wrong. A carnival mirror image of Miles' magic, refracted through the cold light of infernal power. Esme could feel its intense, undeniable, impossible power.

But this was *Seren*.

The bones knit themselves under Seren's hands, a sickening *click* accompanying each connection, and, like serpents returning to their burrows, his flesh wiggled back into place.

A whimper of relief, mingled with confusion and her darker feelings, escaped Esme's throat. "How?" The word barely made it past her lips.

Seren withdrew her hands, her eyes avoiding Esme's. The woman's usual confident facade cracked for just a moment, revealing the burdens of years, worries, and a deep weariness within. "Only ask questions you're prepared to carry the answers for until you die and beyond." Seren wiped Miles' blood from her hands onto her black trousers with practiced movements. Esme was beginning to understand her fashion choices.

Miles stirred, his eyelashes fluttering slightly. Though her hand reached for him, Esme's mind was racing, replaying each of Seren's cryptic comments and every dangerous situation she'd led Esme into. And now, this impossible magic.

The accusation in Esme's eyes was impossible to hide as hers met Seren's suddenly guarded gaze.

"I care about my assets. Don't mistake necessity for sentiment." Seren's eyes flashed with her usual fiery intensity of spirit, of personality. "I *am* the Citadel," she said, her voice ringing with a dangerous finality.

As she straightened her spine, Seren's composure returned. It fell over her face like a veil—one of mourning if Esme had the right of it. "You've seen nothing tonight. Remember that."

Miles woke slowly as Seren stood over him, as silent as the grave. Esme cradled his face, searching for any lingering injury. Despite his obvious confusion, he awoke, whole and coherent.

"What happened?" Miles asked, touching the still-sticky blood on his scalp.

Esme's glance fell upon Seren, who watched them with an inscrutable expression. Esme suddenly understood that Seren hadn't helped Miles out of generosity or human kindness; she had ulterior motives. But what? Given her history of reckless endangerment, why did Seren's expression now hold a hint of… possessiveness?

"A fachan," Esme said carefully, watching Seren's face. "It attacked us. I killed it. I'd like to know why these Scottish Fae fuckers keep turning up in sets…"

"And your head wound is healing nicely," Seren added smoothly. "Your own magic kicked in, though you were unconscious. Fascinating ability."

Seren lied effortlessly, as if she'd done it a thousand times before. Miles nodded slowly, accepting the explanation without question.

As they helped Miles, still a bit woozy, from the car, Esme caught Seren watching her, not with the usual calculating glint, but with a deeper, almost sorrowful expression. For a fraction of a second, Esme glimpsed a silent intensity that sent a shiver of unease down her spine.

"I've always looked after what's mine," Seren murmured, so quietly Esme wasn't sure Miles could hear. Then louder, she added, "The car is beyond saving. I'll take care of the body. Go, now. That's an order."

"An *order* order?" Esme's eyes were narrowed.

"Yes, a bloody order!" Seren exclaimed, her usual composure replaced by unexpected anger. "Get walking. Your presence will only make my task harder. Call for a ride share; go straight to the hospital. I don't care. Just *go*!"

Miles used his prothesis to nudge Esme, indicating they should proceed. So they just walked away—from the still-bleeding mess of flesh that used to be a fachan, from Esme's dead car, from the woman staring after them like she was half a heartbeat from losing her temper in a truly terrifying way.

Seren had turned on them just like that. Like she hadn't returned Esme's home, her comfort against the storm of life, as if she hadn't just returned Miles to her with magic that shouldn't exist.

Not human indeed.

They walked a block and found a bench to rest on.

Esme tightened her grip on Miles and pulled him into herself. It didn't matter if he outweighed her by sixty pounds. She needed to feel him *alive*. She needed to feel the heat coming off his skin, to hear his heart beating and his lungs breathing as she held him close. She needed proof that death hadn't stolen him too.

Holding on to the man that had captured her heart, Esme saw it clearly. Seren was playing a game. And Esme had just become a piece worth protecting. *Or* sacrificing.

She ran her fingers through Miles' blood-soaked hair where his wound had been. "What is the 'Citadel'? Is it like the 'Bastion'?"

"Did Seren get to talking while I was passed out? She's the Citadel. The last defense that might stand at the end."

"The end of...?" She let the question hang.

"Hope, lovely. The end of everything."

Her question had caused the atmosphere to shift. His searching eyes met hers in the dim lighting. "You've done it again," he whispered. "You saved me."

Esme had witnessed something that evening she was never meant to know about. But Esme wasn't bound to keeping a promise she'd never made. She wouldn't be made a fool again.

There would be no repeat performance of what had happened with Leon.

Esme shook her head. "Seren did."

She leaned her forehead against his, feeling the steady rhythm of his heart through the contact. And this time, she didn't keep the secrets. Not from him. Not again. She told him everything.

They sat like that for a long moment, enjoying the togetherness.

Until a wave of frigid death magic, like a howling arctic wind, slammed into them from down the street.

Chapter Twenty-Five

The Dead Don't Forget

Gwyn

"Thanks for accompanying me while I walk it off."

Gwyn pulled Abby closer as they walked hand in hand through Pioneer Square, not far from the Sanctuary of Spirits. The cool night air was refreshing, like the city was slowly waking up from a long winter's nap. New leaves, bright and trembling, clung to the skeletal gray branches above like hope on the verge of faltering. The dim yellow glow of old-fashioned street lamps cast long shadows as their footsteps echoed softly on the uneven cobblestone streets.

"I think we missed the last bus anyway," she added. "Let's relax here for a few. Then call a cab home."

The wrought-iron and wood benches under the antique pergola sat empty. Selecting the one least covered in pigeon droppings, they curled up together for warmth. The square was nearly empty, only a few stragglers passing through.

Gwyn draped an arm over her shoulders, his thumb tracing idle circles on her sleeve. "Finn's lessons going well?"

"Yes." Abby turned toward him with a small smirk. "Actually, I think I'll try something. We've been trying to figure out if I can use a Fae charm to divert mundane attention."

Gwyn arched a brow. "And it works?"

"Only one way to find out."

A subtle shimmer in the air, so faint he might have imagined it, and the world shifted its attention elsewhere.

Gwyn laughed, an exceedingly rare sound even to his own ears. "At least the leprechaun has proven himself to be of some worth."

Abby snorted, nudging him. "Don't let him hear you say that. His ego is big enough already."

She looked around like Finn might show up at any second.

One moment, he was content. Abby was there, the gentle rhythm of her breath against his chest, a slow, steady presence that warmed him better than any hearth fire.

The next, a chilling wave of dread washed over him, stealing all of his joy—and his next breath. Gwyn's vision blurred.

Abby said something. He tried to move his head to hear her better, but his muscles wouldn't obey his commands. His hearing was failing too.

The pain that ripped through his chest next was all-consuming, a burning agony that stole every bit of his attention.

Then, like a harp string stretched too tight, something snapped inside his ribcage, instantaneous and irreversibly final.

Gwyn barely registered that he was crumpling sideways onto Abby's shoulder. Even though she was right beside him, her voice sounded far away as she repeated his name.

Holding her, Gwyn succumbed to the encroaching darkness, dying for a second time.

When awareness returned to him, he found himself floating once again above a distant battlefield, separated from the people below by time and thousands of miles. This was not a repeat of the Battle of Arfderydd. This war was older, messier, fought in the misty valleys of Wales.

This was a battle he had fought not as a legend but as a man of flesh.

Ruined bodies lay scattered across the ground, their faces contorted in agony. A muffled clang of metal echoed as if underwater. Shadows lingered above each of the fallen, whispering all at once in Brythonic, familiar and yet utterly unintelligible.

Was he witnessing the first time he had felt the pull of death? Left with no memory of using necromantic powers during his first life, Gwyn could only guess at the significance of what he was seeing.

The vision reverberated with his name, a hopeless, echoing sound that felt like a desperate plea laced with magic. "Gwyn!"

The real world snapped back into focus. Abby's hands were on his shoulders, her face inches from his. Her hand was on his neck, checking his pulse, her expression pinched with concern. "Come on, come on—damn it, Gwyn, no, no, *no*."

Her pale face hovered above his, caught between terror and disbelief. Her other hand was fumbling with her phone, dialing. He wasn't seeing her through his own eyes. It was as though he hovered above himself or had slipped into someone else's memory—yet it was his.

All at once, his lungs pulled in a great burst of life-giving air.

As his body involuntarily jerked upright, the movement knocked Abby off-balance, sending her sprawling onto the cobblestones. His heart jolted back to life as cold air filled his lungs.

I'm so sorry, Abigail, he thought. But he couldn't speak yet.

Sound and sensation came flooding back as Abby said his name again. His eyes rolled automatically, locking his gaze on the space beyond her shoulder.

A sharp, penetrating chill swept through the square, a cold that reached deep into the marrow of his bones—a cold that only magic could cause.

Abby stiffened seeing his expression. Slowly, she turned her head, following Gwyn's line of sight.

A figure stood under the lamplight, as still as a statue. The shape of a woman gleamed faintly like moonlight trapped in shadow. She wore a flowing robe that was cinched tightly at her waist. A delicate crown of flowers adorned her head. There was an unearthly beauty to her blurred, ethereal features.

If she was a ghost, she wasn't the type that was all rotting flesh and bones. She appeared alive and human. First, she inclined her head to Abby. Then, her attention fastened on Gwyn. Her scrutiny was almost painful, as if she could see through his skin into his soul. She inclined her head once again.

Impossible. Ghosts could not cross the threshold. They didn't exist like this.

But this one had. She was tethered to him, like an echo of something he'd forgotten.

And the way she looked at him made Gwyn feel like he'd broken some unspoken rule of the universe—again.

Abby's shock was so great that she hadn't flinched since turning to see it with her own eyes. The only indication that she had seen the same thing was her quick, sharp intake of breath.

Gwyn's hand lifted on instinct. Energy that he pulled from the deepest recesses of his magic coiled around his fingers. The ghost, if that was what she was, reacted instantly. She stepped closer with a smile on her face. His energy sharpened her blurred features. The outline of her shoulders, cheekbones, the details of her hair, formed from the haze.

She paid her respects, performing a perfect curtsey first to Abby and then Gwyn. "Lady, I greet you once more. Gwyn ap Nudd, hasten your progress."

It sounded like an order.

"I'm bending too many rules by being here, but I need to impress upon you the urgency." The ghost took a step toward Abby.

Gwyn felt Abby's reaction as strongly as he saw it. A wave of calming magic crashed over the square in a flood as she tried to remove a potential danger through peace instead of violence.

In response, the ghostly figure grew unnaturally bright, as though lightning had struck her form from within, intensifying her image with raw power. Gwyn felt his muscles loosen, the tension within them drain away. But as he relaxed, their visitor flickered. As her form lost solidity, the ghost smiled.

One moment the beautiful woman stood before them, spectral but holding the outline of a human. The next, she was a blur of white and burgundy mist. She vanished in a burst of light and necromantic power.

Quiet returned to the night, but this time it was the bone-chilling stillness of revelation.

Abby turned to Gwyn, her hands suddenly gripping his face as if removing them might allow him to disappear too. "What the hell just happened?" Her fingers trembled against his skin, and her voice shook. "Your heart stopped!"

A lump formed in his throat. He could only manage a strangled cough at first. Gwyn suspected that his pulse hammered a frantic rhythm beneath her fingertips. "I—"

Gwyn hesitated a beat too long for her patience.

"I need to find Miles." Abby was already collecting her belongings that the stumble had scattered from her purse onto the pavement. "Stay here; don't move. He can heal you."

His hand shot out, stopping her. "No."

For a moment, she glared at him, seemingly on the verge of screaming, before a sudden comprehension dawned on her face.

"This... wasn't a surprise to you," she pressed, now verging on angry.

He admitted, "I had a dream. A memory. I knew I could use necromantic powers while I was ascended. I thought..."

A sharp breath escaped Abby's lips as she stood. She paced in tight, restless circles. "Gwyn," she said, voice hushed. "I understood her. It felt like she was speaking to me from inside."

He closed his eyes briefly. "Death transcends language."

She froze and stared at him like he was a ghost. "What the—Gwyn? How do you know that?"

"I—" But no answer came. It was yet another example of his ancient past intruding on his present consciousness.

Approaching footsteps interrupted their argument. Two figures emerged from the darkness, moving slowly but determinedly their way.

"Oh good, you're alive." Esme was half carrying Miles toward them. His pale, blood-streaked face showed his exhaustion. Despite the strain of holding him up, her knuckles showing white with the effort, Esme smirked. "We got attacked. What's your excuse?"

Abby narrowed her eyes. "Well, his heart stopped beating. Apparently, *ghosts* exist and are multilingual."

"I don't know if that was a ghost, Abigail..." Gwyn argued quietly, so quietly he wasn't certain anyone else heard him.

"Well, hell." Esme halted. "Y'all win on weirdness. We just had another fachan show up."

Miles, weary but dryly amused, managed a weak grin. There was a bit of blood dribbling down his beard, making the sight a bit grizzly. "Keep this up, mate, and I'm dragging you to a cardiologist myself."

"*Keep this up*?" The intensity of Abby's glare could have melted steel. She nearly screeched, but caught herself. Even so, her voice climbed an octave. "This has happened before?"

Miles closed his eyes and sighed one of those slow, tired exhales that carried more weight than words ever could. At nearly the same moment, Gwyn did the same.

Both women stared at their respective partners.

Then Abby threw up her hands. "Is there a curse on thirty-second birthdays, or is it just us?!"

***

The lateness of the hour and everyone's exhaustion prevented immediate attention to the night's events. A heavy silence hung in the air as both couples shared a taxi, the only sound the gentle hum of the engine.

There was no question. Gwyn was staying with Abby that night. He knew from watching television shows that her clandestine attempts at practicing fulminomancy when she thought he wasn't watching were to restart his heart if it stopped again.

He had no idea what was causing the "heart attacks." Had the first instance when Miles had come over to heal him also been related to a ghost, or was that merely coincidental? And what sort of "progress" was he supposed to make? Something to do with his necromancy? Nothing about this made sense.

What did make sense was how seeing random things kept triggering forgotten memories from his past, memories he'd believed were gone forever. It had already happened several times since he'd gotten home with Abigail an hour ago. Was it too much to hope that he was truly, finally, regaining his past?

As they lay together in her bed, he explained everything about the dream he'd had of killing Gwenddoleu ap Ceidio hoping it could bring about peace. He told her about his folly in believing war could ever stop. He described how he'd only left his bed the day after this dream to feed and walk Cerys. Then Miles had come pounding on his door later that afternoon due to something a Likho had said.

Gwyn's new reality prompted him to be honest with her. "You were right, Abigail. I think Miles and I are... friends. For the love of all things sacred, *do not* tell him that."

She giggled, just as he'd hoped. But she couldn't know how strange it was for him to say that about a man who looked exactly like his father.

The tiny strands of Abby's hair tickled Gwyn's nose as he lay comfortably nestled with his face next to her neck, ready to fall asleep in his favorite spot. Then she suddenly flipped around, startling him.

"Gwyn," she whispered. "That ghost. I know you've always been different. But, you're... you're a necromancer."

His palm moved to smooth the curls framing her face. "Yes."

She studied his face for a long moment, evidently saw something she didn't like there, then switched topics. "Did you notice that the woman's shape flared when I accidentally used my new power?"

"I did," he said, nuzzling her nose.

"Stop, silly. I can't concentrate when you do that."

Gwyn tried again, but his affections were met with playful rejection.

"I'm serious! What do you think caused it?"

"I have a theory. If I must assuage your worries, I will be comfortable while I do it." Rolling onto his back, Gwyn pulled her with him until she was half atop his chest. "I have long thought that magic's primary responsibility in our world is to maintain balance. Maybe, like Seren said, your magic resonated with hers perfectly. Like two musical instruments playing perfectly in sync."

Abby harrumphed into his shoulder. "Then I messed it up by making you relax too much with my magic."

He massaged her arm, his fingers tracing her soft skin. "Hrmm, maybe."

"Who do you think she was?"

"I don't know, Abigail. But it felt…"

"Important," Abby finished for him.

"Yes." Gwyn pulled her tight to his chest and added, "I love you. You must know that."

Abby stilled in his arms, then energetically wiggled free of his embrace. With a determined jerk, she rose to meet his gaze, her expression a mask of affront. "You're possibly the most over-the-top and theatrical person I've ever met, besides Finn," she muttered, exasperation in her voice blessedly laced with affection. "And *that's* how you tell me you love me for the first time?"

"But I've loved you for nearly two thousand years."

"Now that's exactly how you start a love confession. Keep going. The more drama, the better." Abby flopped onto her back beside him, her smile returning like the first sunbeam after a storm.

"When shadows drown my world and despair closes in, you are the light I follow home..."

CHAPTER TWENTY-SIX

SPY AGAIN

Jacob

Jacob lowered himself into the well-worn recliner with a sigh that drifted downward like settling dust. The chatter of the group reverberated through the room, bouncing off the mahogany paneled bookshelves. With steepled fingers, he watched the young mages sprawled before him, already anticipating a growing headache.

"Do we even have lives outside this library?" Esme grumbled, barely managing a polite pretense while working through a mouthful of food. She waved a biscuit for emphasis. "At least you provide incentives."

Before replying, Jacob fixed her with the cold, penetrating stare that had broken the resolve of mages twice her age. Which, of course, she promptly ignored. "Manners, Ms. Turner. One might mistake you for a feral child." He flicked a speck of pastry off his trousers. "Everything you've told me raises multiple red flags."

With an unusually challenging expression, Miles leaned forward, his elbows resting on his knees. "Jacob, it's time we talk about our pasts. Finn told you the same thing he told us, but you only half accept it. I don't need you to believe it, but I do need you to take it seriously when I say that there's too much coincidence."

Good. Jacob needed Miles to question him more often. Especially with what he had planned for him.

"Well." Jacob cleared his throat, buying time. "For one, these 'backstories' are a bit outrageous. And the evidence for the truth of it is spotty at best." He met each of their gazes in turn. "*Regardless*, you are *my* people and *my* responsibility. My uncertainties are completely irrelevant when weighed against my duty. I will do what is necessary." His tone hardened. "And something must be done about that woman."

Until that point, Abby had been unusually quiet, her silence heavy with unspoken questions and a judging gaze that bored into him. Jacob didn't like it coming from her one jot.

"What?" he snapped before he could stop himself. The O'Malley girl didn't deserve his ire. The look in her eyes, so much like Christi's, triggered a wave of memories from forty years ago. Because she reminded him of the promises he'd made and subsequently broken. He hadn't been there to save Christi, to save Sean O'Malley.

Abby's tone brooked no doubt. "You're afraid of Seren."

"*Yes*, Ms. O'Malley, a sane man would be." His staff thumped the floor for emphasis. Jacob huffed, reining himself in. "Now, stop reading my emotions and let's get on with a plan." He muttered under his breath, "Should've known your mother was part leprechaun forty years ago, with how much trouble she caused in school with Josiah..."

That, at least, renewed the smile on Abby's face. There were times when playing the doddering old man was worthwhile, especially when one was truly grumpy, old, and needing to atone. Pushing aside the irritation at himself, Jacob straightened. "The questions are thus: why does she have the ability to heal, and is it connected to Miles' ability in any way?"

Esme wiped her fingers on a napkin and leaned forward. "It felt like Miles' magic, but it was a totally different color."

Jacob's patience frayed like the edges of his old recliner. "I'm not certain how relevant the color is, Ms. Turner, but thank you."

Her gaze dropped for a moment, as if she was uncertain she wanted to speak. Then she met Jacob's eyes, and her voice came low and far too hesitant for her not to be serious. "Abby and I... we're not convinced Seren is even human."

Jacob's expression didn't change, at least at first. But his posture shifted against his will. He'd had his own suspicions about her for years. "Explain," he ordered.

Abby leaned forward. "Her aura was... blinding. It was like staring into the sun."

"And the way she acted about her healing magic..." Esme added. "Too secretive."

Jacob exhaled slowly through his nose. "You're suggesting she's... what?"

"We don't know." Esme shook her head, frustrated. "My guess is that she's like Gwyn *was*."

Jacob forced out a laugh and lied. "I assure you, Seren is quite human."

He wasn't certain of that. But knowing what she was wouldn't change the outcome since he'd already ruled out Fae and fifteen other possibilities that had convenient rules attached to their use of magic.

His gaze snapped to Gwyn, who had been unusually rigid in his seat. "Mr. Newman, you've been uncharacteristically quiet since you entered my house and you've not even sneered once. Anything to share?"

Gwyn's tightly clenched jaw betrayed his barely controlled frustration, the only visible sign breaking through his otherwise composed demeanor. His eyes flickered, and the old defiance, the arrogance, revived in him as Jacob had intended. "If you don't believe the truth of who I am, I have nothing to add."

"It took you long enough to start sulking." Jacob waved a hand. "No one cares that you have necromantic power. No one thinks you'll start killing mages to raise an army of the dead. Get over it, son."

Jacob paused, letting that barb sink in, then continued, "But it doesn't matter what I think. What matters is that malevolent activity has ratcheted up. And part of that is your fault." He pointed at each of them. "You're all too powerful to be together. But since *mass slaughter* seems the only thing that'll tear you apart, we need a plan. Esmeralda—"

Esme straightened, a flicker of something between excitement and wary interest crossing her face. "What?"

"You're back on enforcer duty." He steepled his fingers. "Seren is hiding her abilities for a reason. First, she tests you, then she *accidentally* reveals she can heal? She's playing a long game."

"I thought the same thing," she said.

"Good. It proves you have a brain that still works." He took in her withering glare and abruptly changed his tone. "Darling, she's grooming you. You'll play the model student. Charm her. Uncover her aims."

"I'm tired of playing games." Esme crossed her arms, defiant already. "I'm tired of *being* played."

Despite himself, Jacob winced. Even though he knew she was referring to Leon, the sting of his past mistakes was a bitter pill to swallow. His empathy was rarely stirred, but several people capable of doing so were in the room. His brief hesitation was the closest he could allow himself to come to gentleness in this precarious situation.

He had to prepare them, even if it hurt.

"You'd enter this situation aware that she wants something. You're not the manipulated. You *are* the manipulator. We need to figure out what she's planning, and your help is key to doing that."

Esme snorted in displeasure, shaking her head. "You'd know an awful lot about that!"

He deserved that too.

Then Esme shot to her feet, temper flaring even higher. "Jacob, none of us knows if you're right anymore. Maybe Seren is right. Maybe the community does need to know about the malevolents. So while I'm spying for you, I'm going to be making up my own damn mind about that."

He wanted nothing less from her. Underneath his stern exterior, Jacob felt a spark of pride. To thrive in this deadly political game of magic, one needed fire burning in their soul; Esme had more than enough.

"It's decided, then." He rose, leaning on his staff, yet another reminder of his shortcomings. "I'll be waiting with the antidote if the viper sinks her fangs in."

Angry, Esme said nothing. But Abby asked, "And what is that, Jacob?"

"Me," Jacob said, a small flame blooming in his palm, "going out in a blaze of glory. Playing the fire starter. One last time."

CHAPTER TWENTY-SEVEN

BASTARD

Esme

The fluorescent lights buzzed with a migraine-bright hum, washing the steel cages in sterile white. All that remained of the malevolent púca was its empty cage. Esme couldn't shake the memory of what had been, and what could have been under different circumstances.

From behind bars, a kiokusaru flashed a smile at her, needle teeth gleaming dangerously. Its ghostly, simian grin stretched wide, a little too wide to be strictly natural. Its fur shone somewhere between gray and pale blue with magic radiating off every piece of fur. A mischievous glint sparked in its empty eyes as they stared at her with a silent promise of violence.

Esme unconsciously made two fists of her hands. She hated this creature. And, more importantly, she hated herself for being here. The kiokusaru flashed more teeth, daring her to so much as blink.

Why the hell did I agree to this? Oh, yeah, those pesky politics I swore I'd never get involved in! I'm not like Seren. I'm not like Jacob. I'm not...

Damn. Now she understood Will's frustration at constantly being dragged in to be their magical lookout. She owed him an apology letter and a box of his favorite protein bars.

"I chose this one because it's mostly harmless," Seren said. "Steals memories as a prank. Sometimes gives them back, sometimes eats them."

Mostly harmless. The little bugger looked like it wanted to bite her!

Esme had once begged Abby to remove her worst memories. Those invisible scars, etched inside her mind by traumas and nightmares, usually surfaced only when she flinched. Unfortunately, Esme had been doing a lot of flinching lately.

Abby had refused, citing ethics, magic, danger. But the kiokusaru? It would devour them gladly, memory by memory, until there was nothing left but a smiling, empty shell.

Seren stood with arms folded, her expression unreadable, but her presence pressed on Esme like gravity. "I'd like to bring it out," she said, not as a request, but a declaration. "Last time, getting your magic to penetrate the wards likely put a strain on you. At least that's my theory why you collapsed. Without them in the way, you can use your infernal conduit on the creature directly."

Esme swallowed nervously. "If it gets out, we'll just have another malevolent to hunt."

Seren dismissed the problem as insignificant, treating it like it was nothing more than a bothersome insect. "I'll kill it before it becomes a problem."

Be the model student. Esme sighed. "Fine."

Just another role to play, another mask to wear. She slipped into it with practiced ease. Returning to her old ways proved too easy.

A small pulse of magic came from Seren as the cage clicked open without being touched.

The kiokusaru slammed its head into the invisible barrier at the opening. It fell backward, a high-pitched chittering screech of pain and surprise escaping its lungs. Esme almost felt sorry for it until it gnashed its teeth at the bars in her direction, staring into her eyes as it bit down on the metal.

Half a second later, the second pulse of magic came from Seren. She then motioned for them both to step back. This released the barrier on the cage, and the kiokusaru shot out in a streak, scrambling for the *still-open* doorway on the other side of the room.

Esme's heart plummeted. It was going to escape.

But then the demon monkey slammed its head into a second invisible barrier, falling onto its back. It shrieked, clawing at the air, then flipped itself upright and scrambled up the wooden walls, looking frantically for an exit that didn't exist.

Finding no way out, the creature settled for hanging upside down in the doorway, watching them with those unsettling eyes.

"Now's the time to focus, Esmeralda," Seren murmured.

Esme reached for the infernal conduit inside her, the dark river she'd learned to channel. It opened like a yawning chasm. But at the same time, the kiokusaru's eyes, dark and glittering with predatory intent, locked onto hers.

As Esme's conduit flared to life, the kiokusaru's eyes snared her in return.

Esme didn't fall so much as *plunge* backward, dragged beneath time's surface like a body drowning in someone else's past.

Her vision swam as a cruel smile stretched across the monkey's face. Time fractured around Esme, and she fell into the past.

Esme emerged behind a pair of foreign eyes. High in the sky, the sun blazed, its golden light heavy and oppressive. The reek of blood, bile, piss, and shit mixed with the cleaner scent of the sun-baked grass into a foul miasma that could be labeled as nothing other than the scent of insanity. It was almost overwhelming to Esme, but her host seemed not the least bit disturbed by it.

The eyes Esme saw through studied a young woman standing amidst the carnage, her honey-colored hair stiff with drying gore. Crimson dripped from the well-maintained farmer's sword she clutched, trembling, giving what little water the blood could grant the dirt. A number of men lay at her feet, their bodies ripped apart, their limbs scattered like broken toys in a macabre display.

The young woman gasped for breath, her chest heaving, each inhale a ragged, desperate sound. Her rage, her magic, was fading, leaving only horror in its wake.

Esme's host's eyes walked through a haze of branches to carefully emerge from the edge of the copse she'd been standing in. Esme could feel her host's unrestrained joy at the carnage; it was so palpable it radiated from the memory.

"Impressive." She felt her mouth form the word.

The blood-soaked young woman flinched, a different type of terror causing her to freeze. The stench of death wafted as she turned, her eyes wide at the sight of Esme's host. Her presence seemed to intensify the young woman's horror over the massacre.

"You've done well for one untrained," Esme's host said, stepping closer. "Messy. But you've embraced your birthright! And you have avenged your parents' deaths."

"Who—?" the young woman started.

"I am Morgana. Though I am called Morgan le Fay." She stepped into the blood-soaked clearing. "But to you, I was supposed to be 'Mother.'"

Morgan le Fay? What was this? Was Esme hallucinating?

"No," the young woman whispered, eyes turning wild with alarm.

"Yes. Your parents always told you that you were a divine gift." Esme could feel her host smiling. "They were correct, Elena."

Hearing the name, Esme finally understood the full extent of the reality unfolding before her eyes.

The sword slipped from Elena's fingers. "That's not possible." Her clothing was still dripping with the blood of the men nearby.

Morgan stepped forward, unconcerned by the filth surrounding them. Her voice softened. "It is. The magic I placed upon you before your birth suppressed your power and shielded you until you were a woman."

"...my parents," was all that Elena managed.

"They loved you as their own. It was necessary. There was a—"

The smallest amount of emotional intelligence should have made it clear that Morgan was placing too much, all at once, on a woman deep in the throes of fresh grief. Not only that, Elena was still reeling from a devastating demonic rage.

What was Morgan thinking? A second later, Esme's thought was proven correct.

"I don't care!" Elena's voice broke. Tears streamed down her face as the crushing weight of her loss and the guilt of her actions finally caught up with her. The truth exploded out of her as Elena *fell to her knees. "You think this is some gift?" She clutched her head like she could rip the magic out with her bare hands. "I killed them!"*

"You are my blood, Daughter. You are a cambion." Morgan's hands raised in a calming gesture. "The rage can be controlled."

Morgan reached for her, but Elena recoiled. She staggered backward, gagging, then collapsed to her knees. Bile, mixing with the blood and gore, landed on the ground as Elena vomited out her whirling emotions.

Esme's awareness of herself versus the memory had been gradually returning, bit by bit. The kiokusaru, she realized. Her conduit to it must have interacted with its feeding on their memories to trigger this vision.

Certainty hit Esme like a bolt of lightning. Her voice. The way she moved. This had to be Seren's memory. Seren was Morgan le Fay, her namesake, Morgana.

In the memory, a surge of magic so great it nearly took her breath away erupted from her host. The filth on the ground, on Elena, even the corpses—it all disappeared with the simple wave of a hand.

There was only one explanation. Seren, Morgan, had been an ascended being like Nudd, like Gwyn.

Esme must have missed a portion of the memory in her distraction. Time seemed to have skipped forward.

Elena was clean, her features clear for the first time, but now she was standing, trembling mere inches away from the sorceress.

So close now, Esme could see that Elena's face mirrored Seren's across time. Her eyes, hair, and nose were perfect facsimiles.

And, because it was impossible to deny it now, Esme was the echo.

It wasn't hard to tell that she and Elena had more physical similarities than differences. Abby had told her that much from seeing Nudd's and Leon's memories. She'd put it down to being cambion, but now... Now Esme wondered if she was the result of something ancient and unresolved—something she was seeing play out in a memory through her own eyes.

"Goddess, there must be some mistake," Elena gasped out.

Morgan cupped Elena's chin. "A prophecy forced me to leave you. 'Love for the bastard of scales and flesh will bind magic beyond all reach.' I'm so sorry, Daughter. I had to."

Morgan pulled down the neck of her dress, revealing a twisting viper made of living ink coiled loosely around her shoulders. It appeared interested in Elena.

It was even the same tattoo as Seren's.

Morgan said, "I wasn't allowed to love you. But now you're grown. Now you can claim your birthright."

Elena had been calm, but at those words, her breathing picked up.

"If my birthright is insanity, I want none of it!" Elena answered, seething fury reigniting to pump adrenaline through her blood. "You did this! You—magic—it made me into a monster!"

"I can teach you control." Morgan's voice was almost pleading. "But I must give you a choice. Claim your birthright and learn from me. Or... Or walk away. Either way, you cannot ignore its existence."

Elena looked at her hands like they should still be dripping blood. Raising her gaze, she then looked up at her birth mother before spitting directly at the demigod's feet.

"I reject you." The young woman's hands curled into fists. "I reject magic. I will find my own way. Something noble, something

good. If I must rage, I will do it for righteousness to make up for my sins."

Her host's motionless body couldn't mute the memory's power. Grief washed over Seren/Morgan le Fay, creating an inner tempest of sorrow that could make a mountain tremble.

Pain pounded in Esme's skull as she surfaced from the memory. She blinked, trying to clear the haze from her vision, but quickly realized only time would heal it. She was lying face down on the cold concrete of the warehouse floor. Feet away, the kiokusaru lay dead, impaled by a weapon not visible to her from that angle—probably a conjuration.

Seren's face showed genuine worry as she crouched, her eyes wide with apprehension.

Esme pushed herself up, and the floor tilted beneath her. Centuries-old grief and rage that weren't hers still leaped across the synapses in her mind. *How could Abby cope with Leon's terrors*, she wondered, *when I'm so shaken by just one vision?*

"Was that your memory?" she demanded.

Seren, still crouched over her, said nothing in reply but helped Esme sit mostly upright.

Esme's voice cracked. "I saw a young woman named Elena waking up from a demonic rage. To Morgan le-fucking-Fay telling her that she's her mother. Is that *you*? Are you Morgana?"

Seren remained silent.

"What is this?" Esme shoved Seren, voice cracking. "Trying to make up for past mistakes?"

Seren's watery violet eyes met Esme's as she finally lifted her head.

"A second chance with your dead daughter? A do-over using *me*?" Esme's heart was racing a million miles per minute.

Seren still didn't answer.

Esme couldn't stop herself from shouting it. "I'm not Elena!"

"I know." Seren's tone was precisely, deliberately flat.

"Then *what*?" Esme's voice broke on the last.

Seren's voice rose as Esme's fell. "Who else will keep you alive?"

"Me!" Esme snapped, jumping to her feet. "What the hell does that even mean? Why would you say that?"

More silence. Seren's expression remained unreadable.

And, damn it, Esme had no idea what to even do at this point. She was furious. Spinning on her heel, she marched toward the exit, her steps heavy with barely controlled emotion.

As she neared the doorway, Seren's near-inaudible whisper reached her ears. "I'm sorry."

Esme hesitated. But only for a second.

Then she kept walking. It was too much for her to handle with Seren in the same room.

She was in a state of mental chaos. Tasked with a simple job of spying on Seren, Esme was wholly unprepared for the discovery of their close family ties. The dangers Jacob had described, fear and misused power, warred with the undeniable truth: Seren was Elena's mother. She had waited centuries to be reunited with her, only to be rejected by her echo, again.

Seren had lied and manipulated her, had hidden truths behind half-smiles. But the memory of her all-consuming grief at losing her daughter stubbornly refused to leave Esme. It had wrapped around her heart like it had become her own emotion.

And Esme had absolutely no idea what to do with that. How could the woman who mourned her daughter like that be the monster Jacob warned her about?

She and Seren had an undeniable connection that went deeper than the fact that they were both cambion women, that they were both conjuration mages. And even if Esme couldn't remember a single moment of her time as the other woman, she knew Miles was right.

Elena's death hadn't cut her connection with Nudd. Nearly two thousand years hadn't erased the fact that Esme was going to fall in love with Miles all over again.

And now, with Seren... She sensed a connection between them, had since first meeting her if she was honest with herself. It was messy and convoluted, and Esme didn't know if their relation was a good thing.

But it was undeniable now.

And how could Esme decide who to become when every choice she had felt like a betrayal of someone she'd loved?

Every choice she had at this point would force her to cut away a part of herself. Did she betray Seren, a deadly, dangerous, manipulative but grieving woman who was clinging to the last vestiges of her daughter? Jacob, who might be wrong about the dangers of telling the truth but had supported her for years? Or herself, by ignoring her new reality?

Chapter Twenty-Eight

Kill Room

Miles

Miles had tried to hold back, to let Esme approach Seren on her own terms. But watching her fall asleep crying for the second night in a row had broken his resolve.

He stepped into the kill room and shut the door behind him quietly. Sometimes silence could unnerve an opponent better than any threat, and Miles needed every psychological edge he could get. The overhead lights threw sharp reflections across the blood-slick floor.

Even Esme didn't know of this room's existence. There were three reasons: he didn't want her to, she didn't *need* to, and his oath to the Corded Brotherhood made it non-negotiable.

He stopped a few feet in. The silence was broken only by the drip, drip, drip of blood from the ceiling. Liquid-proof plastic, reinforced with soundproofing, formed the four walls. A drain sat in the center of the room, swallowing the grisly offering with the greed of a hungry mouth.

Seren—no, Morgan le Fay—stood amid the wreckage of something that had, until seconds before, been alive. He'd entered a minute too late to know exactly what because the carcass was too mangled to identify. At least it wasn't a human... probably.

"Your idea of 'training' seems a bit... unconventional," he said, crossing his arms.

Years ago, he'd seen Seren as this terrifying figure who barely tolerated his existence. Her importance in his life had faded into almost nothing until she came to Seattle. His first thought had been that she could act as Esme's guide and safeguard her from others who might seek to exploit her. Now?

Fuck, he still didn't know.

"I had some frustrations to work through." Seren didn't look up immediately. The rag in her hand was already stained red. She folded it in thirds with a surgeon's precision before tossing it into the bin beside her. "You won't suffer the same gruesome fate as that oni. I know why you're here, Miles, so get to it."

"You already knew," he said, voice even. "Didn't you?"

Seren still didn't look at him. "Be specific, Dr. Goodwin. I know many things, most of which you are not ready to hear."

He walked another step closer. "You knew who she was. Who I am."

That made her turn. Her violet eyes, too old for her youthful face, locked with his. There wasn't any surprise in them, only assessment. "Yes."

Seren's tone remained maddeningly calm. She scrubbed the blood from her arms in the industrial sink. Somehow, she'd only managed to get a bit of the oni's blood on her. While it, on the other hand, was painted across three walls and the ceiling.

Seren hesitated by the sink, her wrist trembling subtly as if an unseen force weakened her resolve. "I only knew about *you* until David Abington leaked her picture and description."

Every time he learned something new about David, Miles felt a bit better about skipping out on his funeral. *Fuck him.*

"Have you been watching me?" His chest rose and fell slowly, maintaining control.

"Of course," she replied, reaching for a paper towel to dry off. "Skip to the real question, Miles."

"Fine. You watched her fall apart in that warehouse. You saw her break with the wendigo, and still"—his voice cracked with fury—"you said nothing."

"And yet she came out of it stronger." Seren's chin tilted up, as elegant and dangerous as ever. "Do you think truth is always a kindness, Miles? You, of all people, should know better. Some truths need to be kept until the right time. Unfortunately, this one came too early."

Miles stared at her. "So that's it?"

"I gave her what she needed." A momentary flicker of regret briefly darkened her eyes, then vanished. Her jaw ticked in defiance. "Not what she wanted."

"And who made you the arbiter of that?" Miles snapped, stepping forward again. "Not in this life. You're not her mother here. You claimed you wanted to protect her, but your manipulations are as obvious as the strings you're pulling. Are you setting her up as a bloody chess piece?"

"I'm guiding her toward survival," Seren replied, a quiet strength in her tone. "You have no idea what's coming."

"Bullshit justifications! I'm not your pupil. I'm the man you looked at through the mirror. You threatened Nudd. Now you're here putting her in danger when you claim the opposite."

The edges of Seren's control frayed. There was the slightest hint of a break in her expression. A twitch of her fingers smeared the still-wet oni blood from her sleeve back onto her cleaned hands.

"I did not threaten Nudd." The words came out too fast, like she'd been waiting centuries to say them.

Miles narrowed his eyes. "No? 'Her fate is braided with yours,' you said. 'I will not see it severed.' You glared through the mirror like a goddess passing judgment. You were trying to scare me."

Seren flinched. Was it because he remembered the exact wording or something else?

"I was trying to *warn him*." Her voice sharpened. "And you've proven exactly how little you remember."

Miles closed his eyes, taking a slow, deep breath, forcing some of the tension to leave his body. "So you do remember."

She paused, a beat of silence hanging in the air. Then a quick nod signaled her agreement. "I am not like Gwyn."

"That makes your silence worse," he accused.

"You're afraid," Seren said, a gentle but firm statement of fact. "You want someone to blame. That's why you're here. You're speaking from a place of emotion."

"Damn right I am," he said. "Because I actually see her. As *Esme*. You remember her as a daughter. I wake up next to her every day. I refuse to let you make things needlessly difficult for her. I can't make you leave. But I also *won't* allow you to exploit her."

The silence between them crackled with magic and simmering frustration.

Then, all at once, the fight left Seren. She asked quietly, "And what would you do instead, Miles?"

His gaze remained fixed on hers. "The decisions Esme makes scare me half to death sometimes, but I've learned to trust Esme's instincts, to trust *her*."

Miles imagined Esme, Elena, even Nudd standing between the two of them, stitching together the past and the present with heartstrings.

After a long, tense pause, Seren finally let out some of the tension she'd been holding on to, the air leaving her lungs in a slow, shuddering sigh. "You sound just like him."

"Maybe I've seen enough of his pain, his misjudgments, to know when someone else is teetering on the edge of making a new mistake based on old ones."

That struck home. Seren's jaw tightened, her arms crossing defensively, a silent challenge in her posture. "Do you really think I'm a danger? That I'm the villain in this story?"

"Not exactly," Miles said. "But I think you're trying to rewrite the ending. I saw Elena tell Nudd that you gave her a choice whether to be your student in magic. I have a feeling that you weren't allowed to take that choice away from her then. So don't do it to Esme now."

A pause of consideration, then she said, "You want to make sense of this mess. I get it. But it has to play out, Miles." For some reason, a shadow of sadness seemed to fall across her face. "It has to play out..."

"Bloody hell, Seren, you're still pressing this. Esme is *not* your redemption."

The words struck her like a spell. Seren staggered into the nearest chair.

With a heavy sigh, Seren dropped her head into her hands, her shoulders slumping. "You have no idea what I've had to become to get to where I am today. And still, I kept my distance then. Even when every instinct screamed at me to intervene."

A thin, tight line formed on Seren's lips, the corners downturned in a subtle frown. "Esme and Abby are quite different from their predecessors. You're too much like him, you know?" she asked, voice low.

So, she knew about Abby too. Of course she did.

Seren was too caught up in her own memories to notice that realization dawn on Miles' face. "You need Esme just like he did... Elena kept him... human, in a way. I sometimes suspect that without her, he might have gone down a dark path, convinced of his own moral high ground the entire journey."

That did feel like a possibility for Nudd, Miles too. Hoping for a response but cautiously managing his expectations, Miles asked a question. "Why do I resemble him so much, unlike them? What makes me different?"

"My guess is that it is because you, well, *he*, died while ascended. That... would likely leave a lasting mark."

"That's *it*?" Miles let his arms drop at his sides.

"The simplest solutions tend to be the most accurate, Doctor Goodwin. Magic has her own rules. I'm fairly sure your existence breaks one of them."

"And yours? Gwyn's? Shouldn't yours also break rules?" None of this made sense.

"We've balanced magic's scales by losing our near immortality." She slid one perfect fingernail across her palm hard enough to draw beads of red blood. As proof of her fallen nature, Seren presented it to him.

Human, then.

She closed her eyes and palm. Miles felt it before he saw a dark light tinged with silver seep out from between the cracks in her closed fist—healing magic.

He couldn't do anything but stare at her palm until she spoke again.

"She rejected me once," Seren said quietly. "I made peace with that. But I will not let her die again."

"Now *you're* speaking from a place of emotion," he said. "I won't argue against you protecting her. But that's entirely different from making decisions for her. Remember that."

"You're infuriating," she said at last.

"I've been told. Repeatedly." Mainly by Gwyn.

"I misjudged you. I apologize for that."

Miles gave a small, sardonic smile. "Been a lot of that going around."

A hint of what he hoped was respect momentarily flickered across Seren's face. As he turned to leave, Seren's voice followed him. "Miles."

He paused at the threshold.

"I could never forget what kind of man Nudd was. But I never thought I'd see his heart walking around in another man's chest."

Miles didn't turn. He offered a quiet, sincere, "Thank you," tinged with apprehension about the implications of what being like Nudd meant.

And it left him more terrified than he could express. Because it meant Seren still saw too much of the past to ever let it truly rest.

CHAPTER TWENTY-NINE

INTERDICTION

Seren

Seren withdrew her hand from the cage, the faint tremor in her fingers the only outward sign of the toll the magic she'd just lost took. Only those who knew how to listen would notice the faint pulse answering her magic like a heartbeat under glass. The type of ward she'd used to contain this creature was unique.

A chilling dampness clung to the concrete walls of the underground mechanics room, thick with the scent of rust and magic. Cold from the concrete walls clashed with the heat from the steam pipes, turning the room into something between a tomb and a Turkish bath. The malevolent inside was still in stasis. For now.

She had given a bit of time every day since arriving in Seattle to siphon her power into the bindings, delaying its full emergence. Few knew the room under the Assembly's headquarters existed, and magic easily controlled the human workers who needed access to the area.

Of all the roles the world had forced her to play, the unflinching, neutral version she wore as "Seren" was the cruelest illusion. Yet somehow, it was the one that fit best—at Council meetings, in Assembly chambers, even across the table from Esme. In some ways, it was more *her* than she'd ever been before.

In her past life, she'd had to lie, cheat, fuck, and murder to get what she wanted. Seren still did all of those things, but not because she was forced to do so. Each day in this era, she woke to a life where her choices were her own. She chose her name, her personality—everything down to what she ate for breakfast each morning.

Freedom for twenty-five years had been a blessing. But she'd bartered freedom for loneliness, and loneliness always demanded payment in full. A sword of Damocles was hanging over her head every single time she looked up. The blade had never stopped glinting, only dulled by years of looking away. And now it was growing ever closer to her head.

Unfortunately, simply informing people of a problem rarely led to actual change. A more effective approach involved demonstrating the issue to them. What she was planning might make her a monster. That wasn't new, but it was the first time in ages she had something worthwhile at stake. With everyone's futures hanging in the balance, fear and second thoughts were a luxury she simply couldn't afford.

Seren's heels echoed softly down the narrow corridor, past cages that whispered of violence. These were less dangerous than the vault's prisoner, but no less eager for blood. One hissed—a soft, wet sound like water being poured onto hot coals.

Even they hated her.

Or, equally likely, the surge of necromantic magic nearby a few nights before had left them all on edge. It had taken her walking less than a block away from the scene of the fachan attack to confirm what she had already suspected: Gwyn had finally rediscovered his power.

A subtle pulse of magic flowed from Seren's fingers, silencing the mundane and magical alarms like a lullaby did a sleeping beast.

Seren's twenty-five years of making whatever choices she wished were drawing to a close. All that time, Jacob had hidden Esmeralda. All that time, Seren could have been making a difference. She could have been making the ending of Morgan le Fay's story that much neater.

The sting of betrayal and anger she felt toward Jacob was only lessened by her awareness of his ignorance. Grudgingly, she admitted she owed the old man a debt for his unwavering protection of Esme and the ignorance that made it possible. Considering how long he'd lived with his blessing, Jacob's understanding of his own secret, of his own connection to the past, was surprisingly scant.

Well, life had never been fair. There was only what she could do next. She'd tell him eventually, but not yet.

Esme had already seen too much, too soon. Whether it was accidental or intentional, her memory and one of her hidden abilities were now out in the open. Some magics had wills of their own, and grief was a powerful force that could shape magic—exactly like choice.

What Esme would do with that knowledge was yet to be seen. But it did mean that she needed to escalate her plans for preventing catastrophe.

Seren had spent two lifetimes protecting her heart. And one soul had managed to tear it open in seconds during both. Elena was gone. But Esme was a living echo of the past.

Esme had shouted at her. Pushed her. She'd called Seren by her old name but had stopped short of rejecting her. Seren had seen the conflict behind Esme's eyes, even through her fury. There was hope in that.

Her secret was probably safe for now, safe in the way only unbelievable truths could be. Morgan le Fay was a myth, not a committee member with perfect nails and a seat at the Assembly's high table.

Jacob's unwillingness to acknowledge his own truth was creating extra challenges for everyone without any of them seeing it. Gwyn's secret, however, would not remain so conveniently buried. Any seasoned magic-user would instantly identify the magical surge he'd created downtown as necromancy.

She would call a meeting. Jacob would expect it. It was likely he'd already warned them. That was fine. This wasn't a trap, not in the traditional sense. It was an ultimatum dressed in happenstance.

This was an opportunity.

She'd tried compassion before, and it had cost her a daughter. Now, if fear bought survival, she'd make everyone chip in. This time, they would learn through fire. She had warned Arthur many times and had been ignored. That mistake had cost hundreds. This time, they would listen—even if it meant hating her for it.

Gwyn's secret would serve her purpose, but she refused to let it be his undoing. Arawn had ensured that much. Besides, she didn't want him broken. Not Gwyn. Not any of them. Especially not Esme.

The most critical revelation of all was already in motion, uninterested in receiving their consent, uncaring of their fears or their fragile alliances. They all had a part to play in ensuring that it wouldn't end civilization as they knew it.

Miles

With the sun setting, casting orange and pink across the sky, they basked in the warmth of the clear spring evening. What had started as a casual double date, orchestrated by Esme and Abby, had turned into Esme finally dropping the bombshell of who Seren was on Gwyn and Abby.

"I should be spiraling, but this chicken? Mind-blowing," Abby said, licking her fingers with zero shame.

"I know, right?" Esme managed around a mouthful of fried chicken drenched in a slightly spicy, slightly sweet sauce.

"I really get what you meant now. These endless revelations are *truly* exhausting. You could tell me almost any life-upending fact, short of someone dying, and I'd just shrug. I'm too worn out. At this point, I'd take it as fact; I don't even bother questioning it."

"Honestly, how important is it anymore?" Miles said, hating the hollow note in his own voice. "Maybe Abby is right. This is just one more body on the pile of people who shouldn't be here. We don't know why *we're* here. Maybe she doesn't either."

A spark of something uncomfortable and full of nervous energy flashed across Gwyn's face before vanishing as quickly as it had come. Miles only noticed his new friend's subtle shift in demeanor because their reconciliation was fresh, leaving him hyper-aware of Gwyn's every reaction.

"I hope you're right." Esme squeezed Miles' thigh under the table. In the midst of the world unraveling around them, the small gesture provided a moment of silent, reassuring stability.

Esme added with a bit more cheer, "I finally got to join the 'I've seen ancient history' club. Was honestly pretty nasty, though."

Abby quirked her head in question.

"Oh, you do not want to know right now." Esme squinted her eyes and shuddered. "Let's just say that Elena finished the job... messily."

"Noted. Though... I don't know," Abby murmured, her gaze distant. "I did a comparative study of *Le Morte d'Arthur* with earlier Arthurian tales in college. Early versions of Morgana showed her as a benevolent healer. As time went on, tales of her became more and more complicated, more misogynistic. Her character changed from generous to highlighting her manipulative nature and envy of Guinevere."

"So which version is right?" Esme asked, leaning back while dabbing her sticky fingers with a napkin.

Miles watched as Gwyn leaned over and gently squeezed Abby's hand a few times. He relied on her as heavily as Miles did Esme.

"The men who have written history seem to love to vilify women." Gwyn had been unusually quiet since his second myocardial incident, so when he finally spoke, they listened to him with rapt attention.

He went on, "There's been too much coincidence, too much fate masquerading as chance. What are the chances that Abigail and Esmeralda were born in the same city at nearly the same time? Miles, what are the chances that you moved here, out of everywhere you could have gone? Even Cerys, showing up like she did in the mountains? Seren, Morgana, whatever we are calling her, her being here matters... somehow. I sense we're being driven towards something. The only question is whether it is catastrophe."

"Ugh," Esme groaned. "Damnit, Gwyn. Dropping existential truth bombs *again* like that."

Gwyn's brow tightened in confusion. Abby opened her mouth, probably about to explain "truth bomb," then stopped. She likely decided it wasn't the time.

Then a call from Jacob came through on Miles' phone. He had to open one of the provided wet wipes to clean his hands before he could answer it.

"Jacob. How are you?" Miles asked politely.

Esme rolled her eyes and kept eating.

"Miles, I am doing well." There was a long pause before he spoke again. "Actually, my boy, that's a lie. I'm miffed. It's evening, so I'm guessing you aren't alone. Pass this message on for me. Seren's called a bloody emergency meeting—something about necromancy, surges, and that damned bukavac. Abby will be getting the text soon. Bring weapons, Gwyn, and Esmeralda. I have to make a few more calls. This might get ugly."

Esme stopped eating because she'd clearly heard the conversation even though it wasn't on speaker. As he said goodbye to Jacob, Esme explained what she'd heard to the others.

"Gwyn, if you remember anything about Morgan le Fay, now is the time to lay it out for us." Miles checked his watch. "We have less than two hours until everything changes... again. Jacob said we need to go home and gear up—I have no idea what for."

Abby pointed at Gwyn. "Probably to keep him out of or break him out of Assembly jail."

Gwyn's knuckles blanched against the tabletop, his grip so tight it looked like the table might crack first. He closed his eyes for a long second. When he opened them, the intensity that usually only blazed during fights was there.

"Okay," Gwyn said, releasing his death grip on the table. "Beyond her identity, the rest of my memory is a frustrating blank. These gaps in my memory have driven me mad since my emergence."

With both Leon and Seren remembering more than Gwyn, the possibility that something had happened to him or, more worryingly, that someone had deliberately erased Gwyn's memories seemed increasingly likely.

Gwyn's heavy confession filled Miles with compassion, yet the rapid string of curses still overwhelmed his thoughts. Miles wanted—no—he *needed* some straight answers for *once*.

All that was true. But what he said, what they needed to hear, from a voice steady and reassuring, was, "We've made it this far. We'll figure out the rest together."

Even if he didn't believe it yet, they needed to.

CHAPTER THIRTY

THE ESCAPE

Abby

No matter how many secrets it hid, the room looked like any
other bland downtown office. Drop ceiling. Pixelated gray
carpet. Bad lighting. It was the kind of room that seemed
more suited to host a quarterly budget review than a magical
security crisis. This was the last place Abby wanted to be on
a Saturday night.

Thanks to Jacob's warning, they were mostly ready. Almost everyone at the table was unnervingly still as Seren
spoke. Something about her commanded attention, and she
had a quiet, deliberate presence that made you second-guess
interrupting. She seemed to walk through life like she could
own anything she touched. From what Abby now knew
about her, it might be true.

Abby was once again seated next to Miles and Josiah. Jacob
sat at the head of the table, his expression unreadable, which
wasn't surprising. What was surprising was how calm Seren

appeared for someone who'd said the words "necromantic resonance spikes."

"...three inside the city and at least two larger ones to the east," Seren was saying, her voice smooth and clipped. "The pattern suggests either a coordinated effort or something breaking through containment. Possibly multiple somethings."

Abby would have been sweating if she hadn't known it was coming. Still, she couldn't help but tense.

Josiah's shoulders shifted with discomfort on her other side. "No undead sightings, right? So what if this is just some punk kid showing off their new edgy tricks? Send an enforcer out and be done with it," he suggested, scratching at the stubble of his sparse beard.

"If this were simply a *punk kid*, I'd have sent an enforcer and been done. This is rogue work. Or something far worse," Seren replied.

Maureen crossed her arms, brows knit. "Why did you not bring this directly to the Brotherhood? It's fifty-fifty that this is a malevolent, which would make this a problem within their area of responsibility rather than an Assembly-wide concern."

Seren didn't answer directly. Abby noticed the faintest flicker in the woman's expression—uncertainty, maybe? Or irritation.

Jacob, appearing impeccably composed in his robes of office, finally spoke. "I cannot blame Seren for taking her job seriously." He gestured to his right, where Gwyn and Esme sat like wild cards at a poker table. "Which is why I invited guests."

Gwyn's glowering expression proved he wasn't happy to be there. Abby couldn't blame him.

"I brought Esmeralda because she's now Seren's apprentice and she was present at the most recent necromantic event. But that's incidental. The real story is about our newest Brother, Gwyn. He *is* the necromancer in question."

Gwyn offered a small awkward wave, accompanied by the gentle smile they'd practiced together. Abby had hoped it would disarm everyone with its innocence, but the final product was too on edge for that.

Jacob explained, "During a hunt on the eastside, he awoke a previously dormant affinity for necromancy. This, without warning. Without training."

Jacob closed the notebook he'd been scribbling in. "The most recent occurrence was due to an undead malevolent emerging in Pioneer Square outside the Sanctuary of Spirits. A medical emergency unfortunately occurred simultaneously with the malevolent attack. The unfortunate medical event triggered Gwyn's new affinity as he dispatched the malevolent."

The room roused into a low chorus of murmurs and raised brows. Abby didn't move. Didn't breathe. Her fingers dug into the chair until the cheap wood bit back.

In the growing hubbub, Jacob added, sarcasm lacing every word, "In case anyone cares, the person who suffered a cardiac arrest is doing just fine. Thank you all for your overwhelming concern."

Gwyn leaned back like he didn't care, but Abby knew better. His arrogance was armor, always had been.

Seren said nothing. That was telling. Had Jacob successfully undermined whatever plan she had working?

Ved stood, feathers ruffling. "That is unacceptable." His voice was cool, but there was real anger beneath it. "Necromancy is not some parlor trick to stumble into. He must be screened."

Of course it was Ved. To the Garuda, necromancy was a perversion of the cosmic order, a tearing of the fabric of life and death's natural harmony.

"Screened?" Maureen's voice cut across the table like a blade of ice. "What are you expecting to find, Ved? A pile of rotting bodies he's buried somewhere? He's been with us for months!"

Only one body, but it was buried by a friggin' leprechaun, not a dark and oh-so-evil necromancer, Abby thought sardonically.

"Then he should make a binding oath," Ved continued, ignoring half of Maureen's argument. "He must vow to use this power only against malevolents, and even then *only* under supervision."

"I'd be happy to—" Gwyn tried to speak up, but the in-fighting was already underway.

"Who is going to provide that supervision? Huh? We're short-handed enough as is," Maureen snapped.

There was silence for a beat, then all eyes turned to Abby. Honestly, she was surprised it had taken them this long. Even so, Abby kept her mouth clamped tightly shut.

Speaking up for Gwyn now would only jeopardize any power she might wield in his favor later. She was too close to the issue. Sleeping with the necromancer in question was already enough to render anything she said biased in their eyes.

She managed a smile. Then forced herself to keep breathing. Abby prayed that Miles would say something to save her, to save Gwyn.

Gossip spread fast in small communities, especially when powerful people were being discussed. Everyone was aware of the history of friction between the two Brothers. Miles' words would carry far more weight if he spoke in Gwyn's defense.

Miles began, "I—"

At the same time, Jacob's uncertain gaze cut to Seren again. She clearly saw her opening.

"I'm happy to take him into custody for an oath," Seren interrupted, hands slamming onto the table with more force than was strictly necessary.

"Very well," Seren continued, without seeking an ounce of feedback from anyone in the room. "Since that is settled, let's move on to my second topic. There has been a major breach in the veil of secrecy around the malevolents. No fewer than fifty Nisse—let that number sink in—saw a bukavac rip one of their friends apart. That is not a memory easily forgotten."

Seren folded her hands neatly on the table, eyes scanning the room. "If secrecy is still our aim, we may not have the luxury of delay. Fifteen powerful mages have died while fighting malevolents in the past six months alone."

Jacob came perilously close to guffawing. "You just so happen to have been less than two hundred miles away each time one of them has fallen. No matter what continent. Now you're here just as our problems worsen."

"My life is travel, Mr. Spencer," Seren snapped.

Abby grimaced, and she was thinking another verbal spar was about to break out when a sharp rap resounded from the far door.

"Come in," Seren called out.

The door creaked open. Abby turned, expecting some grim-faced Brother she'd never met before. Instead, what stepped through was tiny, pale, and terrified.

Nisse children.

There were a half-dozen of them, maybe more, peeking out from behind two adult Nisse attendants. Their tiny feet were silent on the floor as they were brought inside, huddled together like frightened baby birds. They were impossibly small, barely one foot tall, with enormous sad eyes and soft, downy hair shimmering in shades of silver, white, and gray. One girl clutched a knitted doll, its fabric worn from years of affection. Another a well-loved blanket.

The meeting room went deathly quiet.

Winnie zipped over without being asked to distract the children from the proceedings. The aziza flitted about, making illusory magic fly while speaking in a singsong voice that made a few of the kids smile.

"These are the... witnesses," Seren said. "Of everything graphic you can imagine in such a scenario. Most are too young to understand what they saw, but not young enough to forget it."

Jacob sat back slowly in his chair, hands steepled, mouth a grim line. Murder was in his eyes. Even Maureen, who had the personality of a honey badger, had the decency to look stricken. Esme seemed poised to duel Seren, conjured sword in hand.

"They're babies," Sorcha whispered, eyes wet.

"They are security risks," Seren corrected. "And, more importantly, they are suffering. Inaction will leave them with those memories forever. They will dream of it. They will wake screaming in the dark. Fear every shadow. If the room is willing, I propose we aid Abigail in removing the memories."

Her magic curled tight in her belly like it sensed the trap before her mind did. "What?"

"Wipe the memories," Seren said, not unkindly. "Ease the pain. Seal the trauma. Give them something kinder to remember than the truth."

There it was, her real play.

What Seren got out of her joining the closed board was now crystal clear: a tool. Abby's heart thundered against her ribs. Sure, everyone knew what she was, but what she could do was illegal by international mage law.

"So this is what it looks like at the top? No privacy, publicly crossing lines?" Abby snapped, louder than she meant to.

The children shrank from the spike in Abby's voice, and guilt crushed her. Miles placed a gentle hand on her shoulder, not chiding, but reassuring.

"I'm not saying I won't do it," she added, quieter now, forcing her breath to slow.

Even as Seren went on espousing the virtues of her plan, Abby couldn't stop staring at the children. She wanted to scoop them all up in her arms and make all of their problems go away. That thought alone decided for her. She'd do it.

Boom. The silent alarms blared, an almost deafening cacophony of magic that vibrated through the floor and up into her teeth. The wards around the Assembly headquarters exploded.

Not literally, but it felt that way. While a mundane person might feel it as an intuition, like a cold wave of dread that skittered up their spine, the magically sensitive felt it in every pore. The feedback from the magic was so great that the most sensitive of them all, Winnie, had fallen from the air onto the carpet in a tiny pile of wings.

"Too many!" she shrieked, one wing crumpled, broken, beneath her. "Dozens. Maybe more. Breaching the… stairwells above, below, elevators, *everywhere*!"

Malevolents. She had to mean malevolents.

While the adults of every species clutched their chests from the invisible, silent magical explosion, the children wailed. One tried to run, but Finn, appearing as if from nowhere like normal, quickly scooped up the child and held him to his chest. Finn shouted, "With all the exits blocked, how will we get the weans to safety?"

A grim scowl settled on Jacob's face as he studied the children. "Abigail, I'm going to need you to give me some magic. Winnie, I'll need you to take them through the portal."

Abby asked, eyes wild, "Portal?" What the hell was he talking about?

"I-I can't fly, Jacob," Winnie was breathing hard, crumpled on the ground. "I'll need my magic for defense if it comes to it."

The truth in that was nothing to scoff at. Winnie's shields were nearly as strong as Miles'.

"I'll take them." Speak of the angel, Miles was there in under a second. Everyone else was shoring up the defenses of the room or making plans of attack and concealment. It seemed a fight was imminent in downtown Seattle. The world did *not* need to know about it.

Gwyn was right behind, fear and fury reflecting in his gaze. He'd said he'd suspected Seren would pull something more than trying to get him locked up during this meeting. Whether she was responsible for whatever was coming at them was undetermined.

"No." Abby was adamant. "I'll give you the magic, and I'll take Winnie and them with me. I can keep them calm like no one else can."

Jacob turned to her, face like stone, voice not budging an inch. "You'll do no such thing."

That shut her up.

"Selkies aren't effective fighters outside of water," he went on, already scanning the room. "She's faster than anyone else here and can melt into shadows if something follows. I'll send them to the pier."

Jacob casually spoke of using magic to send ten people a *mile* away as if it were no big deal. Esme had thought mist walking was tough for him, but now Abby wondered if he'd been totally honest with her. Knowing Jacob had lied wouldn't surprise either of them.

Sorcha, silent and intense like a mother hen, moved forward at once. Her face gave nothing away, but her eyes darted to the kids—Abby saw the worry there. "Understood. I will also give what magic I can."

A pained "I'll help," was all Winnie could manage.

Jacob nodded. "No delay, then. Ms. O'Malley, Ms. Donu, Ms. MacDonald, let's begin. This will be far more demanding than any other portal I've attempted. My magic is willing but my body has grown frail. I may collapse. Miles, shield the doors."

Not a half-second later, the doors rattled on their hinges with a resounding *boom* that was so loud Abby feared people outside the building could hear it.

Sorcha scooped Winnie up in one arm, trying to ignore the pain she was obviously causing her best friend. Abby and the other two women got into position, making a triangle with Jacob at the top. The children were crying, but their caretakers were doing an admirable job of distracting them.

The moment Abby extended her hand, she felt Jacob's magic. It wasn't a gradual thing. One second, he was a stately, elderly man in layered robes who was impeccably composed, even under pressure. The next, she was crushed by his force. The room was caught up in the landslide of his power.

The room folded in on itself. Words died mid-breath. Even the air tightened like a noose, strangled by the undeniable gravity of Jacob's magic. The crying children fell silent under the weight of it, their fear momentarily forgotten in their wonder. Magic was a friend to these nonhuman children, and they were witnessing something few had ever seen before.

Abby pushed her magic into Jacob, but it was like forcing water into a full barrel. Her own magical reserves slowly drained. One misstep and she wouldn't be any use in the fight to come. Winnie, still shaking, added her strength with a low hum in her throat.

Jacob didn't move, but his eyes *burned*. They were alive with the kind of power she'd dreamed of as a child. It was more power than Abby had ever felt in her entire life. This was the kind of magic that only the ascended were supposed to be capable of, not ordinary humans.

The floor beneath them began to vibrate. It felt like a mountain-sized tuning fork had struck the world. The pressure suddenly became unbearable, causing the children to cry out in unison.

Abby's heart thundered. This wasn't magic anymore. It was more like a tectonic shift in the fabric of reality. Her organs shifted inside her belly with the force of whatever was shifting the fabric of reality in front of their faces. Jacob was tearing a hole in the world with his bare will.

And then, impossibly, the floor simply... split.

It opened silently, like a blind being slowly drawn upward. A rectangle peeled open, impossibly thin and impossibly deep, revealing the... bridge to the West Seattle water taxi?

It didn't matter. It was away from danger.

Jacob's voice came out in a rasp, barely holding together. "Go."

Finn handed over the little boy he was holding to one of the adult Nisse. The children's caregivers didn't need to be told twice. To most of the magical community, Jacob was basically a demigod, so they trusted him without question. They ushered the children through first and disappeared through the impossible portal with as much haste as their legs could handle.

Sorcha and Winnie cut off their flow of magic, making Abby gasp at the power she needed to add to help sustain the portal. The pair disappeared with a wave, and the floor sealed behind them without a sound.

As soon as the portal was gone, Jacob collapsed like a marionette whose strings had been cut. Abby just barely caught him in time. He was of average height for a man, while she was, well, part leprechaun, so it was no mean feat. He wasn't unconscious—yet. But in her arms, he felt like a collapsing star: all heat, no light, burning itself out for the last time.

"Jacob!" she gasped. "Here's a bit more. We both know I'm not as much of a fighter as you."

His voice was barely audible. "They're safe."

"I hope to hell you're right," she whispered, holding him upright as the next thunderous boom hit the door like the devil had finally found their address.

CHAPTER THIRTY-ONE

SIEGE

Esme

Time sped like a god had hit fast-forward. Mortals could catch up or die trying. At least it felt that way to Esme.

"Keep your head straight, lovely." Miles' voice stayed calm—too calm. He was afraid. That scared her more than anything else.

The kiss he gave her was brief but searing. It was a promise, a prayer, and an "I love you" all wrapped up in one breathless moment.

That kind of kiss could mean many things, but it definitely meant he was about to do something stupidly noble, possibly even fatal. Still, she didn't stop him. They had their duties to attend to, and respecting each other's power had always been an important part of their relationship. He turned and strode toward the others.

This was supposed to be nothing more than a politically inconvenient meeting. Not a godsdamned war zone.

With Miles busy playing protector, Esme turned her attention to the corner where Seren was probably causing problems. The woman had been a walking red flag since day one, and Esme wasn't about to let her wander around unsupervised. She didn't trust Seren's motives for a heartbeat. And this attack? It was too big, too sudden, and too damned *convenient*.

Esme jogged over in time to catch Josiah, arms folded across his hoodie, saying, "We're sure you can handle this alone, Ms. Lewis, but you aren't exactly subtle." He gestured sharply at the floor, all business—totally unlike his usually relaxed self. "We're in the middle of downtown. We need you to hold back."

"I see your point." Seren let out a dry, unconvincing harrumph. "Mr. Garuda, could you conjure a large enough illusion to engulf any areas a member of the public might see outside? Perhaps also store up the wards dampening the sound?"

"Yes, but I need to get outside to be most effective." The Garuda's voice turned into a sharp screech—fitting, given his beak. "Jon!"

Poor Jon Doe, sitting where the meeting had left him, had the look of a man who'd been told the sky was falling. Which was, well, *fair*. Hearing his name snapped him out of it, and he stood on autopilot. Thin, mild, and thoroughly unprepared for monster attacks, he shuffled over in a daze.

"First," Ved said, talons clicking against the floor, tone shifting to something more clipped and commanding, "seal the doors. Rearrange the seams. Buy us time. Miles will shield you. Then open that window. I need an exit."

Josiah jumped in. "After that, you're on sharp-object duty. Hunker down, make weapons, maybe hurl a few if you're feeling spicy. I'll be feeding Ved juice and doing what I can to slow the flow."

Jon didn't answer, only nodded, already moving toward the door.

"I'm gonna send out a few scouts," Esme added, half raising a hand like she needed permission. "Critter recon."

"Do it now," Seren said with a decisive nod. "I'll be twiddling my thumbs until the door breaks, then I'm walking out and discreetly—*discreetly*—killing anything not on this floor."

She shot Josiah a glare so sharp it might've cut him had Josiah given a single fig. Esme fought back a snort. Pressure had a tendency to make her hysterical in the worst moments. She started working right away.

Magic pooled within her, coalescing into four quick-footed shapes—her little spies, her business of ferrets. Thursday, Friday, Saturday, and Sunday emerged with twitchy noses and slinky little bodies, each sniffing the air as if smelling danger on it. The air already reeked of wrongness.

As one, they scurried up the walls and vanished into the gaps of the loose ceiling tiles.

Esme closed her eyes and focused on the echoes they sent back—not sight or sound exactly, but impressions. She wasn't looking for the telltale crimson glow of malevolent magic. She expected it, so she didn't bother with her new ability.

Friday was first. He peeked through the ceiling above the door Miles had shielded.

A *thing* crouched at the door—bigger than the dire boar and somehow worse. All wrong. All *wrong*. A grotesque fusion of man, bull, and goat. Thick muscle corded its entire body. Its back was too broad, its face too long, its arms too horrifyingly human. Curved horns, nearly as big as she was, jutted from its skull.

It was feeling at the door with its too-human hands, trying to find a way in...

Horrified, Esme pushed Friday's feedback to the back of her mind, bracing herself for more bad news. Thursday skittered farther across the ceiling, Saturday veered left, Sunday right—but the feedback was muddled, the wards in the building and the distance warping her connection. All she got were flashes of movement. Shapes, some large, some small. They were scratching at doors, trying to climb up walls, peering out of windows where office doors had been left open...

Too many. Far too many shapes. The only thing she could be grateful for was that most were smaller than dogs.

Esme ground her teeth, and she dismissed the ferrets. Her mind snapped fully back into her body on a sharp exhale. She whirled back to the group just in time to be nearly knocked off her feet.

Jacob's magic ripped a hole in reality only fifteen feet away. Sure, her magic ripped a hole in reality, but it didn't *displace* space. But her magic couldn't do this. No one's could. For a second, all her sarcasm burned away—Jacob was terrifying.

Gods above and below, Jacob had created a *wormhole* to save a group of preschoolers.

Another *boom* at the doors refocused her.

"There's a thing at the door—a bull-goat-man monstrosity," she blurted, choking on the rising fear. "And more, way, *way* more of freaking everything filling the halls."

Miles

The second Esme spoke, Miles' head snapped up. He was already heading their way after settling the plan with Jacob and Abby.

"A chort," he said, loud enough for the room to hear. Centuries had passed since one had appeared, making any reliable data available on them less than ideal.

He looked across the room to Jon, who had just finished rearranging the seams of the window to let Ved out.

"Jon, I need a spear. Big one. Heavy-duty. Reinforce the shaft. This thing is going to hit like a wrecking ball."

Jon was already grabbing items scattered throughout the room to melt with magic into Miles' desired weapon. Jon was a fighter, in his own way, but not the type to be on the front lines. But once he got going, he didn't stop.

Miles glanced around again to see no sign of Finn. Of course, the leprechaun always picked the worst times to disappear.

"Maureen," Miles called, turning to the ice evocation specialist. "Want to try a repeat performance of the dire boar?"

A steely glint shone in Maureen's eyes as her answering grin stretched across her face. "Hell yes."

"That won't work." Gwyn finally spoke up. The former prince's expression was grim. "Unless it's very diminished, it can move in and out of the mists."

Miles swore. "It can bloody mist walk?"

He hated it when Gwyn used his arrogance to deliver bad news—especially when he was right.

"Only parts of its body will dip in and out of the magic. It will be like stabbing smoke."

"Bloody hell," Miles muttered, already reassessing. Everything about this had just gotten worse. And they still had no idea what else was out there, trying to figure out a way in. That, at least, was one benefit. Their combined magic was acting like a homing beacon, keeping the malevolents away from mundane humans, while they prepared to fight.

Seren rose slowly, like a snake shedding its skin. The pout disappeared and eagerness took its place. She rolled her shoulders like a fighter preparing for the first round. "This changes my plan. Get the chort in here. I'll handle it instead of the halls." Her gaze flicked toward the door, nostrils flaring. "More are flooding the halls. I can sense them. Lucky for us all that someone else has already begun to handle that."

Her grin was all teeth. She was terrifying, but maybe terror was exactly what they needed. He didn't trust her, but at least she was fighting with them. Maybe she wasn't behind this disaster after all.

Seren's eyes flicked toward the mages preparing defenses. She didn't wait for any debate. "Esmeralda, protect Josiah and Jon. They need safety to work."

If Seren really was Morgan le Fay, she might be able to solve this entire problem all on her own. But Josiah was right. She wasn't exactly *subtle*.

Abby's voice cut through the din, strained. "Jacob's half out of it. Pulse is steady, but he might not wake up enough to fight."

Miles didn't need to ask what that meant. There would be no backup portals, no escape. And the Bastion needed to be protected.

"With Jacob out, plans have changed!" Seren shouted above the din of the malevolents trying to break in through the door and walls. "Jon, weaken the framing of that wall, top and bottom—not the drywall. Josiah, prepare to push that section of the wall outwards. I want two funnels into this room."

And that was that. There was no time to plan further. The door boomed again, the sound shuddering through the room.

Everyone moved. Ved ducked through the open window, wings snapping wide as he soared upward. Josiah pressed a hand to the wall and murmured something. The way he did magic was strange, but Miles felt a tingle of something warm move throughout the room. Maybe he was reinforcing the sound dampening while Ved started outside?

Jon's hands trembled slightly as he stepped forward and offered Miles a newly forged sword, its tip still white-hot. The weapon was a motley of colors: silver, brass, something like iron. It was a bit heavy, but it would keep him alive if he needed to maintain some distance between him and whatever he was attacking.

Astonished by the gift, Miles murmured, "Thank you, Jon. This is perfect."

Jon's gaze was serious, his step deliberate as he sprinted away from Miles, off to weaken the wood framing that kept the interior wall upright.

Abby crouched over Jacob, pushing magic into him, willing him to wake. Esme moved into the corner next to Josiah and stood, arms outstretched at her sides, ready to summon a blade at a moment's notice. She was gorgeous, his modern-day Amazon.

Seren stood at the center of it all, eyes bright with something almost feral. "Are you ready, Josiah?"

Miles' eyes followed Josiah as he walked to the wall where Jon was working. "Give me fifteen seconds," he mumbled.

The warm, humming sensation in the room pulsed stronger as Josiah pressed his palm to the wall and closed his eyes. Maureen climbed atop the conference table, hands raised, ready to cast ice as sharp as blades at the incoming horde. Gwyn took up a position in front of Abby and Jacob at the other end of the room, sword that he had glamoured to be invisible before now outstretched. To give Maureen a clear killing field, Miles positioned himself between Gwyn and Seren at the front, daggers at the ready.

Seren's hand rose. Her lips moved in silent countdown, fingers curling like a warlord calling for blood. Magic thrummed around her like a coming storm.

A sharp *crack* resounded from multiple points on the wall as Jon scurried away, running into the far corner where Esme was waiting.

The increase of magic in the area intensified the scratching and scrabbling on the other side of the wall.

"I tear Jon's seal in three," Seren announced, voice echoing. "Two…"

At two, a riot of new growth, thick and impossibly fast-growing, exploded from the wooden wall framing.

"One…"

A tangle of green shoots and leaves pushed upward at the ceiling, heaving the weakened wall frame outward—directly onto the heads of the scrabbling malevolents on the other side.

At the same time, Seren's violent detonation ripped the door from its frame.

The room exploded—sound, motion, magic, screaming steel. Chaos, unleashed.

CHAPTER THIRTY-TWO

BATTLE ROYALE

Gwyn

As some of the malevolents cried out, crushed by the wall, the first of the uninjured ones crawled over their fallen comrades to surge through the opening. Gwyn immediately recognized a basilisk, its scaly, reptilian body scrambling his way. It was a sinuous coil of muscle and jagged scales as it lunged from the wreckage, jaws unhinging with a hiss that smelled of rotting meat.

Maureen's ice shards punched into its flank, freezing the surrounding air in glittering fractals. The creature shrieked, twisting, but Gwyn didn't wait for it to recover. With one swift, clean strike of his sword, he severed its head. Dark blood sprayed, steaming as it hit the floor where Maureen's ice magic had frozen.

This creature was likely smaller than the one that had caused Colin and Will so much trouble in Portland because that had been far too easy.

The onslaught of gnashing teeth and clawed limbs continued its advance, showing no sign of stopping. The second malevolent was on him in second. This one was the size of a large dog but feline in build, except that its legs were far too thin and its eyes glowed a telltale malevolent red.

Gwyn's sidestep away was a beat too late. The creature's claws grazed his ribs before his sword found its belly. Even after a year of this, he was still too used to fighting with armor, and now he was paying for it. White-hot agony lanced through his ribs like a second kiss of the Dullahan's whip, each breath scraping against broken flesh as his lighting seared through the creature's belly. The thing screamed, thrashing as its limbs spasmed against the current.

The coppery taste of blood filled his mouth. He'd bitten his lip without realizing it.

As he was pulling his sword from the creature's belly, a searing wave of magic slammed into his back. His ribs screamed in protest as the force hurled him forward, the force of it knocking him nearly off his feet. The shriek of a projectile that whistled through the space where his head had been quickly eclipsed his searing pain. Half a breath later, he caught the shimmer of shield magic pulse around him. The missile embedded itself in a red body that landed where he'd been moments before.

Nothing served as a better reminder to look *up* than his allies having to save his sorry hide.

Gwyn only needed a quick look to identify the body as some sort of monkey's. The shield had been Miles', and the forceful blow had been from Abigail. But the projectile weapon was a mystery until he turned to see Jon, crouched in the corner with a little smile on his face.

The alteration mage kneeled with random bits of office supplies and scraps of furniture around him. He was crafting weapons from a mixture of wood, steel, and shattered glass. A torrent of creations, each propelled by raw telekinetic energy, erupted from him one after the other into the crowd of malevolents.

Josiah, hand on the window frame, fed his magic out to the waiting Garuda outside. Ved's wings shimmered as he wheeled through the sky, silent as the night. In waves, Josiah's free hand would sweep toward the battle, sending a gust of wind at a charging monster to knock it off course.

One of Esmeralda's conjurations—it looked a bit like a green-skinned ogre—burst into being nearby. Grabbing a chair, the ogre hurled it at another of the slender-legged feline creatures. When it missed, it roared, then promptly hammer-threw the malevolent across the room. The cat made a splattering sound as it shattered on the far wall.

"You're welcome," Miles said, panting. He surged past, daggers a blur of motion.

"I had it," Gwyn muttered.

Miles snorted. Gwyn, an avid reader on malevolents since arriving in this era, was clueless about Miles' opponent. It looked a bit like a bird but had scales and a nearly human head. Gwyn sent a burst of fire at its back and moved slowly toward Abby and Jacob. *Now you're welcome.*

Maureen was busy with a whole swarm of creatures that looked like enormous centipedes with razor-sharp grasping mouthpieces. More and more of them were continuously crawling out from beneath the fallen wall in small groups.

Gwyn felt each death as a cold fist clenching around his heart. Even though he wanted to push the power away, to reject it, it gathered within him in a dark, swirling vortex.

Then a low, grinding growl vibrated through the entire room. Gwyn's head snapped toward the doorway where the chort stood.

Until then, it had remained in the hallway, observing, waiting, and worst of all, *studying* them. Gwyn caught sight of it in the corner of his vision, ten feet tall at least, quadrupedal, thick-skinned and sleek like a demonic over-sized man-bull.

It hit the floor like thunder, snarling with a mouth that seemed to tear upward through its face, not down. It disregarded Seren's attempt to block its path, hurtling instead toward the fallen Jacob.

It only made it three steps.

Esme

Enormous inky black tentacles erupted from the floor, halting the beast mid-charge. It howled in rage as the tentacles wrapped around the chort's legs, throat, and midsection.

The pressure in the air shifted as the rush of its malevolent magic flooded the room. The chort was trying to phase itself out. But Seren was holding it here, trying to force its existence fully into their plane.

Was it truly a demon? Did her bloodline have something awful like that in it? *Ick.*

One slick tentacle forced its way down the chort's throat, and even Esme, who wasn't squeamish, flinched at the wet, horrible sound of it gagging.

But it wouldn't go down so easily. The damn thing phased its head in and out of their reality, likely gasping for air. Seren stood in the center of the chaos, like some eldritch priestess, arms outstretched, eyes as black as a starless night.

Watching, Esme experienced the pull of her power. The thought of that much strength was almost seductive.

Esme's own conjured orc was nine feet of green fury and bad attitude. It had been a long time since she'd summoned him. He was the muscle she'd used while trying to conceal her identity for Assembly enforcer work, so using him now just felt *right*. Chuck worked by her side like a loyal bouncer, using his hands and anything she could have him grab to stem the invasion.

She'd also summoned her sword, now more comfortable in her hand than she'd thought it would ever be. A flash of motion, a flicker of shadow and a glint of malevolent red, drew her eye.

"Shit—" she muttered.

A xolotl came from the wreckage at full sprint. The sleek hell-black blur with too many teeth and not enough conscience moved like hate fueled it. Its paws fell silently on the wreckage of the meeting room as it leaped straight at her.

While Esme would like to say that she didn't flinch, she absolutely did. Chuck successfully snatched it from the air with one hand around its throat. He slammed it into the floor hard enough to break most of the bones in its body. The orc didn't wait. He lifted one foot and stomped the thing's head in like squashing a bug.

Only after it was dead did Esme realize the possible implications of that creature being there. Had the malevolent containment on Maury Island failed? From her understanding, xolotl weren't that common. What were the chances?

Esme did not like the conclusion her mind was leading her to.

Orange and yellow flames burst out in the hallway. Esme's attention snapped toward the light, catching a glimpse of Finn's silhouette stalking outside the conference room.

With a shriek, two gaunt, rat-like malevolents, their thin bodies barely cloaked in scraggly fur, launched themselves at him from opposite ends. Finn's arms thrust outward like a vengeful deity's judgment, twin pillars of ifrit fire erupting with a roar. The very air screamed in protest as it superheated with his fury. One monster, caught in the full force of the blast, shrieked a horrifying sound as its flesh burned. The other creature tried to leap away, but Finn pivoted, another burst of searing flames catching it on the tail.

The leprechaun turned and stalked farther into the hallway.

As her attention switched to dangers closer to herself, Esme heard the wail.

It wasn't the roar of the chort, nor the more common yelps of pain or rage coming from the dying malevolents, but something high, wrong, that sliced through the battle like a knife made of sorrow.

The banshee's wail had barely faded when Jon folded. No gasp, no cry. He'd just collapsed. Esme turned in time to see Josiah's hand drop. He'd begun to hurl a blast of wind too late to stop its attack.

The creature looked as if it was made of shadows and light, grief and malice. The banshee looked more like a specter than anything living, shape fading to almost nothing at the edges.

Esme was experiencing a moment of panic when a flare of pure energy lit the air.

Prostrate, pale, and sweating profusely, Jacob managed to raise one trembling arm upward. A crackling bolt of undiluted magic shot from his staff, hitting the banshee and blasting it backward against the wall. It dissolved with a hiss.

They'd been too slow. Blood trickled from Jon's ears, streaking the still-smiling curve of his lips as if death had caught him mid-thought. He hadn't even turned around.

"No—" Esme's breath locked in her throat.

Miles was moving before she could blink. He wasn't running, but collapsing, knees hitting the ground beside Jon's body like he'd been dragged down by grief. His hands glowed. Miles didn't scream or curse. He just *tried*. But even from where she stood, Esme could tell that it wouldn't be enough.

The silence that followed made it clear. The smile remained frozen on Jon's lips, frozen in eternal amusement. Miles' glowing hands pressed uselessly against his still chest, the light reflecting in the pooling blood of the malevolents around them.

She'd been close enough to touch him. Josiah's wind, Jacob's magic, Miles' shields. They had all been useless.

Jon's blood seeped down his face, soaking the collar of his shirt. His hand fell, scattering the pile of his half-made projectile weapons.

Something inside her ruptured. It was louder than grief and sharper than rage. Her heart broke with a flare of power that answered the banshee's call in kind. The world narrowed to tunnel vision, every beat of her heart pumping liquid fury through her veins.

Her magic responded like a starving beast, crackling along her skin with electric hunger. Her blade burned colder in her hand. Anger made it easy, easier than it ever should've been. Easier than it usually was.

She was done holding back.

Somewhere between one breath and the next, she dismissed her orc in favor of *feeling* the fight. The nearest malevolent, a crawling insect-thing with too many limbs, turned toward her in time to be cleaved in half. Another, some kind of gremlin with one broken wing, shrieked as she hurled a conjured spear through its chest.

From the corner of her eye, Esme noticed Abby, her breaths ragged as she stood over Jacob. Esme couldn't see her face, not fully, but there was something brittle in how her shoulders squared. Like she was holding herself up by sheer will alone.

As Abby shifted, a strange pressure twisted the air in the room. Esme's mouth dried instantly.

And the battlefield changed.

All across the chamber, the malevolents staggered. They lurched sideways, snarling at imaginary foes, their eyes darting wildly as if hallucinating. Some twitched. Others recoiled like they'd been struck. A moan, not a roar, escaped one's lips as it clawed at its face. A huge, grotesquely malformed dog-like creature flattened itself on the ground, its tail thrashing, ears pressed back, as it whimpered in terror.

The air itself seemed to bow under Abby's aura, a visible distortion radiating outward like a heat haze. The supernatural tendrils of her magic pressed into every living thing nearby, not harming them, but suffocating them with the weight of her blessing, with her will.

This wasn't simple power. This was her wrath. And something else, something a bit more terrifying. Esme thought it was a glimpse of the goddess within.

Seren

Jon's death registered as a flicker, a candle snuffed out in the middle of its burn. It wasn't grief that made Seren's fingers twitch, but calculation. He represented a piece removed from the board, a cost incurred, a *miscalculation*. It wasn't ideal, but that was now their reality.

The soft-spoken alteration mage's life, though not crucial in the grand scheme, was significant enough that its loss would likely incur unforeseen consequences.

Worst of all, it was a risk that could have easily resulted in another casualty. Seren's eyes flicked toward the young woman raging, her sword now cutting through one body and then another. Had she been even a second slower, or mistimed a step...

Bound and struggling, the chort thrashed, its limbs flailing against her magic as it tried to slip in and out of reality. Seren anchored it with another thread of infernal magic, forcing the tendrils of her magic deeper into its hide. The effort was considerable. This creature was old and powerful, and far more intelligent than she had first suspected.

But she could kill it. She could rip it to pieces easily. In the blink of an eye, her infernal arsenal could raze this building—windows, concrete, and steel reduced to rubble, leaving only silence in its wake.

Except that would draw attention. Ved had continued circling the sky outside, cloaking the building from mundane eyes. Too much noise, any structural collapse, and even a Garuda's magic couldn't mask it.

Seren's eyes swept the battle royale. Abigail slumped beside Jacob, pale and shaking. Her spell's wave had broken. Seren suspected that was only a fraction of what she could do, given a bit of time and practice. But the princess wasn't done fighting. With one hand, Abby lifted a broken chair leg. With her mind, she sent a filing cabinet crashing into another small animal.

The remaining malevolents, briefly subdued, had returned to the fight with renewed bloodlust. Miles was using Jon's sword now. His weapon work was so familiar it nearly transported her back in time. Gwyn was his mirror, faster and more precise in his movements but with less power behind each strike.

It was time for Seren to put on her own show. She allowed a slight tremor in her voice. "Gwyn, please." His name was a hook, and she yanked on it.

He was already moving toward her, sword held low, fire at the ready in the other hand.

"Steel is useless," Seren snapped. "Necromancy."

Gwyn's stride faltered. His eyes, always too perceptive, narrowed.

"You can," Seren said before he could dispute her. "You *must*."

She purposefully allowed her control to slip the smallest bit. Muscles rippled beneath the chort's thick, mottled hide as it thrashed and snarled. It swerved violently, almost hitting Miles where he'd been fighting, before she wrestled it back under her control.

"We must overwhelm it," Seren said. "It phases when struck. But it cannot phase through dozens of attacks at once."

Gwyn didn't move. He looked at her again, truly looked, with a question in his gaze.

She let him see past the mask. Stripped of pretense, she laid bare the truth: she was using him, but he only stood to gain from it.

Gwyn bared his teeth in an expression that was not quite a snarl but also not quite surrender. He wordlessly acknowledged, albeit grudgingly, that the choice was sound.

The moment he unleashed the magic, she sensed it like a thousand tiny ants made of ice crawling across her skin. A glance proved Esme did too. She slowed her rage and inched closer to Miles.

Freezing-cold static snapped on Seren's skin. Across the floor, the dozens of maimed, mangled, and bloodied malevolent corpses twitched.

As one, they rose like puppets pulled on a thousand strings.

A feline thing, body split at the ribs. A centipede-like horror with only half a head. The crushed xolotl. The winged gremlin. A basilisk missing part of its chest. All of them animated, shuddering, crawling, dragging themselves over shattered furniture and splintered walls.

Sword in hand, Gwyn inched closer to the chort. There was no fancy display of light. His eyes didn't flash crimson, nor did necromantic fire pour out of him. But the dead obeyed all the same.

As the dead sprinted forward, Gwyn's face froze in quiet horror at his own work. The chort roared in dismay as the dead swarmed it. Clawed hands latched onto its limbs. Snapping jaws sank into its flesh. Even as it began to phase, to blur, to vanish—the attacking zombies clung.

One would fail. Another would miss. A third would strike too late. But the fourth would land true.

The bull demon let out a shriek of pain. Seren's bonds constricted, holding it here, yet Gwyn's resurrected army was its downfall. They covered it in a writhing, grotesque mountain of claws and teeth.

"I'm going for the kill," she announced, putting on a show of the effort it took.

Gwyn nodded, and one tiny flicker of thought from Seren ended the chort's life. With it, the risen dead collapsed. A dozen bodies hit the floor in unison, making a grim, wet sound.

Free of that task, her tentacles erupted across the room. As one, they obliterated every single remaining malevolent.

"See, subtle," she murmured.

But Miles was already moving toward her. Miles' roar shattered the silence, carrying a grief too vast for his human frame. "This is how we die, Seren!"

Blood dripped from Jon's sword in his white-knuckled grip, each drop a crimson accusation against the floor. His chest rose and fell in ragged bursts. "You've seen it firsthand here, now. If we can't cover this up, you'll get exactly what you've wanted all along! The truth out! Are you *bloody* happy?"

The words echoed in the sudden stillness. He had all but come out and accused her directly of the attack.

Somewhere across the room, Josiah slumped to the ground, spent from giving so much of his magic to Ved. Gwyn collapsed against the wall, eyes averted from the mass of corpses, looking shamed.

Miles' voice cracked, thick with grief. "Jon trusted you."

Esme was there instantly, tugging on his arm. "Miles—" she said as she urged him away.

He didn't shrug her off, but his entire body vibrated with restraint. Miles shook from the rage and despair of having witnessed countless losses and having found himself powerless to save one more.

Seren couldn't speak. Her eyes met his. He deserved to see the truth of what she'd done.

What she saw there made doubt creep into her certainty. He knew, maybe Nudd knew, like Gwyn. Yet he judged her for it.

If it were anyone else, even Esmeralda, Seren would have shrugged off her loss of face as simply collateral damage. But he was infuriatingly noble and straightforward in his right-eousness. In their past life, he had been a constant, irritating reminder of her own compromised morality.

It seemed that he was determined to be that reminder in this one, too.

But she'd had to make one more dramatic, final push to get them to understand. They *had* to see how bad the problem was so that action could be taken. They had to be convinced so that the worst did not come to pass, even if it meant a few more had to die in the process.

Seren's gaze dropped to the floor where Jon had fallen, body crumpled in on itself. The magic in the room had begun to settle, leaving only the smell of blood and scorched flesh behind. Their victory had created a scene of carnage: slain monsters, shattered glass, and the wide-eyed silence of those who had survived it.

Esme stood beside Miles, one hand lightly on his arm after giving up on dragging him away. The mix of worry and exhaus-tion in her expression stirred up old emotions in Seren.

It had been necessary, but...

She saw them all now. Gwyn, his face pale and closed, avoid-ing her gaze. Abby crouched over Jacob with one hand, check-ing his pulse, surrounded by the debris she had hurled. Finn had just walked back in, his coat singed and a fresh gash on his cheek. But his eyes were storm-dark. There wasn't a trace of humor in his expression. Even Ved outside, wings beating slowly, straining to maintain the concealment.

She hadn't protected them. She had wielded them as she would a blade or spell, not as people. Not as Elena's people.

Her plan had been simple in its logic: provoke the threat, expose the truth, show the Assembly that secrecy would only lead to ruin. She had believed this fight would *galvanize* them.

But all she had done was use them. Her daughter's soul reborn, her daughter's allies, lover, kin-by-choice—all bent to a purpose they hadn't chosen. Her choices had exposed their secrets while using them as blunt instruments.

And now they knew it.

The Assembly would have to face the truth. But so did she.

For the first time in an age, Seren felt something she thought she'd buried on that hillside in Wales. It wasn't the flicker of regret that normally accompanied collateral damage, nor the detached recognition of error.

It was guilt. Centuries of carefully constructed detachment crumbled in an instant.

Esme didn't speak to Seren. Yet her look was far colder and more cutting than any of Gwyn's undead magic. That silence said everything.

The weight of their accusing stares pressed down on her like a physical force. She had won, but not without paying a steep price.

CHAPTER THIRTY-THREE

A MATTER OF COURSE

Gwyn

Gwyn slumped amidst the wreckage, his hands clenched into white-knuckled fists, one around a sword, the other still burning from flinging fire. After Miles' outburst, the silence was broken only by the slow, rhythmic drip of Maureen's melting ice spikes. Each drop echoed cruelly, a pointed reminder of how quickly magic became aftermath. Acrid smoke, blood, and burning flesh filled the air.

The stench clawed at his throat, but worse was the crushing pressure, like death itself was trying to crawl out through his pores. The insistent hum of death magic was squeezing his organs, making it feel like his heart was skipping beats and making his ears ring.

He still felt them. Each corpse was a knot of tension in his mind, the weight of their silent presence pushing behind his eyes from the inside. Worst of all, it wasn't just the malevolent corpses he could sense.

He could *feel* Jon. He could feel what was left of him. Gwyn's stomach churned violently, threatening to send its contents flying.

His gaze flicked once to the corner where a coat had been draped over Jon's body. He hadn't seen who had done it. Probably Josiah.

Gwyn could still remember the faces of many men he had killed. He was likely a more prolific killer than almost anyone standing with him in the ruins of the conference room, possibly even surpassing Jacob in that regard, but likely just behind Seren in body count. So it wasn't Jon's death that bothered Gwyn.

It was that he wanted to reach for the power again.

He had braced for it this time. He had expected the magic to flow from each body toward him with the speed of a striking serpent. Then Jon had fallen. And try as he might, Gwyn hadn't been able to stop his death from sinking into his pores. Hadn't been able to stop it from filling him with its poison that transformed into a potent elixir that surged through him, electrifying every cell.

It was like his encounter with the ghost had irrevocably altered something inside of him.

Necromancer. The word, an ancient malediction unearthed and stained with blood, was now undeniably tattooed on his skin for all to see.

He thought he had come to an understanding before about why Nudd had never trusted him, but *this* was the true reason. Necromancy was like blinking. It came as naturally as breathing to him.

Nearby, Seren snapped her fingers and shouted names. The sound pierced the fog in Gwyn's mind.

"Cleanup begins now," she called, transformed into a woman in command once again, a far cry from the moment of stunned tolerance while Miles shouted at her.

Unblemished by the fight, Seren stood amidst the carnage and blood splatters on the floor, her dark eyes traveling over the ruins. "The Nisse will handle most of it, but we can't leave the bodies here."

Esme wheeled on her. "Haven't the Nisse been through enough recently?"

"Yes, which is why they need the work," Seren replied without missing a beat. "They trade cleanup for goods, Esmeralda. Goods they use to feed their overgrown families. Would you rather they starve? Or *steal*? We all know how good Fae are at getting into trouble."

She wasn't wrong. The Nisse thrived on work, but the way she said it, a low, emotionless hiss, made his skin crawl.

"I'll move them," Gwyn said, his voice coming out a rough rasp.

Seren's gaze flicked to him, assessing. Then she nodded.

Gwyn released his white-knuckled grip on his sword, the cold steel clattering to the ground with a sharp clang that echoed in the ruined conference room.

He wanted to reject the power. But the dark energy inside him pulsed like a trapped beast, a restless churning in his very core. If he could expel some of it, maybe the pressure in his skull would ease, like draining poison from a wound.

"March them into the elevators and our offices," Seren ordered. "We can lock the elevators for *maintenance* and each ward our rooms."

He reached for the chort first, black blood oozing from a million cuts. With a mere flick of his will, the beast shuddered, its limbs seizing and locking rigidly in place. He forced it upright, then made it drag several other malevolents toward the first office, their broken bodies leaving smears across the floor. It was grotesque but efficient.

The entire time, Jon's body pressed against his mind as a silent, dreadful presence coming from beneath the jacket. He could feel their eyes watching him, evaluating his mental stability, his *threat*. Gwyn squeezed his eyes shut and turned away.

Miles had said it: *"If you can't trust yourself, how the hell are we supposed to?"* He'd meant it as a challenge.

Gwyn had risen to the occasion and used his power for good, but would it be enough to assuage their concerns?

Some time later, Abby spoke, soft but firm. "Gwyn."

He flinched but didn't look up. She was there, standing next to him as he closed the elevator doors one last time.

"I think that's enough," Abby said, more to the room than him. The gap left by the demolished wall now provided easy communication. "We're leaving. *Now*."

No one, not even Finn, uttered a single word in their wake.

***

Whatever the others did after he left with Abby, he never asked. Their exhausted walk to the pier started out quiet. The city's usual nighttime glow went on around them, the people completely unaware that just blocks away, monsters had attacked en masse.

Abby easily kept pace with his dragging steps. "Tell me what's on your mind," she said.

He exhaled gently.

"Gwyn," she said again, understanding but insistent.

So he told her all of it. About his feeling of revulsion, the stolen magic, the fear that this power would twist him. That he was becoming something even Nudd had despised.

"It's disgusting." He couldn't meet her eyes. "It's wrong. I hate how terribly simple it is for me."

She stepped in front of him, small but mighty, halting him. The city noise faded around them. Abby grabbed his face, her warm fingers forcing him to meet her eyes.

"You didn't choose this," she said, gripping his face like she could press the truth into it, fierce and fragile all at once. "But you *did* choose to save us. Magic isn't the enemy, Gwyn. It's how it's used that matters. You didn't pull power from Jon out of greed or raise those monsters to hurt us. You say it's disgusting, but you saved us. You cleaned up so we didn't have to carry those bodies in our minds when we try to fall asleep tonight."

"Miles said the same thing about choices." He swallowed hard. "Even so, it still feels wrong."

"Of course it does," she said. "Because you're not a necromancer like the ones you scorn. That's why *you*, not them, ascended in the first place, dummy. Why can't you see that by now? Need one of Esme's trolls to hit you over the head for a third time with the same message for it to sink in?"

Abby was smiling by the end, trying to lighten the mood with a bit of dark humor. How could he have gotten so lucky as to find her *again*?

He closed his eyes, allowing her touch to anchor him for just a second longer. He wanted to believe her.

Then he changed the subject. "What are you going to do for the Nisse kids?"

Abby dropped her hands, studying him for another long moment, and began walking again. "They'll remember singing for the closed board. They won't remember the bukavac or the wards going off. This trip will give them plenty to smile about instead."

Gwyn nodded. How could he ever deserve her?

He marveled at her compassion. At how much she took on to save others from the mental terrors she had to embrace. Though he knew she felt uneasy about it, her act of erasing their memories was an act of kindness.

He saw it then. He'd been a self-important *fool*. Her magic suffered the same disdain as his.

They were truly in this together, in magic, in their secrets, in *life*.

Maybe she was right. Maybe Miles was, too. He didn't have to like the power, but he could choose what to do with it.

And from now on, he would choose how he used it with open eyes.

Abby

Morning light had streamed through the gap in her curtains as she'd woken to Gwyn's thrashing. Normally, after expending as much magic as they had the day before, they'd both be boneless heaps in their slumber, but this was different.

"Gwyn, wake up!" For at least five minutes, Abby had tried everything, shaking, slapping, and ice, but nothing was working. Something was wrong. It was like he was trapped in a dream. She knew it in her gut.

Damn it. A single moment's hesitation, then she steeled her nerves. *I'm going in without permission.*

Hand holding his wrist, Abby entered Gwyn's mindscape. His mind was completely defenseless to her intrusion. It had flung itself open at the first touch, like it had been waiting for her arrival.

It wasn't lit with a golden light like Miles' was, but Gwyn's was... enormous for a lack of a better word. She could see one row after another of memories. A huge section looked like it was blank—not missing like in Leon's mind, but emptied or locked away. The memories held there were lifeless and devoid of whatever powered thought, but they were present. That seemed important.

She knew at once he might recover those memories, and she would spare no effort to help. But not right now, not when he was trapped in a dream.

Right at the forefront of his thoughts was a door. A tall, ancient-looking, dark wood door loomed at the forefront. It was nearly identical to the one she'd seen in Miles' mind during their fight with Leon, but this one made her eyes ache to look directly at it.

Rich burgundy and gold pulsed from within, bleeding through the cracks like sunlight and wine. That was unsettling, but she'd lived through Leon's horrors. She could do this. She was determined to find Gwyn.

Without another moment's hesitation, Abby reached for the handle and pulled. The moment she touched it, the door pulled back. It yanked her forward, and she tumbled into a world of swirling light.

A brief moment of weightlessness, and then Abby was suspended in a void, the absolute black pressing in on her from all sides. A moment later, she emerged behind Gwyn's eyes. He stood on a narrow path of black stone surrounded by a blank abyss.

Overhead, the sky churned with the same burgundy and gold, like the gods had spilled wine and magic across the heavens. It was neither day nor night, but something beyond either. Powerful energy filled the air, smelling something like the soil after rain. And there, standing above them like an ethereal monument to death, was another door.

Based on Gwyn's description of his first memory as an ascended being, Abby knew this was the entrance to Annwn. Unlike the door that had pulled her into this dream, the threshold to Annwn gave off no sensations whatsoever. It was as senseless as a black hole. Even though she was safe in this vision, she instinctively recoiled from it.

The unnatural setting was a clue that this wasn't a normal memory, but the feeling of experiencing the world from within his body made it a certainty. She was not seeing through the eyes of the man asleep in her bed. This was Gwyn ap Nudd—psychopomp, leader of the Wild Hunt, the demigod.

A mage learns early to recognize their own magic. His entire body seemed like it was made of it.

Abby almost lost herself in the warmth. Then she heard a tiny gasp.

Gwyn's right hand held an unfamiliar obsidian black sword. But dangling from his left, gripped by the collar of his tunic, was Finn.

Her great-great-great grandfather looked younger, his clothes of a style she'd never seen before, his face less lined. Yet his eyes were the same. Those blue orbs, keen and intelligent, remained fearless despite his obvious state of disadvantage.

"You've been following me," Gwyn snarled, his voice tinged with anger and echoing in a way that wasn't completely human. "Do you have a death wish, leprechaun?"

Finn grinned, even as his feet kicked uselessly, suspended over the abyss. "Wouldn't be the first time."

Gwyn's grip tightened, and Finn's face reddened. "This is a convenient place for it, then. Not much walking for either of us."

Abby bit back her gasp, forcing herself to remain silent. Selfishly, she wasn't quite ready to stop watching this yet. If her Gwyn was here, he hadn't noticed her yet.

The demigod's emotions rippled through her—anger and frustration, but something softer beneath. Gwyn was bluffing. And from the way Finn's smirk didn't waver, he knew it too.

Without warning, something shifted in the damp, earthy air of this unnatural space. It became heavier, charged, colder. Finn's grin vanished.

Dozens of spectral hands tore through the darkness. Their long, skeletal fingers matched the ghostly burgundy swirls in the sky. All at once, they surged forward, grabbing Finn by his legs, arms, and torso, and pulled the leprechaun from Gwyn's grasp.

The demigod's eyes widened, and for a split second, Abby sensed his genuine fear.

It happened so fast she almost didn't realize they were moving. Gwyn ap Nudd raised his sword and charged. The air itself seemed to vibrate with the force of his sword cutting a clean line through the door. As dream Gwyn disappeared through the gap, Abby's vision went momentarily black.

Did she allow the dream to unfold or break him out of it? With a quiet type of certainty, she knew she could free him from it at any point. Yet anticipation kept her watching, waiting. Though she could feel her own body trembling in the real world. The strain of holding herself in the dream after the fight and with no sleep was becoming a strain.

Why was Finn there? *How* was Finn there?

As soon as she had that thought, her demigod dream host emerged on the other side of the door. Abby's expectations of the afterlife were utterly destroyed by what she saw there. It was... strangely normal. Not like the swirling abyss outside at all.

Blazing torches illuminated the stone floor. Magnificent tapestries hung on every wooden wall. It was enormous, resembling Nudd's keep but on a far grander scale. Despite its size, the space was oddly cozy.

Nevertheless, Abby felt a strange fear grip her demigod host. That made her decide she'd been a voyeur long enough.

"Gwyn!" she prompted. "Do we need to get out of here?"

She sensed his focus shift to her almost instantly. "Abigail?" he said, surprised.

"You were stuck in the dream." Abby mentally swallowed. "Nothing worked, so I had to wake you up from the inside. Babe, what the actual fuck is Finn doing there?"

The unexpected sound of a light male tenor coming from outside—a stark contrast to the more baritone voices of Miles and Gwyn—silenced them both.

"Welcome, son of mists," the voice greeted. The voice was calm, but it carried weight like it didn't need to raise its volume to be obeyed.

Abby felt Gwyn mentally straighten. She understood then, probably through some strange effect of being inside Gwyn's head, that Gwyn ap Nudd was operating outside his domain. He held less power in this place, substantially less.

"King." Gwyn's dream self greeted with a courtly bow. "You took the leprechaun."

From the edge of torchlight, a shape peeled itself from the dark. It was gaunt, almost skeletal in proportions, and draped in thick shadows. The tenor voice came once again from the figure. "As is my right. He ventured too far."

Sitting in a roughly hewn chair, Finn appeared as if he'd been teleported there. The leprechaun was unnervingly silent and subdued, his usual bravado stripped away. He seemed... almost ashamed. On top of that, his face was ashen, eyes wide with terror.

Finn was utterly petrified.

Gwyn ap Nudd argued, "My father is to blame, not the mortal."

"I understand his reasons for coming, but I also understand yours. We should address your wishes before discussing the consequences you will both face... I want something from you."

She couldn't see his face, but she already suspected that this was Arawn. Gods above and especially below.

"From me, lord?" Abby could feel demigod Gwyn's hesitance. "I have already taken over the Wild Hunt. What else would you ask of me?"

Something in the god's tone suggested he was smiling behind the ghostly hood that covered his features. "We want the same thing. My lady queen sees too little of me. You want your princess back."

"King Arawn, I do not know what you mean." Her Gwyn was just as confused as the demigod version of himself.

Arawn explained, "My wife has... become enamored with your quest for love. I am powerless to deny her wishes. Yet I must also uphold the balance of magic and serve justice."

They both felt the strange bubble of hope bloom in Gwyn ap Nudd's chest. He took a half step forward. "King?"

"I... cannot explain it all." The dark ghostly figure waved a cloaked hand. "Suffice to say that your father has a scheme in the works that will change the balance of magic forever... and I aim to help him."

"My father?" Gwyn asked.

"Again, I cannot explain it all. Your punishment, and the leprechaun's, will coincide with your father's scheme. You will get your princess, nay, your queen, back thereafter. After your deaths, you and she will ease my and my lady's burden here by taking over our duties."

Arawn's face, as pale as bone and as sharp as a skull, showed something like empathy as he looked straight at Gwyn for the first time. "Are we agreed?"

Wait, what?! Abby reeled. Was Arawn talking about her?

Gwyn ap Nudd's gaze, as sharp as a hawk's, locked onto Finn as he roughly demanded, "What will be his fate?"

"The leprechaun gave up his right to choose what comes next when he ventured too far. So he will guide you when the time is right." Arawn pointed at Finn. "But even he will have help. You will not be alone."

Her Gwyn angrily muttered something incomprehensible to Abby's ears in their shared space within the dream. So maybe Abby's first assumption had been wrong. Maybe her Gwyn hadn't known from the very beginning that Finn was involved in all of this.

Gwyn ap Nudd nodded slowly. "King Arawn, you are a fair ruler, so I must believe that the leprechaun will not suffer unjustly." It was a question.

"He will not. I have already frightened him enough. He will enjoy a full life, making whatever choices he desires until his debt comes due. This I promise."

Gwyn ap Nudd tilted his head in the same nearly canine way her Gwyn did when he was thinking. "Then name your price. I'll pay it, whatever it is, if it brings her back to me."

She somehow knew Arawn was smiling, even though she couldn't see his face. "This will please my queen greatly. Your lady has already agreed to the proposed terms."

She what?!

Just as Abby had that thought, the world shattered into a million tiny pieces.

Abby fell back into her body with a lurching gasp. She flopped down onto the bed as the magic holding Gwyn within the dream violently released them both without her needing to lift a finger. The pain of being released by the magic after expending so much the day before hit Abby hard and fast.

Next to her, Gwyn bolted awake with a choked sound, his hand flying to his chest like he'd been stabbed. A moan of pain escaped Gwyn's lips. Then he said, rough with sleep, "Cariad."

They stared at each other across the sheets, breaths ragged, waking from a shared nightmare into the same storm.

"I have bartered away our future. One lifetime of distance for a chance at eternity. By all the magic, Abigail, *I'm so sorry*."

"Then don't waste it," she whispered, her voice too thin to carry any of the anger she felt at past her choosing her future.

As she pulled the covers up to her chin, she said, "Right now, I just need to feel you breathing here, next to me."

Gwyn, already halfway asleep, murmured, "I'd still make the same choice if given it today."

They both fell back to sleep, clutching each other's hands beneath the sheets.

CHAPTER THIRTY-FOUR

A DEADLY OBLIGATION

Jacob

The portal spell had left Jacob drained, his mind foggy, his body aching, and his spirit weary. He was utterly depleted, like a dry husk left to wither in the sun, every ounce of verve desiccated.

He'd drifted into the kind of sleep that was as close to a quiet death as the living could come naturally. For once, when he closed his eyes, there was no screaming, no dreams, only the void where his pain surrendered. He woke to the scent of peppermint and the sight of an uninvited figure lounging beside his recliner, cradling a steaming mug like she belonged in his library.

"*Bonjour*, Jacob," Seren purred, her presence already an intrusion wrapped in silk and civility.

Sunlight filtered through the library's tall windows, but it brought no warmth to Jacob's bones. Every inch of his body and his mind were weary. He truly was getting too old for...

everything. If not for the physical toll of years of war, his aching bones and weary muscles wouldn't plague him so severely.

Jacob didn't bother to sit up. He simply arched a slow brow, signaling that she wasn't worth the effort of getting irritated. "I don't remember inviting you in, Ms. Lewis."

Though attired in her customary somber black, the Citadel herself was stunning that morning. Her ears, neck, and fingers were ablaze with a dazzling array of purple gems, their facets catching the light whenever she moved her head, making her look every inch like the dark queen of magic she was.

"Miles and Gwyn carried you in last night, Esmeralda barking orders the whole way. It was quite the sight."

Her sudden bright smile flashed like a conjured blade. If it was meant to disarm, she'd achieved the exact opposite. "Seren, why are you here? Did you convince them you needed to stay the evening?"

"I did *not* stay here all night. My view is better. Anyway, first things first. I promise, upon my magic, that I mean you no harm in coming today. Can we please have a civil discussion? I need something from you."

"Are you capable of genuine honesty, Seren? Your schemes have dipped so far below board they're practically scratching Hell's floor. I should be calling for your head, but I haven't figured out the play you're making yet."

"Yes." The look she gave Jacob bored into his soul. "I'm afraid that we've come to a point of no return. Your suspicions about the attack on the meeting are correct."

Jacob mused that if she was going to kill him, at least he'd die in his favorite spot. Jacob's fingers curled into the frayed armrest.

A tremor, barely audible, ran through her voice. "The Assembly had to understand that secrecy and silence would doom them. That their children were already fighting this war. I thought... if the hardest hit saw it with their own eyes, the world would finally stand together. *That* would be worth the cost."

Fearing uncontrolled fury, Jacob rose slowly and cautiously in his seat, each movement measured. "You used us to prove a point? For what? Political theater? Here you are again, thinking that the ends justify the means. Another sacrifice that's *worth it*!"

A muscle twitched in her jaw. "None were meant to die this time. Consider what I'm about to say." With a snap of her fingers, Seren created an impenetrable ward of silence around them both. "On my magic, I swear—I am the Morgan le Fay of legend."

First his heart skipped a beat. Then Jacob stared at her, half expecting a punchline.

When one didn't come, he was forced to consider. The Morgan le Fay? Speaking with Finn and even level-headed Miles about their supposed pasts should have prepared him for this level of lunacy, but apparently it had not. There was no grand performance in her voice, only the brittle edge of desperation.

Desperation, Jacob knew, was more dangerous than any lie, especially in the hands of someone like her.

Jacob's first instinct was suspicion. He could see her, of all people, finding a loophole in the oath, but dismissed the notion as impossible. Even with magic ringing in her voice, he doubted the veracity of her statement. Might as well hear what she had to say.

"Go on, then. If I must die dressed in yesterday's clothing, at least tell me something interesting first."

"I'm significantly older than you, so please stop complaining." Seren rolled her eyes. "I already made an oath that I am not here to harm you."

A grunt of sarcastic laughter came from Jacob. "By all means, Lady Le Fay, enlighten me."

Seren's smile curved viciously, her voice dropping into a growl as her civility peeled away to reveal her darker side. "The mockery is unbecoming, Jacob."

Straightening her shoulders, she wiped all expression from her face and returned to her prior topic. "Like Gwyn, I was released from a malevolent prison. Llefelys, *Leon*, that swine was the same. I should have been here to kill that piece of shit, but I am human now and have never been omniscient."

Like Gwyn? Maybe the application of logic, devoid of emotion, would finally break through whatever manipulative game she was playing.

"If you are Morgan le Fay, why do you care about four young people whose supposed pasts seem unconnected to your history except by geography and Gwyn ap Nudd's shenanigans with Knights of the Round Table?"

Seren's answer was immediate, though the words were slowly spoken. "Esmeralda... Elena. Elena was my daughter."

Jacob blinked. The urge to laugh was there, a twitch at the corner of his mouth, but the sadness he saw in her eyes suppressed his ability to give in.

"Why are you telling me this?" Maybe it was the fatigue, but he couldn't fathom the endgame she was aiming for with these lies.

"I need your help."

"...Why?"

"Because magic is out of balance, Jacob. It will come crashing down on all our heads soon if we don't do something about it."

That was a worry he'd secretly held for some months now. The signs were undeniable if you knew where to look. And, unfortunately, Seattle seemed to be ground zero for the problems magic being out of balance was creating.

"Explain," he ordered, nervously clearing his throat.

"So, you've noticed it too... Your assumption about me is correct. I was present for all the recent deaths among the powerful." She began to speak more rapidly. "An overabundance of power concentrated in too few hands, coupled with the sheer amount of time the magic holding the prisons together has been active, has brought us to where we are today—screwed, gaffed, *fucked*! All those words describe our situation."

Jacob's attention sharpened. "Tell me, did your conversation with each of your victims mirror the one we are having now?"

"No!" Seren snapped, her eyes briefly flashing black before settling back into their usual violet. "Unlike you, they weren't granted the privilege of my honesty."

"Did you kill them?"

"If I had, you wouldn't have been able to find their corpses." Seren scoffed. "No, Jacob, our compatriots truly died fighting malevolents. I merely changed the number of boots on the ground so they would be entering a zero-sum game, magically speaking. I ensured that powerful threats on both sides of this war would be taken out each time."

Many unexpected truths had been thrust upon Jacob throughout his life, but this one stood out as both unbelievable and utterly true simultaneously. "Powerful threats? Both sides? *Seren*, what are you saying?"

"I am saying that magic is a force of balance, Jacob. I am saying that *you* are part of the problem. Miles and Abigail are not the only ones with a blessing, old man. You've been walking around with a halo for probably eighty years without realizing it. It's been there so long it's sunk into your aura."

"A... halo?"

"Yes, you have one that reminds me of Merlin's. Which is probably why I find you so incredibly infuriating. You've been following in his footsteps, even if you didn't realize it."

Jacob was momentarily rendered speechless. *Can that be true?*

What did it mean that he carried the aura of a man who was great, yes, but was also a manipulator of kings and a liar with a secret agenda? He had an immediate urge to refute the statement, but a strange sense of certainty settled upon him, making him hold his tongue.

Merlin. The archmage who'd orchestrated Camelot's glory and ruin. Who'd groomed Arthur as both king and sacrifice. A visceral reaction to the comparison seized Jacob as a parade of his choices—lies, the hands forced, and steering his children toward battles they'd never chosen—played out in his mind.

His stomach turned to lead. For eighty years, he'd feared his compromises were carving away at his humanity. If he bore Merlin's halo, maybe it wasn't a blessing at all. It could be a reckoning, the crown on top of every sin he'd buried. Every manipulation, every calculated betrayal, had corrupted his aura and his soul.

Something cold crawled into his chest, because he realized... Bloody hell, he realized he *believed* her. He didn't want to, but he did.

Yet if magic needed balance and he was tipping the scales, then... "Again, what do you need from me?"

"You have successfully shielded Esmeralda from the Assembly's notice for years. I can see how much she cares for you in the way you interact. You've clearly been looking out for her for a while now. For that, I'm grateful. I need you to do one more thing for her, Jacob, for all of them."

His mouth went dry. He already knew the answer. He just needed to hear her say it. "What is that?"

"I need you to die."

Chapter Thirty-Five

A Night for Remembering

Miles

Miles felt his hands, one of flesh, one of silver, run through damp hair slicked with sweat.

Except it was cold. The scalp that should brim with the heat of life beneath his touch wasn't simply cool, it was corpse-cold, a final, unforgiving stillness that made his stomach twist. This time, Nudd was too late.

"You always reminded me of summer. Burning brightly, full of light and hope."

When Nudd opened his eyes, Miles saw that he was cradling a woman's broken body in his arms. Even in his dream, Miles felt a sickening plunge in his stomach. The hair, the armor—it was Elena.

The tilt of the mouth, the faint furrow between her brows. To him, it was also Esme. The same soul, but in a different life.

Gone.

"I should have told you to stay."

Inhabiting the demigod's memory, Miles experienced sorrow that would bring any mortal man to his knees, yet Nudd's immortal flesh felt none of the strain. Nudd's arms remained steady, silver hand unshaking beneath the weight of Elena's broken body. But inside, Nudd was screaming with the part of himself that still remembered what it meant to be human. The part that grieved through clenched muscles and choked breaths.

It was terrifying, utterly inhuman, to feel such devastation while the body that housed it remained unburdened by his grief. While Nudd could weep, as he probably had been for some time, he experienced no physical release from it. Nudd needed to collapse, to fall undone. But this body wouldn't let h im.

This was... torture. Not of the flesh, but of the spirit. Elena's death and the accompanying regrets were too much for a man with no outlet for his grief.

Fuck.

He heard Nudd say, "I should have given up my kingdom years ago. I could have."

Nudd's anguish bled into Miles. It was an almost physical thing, how hard it pressed down on his heart, his lungs, his... everything.

"I could have disappeared with you. I could have shown the same courage Gwyn did with Creiddylad. In so many ways, my son has been a better man than I. I should have taken you as my wife. I should have..."

The pressure was becoming unbearable. He was going to need to take a sedative when he woke up. It would make him a shambling zombie for the rest of the day, but he might be able to function with his nervous system suppressed.

Miles could practically feel the fine hairs on Nudd's neck prickle with a warning right before static charged the air. The magic arrived as a crashing wave, washing away the crushing weight on Miles' soul and replacing it with a sense of foreboding.

The same violet eyes that had haunted the mirror now watched him from a younger face. It was Seren, impossibly young, across the clearing, eyes gleaming with unreadable sorrow. Her eyes seemed to pierce him even from this distance. Yards of gossamer-thin black fabric swathed her body, and jewels glittered on her ears, neck, and fingers.

"Silver hand," she greeted, voice held low for the solemnity of the moment. "I am not here to blame you. I know, knew, her mind. She was as annoyingly stubborn as her mother, as valiant as her father."

Looking closer, Miles could see that Seren's eyes held a somber, watery gleam that spoke of hidden sorrow.

"I am not here to add to your grief. I share in your suffering."

"Morgana." All Nudd managed was her name.

"I know you loved our Elena. And she, you." In a flash, her tone changed from somber to bitterly reproachful. "You're right about what you could have done. A more forthright approach might have given you a happier ending."

Nudd looked back down at his beloved. She was so cold.

"Your son has led her to the threshold." Seren's footsteps were growing closer.

Miles understood that Nudd already knew this, but he remained silent.

"I'm going to get her back." The way Seren spoke made it sound like breaking cosmic rules was as unremarkable as enjoying ice cream for breakfast.

Nudd's head whipped upward, his neck muscles tense. "What?"

"In one stroke, we can get her back and also make your plan to lock all the malevolents away a reality."

She couldn't mean it. Miles braced for Nudd's fury, his refusal. Miles waited for the rigid, uncompromising morality that Nudd had used to build a kingdom. But it didn't come.

Instead, Nudd asked, "How?"

"You have to die. That's the cost."

Nudd stared back down at Elena's too-still face and made a decision. "Please... tell me more."

If Miles had had eyes in the dreamscape, they would be as wide as saucers. He could feel the dark truth that Nudd would rather die than live in a world without her—if only he could.

Nudd Llaw Eraint, the demigod who had forged his legacy on duty, whose name meant Silver-Hand but whose will was iron, was bending.

No, Miles decided. He'd broken the moment her spirit left her body.

Was dying for love noble... or desperate? Miles had been willing to do it once. And now he knew Nudd had made the same decision.

Miles didn't know what unsettled him more: that Nudd would abandon his principles so easily or that Miles understood. Miles almost felt relieved. And that understanding, that quiet, shameful kinship, was what truly shook him. Because if even Nudd could choose love over duty, then maybe Miles wasn't as far gone as he feared. Maybe David hadn't poisoned him irreparably.

Or maybe the foundations of his moral frailty didn't come from outside at all. Maybe Nudd's vulnerability had always been there, lying in wait until he was broken enough to make the weak choice.

Miles jolted awake, lungs convulsing around a sob his human body had tried to release for Nudd but hadn't finished. His body was leaden, each shift under the sheets a painful reminder of the previous day's magical and physical struggle.

Esme was already at his side, one hand pressed to his chest. "Hey, hey, it's okay. You're back." Her voice was quiet, her thumb brushing a small circle over his sternum. "I woke you up because you were thrashing like you were fighting off an entire pack of ghouls in your sleep."

He blinked up at her, the enormity of what he'd witnessed crashing down on him all at once.

"Miles?"

"It was her," he said, breathless.

"Who?" Esme smoothed a lock of hair out of his face. He'd let it grow too long these past few months.

"Seren," he said. Then, with a sickening twist in his gut, "Morgan le Fay."

Her concern vanished, replaced by a bleak alertness he'd seen each time they had walked into a fight with unfavorable odds.

"She was there after Elena died. She came to Nudd. Told him they could get her back. Told him they could create the magic that imprisoned the malevolents."

If Seren was willing to rewrite the world for Elena once, she might do it again—for better or worse.

Esme blinked, a rapid, analytical expression crossing her face as she processed the news. "Shit."

"Exactly." He sat up, swinging his legs over the side of the bed. His head was full of cobwebs, but this was too important to be dragged down by his body screaming out at him to stop. "We need to talk to Gwyn and Abby."

Esme didn't argue. She was already changing her clothes.

"Let's go," she agreed. "Whatever Seren's playing at... Damn it, we're ten steps behind *again*."

"No," he breathed, realizing all at once that he couldn't delay any longer. "Esme... Wait."

She stopped, one foot caught in her trousers, her brow furrowed as she looked over her shoulder. "What is it?"

Miles didn't answer. He moved like a man possessed. He didn't care if he was acting out of clarity or desperation. The weight of eternity had crashed down upon his chest. He just wanted to cling to what gave his life meaning.

His body ached, but he pushed past the pain, stumbling to the safe where he kept his guns. His fingers trembled as he typed in the combination, ignoring the pulsing in his temples and the dull, bone-deep ache in his limbs.

"Miles," Esme said again, worried now, "a gun isn't going to make a bit of difference with Seren."

He couldn't answer. Not until he found what he was looking for: the small, matte navy-blue box hidden behind the foam. His hand closed around it like a drowning man finding a buoy in the middle of the ocean.

He turned, dropping to the floor, not in a fall, but in a purposeful, reverent descent, hand clasped tightly around the box. He moved forward on his knees. It wasn't quite crawling, and it wasn't quite kneeling either. It was somewhere between a bow and moving supplication.

When he reached her, he stopped inches from her legs. Still kneeling, he leaned into her, wrapped his arms around her waist, and buried his face against her stomach. He inhaled deeply—her scent, her warmth, the living proof that she was here and not the cold shell he'd held in the dream.

Alive and *his.*

"Esme," he whispered into her shirt. "I can't live without you."

She froze, allowing him to hold her there. Then her arms came around his shoulders, cradling him. "Mmhmm. I love you too," she said gently, a smile in her voice. "But I thought we were about to go to Abby's. What's up, babe?"

He shook his head against her. "There's never going to be a right time."

If the man who had built his legacy on duty could choose love, what excuse did Miles have left?

His breath hitched. He was shaking with the effort of holding in the need, the love, the *grief.*

He drew back just far enough to shift into the formal position: left knee down, right knee up. The box was in his hand, held out between them like an offering. His prosthesis reached out, fingers artificially steady, and opened it.

The ring inside caught the light.

But his eyes never left hers.

Like the moment when he'd laid himself bare beside her bed that first time, he spoke again. This time, the same reverent truth that had driven his first confession drove his urgency. "You asked me once if you were really my choice or if I was merely following someone else's story. I told you then that he never chose love... but I did. And I still do."

He swallowed hard.

"I didn't know I needed you until you walked into my life. Since then, I've needed you in every way. When I wake up next to you, I remember what it feels like to be a person again. You remind me who I am. You remind me I have a heart that still works. You bring me back from things I didn't think I could survive."

His voice cracked, and he didn't fight it.

"I need your laugh, your rage, your tenderness. I need the way you don't let me retreat into myself. I need the way you see me, not who I'm supposed to be, not who they made me into, but *me*. Just Miles."

He looked up at her then, utterly unguarded. "I want to build a future that's ours, not built on duty, not haunted by the past. I know this world is cruel and uncertain, and I can't promise you safety. But I can promise you *me* as long as I'm breathing. Please, Esme." The last words came out like a prayer. "Let me have you. Will you marry me?"

Her eyes were wide, wet with unshed tears.

Then she laughed, soft and disbelieving, and dropped to her knees in front of him, cupping his face in both hands. She laughed again, the sound somehow both a sob and a wonder to his ears. "Golden boy," she whispered. "You've done it again. That was *so good*."

And she kissed him, fiercely, tenderly, like he was air and water and home and everything she needed to survive.

He melted into her, arms tightening, heart finally releasing a little of the weight he'd carried for too long.

When they broke apart, she grinned through her tears. "Yes. Of course, yes."

Chapter Thirty-Six

Damned Leprechaun

Abby

The sheer amount of illusion magic in the air made Abby want to claw at her eyes. It clung to her skin like static, buzzing just beneath the surface of perception. She hugged her arms tightly across her chest as she and Gwyn moved in silence down the alley behind the Assembly headquarters.

Ahead, a rust-red shipping container yawned open on the building's loading dock. Its paint flaked in long, jagged strips, the metal beneath scarred from time and weather. Beyond, barely visible under the glamours masking them as bored teenagers in neon safety vests, a half-dozen Nisse rattled carts toward the container. Each cart bore a grotesque load: limp, blood-slicked malevolent bodies piled like discarded mannequins.

From a distance, it might've looked like they were hauling out broken office furniture. But up close, the coppery stench made any such delusion impossible.

Finn sat on the only real piece of office furniture in sight. The battered desk chair creaked obnoxiously every time he spun. His feet almost brushed the concrete with each rotation as he whistled a jaunty tune entirely at odds with the carnage around him.

When he finally noticed their approach, Finn popped up, clipboard in hand, and gave a too-cheerful wave. "Well, now. If it isn't one of my favorite descendants. Come to inspect the merchandise, Lady Boardmember?"

"Don't," Abby said, voice low but set to cut. Though Gwyn probably knew it was a futile effort, he placed one warm hand on her shoulder as if trying to calm her.

Finn's smile didn't vanish, but it did lessen in brightness. "Alright, then. I'm bein' ambushed." He folded his arms, expression dimming to something more guarded. "I see you've come to fight. Say your piece on the walk upstairs. I've already spent a lot of magic keepin' this mess contained."

The stairwell was a grim reminder of the battle they'd fought only the day before. Scorch marks lined the walls. Blood had dried in thick, crusted streaks on the floor. Whatever stray malevolents hadn't made it into the conference room, Finn had clearly taken care of himself.

Abby could feel her heartbeat in her fingertips.

At the landing, Finn held the door, but Abby didn't wait. "Gwyn was trapped in a dream this morning," she said. "An *old* one. You were there."

Finn's brow creased. The smirk faded. His gaze darted past them, toward the alley behind, scanning for glamoured ears. His next sigh was long and labored. The past had finally caught up to him.

"You were magically frozen," Abby continued, stepping in close now, her voice beginning to rise, "while Arawn explained that *you* were going to be Gwyn's guide. It seems *we*"—she gestured between herself and Gwyn—"are expected to take on some of his and his wife's work after we *die*!"

She spat the last words like acid.

Finn staggered a half step back, eyes wide, like the news had reached into his chest and sucked away all the air. His hands slackened at his sides, clipboard nearly slipping from his grip.

"Well," he rasped, once he had enough breath, "no use denying it now, is there?"

Finn grimaced. It was an expression that might've passed for sheepish, if not for the fear flickering underneath. "I don't remember any of that. He wiped that memory too."

Abby tapped her foot, trying to rein in her temper.

"Maybe plans have changed, then…" he muttered, more to himself than to them.

But Gwyn closed the distance Finn had created, interrupting his musings. "Arawn erased your memory?"

Finn stiffened, then nodded once. "Aye. Responsible for yours too."

At Gwyn's sudden inhale, Finn's hands flew up in surrender. "Now don't go hurling me into a wall, lad. It wasn't my idea. I had no choice about it!"

Instead of laying into Finn with the vitriol he most certainly wanted to spew, Gwyn turned around on his heel and unleashed a string of Brythonic curses into the air like verbal shrapnel.

Abby stared at Finn. He'd entered their lives only a year before but had changed everything in that short time.

Maybe she didn't know him nearly as well as she'd thought, or maybe she wasn't being fair in holding him to human expectations. Regardless of whether one or both things were true, her voice cracked with the effort of containing the hurt. "Why didn't you tell him?"

More than anything, she was hurt the deepest by his ongoing circumvention of honesty. It came naturally to leprechauns, but he seemed very dedicated to the idea of them being family. Honesty and trust held a family together, yet he kept doing things that went against that.

"Tellin' him who did it wouldn't have changed it," Finn said, shrugging one shoulder. "*And*, as I've already explained *to him*, knowin' about the big man's meddlin' wouldn't have done one lick of good when he and Miles were at each other's throats."

"Why did Arawn do it, then?" she pressed, needing to understand something, *anything*.

Finn tapped the clipboard against his palm. "I don't think his type was supposed to meddle as much as he did. Maybe he did it to cover his tracks. Maybe it was some sort of fecked-up penance to keep the cosmic scales balanced. I don't know."

A rare, fragile guilt, so unlike him, weighed heavily in her grandfather's eyes as he looked back at her. "I've known for a while that I was meant to guide him. I knew I needed him to get his powers back. Anything else..." He shrugged again.

Gwyn, having thoroughly vented his frustrations, seemed far less inclined toward third-degree murder when he rejoined Abby and Finn by the window. The three of them stared down at the container where a Nisse adjusted the illusion in time to make a grotesquely twisted monster arm appear to be the leg of a broken table.

The concrete of the loading bay was suddenly stained with a dark, viscous fluid as a particularly bloated corpse, accidentally dropped by a Nisse, ruptured upon impact. *Gross.*

Abby let out a strained breath. "No more half-truths. How the hell are you this strong?"

Finn blinked. "What, these tiny things?" He flexed unimpressive biceps with a grin. "Strong indeed!"

"Damn it, Finn," she snapped. "You know I meant magically."

"Ah. That." He looked down, scuffing a miraculously pristine shoe against the tile. "I suspect we can blame Arawn, or this one here"—he jerked his thumb at Gwyn—"or even ole Nudd. One of 'em must've juiced me up so I'd survive long enough to do my job. Got the ifrit magic on my own, though. That bit's all me."

The arrogant grin was back on Finn's face.

Mentioning Nudd brought up another one of her questions. "Arawn also said something about Nudd having a scheme in the works. Do you know what it is? Gwyn thinks it's tied to the malevolent prisons."

Finn sobered immediately. "I don't know for certain," he admitted. "But... aye. Wouldn't be shocked if it's all connected. Nudd had a peculiar way of seein' right from wrong sometimes."

There were still two puzzle pieces the dream hadn't explained. "We think whatever Nudd was up to must be why Esme is here too. Gwyn didn't make a deal with Arawn for Elena's soul, only mine."

"Well." Finn seemed genuinely shocked at this news. "That's... new."

Maybe he didn't know as much as she thought. Abby crossed her arms again. "Arawn also said you wouldn't be alone in helping Gwyn. Do you know who else he meant? Please tell me it wasn't Leon."

Finn hesitated for too damn long.

Abby stepped in front of him.

The classic grin that Finn used when he was trying to appear sincere but doing a poor job of it stretched across his face. "Really, I should get back down there and help the lads. You've already seen the mess they've made!"

Gwyn flanked him from the other side, arms folded, posture just short of threatening.

Finn's shoulders slumped. "Fine!" he snapped. "Seren, alright? She's the one who receives word from Arawn."

Receives word?

Abby's eyebrows climbed up her forehead. "What the hell does Morgan le Fay have to do with Gwyn's deal with the king of the Otherworld?"

Before Finn could reply, Abby's phone chimed. She pulled it from her pocket and glanced at the screen. It was a message from Esme. She slowly and deliberately exhaled, calming herself as her brow furrowed while reading.

"Well," Abby muttered. "Seems like the grandpa leprechaun is telling the whole truth after all. Esme and Miles have been asking the same questions."

Gwyn

Gwyn trailed behind Abby, as silent as a ghost, blanket in hand. He pushed open the heavy access door and stepped out into the cool dusk. A soft blur of lavender, orange, and gray painted the sky, clouds trailing like smoke, their edges tinged with the faintest hint of rose. On the rooftop garden, the world felt suspended, like the world had paused to let them catch their breath.

Down below, lights flicked on in windows. A dog barked at a seagull that landed on a porch across the street. Life carried on.

They were sharing a bench, all alone—a rare thing on an evening as perfect as this.

His muscles ached from a day of constant tension, each fiber bound into knots. Feeling her lean into him as he spread the blanket out seemed to unravel half of them at once.

"There should be a limit on the number of people magically dumped into the present," Abby said. "Leon and Seren, I could do without."

Despite their history, a wave of self-doubt washed over him, chilling him as he hesitated to speak. "And me?"

"Oh," Abby said, a bitter laugh escaping her lips, "I'm still upset you didn't tell me about Finn's connection to your past sooner, but I know you only kept quiet because you weren't sure yourself. It's becoming a pattern with you. You really should start talking to me earlier. We *can* figure things out together."

Gwyn pulled her closer, seeking comfort in the press of her skin against his and the soft rhythm of her breathing. "You're right, as always."

Miles was right. Gwyn was an idiot in countless ways.

"So what do you think about Miles proposing to Esme?" Abby nudged him with her elbow lightly. "I can't wait to see you in another suit for the wedding, because he'll definitely ask you to be the best man."

The title "best man" appealed to Gwyn, despite his ignorance of the position's duties. It didn't matter in the end. He'd support his sister in spirit, Esme, and now his friend in truth, Miles, in any way they desired. "I think..."

He struggled to answer Abby's question. How could he find the words? There were no right words for grief that circled around into joy and back to grief again.

His relationship with Miles had finally lost all the rage connected to his father, but in times like this, it was impossible to ignore the fact that Miles was fixing his father's mistakes. Gwyn settled on saying, "I think they'll be very happy together."

Abby chuckled. "Their children are going to be terrifying."

"Utter terrors." Gwyn joined in the laughter. "I can already picture a far-too-grave-mannered toddler, his tiny brow furrowed in displeasure as his five-year-old sister throws a cambion tantrum."

"They're going to expect us to babysit." Tears welled in Abby's eyes as her giggling escalated into unrestrained mirth, her shoulders shaking with each burst. "They'll absolutely use you as a jungle gym and sneak Cerys more treats than Esme already does."

The news of Miles and Esme's engagement, of Seren's connection to the magic imprisoning the malevolents, of his deal with Arawn—it all pointed in one direction: the future. "If I must play nursemaid to the Goodwin children, I cannot think of a better person to do it with."

"Ha! That answer surely has nothing to do with the fact that my magic is specifically designed for control, right?" Abby winked.

A boyish grin spread across his face as he laced his voice with sarcasm. "Not at all."

Calmer now, Abby tucked her head back into his shoulder and asked, "So what now? We get dragged through one lifetime of bullshit. Then we die for real and go work human resources in the Otherworld? What the hell qualifies us for that task, anyway?"

The wind toyed with her hair around his face. The silence stretched. He didn't know the answer. He could feel her gaze flick to his face and away again.

"I don't know," he eventually said. "But I know I'm not doing it without you."

Abby looked at him sidelong. "Because the ghost king told you to?"

"No." His voice was quieter now. "Because I want to. I would suffer another thousand years in that prison for you, Abigail."

Her arm looped around his underneath the blanket and squeezed tighter. "Maybe you did such a good job with the Wild Hunt that he thinks you're ready for a promotion."

She'd said it in a lighthearted way, but he couldn't rule out the possibility. "Though it sounds like you must have been talking with his queen in Annwn, so maybe *your* meddling had something to do with it, *dove*." He mimicked Finn's accent on the final term of endearment.

That made her smile.

"What happens with Esme and Miles?" she asked. "Will we be stuck in Annwn and them somewhere else? What about my family, our other friends?"

Gwyn shook his head, trying to make her understand that he didn't have all the answers. "Something tells me it's only the way we perceive the afterlife that changes things for us. We're all in this world together, sharing the same joys... and sorrows. Why would that shared connection be broken after death?"

"That's a lovely way to think of it," Abby whispered.

"I hope I'm right," he said, giving her a quick squeeze of reassurance.

With a sardonic tilt of her head, she asked, "You know it's like how you said 'death transcends language' all spookily?"

Gwyn let out a small, breathy laugh. "*Spookily*. Now you sound like Esmeralda making up words."

"Hey!" Abby chuckled. "Spookily is a legitimate adverb. You know who is spooky though? Seren. Do you think she had something to do with the horde of malevolents attacking?"

"Yes. I do."

For a long, quiet minute, they sat under their warm fleece blanket, feeling the gentle chill of the evening air as the sun dipped below the horizon, thinking about far too many, far too heavy things.

"Gwyn, what are we going to do about her? If she and Arawn worked with Nudd on the magic that imprisoned the malevolents... What could a flippin' god possibly want now?"

Gwyn rested his head on hers. That Finn knew Gwyn would need his necromancy for something was telling. Whatever came next involved death.

He only hoped it wasn't theirs.

"I don't know, Abigail. Being with you is all that matters to me."

Abby went quiet again. But the subtle shift in her weight as she leaned even further into him reassured Gwyn that she might feel that way too.

The stars were starting to show, blinking lazily through the haze of city lights and clouds.

"Promise me something?" she asked, voice low.

"Anything I can give, I will."

"Promise we will both stay true to ourselves. No matter what the gods want."

They were certain of their values, but their control over their choices was another story.

"I can promise you this: if I have a choice, I've done it for a very good reason."

CHAPTER THIRTY-SEVEN

PREPARATIONS

Jacob

Jacob's eyes didn't leave the photograph in his hand when Maureen stormed into his office. It was of him and Esme on her first day working in the bar. Her smile rivaled the noon sun's brightness, while he had struggled to mask his scowl.

He turned it facedown and tucked it into the desk drawer.

"Alright, old man," Maureen snapped as she slammed the office door behind her hard enough to shake the frame. Her heels stabbed into the Persian rug like accusations. "What the hell's so urgent it couldn't wait until after the damn funeral?"

"Good afternoon to you too, Mrs. Mitchell."

Her dismissive snort echoed in the wood-paneled room. "Yeah, because you summon me the day after a battle because you want niceties. Don't bullshit me. What's going on?"

"Have a seat." He gestured toward the chair across from his desk, then slid the papers toward her. His expression remained neutral. "Your *no bullshit* attitude is exactly why I need you to sign these."

With a pointed avoidance of the papers in front of her, Maureen asked, "Is there going to be an official response to Seren unleashing all those malevolents?"

"No," Jacob answered, his voice tight with barely suppressed anger. "We can't prove it anyway. This is something else. I have to travel again."

With a slight telekinetic push, he inched the papers closer to her.

"Okay," Maureen said, but the word was slow and already too suspicious. She finally seized the papers, read the first line, and then froze in shock. The next page twisted and creased in her grip. By the third, her expression had turned into an angry frown. She slammed the packet onto the desk with the force of a gunshot, sending the crystal paperweight skittering toward the edge.

"Are you sick?" Her tone had become clipped, bordering on a demand, yet still brittle with fear. The faint tremor in her traitorous hands exposed her true feelings. "Or is this simply a reaction to yesterday's events?"

He waved a hand, trying to appear calm. "Maureen, I am one hundred and six years old. You should be more concerned if paperwork like this weren't coming from me."

She leaned forward with a hollow laugh, jabbing a finger at the packet. "You want me to be your estate's executor. I'm touched. Also, *what the actual fuck*, Jacob?"

Jacob gave a long-suffering sigh, aiming for levity, trying and failing to derail the look of panic already forming on her face. "You're just as bad as the active hunters with your language."

"I don't give a damn about my language, Jacob." Though barely audible to his failing ears, her hissed whisper held the power of a scream. "Jon hasn't even been cremated yet. We just lost Sylas. And Philip before that. Now you're handing me funeral instructions and asset allocation documents like this is a catering order for the next meeting?" She shook her head and flicked the papers with one trimmed fingernail. "For fuck's sake."

She was right. There were too many ghosts haunting their recent pasts. But Jacob couldn't bear to add more names to that list without doing something to stop it first.

"Level with me," he finally said, the pleasant expression falling away like a mask he was too tired to wear anymore. "Should I name someone else?"

She didn't answer right away. Instead, she stared at him for a long moment, frustration and grief mixing into bitterness on her face. Finally, she exhaled hard. "No. You know I'll do it, *damn it*. I think you're doing right by the kids with this. I'm only... surprised your golden boy isn't on the list."

"It's easier to grant him my U.K. holdings since he already has citizenship. That's already been taken care of."

"Makes sense..." She hesitated, then added, "You know Esme's going to turn that bar into a circus."

"She manages the whole operation already." With a faint, almost amused shrug, Jacob responded, "Maybe she'll update the place for the better."

Maureen snorted. "Where are you headed?"

He must have taken too long to respond because she accused, "You're hunting something. *Why*?"

He didn't answer but nodded his head once.

"You have lost your damn mind!" She grimaced, suddenly lowering her voice, embarrassed by her outburst. Maureen set her coffee down gently. "Something you think our operatives can't handle or what?"

"A type of wyrm."

"With a 'y'?" Maureen asked slowly. Her mug hit the table a second time, but this time because she'd sputtered coffee all over herself. "As in *dragon* wyrm?" The word cracked, as thin as glass.

"Technically, not a dragon, but yes. Dangerous enough that I won't send anyone else in."

"Jacob, you're too damn old to start parsing technicalities. The papers." She wiped her mouth with the sleeve of her blazer, glaring. "You're going to get yourself killed."

"Possibly," Jacob said, with all the emotion of a man discussing what was for lunch. "But I won't go down alone. Or did you think I was joking about going out in a blaze of glory?"

"No," Maureen sighed. "I guess I knew you weren't joking. Can I go with you?"

"Absolutely not!" His shout rattled the windows. The old fire, the old Jacob, flared in his chest before age doused it again. It faded quickly, replaced by the tired bureaucrat. "I need you here. We have a lot more paperwork to get through, so get comfortable."

The publicly prim and proper hedge fund manager in her fifties, with a secret penchant for profanity, simply looked at him and rolled her eyes. "Fine. If you die, it had better damn well be worth it."

Esme

A dragon emoji blinked on Esme's phone screen. She stared, confused. *What the…?* The message was from Maureen Mitchell, of all people. With her car in the shop, Esme rode shotgun in Miles' car as they left Abby's apartment.

Maureen: *I know your boyfriend and Abby have to work tomorrow, so I got a puddle jumper for you and the zombie-lover to fly to Lake Chelan Airport in the morning. I've been forbidden from going.*

Zombie-lover? She had to be talking about Gwyn. Esme stared at the message. *What the hell?*

Another message pinged in from Maureen: *I can't say in text and I can't call right now either. Suffice to say, I need you two to save one very grouchy old man from getting seriously hurt. Bring everything you need for hunting big game.*

A dragon emoji punctuated the last message. *You've got to be kidding me.*

Esme glanced up from her phone and asked, "Miles, do you *have* to work tomorrow?"

Eyes locked on the road, he replied, "It's procedure day, so yeah."

Damn. Abby was in the same tough situation. She'd dropped her work hours, which meant that she couldn't take off work as easily as she used to. If Esme was right, Maureen was talking about Jacob hunting a malevolent. But the dragon emoji? Weird.

Esme: *I'm in even if the zombie-lover isn't.*

Maureen: *Good. Old man says he's got it, but he's also making me co-sign his will right now. I don't like it. I thought you two being there could tip things in his favor. Don't tell him you're coming or he'll find some way to keep you home!*

Her stomach finally dropped like a stone into the bottom of a very deep well. His will? Gods, what kind of nightmare was Jacob walking into? He was far too old to be hunting malevolents.

Esme: *Will you meet us at the airport in the morning to tell us the situation?*

Maureen: *I can't; it's earnings day. I'll have a sealed letter explaining everything delivered to a flight attendant. Oh, and Esme, I wasn't kidding about the big game thing. Be prepared.*

Esme: *Okay. Thanks for the heads-up.*

She was clutching her phone like a weapon. She finally released it when her hand started to ache. If Jacob thought he could ghost his way into a noble death, he didn't know her at all.

Maureen: *Just... Keep him alive, okay?*

Esme's head fell back against the headrest. She released a shaky, frustrated sigh. "Hey, babe," she said, voice low. "Gwyn and I are flying to Lake Chelan in the morning. Jacob is trying to get himself killed hunting a malevolent."

Miles cursed like a sailor and slammed his foot on the gas.

Gwyn

Gwyn wasn't thrilled to be standing in the drizzle at a small, private airstrip outside the city. His wardrobe had come a long way over the last few months, but he hadn't thought to buy backpacking gear. He'd borrowed from Miles again—and minded less this time.

A glamour disguised his sword as a bedroll and his crossbow as a bear-proof food container. He'd assumed Esme's warning about bears had been a joke—until a quick search on his phone had convinced him otherwise. Part of him almost welcomed the idea. He'd never seen a bear in person, and at least it would be a mundane encounter.

Esme stood beside him, pale and grim in her well-worn hiking jacket, her hair tied back in a rough knot. Dark circles underscored her eyes, and her face was pale, making it clear she hadn't slept. Everything about her attitude that morning was focused, bordering on bleak.

The night before had been illuminating, but nothing prepared him for the sight of their so-called aircraft. Esme had called it a *Cessna*, but to Gwyn, it looked barely larger than the male roc they'd fought only weeks earlier. The idea that it could carry three people and their equipment bordered on absurd. It didn't feel like flight—it was trusting one's life to a tin can with wings. He half expected to fall out of the sky the second they lifted off the ground.

His only prior flight between London and Seattle had required significant self-control for him to not show everyone around him the sheer panic he'd been experiencing.

With characteristic perceptiveness, Esmeralda gave him Maureen's promised missive as a distraction once he was buckled in. Her lips were pressed into a thin line, her fury brewing. Jacob was its eventual target.

As the engine roared and the Cessna lurched down the runway, Gwyn clenched the armrest, fighting the urge to call on magic. His panic wanted to make him crack the plane with lightning, to melt his armrest or seatbelt, anything.

He unfolded the letter. Maureen's familiar, spiky handwriting flowed across the page:

All Jacob told me is that he's fighting a "wyrm." He said it wasn't a dragon, but I call bullshit on that. He said it was making its way toward Seattle and that if he didn't get there by today, it would reach a populated area. He said it was too dangerous to send out any teams. I think he's being overly cautious and I can't understand why. Maybe something about the HQ fight, about Jon's death on top of all the others, finally shook him. I don't know. If you can help it, don't let him die. I'll know you gave it your all, regardless of the outcome. You're a good kid, Esme.

Sincerely, M.M.

Gwyn's sharp intake of breath at the first line was involuntary. A wyrm would be trouble enough. But if it was actually a dragon...

Legends said his father slew two dragons. If that was true, it had happened after his ascension. The ancient beasts had enough raw power to split entire keeps asunder. The stories said that the very air would shudder when a dragon roared, lighting would strike, the mountains would quake.

The giant beasts' deaths were considered epochal events. Alone, Jacob didn't stand a chance against it.

Even together, he couldn't see how they could win. He met Esme's eyes across the narrow cabin. Neither of them needed to speak. A shared understanding flickered in her eyes, confirming that they were thinking likewise.

Gwyn refolded the paper with care, sliding it into his jacket.

He worried about Esme's reaction if they failed. She had become a valued friend, more than a simple ally, much like Elena had in times before. But she was far closer to Jacob than the rest of them. Jacob's death would either strengthen her resolve through the crucible of sorrow or, however momentarily, cause her to fall apart.

We're going to get there in time, he promised himself silently.

By all the magic, he hoped he was right. It didn't take much thinking for Gwyn to realize that his current life, the happiness he'd found, was only possible because the man they were being sent to save had decided to take a chance on him. Jacob had trusted him with dangerous secrets, and when Gwyn had found successes, it had only been because of the people Jacob had brought into his life.

Gwyn couldn't, he *wouldn't*, fail Jacob now.

CHAPTER THIRTY-EIGHT

TWO DRAGONS, GONE

Jacob

Even in spring, the land east of the mountain passes was bone-dry. Dust threatened to cake Jacob's nostrils as he tried to use what little was left of his physical prowess to save on his magical reserves. The rocky landscape presented a challenge, but his staff helped him navigate the rises and drops, the rhythmic *tap-tap-tap* of the stick his only companion.

The shade of the pine trees only did so much to prevent the sun from sapping his strength. He pulled the hood of his robe up to help, but the robes were mostly theater. They were fitting for a man staging his own exit, should Seren get her way.

The wyrm's trail was easy enough to find. He'd accessed drone footage, then rented an all-terrain vehicle to get him most of the way to its nest. From the air, he'd searched for oddly patterned burned or downed trees. On the ground, he'd scanned for trails of magic and hunted for deep gouges in the soil. The beast hadn't bothered to hide its passage. He had quickly found footprints that crushed saplings like matchsticks.

He'd abandoned the ATV, choosing instead to meet the creature on foot since the ATV's noise would alert the creature of his arrival even before his magic did and Jacob didn't want it flying off before he had a chance at it. Jacob wasn't here to escape. He was here to end this, even if it meant trading his life for those who still had a long road ahead of them.

Staff punching into the brittle earth, he crested a low rise. It was the perfect spot to survey the landscape ahead. Before him lay a scatter of sunbaked boulders, their light-colored stone speckled with the dry soil. He was turning to go back to the ATV, thinking of using it to skirt the rocky area, when the largest of the boulders moved.

The dry dirt covering what he'd assumed to be boulders fell away with a soft crumbling sound, revealing something darker beneath.

It was scales. Where the scales were weathered and scarred, they were a storm-cloud gray. The rest were obsidian, so dark they almost seemed to absorb the light.

A massive form uncoiled itself with a terrible grinding sound that reminded Jacob of sandpaper rubbing on glass. A single, slit-pupiled eye, yellow encircling black, snapped open, its burning glare fixating on him directly.

Seren's report had been wrong. Maureen's guess, right. This was a *dragon*, not a smaller wyrm.

Whether Seren's misreporting was intentional was no longer of any consequence. Because with a roar that cracked the air itself, the dragon surged upward on two massive wings. The air shifted around it, blasting Jacob with a spray of dust. Then thousands of pounds of muscle and ancient fury lunged.

Jacob barely had time to react.

He slammed the butt of his staff into the ground, pushing energy into the earth. A column of stone erupted from beneath the creature, throwing it sideways as it barreled toward him through the air.

Next was an aegis around himself. The shield blossomed to life as the dragon's tail lashed forward in retaliation. It slammed into Jacob's shield like a battering ram. Even the air cracked with the impact. His aegis held, but only barely. He was hurled backward like a rag doll.

He hit the rocky slope hard. His staff clattered away. He tumbled down the incline, limbs twisting, robes tangling. A jagged stone tore through his side with a wet ripping noise that stopped his breath in his throat.

White-hot pain ripped through him, burning its way along nerve and bone until there was no breath in his trembling body. He rolled to a stop in a cloud of dust, the gritty particles stinging his eyes.

For a moment, everything went still except the ringing in his ears.

He tried to sit up. Pain lanced through his torso like claws. His side was soaked. The robes clung to him, sticking to the gash. When he touched it, his fingers came away slick with dark red blood and smelling of too many violent memories.

Age had turned his skin to paper, and the rock had torn through it. But it had gone deeper than that. It had penetrated through the muscle, through the membrane that held everything together inside. He could feel it in the hollow way his body moved now, like something fundamental had come undone.

He'd seen wounds like this before. *Inflicted* them, too.

If he were fifty years younger, with an emergency evacuation already on the way, he might have a chance. But *no*, not now. Even if Miles had been here, he'd have no chance.

His left hand was shaking. His right recalled his staff with a flick of telekinesis.

With a low growl that vibrated through the very ground, the dragon stalked toward him on four legs. Jacob gritted his teeth against the pain and forced himself to his feet.

Only subtlety and cunning remained. Magic coursed through his body, granting it the ability to *move* through the pain. If he burnt out, at least he would do so fighting.

Without a sound, he split himself into four. Three false images of himself darted across the stony ground in different directions, and he followed but more slowly. The dragon roared, its huge claw scattering the illusions as easily as smoke.

Jacob seized the distraction. He thrust his staff down and called up a wall of wind, thick with the displaced dust and grit. The dragon snapped its jaws, flinching away, but only briefly. It shook its head, smoke curling from its nostrils.

He didn't need the staff to call up the magic, but it helped him focus, helped him mold his will into purpose. With a forceful push, he planted his staff and drove the magic deep into the ground for a second time. Sharp gray stones and brittle, half-dead pine roots, gnarled and stubborn, heaved upward. The roots scratched against the dragon's scales as they wrapped its limbs and wings in a vicious snare.

The beast thrashed, sending chunks of dirt and shattered roots flying. The bindings gave way with an ugly crack.

The old sorcerer staggered back, leaning hard on his staff, sweat and dust stinging his eyes. The afternoon sun beat down, merciless.

A shout in a familiar voice.

No.

Jacob's head snapped up. Across the broken ground, he saw them. Esme, eyes already burning with brimstone as she summoned her minions, and Gwyn with a crossbow drawn, moving wide to flank.

The dragon turned, its interest drawn by the sudden appearance of new prey. Jacob's heart dropped. This was exactly what he had feared. In his haste to protect them, he'd failed to keep them away.

Jacob hadn't planned to survive. But he *had* planned to keep them safe. He couldn't... he couldn't protect them like *this*.

A wave of nausea and anger, the torment of their presence, finally broke through, forcing words from his lips. "Not them," Jacob breathed.

Blood ran down his side in steady rivers. There was no strength left in his body for finesse, only the brute force of his magic.

Jacob drove his staff into the ground one last time, summoning every last spark he had left—not for glory, but to burn a hole through death itself.

For them. For Esme's stubborn brilliance and fire. For Gwyn's impossible loyalty. For the ones they loved. For the ones he'd miss.

Let me be the one who falls. Not them. The yell that tore from his throat was raw and broken.

The sky cracked open. A bolt of blue-white fire lanced down from the heavens, so bright it was blinding, searing the pattern onto his retinas. It struck the dragon squarely between its shoulders.

The creature let out a deafening roar, a sound like the tearing of the world. The collapsing dragon shook the ground as it hurtled forward another twenty yards before collapsing in a smoldering heap, the acrid smell of burning flesh filling the air.

Jacob sagged, the staff the only thing holding him up. The lack of magic left him feeling hollow, while the loss of blood caused a chilling weakness to spread through his limbs. The taste of copper filled Jacob's mouth.

His knees hit the rocky ground. Through ringing ears, he heard Esme and Gwyn running toward him, watched the sky wheel overhead in dizzying circles.

Through the dust, he saw Esme, alive, and Gwyn, steady beside her.

Good, he thought. That was enough for him. A defiant grin stretched across Jacob Spencer's face as he crumpled to the earth.

Esme

The sounds of two titans impossible to ignore reached them first. Roars that didn't belong to anything natural shook the trees, and shockwaves of wind and debris rattled every branch. Esme's lungs burned as she ran, feet pounding the earth, heart hammering like it was trying to outrun her.

She *knew* something was wrong.

Esme muttered a string of curses, again and again, breath ragged, as she and Gwyn sprinted even faster. A faraway shout destroyed her fragile hope that they weren't too late.

They burst from the trees in time to see Jacob atop the ridge. He was holding on to his staff like it was the only thing keeping him upright. With his long, flowing robes, he looked like a sorcerer from a forgotten age. He seemed impossibly old yet impossibly strong, like a relic of the past, like a guardian, *her* guardian.

For a heartbeat, Esme's mind lied to her. Jacob wasn't up there. That was some random sorcerer who'd stumbled into a battle too big for him. The real Jacob was back in his library, sitting in his ratty recliner, scowling at his tea gone cold.

But then the wind shifted, carrying the scent of blood. The lie shattered.

That was him. He was ragged, bleeding, and somehow still standing against a massive, black-scaled, furious *dragon*.

Then everything changed.

A spear of scalding fire lanced down from the heavens, whiting out Esme's vision and almost burning her skin from the heat even at a distance. Molten glass and scorching dirt erupted from the inferno, showering the air with fiery debris. Esme threw herself low, arms up to shield her head as shrapnel, dust, and rock rained down, the roar swallowing her scream.

When the storm cleared, the dragon was a crumpled, smoking ruin. Her ears were ringing from the deafening sound. And Jacob...

Jacob was crumpled on the ground, as though the fire he'd unleashed had burned his magic out like a snuffed candle.

Jacob had never been small. He was larger than life, a sharp-tongued force of nature in black robes. But now he lay broken. His staff was splintered beside him, more shattered than him.

"No," Esme choked out, the sound jagged as she bolted toward him.

She fell to her knees beside him so hard the dry earth bruised her. Her hands shook as she reached out, not knowing where to touch, afraid even contact might break what was left of the man who had stood between them and so much danger.

"Jacob," she gasped, the ringing in her ears subsiding.

He greeted her with a weak smile and a shaky laugh. "Darling," he rasped, his lips stained with blood. "Happy... to see you."

The way he said it destroyed her. Like seeing her was the victory, not slaying a beast of epic legend. Like seeing her there beside him was enough.

"Jacob, no." Her voice came out as a whine. Tears blurred her vision. She touched his shoulder, then his chest, then his hand, trying to hold him to the world by sheer force of will. His robes were soaked in blood.

He forced a crooked grin, intractable even now. Though his voice was rough, it also had a lightness to it. "Too stubborn... to die in bed," he whispered. "Got what I wanted... you safe. That's all I ever needed."

"No," she said. "This isn't goodbye."

"You're my granddaughter... in every way that counts, Esme." His eyes grew soft.

His hand in hers trembled, rough with calluses from holding everyone around him up for two lifetimes.

"Make my tale sound grand for my Brothers?"

Tears slipped free, burning down her cheeks. She nodded. Jacob had taught her to be selfless, like him.

What she wanted to say was, "Don't go. Stay. I still need you." But she swallowed the words, let them burn like his fire in her throat, and gripped his hand harder.

He smiled again as his hand twitched toward her face. She caught it and pressed it against her cheek like she could transfer life between them through skin and stubbornness.

His skin was too cold.

Gwyn hovered at her shoulder, silent, his mouth drawn tight in helplessness, eyes half-lidded in misery. His fists were clenched so tightly that blood seeped from his palms.

"You were the one who taught me not to be afraid of my magic," she whispered. "You made me stop hiding and gave me a life bigger than I'd ever imagined for myself. You stayed when everyone else left."

She wanted to say more. A torrent of words built in her chest, but her voice caught in her throat as she saw the unshed tears in his eyes. This was *his* time for words.

Jacob's eyes shone with a flicker of hope and a lot of pride. "Live big..." he breathed. "Make a fuss."

"I will," she said, even though her throat burned.

"You brighten everyone's life... especially mine."

His hand squeezed hers once. Then released. His body sagged against her.

And Jacob's last breath left him with a soft, defiant laugh.

Something inside her cracked. Not big and loud like usual. Not like shattered glass. She broke quietly this time, like the changing of seasons, slowly and with no ceremony.

It settled into her joints, her lungs, into the hollow of her throat, until even breathing felt like a betrayal. How could she when his breath had stopped?

She wanted to scream. To rip the trees out of the ground. To claw time backward until he was whole again, until he was grumbling about her manners, grunting in displeasure at her recklessness—*alive.*

Esme pressed his hand against her face again, wanting to will his spirit back into his body. She breathed through the shudder that wracked her chest, hoping against hope that sheer stubbornness could turn the tide.

Gwyn kneeled beside her, eyes locked on Jacob's still form. He reached for Jacob's shoulder, then stopped halfway and dropped back to his side like a stone. A tremor wracked his body before his hand hovered in the air and slowly closed Jacob's eyes.

"He saved us," he said softly.

But Esme couldn't answer. Her voice was gone. Her grief was too large for words. Her thoughts were scattered. All she could feel was the hollowed-out place where Jacob used to be. A silence too big for this dry forest to contain.

The world fell painfully quiet around her. He didn't give any political commentary. Nor was there a sigh when she did something impulsive like hug him again. Only... silence.

She stared at his shattered staff, the one he'd carried to remind himself of the heavy cost of his sins. How could he have thought that they still dragged him down when he'd given his *entire life* to protecting the people around him? He'd never married. His entire family was gone. He'd devoted all his time to the community.

Esme realized Gwyn was right. Jacob hadn't meant to survive this. She knew it with a cold, terrible certainty. Every step he'd taken, every drop of magic he'd poured into that final strike, had been meant to ensure that they lived.

He chose this.

She'd been so used to him always being there, as steady as stone. He'd be ready with sarcasm, patience, or fury, whichever the moment required. He was her constant—always the one who stood up for her. Who taught her that her fire wasn't something to be ashamed of. That she could be dangerous and *good* at the same time.

And now he was just—gone. His laugh. His lectures. His support. The way he'd always known when to push her, sometimes too far, but had always been there to hold her hand.

Something inside Esme folded up, making itself smaller and dimmer until it was a tight knot. She thought it would never quite unfold again.

Her world had been reduced. She was smaller in it now. And so much colder without him.

When the time came, when the world stopped spinning quite so violently, she would tell the tale to his Brothers. They would know all the things he had done to protect them for so long.

Esme had made her decision. At least until something changed, she would keep the secret of the malevolents locked away. Because Esme realized now more than ever that he was right. Had her grief not left her so empty, the fury she felt at fate's cruelty would have transformed her into something far more terrible than a malevolent.

Chapter Thirty-Nine

GRIEF

Miles

Esme didn't leave their bed for three days. Miles didn't blame her, not when he could barely function himself. The starched crispness of his white coat had felt like a suffocating shroud the Tuesday morning after his death. Against every screaming instinct to stay, he dragged himself to work, leaving her alone with only Lily curled at her side for comfort.

When he arrived home early that afternoon, deciding to do his charting work at home, she hadn't eaten or brushed her hair. Esme had suppressed all emotion—a dam holding back a torrent of feelings she couldn't, or wouldn't, unleash. Miles saw it in her eyes—the dullness, the snuffed-out light—and knew, with a bone-deep certainty, that Jacob's death had broken something inside her.

By Thursday morning, Gwyn had all but dragged Abby through the door, forcing them both to grieve *with* someone instead of simply for someone. Their togetherness at least got both friends to drink coffee and cry.

But last night he'd seen the first light of hope that she was slowly emerging from the depression stage and into gloomy acceptance.

He'd tried to get her to eat for days with little success. Miles wasn't faring much better himself in that area. But last night he'd had her favorite teriyaki delivered.

Most people would see what she'd done as a red flag. But Miles knew better.

He'd long ago accepted that he was hopelessly in love with a Nergalian cambion woman. She felt things intensely. When her emotions got big enough, they detonated. Even at her worst, Esme was careful not to hurt anyone. She always contained her fury. It was part of what made her so terrifying.

He left the food with her in the living room where she'd been camping out since Abby had come over. About ten minutes after he'd returned to his desk, the silence shattered, literally. First came a low, feral growl, then the unmistakable crack of glass exploding against the wall. The sound of liquid splashing. And finally, something skidded across the floor.

"Fudge-cakes! Shit... sorry, babe!"

He burst out of the office to find her crouched beside a spray of glass shards, eyes full of tears, breathing ragged. The glass had missed the television by inches. Its jagged remains glittered across the floor.

She was trying to scoop them up with her bare hands, oblivious to the blood welling at her fingertips.

"Esme!" His voice snapped sharper than he'd intended. "Drop it before I have to dig glass out of your hands."

She froze. "I'm sorry, I—"

"I know," he said more gently, crossing to her. He flicked the shards away with telekinesis, gathered the shards into a floating cloud, and guided them safely to the trash bin.

"I'm sorry…" she whispered again. With a rush, she closed the space between them. Her scent filled his senses as she sought comfort in his arms.

Miles didn't care about the glass, or the mess, or the rage. It was the first sign that the numbness overtaking her had finally snapped.

Damn the glass. It didn't need to be whole. *She did.*

They needed to get to the Assembly headquarters to meet Maureen in only forty-five minutes. More than half of that would be spent driving this time of day. He wanted to give her a bit more time to push away the world, to feel what she needed to feel so she could process her loss, but they truly couldn't wait any longer.

"Lovely." He warmed his prosthesis so his touch would at least feel pleasant for her, not like the cold metal it was. "We have to be at headquarters soon. Let me help you get dressed. I think seeing you would really help Maureen right now. She's grieving too."

Esme wiped at her face and nodded. "And she's known Jacob way longer than I have."

"It's not a competition." He caressed her shoulder with a veneer of happiness on his face. "But I think hearing that she's won something with you would put a smile on her face."

His clumsy attempt at levity landed better than he'd dared hope. Esme didn't quite laugh, but she did let out a huff of air that was the precursor to one.

"Can I wear one of your hoodies?" she asked, her voice barely a whisper in the quiet room.

"I, uh..." He chuckled. "Didn't know I owned any at this point. I thought they were all yours now."

"Jacob would've picked the Oxford one."

Six soft words—and his heart cracked open all over again.

Once she was out of sight, Miles braced himself on the counter, breathing through his nose like he could will his emotions back. He rubbed at his eyes with the back of his prosthetic. The metal was still warm.

By the time she was back, he'd recovered. Miles helped her pull it over her head, careful not to comment when she breathed in the fabric like it could bring Jacob back.

Esme

Esme shifted uncomfortably in her seat across from Maureen at the Assembly headquarters.

Logically, Esme had understood Jacob's life had been nearing its natural end. His complaining about aches and pains had reminded her of that fact on too many occasions to count. Logic should have made it easier. In some ways, it did. But logic couldn't erase the fact that she had lost another member of her found family so soon after the last.

Maureen grunted in a way that suggested an apology. "Good. Now that we're done with the easy part, let's talk about the hard stuff."

Maureen methodically stirred a packet of creamer into her mug, though she hadn't taken a sip since they'd arrived. Instead of her usual pastel power suit, she wore nearly the same outfit as the one Esme had shown up in. Her bare face, devoid of makeup, and the deep shadows under her eyes spoke of shared suffering and sleepless nights. Maureen wore her grief like armor. With it on, she was flawless, unshaken, except for the tremor in her hand that betrayed everything beneath.

The easy part? If listing every piece of Jacob's life like an inventory was easy, Esme didn't want to see the hard part. Every single line was one more nail in Jacob's coffin.

Esme's disgust must have shown on her face, because Maureen snapped. "At least he was smart enough not to leave you the house. He knew you wouldn't want it."

That was true.

Maureen added, "That's being sold and 'donated' to the Corded Brotherhood's fund. How else do you think we pay our agents?"

A horrible pressure built in her chest. For a second, her vision darkened from fury. She didn't care what was happening to the house. Supporting the Brotherhood was Jacob's life's work, damn it.

Esme blinked hard. Nope, nope, nope. She could not let this happen, here, now, while Maureen was trying to help. And, really, it *was* stupid of her to never wonder where the money for the Brotherhood came from.

Esme's head was spinning. The bar. The stocks. The six-figure sums. Jacob's legacy was being dumped into her lap like ash from an urn.

Miles wasn't doing much better. With a new house in London and a trust fund to maintain it, he had just as much to consider.

Shaking herself free of the spiral, Esme said, "You're right. I'm sorry, Maureen. We're going through the same thing. What's the hard part?"

Maureen settled back in her chair, her old curt demeanor returning. "I've looked through all the Brotherhood communiques. I can't for the life of me find any message about wyrms, dragons, nothing of the sort. Where did Jacob get his tip?"

A sliver of ice slid down Esme's spine. "What do you mean?"

"He barely left his library or either of his offices, Esme. I have access to all Brotherhood communication. *No one* reported a large malevolent. He certainly didn't tell me anything before he left."

A tip from a stranger? From an unlogged Brotherhood contact? A rogue agent? This reeked of intent.

The coffee in Esme's stomach churned to acid as the puzzle pieces snapped into place. The timing couldn't be a coincidence.

"It was Seren," she whispered.

Seren—whom Jacob had accused of every suspicious death for months. Seren, who had vanished without a trace after the malevolent attack down the hall. Seren, who seemed to have a plan for gods damned everything.

The floor didn't actually shift, but her insides did a sickening flip, a disorienting sideways lurch that made the room feel as though it were listing violently.

"Maybe," Maureen said carefully, but Esme could see in her eyes that she'd already considered it.

The grief that had frozen her since finding him bleeding out now crystallized into something edged like a blade.

"They've disagreed since day one." Her voice came out steadier than it felt. "She questioned each of us about his fitness to lead." Her fists clenched. "She said she didn't want Seattle, but was that the truth?"

"Seren couldn't have Seattle if she wanted it." With his usual calm, Miles placed a comforting hand on Esme's leg and said, "There has to be something else at work here."

"What?" Tears pricked at her eyes.

"She sure as fuck won't tell me," Maureen scoffed. "Until a new Bastion is elected, I'll be busy managing everything here."

And just like that, Esme knew what she had to do. Her grief finally had direction, and gods damn it, her grief had fangs.

"She'll talk to me." Esme's fist cracked down on the desk like a gavel. For one startled second, she thought she might've broken it—or herself. Miles' hand on her thigh tightened.

Whatever waited on the other side of her confrontation with Seren would change everything, but she couldn't turn back now. Jacob deserved better than that from her, as did everyone who cared for him.

If she let herself stop—only for a second—she'd remember the way Jacob smiled at her when he brought her a mug of peppermint tea, or the warmth of his voice when he called her "devilish girl." She couldn't afford it now. More grief would come later. Right now, she needed answers.

CHAPTER FORTY

TRUTH BOMBS FLYING

Esme

Esme hesitated, her fist raised midair, knuckles inches from the door. Simmering anger over yesterday's revelation warred with a deep-seated dread in her gut. She'd come seeking answers, but she feared the truth. If Seren had nothing to do with Jacob's death, that would be a relief. But if she did...

Esme would probably spend the rest of her life in misery because she couldn't do a damned thing to get vengeance on Seren.

At best, Seren would be annoyed at her early arrival, and Esme might get to vent some of the frustration that had built up since meeting with Maureen the day before. It was a juvenile, petty thing to think, but Esme figured she deserved some answers from the woman who had inserted herself in the center of their lives without permission.

As soon as that thought hit, Esme reconsidered. Had Seren wrongly inserted herself? Maybe Gwyn was right. Maybe something older and darker was pulling them all together like threads through a needle, ready to be embroidered onto the fabric of the tiny slice of history they occupied together. And maybe Seren had simply seen it coming first.

Screw it, she'd take Miles' lead and be reasonable. Lately, cooperation had yielded her better results than confrontation anyway.

As her knuckles were about to make contact with the wood of the door, it opened wide. Esme's momentum carried her forward—straight into Seren's hastily conjured aegis. The shimmering magic was the only thing that stopped Esme's fist from making contact with Seren's face.

Esme stumbled back. "Shit, sorry."

Seren's lips quirked. "*Bonjour,* Esmeralda. Come, come in."

Esme only noticed then that Seren was attired in a relaxed, loose-knit lounging ensemble, black, of course, but something one wouldn't greet a stranger in because it was basically pajamas. Her hair was pulled back into a floppy bun and she wasn't wearing a speck of jewelry.

Esme wasn't dressed much better; she was wearing a pair of stretchy leggings and another one of Miles' hoodies.

Showing her to the sitting area, Seren said, "You have a mouthful ready for me. Think about it while I make us some *café.*"

The air was too still, like even the room had been waiting for a confrontation.

Leaving to fetch the coffee, Seren mumbled incoherently in French, a low, almost persecuted-sounding murmur that was unintelligible to Esme. Given Seren's uncharacteristic show of pique, Esme was glad she had decided against fighting. While Seren worked in the kitchen, Esme snooped with her eyes.

The view of Seattle and Puget Sound was breathtaking from the thirty-seventh floor.

But Seren was a bit of a slob. The penthouse looked as if a hurricane had swept through—silk blouses draped over chair backs like fallen flags, jeweled hairpins scattered across the coffee table like shrapnel. A half-eaten croissant languished beside a half-drunk bottle of wine.

This wasn't simply a mess. This was the detritus of someone who hadn't slept in days. Either Seren had gone into full hermit-mode, not letting her cleaner in, or she really was this messy on the inside, regardless of how put together her facade seemed.

A minute later, Seren came back in carrying a breakfast tray with croissants and two lattes. As she placed the tray down, a quiet apology escaped her lips. She gathered the dirty dishes before taking them to the kitchen. She sat, movements stiff with tension, and slowly, cautiously, lifted her mug to her lips.

"Alright, Esmeralda." Seren set her mug on the windowsill with a soft clink. "Go on. I can take it."

"Before I go into the topic we both know I want to talk about, did you conjure a giant cobra to fight the wendigo? Or was I hallucinating?"

"No hallucination," Seren said, shooting her a sideways glance, eyes glinting. "But let's not pretend you didn't expect something weird from me."

Esme noted that she hadn't answered her question. But really, she'd only asked because it had been bugging her for weeks and it seemed like a good way to get Seren off the defensive.

"Let's be straight with each other." Esme tried for composed. But her movements were too sluggish, her voice little more than a monotone drone, sapped from grief, unable to convey exactly how *much* she felt in that moment. "I've known for a few months that I might have a bit of Elena in here somewhere. I know how you're connected to me slash her now, thanks to that demon monkey."

"Kiokusaru," Seren corrected gently.

"Whatever." Esme crossed her arms across her chest tightly. "You know about Miles. I'm guessing you already know who Gwyn and Abby are."

While Esme talked, Seren sank into the seat with the weariness of someone much older than she appeared. "Yes."

"But do you know that Gwyn's memory"—Esme gestured vaguely at her head—"is more than half gone? He doesn't remember you at all. Miles has had a few dreams with Morgan le Fay in them, but nothing substantial."

Seren clearly wasn't expecting Esme to show up at her apartment and be reasonable. She visibly flinched when Esme relaxed into her seat, smirking the whole time.

Esme asked, "Please, we, I, want to know about your life... before."

"You want to know why I'm a monster," Seren said, once again half hiding behind her mug.

"Nah," Esme snorted, a puff of air escaping her nostrils—a gesture that seemed to amuse Seren, judging by her sudden grin. "Abby was adamant that history has been unfair to Morgan le Fay. I want to hear your version."

Seren's eyes flickered with false coyness as she teased, "Warming me up before you stick in the knife?"

"Something to that effect," Esme replied, with a chill back in her voice, though the latte had already begun to warm her from the inside, making her more receptive to the conversation.

Seren mused to herself quietly, "So it must not be only genetic, like these modern-day scientists say." Then, louder, she said,

"My life didn't begin with betrayal." This was tinged with a hint of emotion Esme knew too well. What Seren was describing began with anger at the wrongs committed by the universe. Then slowly that anger simmered down to bitterness, only to resolve into the worst heartache.

"Once, a long time ago, I was nothing more than a girl with too much magic. Thanks to my gifts, I was given to a mentor who loved and nurtured me as her own. She was the greatest luck of my early life."

"You were adopted?" Was this a parallel between Elena and Morgan le Fay?

"Not really." Seren made a gentle, slightly dismissive wave of one hand. "Fostered is what I would call it. Common in those days. I'd already met Elena's father and Merlin by the time my mentor... died," Seren said haltingly. "And you... Well, Elena," Seren corrected, a faint, almost mournful smile playing on her lips, "came before the courts and betrayals and battlefields."

Esme shifted in her seat uncomfortably. Seren speaking about ghosts only made her life, Esme's very existence, all the more poignant and unsettling. "Who was Elena's father?"

"His name was Lancelot."

Gods above and be-fucking-low. The name detonated in her skull. Esme lowered her cup as if it might explode in her hands. Lancelot, the golden traitor, the man who had shattered Camelot.

Seren watched her over the rim of her mug, eyes dark with something perilously close to pity. "Not a legend yet. Only a man. Just... mine." She sipped her latte. "Until he wasn't." Her eyes betrayed a hint of sorrow and something else, something... bitter. "The stories get that wrong too. I abandoned him as much as he abandoned me. My mentor also died while I was pregnant. And Merlin sort of... took over her role in some ways. He promised me we could change everything if we worked together. For a time, I believed him." Regret settled over Seren's features like a storm cloud, casting a shadow across her face and in her eyes.

"Why did you give Elena up?"

"You already know the bones of the prophecy from my memory. If I didn't give my baby girl up, I thought I would bring about the end of magic."

Outside, a siren wailed down the wet Seattle street, but the sound barely registered to Esme's ears. Her rage faltered as understanding crept in. The truth wasn't easier than a lie. It just hurt cleaner. But she had come seeking understanding, not reconciliation. So she said nothing.

"Turns out we were fools. We were wrong about the prophecy all along." Her voice fell as if centuries of secrets trailed behind the confession. "Or maybe it was always going to happen. We were blind to the fact that the magic it spoke of was malevolent magic being contained by our own hands, not magic itself."

Seren's gaze dropped to the table where her croissant sat uneaten. "I could have kept Elena, it seems. So maybe I *am* a monster."

A long moment passed as Esme stared. The wall of her anger she'd built for this meeting was forming larger fractures.

All those centuries... Seren's sacrifices... How many lives, spanning over how many thousands of years, had been shaped by one mother's painful decision?

If Seren hadn't misinterpreted those words, *Esme* wouldn't exist. Neither Miles nor Abby—even Gwyn would be dead, given that all ascended beings were probably dead or hiding—no one really knew.

Seren set her mug down. "I appreciate Abigail's perspective on my story. She is right. It was easy for them to make me the villain. I was a mother who abandoned her child, though that's absent from the history now. I was a sorceress who betrayed the shining dream of Camelot. They made me into everything they needed me to be so they wouldn't have to look at their own failings." Seren leaned forward as the fire returned to her voice. "I fought for what mattered. I lied, I killed, I survived. Because nobody else was going to save us."

"Save us from what?" Though Esme thought the answer was going to be a good one. Some stubborn, stupidly desperate part of her wanted to believe there was a simple villain to hate, but more and more she was seeing that wasn't the case.

"From the malevolents. From ourselves most of all."

"How are you going to save us now?"

It was Seren's turn to give Esme a long, searching look. The serpent tattoo on Seren's neck seemed to stir, uncoiling slightly as if waking up from a nap. It stretched itself up her neck. When its head moved closer to her ear, she leaned into it slightly, as if listening.

As intrigued as Esme was by the tattoo, she had to admit that particular gesture was a little unnerving.

Instead of answering Esme's question, Seren asked, "If someone you cared about was in danger, what sin would you not commit to save them?"

Esme knew her answer was nearly the same as Morgan's had been.

At long last, Seren reclined, the weariness evident in the slump of her shoulders and the shadows under her eyes, yet her expression remained undefeated. "The world paints us as monsters because it's easier than seeing the truth. But I'm here.

I'm still trying. And gods help me, I see something good left in the world when I look at you."

Seren's words made it so hard to be cold, but Esme had to know the truth. "Then why didn't you kill the dragon yourself, since you knew about it?" Esme turned her face away, blinking fast to clear the emotion.

"He made a choice. He understood his role in the situation," Seren explained, circling her finger like a planet orbiting a sun.

Jacob's voice: *Too stubborn... to die in bed.*

Could it be true?

"What fucking situation, Seren?" Esme's old anger flared up once more, though she tried to stuff it down. "What could possibly justify Jacob getting himself killed that way?"

"You," Seren whispered, lips forming a tight line.

The word landed in Esme's chest like an arrow with a sudden searing pain. It lodged itself next to all the other shrapnel the past year had embedded there. She couldn't breathe—

"All of you, even that infernal leprechaun!" Seren's mug trembled as she spoke. "To protect you."

"What?" Esme asked weakly. "The dragon was nowhere near Seattle. I wasn't in danger."

"It was on its way. But it's about more than the dragon, Esmeralda. You already know that I helped create the magic that imprisoned all the malevolents. You already know that Nudd helped me."

Esme wasn't sure how Seren knew that the truth had been revealed to them, but she suspected it involved that snake somehow.

Breathing heavily, Seren clutched her mug so fiercely it seemed ready to crack. "Do you know what imprisoning them *cost* us?"

"Of course I don't," Esme snapped. "We haven't gotten straight answers since all of this started!"

Seren kept her voice low enough for it not to travel between floors, but rage clearly vibrated in it. "We had to change the balance of magic. It wasn't a small thing. Hundreds of us had to give up every single ounce of our power to make it happen. The demigods? The magic had to be so great that they had to *kill themselves* to achieve it, Esmeralda. Your Nudd was one of them."

Esme was struck speechless.

"And I had to watch the whole bloody affair. I endured centuries of imprisonment, all so I could fix the magic when it broke again! You were the only thing I got out of this deal, Esmeralda. The only thing Nudd got!"

Seren had bargained for her soul...

A lump formed in Esme's throat, making it hard to swallow or speak. Esme nervously smoothed out her napkin and took a tentative sip of her latte, hoping its warmth could ease some of the constriction in her chest. It didn't, so she abandoned her drink.

"What does that mean, Seren?" she managed, the words tasting like regret already. "And Jacob?" Esme breathed. "Did he..."

"Not like the ascended." Seren waved a hand, dismissing the idea, not unkindly. "I didn't tell him about the dragon with the intention of killing him. Jacob made a choice knowing what his death would buy us if it came to it. What could be more valuable than—"

"Don't," Esme rasped, surging to her feet. The fresh anger after the heartache made her feel dizzy. "Don't you dare make this sound noble."

"Would you rather I lie?" Seren barely blinked. "I bind on my magic that Jacob chose his last fight to prevent another."

"What fight?" Esme snapped.

"A second promise, then. Because I see that you already don't want to believe me. I swear on my magic that the original spell binding the malevolent prisons is *failing*. If magic itself is not rebalanced, the great working keeping all the monsters back *will* fail catastrophically—all at once, and *soon*."

Esme sat back down heavily, her arms folded across her chest.

"Think for one moment." Seren began gesturing wildly with her hands. "It will free all malevolents, all at once. They will be crazed and more than half starved. Entire cities devoured before noon! Such a catastrophe would drive this civilization to self-annihilation in its efforts to remove the monstrous threat. If humanity couldn't defeat a group of dragons or hydras, would they hesitate to use atomic bombs, chemical weapons?"

Seren didn't wait for Esme to answer. "No! Even if humanity miraculously defeated the monsters, who would they pin the blame on for their appearance? *Us*! A few of us would go down fighting, but the rest of us would be dragged out of our houses and shot."

Seren's eyes eclipsed as she growled, "Tell me I'm wrong!"

Silence thudded between them, as swift and heavy as the blood rushing through Esme's veins. The words she needed to get out briefly caught in her throat as the hammering in her chest overwhelmed her.

After a long moment of breathing, of two pairs of violet eyes staring at one another, Esme rallied.

"You're not wrong, Seren," Esme answered quietly. "But gods *damn you*. You should have told us *before* he died."

"I've been trying to protect you!" Seren argued.

"Seren, Morgan, whatever you want to be called," Esme said, her voice bordering on hysteria. "One of the first things I told you was that I could protect *myself*!"

Seren's roar plastered Esme to her seat. "No mother—even one as *horrible* as me—would accept that answer as enough!"

Esme thought of her own mother then, of her father, and she understood what Seren said was true. Her parents had died trying to learn how to control malevolents so that *she* could live in a safer world.

What was right? *Who* was right? Esme's world was turned upside down.

Esme squared her shoulders, either prepared to fight or walk out of the room, head held high depending on the answer. "What was Jacob trying to do to fix magic? What do you, what do *we* have to do to finish what he started?"

"I thought that was obvious." Seren's icy gaze met hers, a chilling stare that spoke of deadly seriousness. That same ice flooded Esme's veins as the words dropped between them like heads from a guillotine. "More powerful people have to die."

Esme's throat closed. "Us?"

"No!" Seren hammered her mug down. "Saving you is exactly the point of all that we've been doing!"

Guilt, crushing in its weight, slammed down on Esme with Seren's words. "I..." Her voice finally broke. "I didn't choose this. Neither did Abby or Miles. How could you throw Jacob's life onto my conscience like that?"

The smirk on Seren's face was a bitter, thin line that didn't reach her eyes. "Because it's my apology, Esme. It's Jacob's from beyond the grave. We aren't done yet."

Maybe the real monsters are the ones willing to burn everything down to save a world that never thanks them for it.

That was it; Esme had to get out of there. She couldn't process it all at once. She wavered between wanting to return to bed in tears, letting fly another furious outburst at Seren, and violence that would leave her hands either broken or covered in blood.

Esme breathed out slowly, trying to calm her racing heart. "I think I've reached my limit. I can't tell if I want to say 'thank you'... or rip your fucking heart out." She turned, pausing at the door. "I'm going to go blab all of this to everyone. Then we'll circle back like nice adults and plan how to fix magic—together—without people fucking dying, right? Peace the fuck out, Seren." Her fingers formed the appropriate two-finger sign.

Seren didn't nod, shake her head, or even acknowledge Esme's final question. Seren only stared at her, eyes returning to their normal violet shade, mouth set in a straight line.

Jacob would've had something wise to say right then. She'd let Seren stew. Esme had people to warn.

Esme slammed the door hard enough to rattle Seren's mountains of jewelry and clothing. The sound was like the final punctuation to fifteen centuries of unfinished arguments.

CHAPTER FORTY-ONE

DO YOUR DUTY

Seren

The faint smell of rosemary and burned orange peels lingered in the air. Seren didn't know the bartender on duty. She was simply glad it wasn't Esme. She wasn't sure she could face Esme so soon. The sting of their earlier conversation hadn't faded. The plan she carried twisted in her chest like a blade made of dread, cruel and impossible to ignore.

Hundreds of bottles stood behind the bar, their labels a rainbow of colors and lettering—each a silent siren song. She sat alone at the far end, fingers curled around a sweating cocktail she hadn't yet tasted. There was too much swirling in her mind, too many pieces to slot perfectly into place for her to properly enjoy what little time she had.

She finally sipped The Last Word, a fitting cocktail for what she was there for. It was identical to the one Esme had made when they'd first met, but the taste was somehow flat, the vibrant citrus notes muted.

The serpent stirred beneath her skin, its phantom fangs pricking at her throat in a silent, knowing protest. Or perhaps a farewell. It always sensed the end before she did. Damn thing liked goodbyes too much.

Seren didn't want to be here forcing a meeting, but the situation was slipping out of control. With each passing moment, the pressure intensified; time was running out.

She didn't need to see his face to know he was scowling; the shift in magic told her. The air was slightly warmer, and something like peat smoke wafted off of him when his ire was raised.

"I'm here, yer highness," he muttered, sliding onto the stool beside her. His voice was relaxed, a grin already spread across his face. But he didn't offer his usual wink. That alone told her he knew what was coming.

"I'm so sorry to disrupt your television shows," Seren scoffed.

"I was watchin' Eurovision announcements!" he grumbled. "Now I'll have to watch the recaps online."

"Yes, well, some of us won't be able to catch this year's winner," Seren snapped.

"Aye." Finn's attitude sobered. "At least allow a man to have a spot of whiskey for this conversation."

Seren rolled her eyes. With a flick of her fingers, top-shelf whiskey rose on unseen currents and glided toward them. The bartender's eyes widened, taking in the theft happening in front of his eyes. Then they grew even wider as he recognized the person the bottle was floating toward. Two glasses followed the bottle, landing in front of their seats.

The bartender wisely went back to work.

Finn didn't wait for an invitation. He uncorked the bottle with his teeth, spat the wooden topper onto the bar, and poured two generous fingers into each glass. He slid one toward Seren, but she didn't touch it.

"You're makin' this feel like a funeral, and not the good Irish kind," he muttered before knocking his back in one swallow.

Seren watched the amber liquid disappear from his glass in one long pull. "You know why I called you here."

Finn refilled his glass, slower this time. "Aye. Doesn't mean I like it."

The serpent coiled tighter around her collarbone, its tail flicking against her pulse point. She wondered whether it was meant to be a warning or a reminder. Damn thing wasn't always the greatest communicator.

"But first." She leaned in. "I need you to steal something."

That, oddly, made him laugh. "Finally. We're back on familiar ground. What am I nicking?"

"Esme's siphoning dagger."

Finn's glass paused halfway to his lips. Then, with deliberate care, he set it down. "That's a shite idea."

"It's the only thing that can draw enough power in a controlled burst. If I use anything else, the explosion might take half the damn city with it."

"Bajesus, Morgan, you're not askin' for a favor. You're askin' for my head on a conjured pike." Finn whistled low. "You want me to steal your daughter's weapon so you can commit murder. Jus' *grand*!"

"She's not my daughter."

But once she had been, and a piece of her was still in Esme.

"Yeah." Finn snorted as he poured himself another shot. "Because you're *definitely* actin' like she's not."

Seren's fingers tightened around her untouched whiskey. "Drop it."

Finn leaned back on the stool, studying her, his fingers drumming idly on the bar. For once, he didn't make a joke. "You're askin' me to hand you the blade and watch."

"I'm asking you to help me make it matter. *All of it.* Every gods damned second of this existence." She finally gave in and swallowed the entire shot in one gulp.

Oblivious, the bar hummed with the chatter of patrons, their laughter a jarring counterpoint to the gravity of their hushed conversation. But the silence stretched between them like a second, unspoken bargain.

Finn leaned his forearms on the counter, glancing sidelong at her. "You always were fond of dramatic exits, Morgan."

Seren's mouth twitched, but there was no humor in it. "This one isn't for show."

That silenced him. His grin faded, and for a moment he looked like what he truly was—old, tired, and far too sharp for the role he played.

"How long have you known?" he asked finally.

"Since the new year." She finally turned to face him. "We're out of time, Fionn. Jacob bought us time... But there's no more dawdling."

Any more delay, and the city would be consumed by the flames of her silence.

Finn closed his eyes for just a moment. When he opened them again, there was something steelier underneath the usual flicker of amusement. "What else do you need?"

"Your magic," she said. "Just enough to satisfy the rest of the Fae and malevolent portions of the working. The rest will come from the dagger."

"Oh, *grand*. All the shit I'm made of." Finn gave a dry snort. "If the dagger has Fae and malevolent magic in it, Esme must not have used it since killin' Leon with it."

"That small fact..." Seren growled. "Her tender heart is the only thing keeping Arawn back from demanding you die too, leprechaun."

He nonchalantly swirled his whiskey, watching the liquid cling to the glass. "Will it be just like giving magic to someone?"

"Yes."

"Is the loss permanent?"

"...Maybe." Seren was clueless about the answer, and Arawn showed no interest in enlightening her.

A long, dramatic sigh escaped Finn's lips, carrying with it the burden of his worry and frustration. "Abby'll never forgive me."

"She won't have to know."

"She'll know." His voice dropped, rough. "You think she won't know with what you have planned for her man?"

Seren's jaw clenched. "Then let her hate me. Let them all hate me. Better that than see the rest of them dead."

"I take it Gwyn's ready to help you with the binding?" he asked eventually. "Because I didn't do the messagin' about that yet."

"He'll help," Seren insisted. "He's strong enough now."

"That distinctly wasn't a 'yes,' *Seren*. Have ya or haven't ya talked to the boy about it yet?"

She met his gaze, not flinching. "After this."

"By all the magic... He'll hate himself for it."

"Then nothing changes for him."

Finn's cheeks were flushed, a fiery red—Seren couldn't tell if it was from the alcohol, his rage, or a combination of the two.

"Survivin' ain't the same as livin', Morgan. And both of them have barely done either!"

"But he'll do it for her, for *them*." Seren let out a breath she hadn't realized she was holding. "I've seen it in his eyes. He has more now than he ever had before."

A low, mournful "Aye..." escaped Finn's lips; the saddest sound she'd ever heard him utter. He stood, smoothing his sleeves. "I've done worse things for dumber people. Let's call this my formal 'bugger off' to the universe."

The serpent hissed softly against her skin, approving.

Seren stood too, reaching out. Her fingers brushed his arm. It was hesitant, brief, and heavy with the unspoken burden they'd carried together.

"Then we're agreed." Seren exhaled. "Thank you."

He covered her hand briefly with his own, rough with time and memory. "You'll still owe me," he said, the grin soft—the kind that comes when the game's already lost.

"I'll pay it," she promised.

Neither of them pretended to believe it.

The whiskey burned on the way down, but not half as much as the lie they had been nursing for years. Somewhere, beneath the hum of laughter and clinking glasses, the clock was already ticking.

CHAPTER FORTY-TWO

NECROMANCY IS KEY

Seren

The Past

Morgan le Fay found Gwyn ap Nudd exactly where she had expected. Alone upon the moor's bleak shoulder, a shadow hunched beside a cairn of stones. Mist crawled through the heather like a patient beast, weaving around him and the monstrous spectral hound that guarded his solitude. One hand was outstretched, touching the rocks in prayer.

It was Elena's cairn. Nudd had selected the spot overlooking the valley for her final resting place. Morgan hadn't held back from spying. This secluded spot had been their sanctuary, far from the watchful gazes within Nudd's imposing keep. Her daughter had been happy here. She approved.

The gwyllgi was gigantic, rime-white fur bristling over muscle and shadow, its eyes glowing red like embers under a wolf's brow. Stepping out of the swirling fog, Morgan saw the beast's head rise, her ears pinned back. But she did not growl. Cerys knew Morgan for what she was, a force of magic itself.

Gwyn ap Nudd's cloak pooled at his feet. Now, one hand steadied him on the gwyllgi's broad shoulder, grounding him between the world he'd guided others from and the unyielding stone beneath his other hand. He remained facing away, but his voice came out as a low rasp that spoke of untold emotions and a long-held silence.

"Why do you show your face to me now, Lady of Avalon? You've haunted other men's dreams, but never mine. Come to watch me mourn?"

Morgan studied him. The hollows beneath his eyes, the slight tremor in his fingers where they sank into the gwyllgi's spectral fur, revealed probably only a fraction of what his losses had taken from him. He appeared too mortal for a prince of ghosts, and far too young for so much sorrow.

As she moved closer, the cool mist enveloped them both, thick and heavy with secrets held for far too long. "Because, dear prince of the Hunt, you and I want the same thing."

He turned sharply, his head snapping around like a hawk, his eyes narrowed as if he'd caught a scent on the wind. In the moonlight, his sharp features were stark, almost hauntingly beautiful in their ruin and despair. He looked more like a statue than a man.

Gwyn searched her face for any sign of deception, but her expression was as unwavering as a mountain.

Morgan kneeled, the hem of her dress drinking up the dew. She laid a sprig of rowan, its berries plump and red, upon the cairn. A second branch to add to the first she'd pressed to her daughter's cold breast—a secret shared only with Nudd.

Though cold, the stones on Elena's grave didn't match the ice in Nudd's eyes as he'd buried her. A man's love and a king's duty had failed Elena. As Morgan had. Just as Gwyn had.

Elena's laughter, once sharp and summer-sweet, seemed to echo from beyond the veil. The world was colder without that sound in it.

"You walked her soul to the threshold?" Morgan asked, though she had no right to press him so. The words escaped before she could armor them in steel. It had been a mother's plea, not a sorceress's demand.

Gwyn's hand clenched in the gwyllgi's fur. The beast rumbled a low, grieving noise in its throat that seemed to echo its master's emotions.

"I did. She mentioned…" He paused, furrowing his brow slightly, as if remembering a riddle that had appeared innocuous earlier. "She said, 'If you see my mother, tell her all is forgiven. I understand now.'"

With a slight sigh, Morgan bowed her head, the weight of the grief once again settling on her shoulders. There it was. Their last fragile thread of love, their final connection, made through a psychopomp instead of face-to-face.

It wasn't right. She'd bend magic itself to give her daughter a happier ending.

When Morgan looked up again, she found Gwyn's eyes fixed on hers, sudden recognition widening them.

"Elena was…?"

Morgan met Gwyn's confusion with stoic calm. "My daughter. My only child."

He drew back a fraction. The gwyllgi showed her teeth, pressing closer to his side as if to protect him from the unshakable realities of the universe.

"All these years… and I never knew."

"It was her truth to tell." Morgan's palm brushed the cairn, wishing for one more chance. "I came to thank you for leading her gently. And to tell you that her death will not be the end. Not for her. Not for you."

The smile that touched Morgan's lips was not a friendly one. It promised destruction on a grand scale.

"I will not forgive myself. Nor the world that bound her to its expectations of propriety. Nor the gods who watch and do nothing. This will not stand, Gwyn ap Nudd. I will not let her story end beneath these stones."

Gwyn breathed out a sound that might have been a laugh if it were not so brittle. "And you think you can change it? Even now? No one has that power."

Morgan leaned in close enough to sense the deathly chill emanating from his living skin. She brushed a lock of black hair from his brow, as a mother might. Though she had never been gentle enough to be a true mother to anyone.

"My vengeance for her death will not take the form of bloodshed. I promise you will not be alone forever, Gwyn. I *will* change it."

Morgan le Fay conjured the fragrance of springtime, of warm bread baking on a hearth fire. The way his fingers twitched in response, as if to grasp a hand no longer there, proved that she had been successful.

The promise of the woman who reminded him of spring was more than enough. The idea she'd planted took root in Gwyn so deeply she knew he would sacrifice his future for it.

Something flickered behind his eyes. The fierce light that shone through the devastation of his spirit took Morgan aback. He looked up. Hope bloomed where she had expected only despair.

"How?" he whispered—a single hoarse word, like he was still unfamiliar with wanting things for himself.

Morgan's answering grin was as sharp and sudden as a blade slicing through the fog. "When the chance presents itself, you'll take it..."

Behind them, the gwyllgi lifted her enormous head and howled, carrying Morgan's vow and Gwyn's hope out across the barren moor. It was so mournful even the dead paused to listen. The hound had been Gwyn's sole companion in his self-imposed exile, a beast bound not by duty but by the understanding that some griefs are too vast to bear alone.

As the last echoes of the gwyllgi's haunting howl died away, Morgan's words cut through the night's silence like a blade. "You might not remember this moment, Prince. When the time comes, you will choose between the world as it is... and the world as it could be. But this time, you won't be alone in pushing the future toward peace like you were with Myrrdin."

Gwyn

The call came at three o'clock in the morning. Though Gwyn's phone was set to silent, the insistent thrumming of his phone on the nightstand was more than enough to rouse him from sleep.

His eyes snapped open as the name on the screen seared itself into his consciousness, banishing the last traces of sleep. Beside him, Abby slept like the dead. The past few days had been exhausting from fighting battles no one should have to fight.

He carefully slid out from under the covers, mindful not to wake her. Sneaking into the bathroom and closing the door, he answered. At this hour, civility was not something he was capable of. "What?" he gritted out.

"Come to your apartment. Now. This is not a request."

"Or?"

"*People* will die."

Such a statement was not an idle threat from Seren's mouth.

Gwyn didn't allow himself to look back as he moved through Abby's apartment like a ghost, Cerys trailing behind on silent paws. With not a car in sight, they made record time across town thanks to a ride share driver who liked dogs.

He'd warded his front door, but that didn't seem to matter. Seren was already waiting in Gwyn's borrowed apartment, perched on the edge of his rickety kitchen table like a vulture watching a corpse stumble into her domain. The inevitability of it settled in his gut. It was his apartment now, technically, though it hardly felt like it. With Jacob no longer managing it, he had no idea how long his current living situation would last.

"Took you long enough," she said.

Gwyn didn't rise to the bait, *mostly*. "You broke in."

The look she gave him said, *dare me to do more.*

He crossed his arms. "What do you want?"

"A favor." Seren stood, brushing imaginary dust off her coat. Her eyes were sunken from lack of sleep but bright with a sort of hunger, and her smile was razor-thin. "Finn told me you remembered your deal with Arawn... I have one of my own with him."

The news didn't surprise Gwyn.

He opened his mouth to ask what her deal was, but then Seren stepped forward, her magic burning around her like smoke without fire. She didn't wait for permission. She seized his wrist.

Visions flooded his mind.

The Wild Hunt let loose again, Dullahan one of their number now, but without a leader to rein in their harvest of life.

Malevolents pouring out of their prisons all at once, all across the world. Men, women, even children falling to their claws.

People he'd met at the bar, dying to teeth, to shots fired by fellow humans. Katia shot in the back as she tried to flee. The last words that reached her ears while living were an insult. "Dirty mage!"

Miles' broken, mutilated body. His form barely obscuring the pool of blood underneath that wasn't his—the bleeding body had Esme's hair.

Finn slumped against a wall, insides now outside. Josiah, Maureen, the selkie not teen feet away in a similar state.

Abby, his Abby... He tried to look away, but he couldn't. She gasped through blood. And he couldn't stop it—again.

No.

Gwyn wrenched free. He demanded, "What was that?"

"A glimpse," Seren said softly. "What happens if we fail. Do you need to see it again?"

"No." His voice was barely a whisper. He could still smell the char of burning magic, still hear Abby's rasp.

"You've already promised your future." Seren leaned in. "I'm asking for your present to prevent everything you saw."

"You truly believe that all the prisons will fail at once?" His voice was hoarse. "And me? What do you want me to do?"

Seren didn't answer. She countered with a question that left the truth bleeding in its wake. "Why do you think Arawn's queen visited you so recently?"

The sudden, chilling understanding of the female ghost's identity hit him like a bucket of ice water, leaving him cold from forehead to toes. Seren knew about the queen's supposed interest in his love story. It was undeniable proof that Seren had a connection to Arawn, to Nudd, to *him*.

Seren dismissively waved a hand, brushing away his unspoken question with an airy flick of the wrist. "I am Arawn's sacrificial cow."

"If you had a deal with Arawn, do you know why he took my memories?"

Seren shrugged and retook her seat. "I wasn't completely honest with Esme when I said that my memories were unaltered. I cannot remember nor perform most of the greater magics from my ascension, thanks to Arawn's meddling. He took them to keep the balance. Or so he claimed." Her voice turned almost threatening. "I tell you this, but do not forget that he has done us both a great service..."

He thought of Abby, of Esme, even Miles and Finn, and couldn't disagree.

All this time, Gwyn had been right in his presumption that magic was a force of balance in the world. He simply hadn't grasped that magic required assistance to maintain its own equilibrium.

Abruptly changing subjects, Seren gave him whiplash. "Your necromancy is needed, *ap Nudd*."

He wanted to reject her use of his patronymic name, but the anger he'd felt about his father had mostly dissipated in the wake of recent revelations, leaving only a faint ember.

"My *necromancy*? What could my necromancy have to do with the malevolent prisons... failing..." Gwyn went very still as he pieced together all that Esme had told them earlier with what Seren was saying now. "You're going to die."

"Yes."

Gwyn's fists clenched at his sides. He was ready to argue, to fight, to run, to do anything but say yes.

She bared her teeth. "Your father did it once for love. Am I worth less?"

"Don't."

"Don't what? Compare myself to the great Llaw Eraint? Too late." She stood, the legs of the chair screeching against the floor. "This is happening, Gwyn. I can't risk Esme or Miles interfering." Her voice softened for a breath. "Or Abby."

Because she might be the only one able to stop you.

"No." He stepped forward. "You sound mad. There has to be another—"

"There isn't!" she hissed, spinning on him. "You think I want this? You think this is easy for me? I *just* found Esme, and it's already time!"

Perhaps he could still dissuade her. "Miles just proposed marriage to her. Did you know? Do you not want to attend their wedding?"

"I didn't..." Seren cleared her throat. "That's... fitting. A beginning and an end so closely intertwined. But I, *we*, have to do this if they are to get that celebration, so long delayed. It doesn't matter, because you owe me, Gwyn. I made your happy ever after possible."

"There has to be another way," Gwyn tried again. It came out soft, desperate.

"There isn't," Seren snapped, her voice wavering. Her hands trembled once, then stilled.

The silence that followed pulsed, thick with promise and peril.

Seren stepped closer, lowering her voice to something nearly kind. "You have already figured out how this ends, ap Nudd. You just don't want to admit it."

"You can't—"

"I can," she interrupted. "And I *will*. Because someone has to."

Gwyn stepped back. The room shrank as the weight of history bore down on him from all sides.

Seren's hand, neither gentle nor forceful, came to rest on his shoulder. She hadn't used magic, yet the power behind that simple touch was unrelenting. "You made your choice years ago."

Behind her, the shadows deepened. Cerys' red eyes fixated on Gwyn before shifting to Seren.

Seren's fingers twitched. A pulse of magic surged through the room. A sudden flash of light was followed by darkness.

Gwyn and Seren vanished, leaving Cerys waiting, watching the door for his return—if it ever came.

CHAPTER FORTY-THREE

DEMIGOD DISAPPEARED

Esme

Esme didn't knock as much as she pushed at Seren's door this time. After a night of tossing and turning, she'd decided to have one more private conversation with Seren before resorting to a group confrontation.

The penthouse was tucked in one of those brooding downtown towers that smelled like wealth and cleaning solutions. Seren's door hummed faintly with invisible wards. Without the slightest resistance, it swung inward.

Locking the door meant very little to Seren in terms of safety. She was quite literally the most powerful mage in the world, Morgan le Fay of legend. But something about the door swinging open freely still wasn't right.

A cold prickle of intuition skittered down Esme's spine.

"Seren?" she called, steeling herself for a shock, a pushback, or some other nasty piece of resistance from the wards as she stepped inside the doorframe.

Nothing happened. The wards were active; Esme could feel their magic humming all around her. Seren must have bound Esme's magic to pass through them freely...

Her voice echoed off the vaulted ceilings. She paused in the doorway, blinking.

There was no answer. But there also wasn't any furniture. The penthouse was stripped bare. Seren's piles of clothes were gone, as was the mess in the kitchen; there wasn't even a fucking coffee stain on the marble countertops. It was like Seren had never existed at all.

"Seren?" Esme called out again.

Esme's stomach dropped. *Oh, you dramatic bitch. What did you do?*

The elevator ride down to the lobby was too slow. Maybe the front desk could tell her something. It was a long shot, but if Esme was tuned to Seren's wards, then maybe she'd left a note for her as well.

The polished doors of the descending elevator reflected Esme's pale face, the usually vibrant violet of her eyes leached out by grief over Jacob and worries over the future. The moment the doors slid open, her phone buzzed with a text message. Abby's name lit up the screen.

Abby: *Have you heard from Gwyn? He left in the middle of the night. Not answering his phone. I thought he was taking Cerys out, but he never came back.*

Esme froze inside the sleek marble lobby. Her fingers flew over the screen. *No. Seren's gone too. Like, moved-out-in-the-middle-of-the-night gone.*

Three dots pulsed.

Abby: *What the fuck?*

Esme didn't bother replying. She was already striding toward Miles' car in the late morning drizzle, heart starting to hammer against her ribs.

Gwyn was missing. Seren had *poof* disappeared without a trace. The memory of Seren's veiled talk of sacrifice clawed its way up her throat.

We aren't done yet.

"Oh, *hell no.*"

She drove like a madwoman. Back at the floating house, Lake Union gray and glassy outside, Esme punched in the code and yanked open the gun safe hidden behind a false panel in the closet. If something was going on between Seren and Gwyn, she could at least arm herself with an extra punch of magic.

Her engagement ring winked at her from the shadows—a glittering promise in a world falling apart. It was only two days ago when Miles had crawled to this same safe like it was the only thing holding back the tide of death.

Esme's finger brushed over the ring. This life, this love, wasn't supposed to be possible for someone like her. A cambion enforcer with too much rage, dangerous magic, and no family to speak of.

And yet here she was. Safe. Loved. *Wanted.*

Esme didn't have time to get emotional. There was someone else who was loved and wanted who needed her.

She rummaged past two handguns, the boxes of ammo, and the utterly unnecessary flashbang (Miles and his paramilitary streak), but her dagger wasn't there. She stared at the empty shelf where it should've been, heart crawling higher into her chest.

A subtle, almost imperceptible tingling sensation grazed her senses, soft yet elusive. The faintest glimmer of residual magic.

Esme closed her eyes, reaching for it with her sixth sense. The trace was tiny but unmistakable. It wasn't hers or Miles'. It was from the man who had been her teacher, so she'd know evidence of his magic anywhere: Finn.

The mischievous little bastard is stealing now?

Her fingers trembled as she called Miles. He picked up on the first ring.

"Hey, lovely," he said warmly. Her breath came out shakily. His voice immediately sharpened. "What's wrong?"

"Finn stole my dagger. Seren's *gone* gone. Gwyn disappeared overnight. Something's happening." She wanted to scream hysterically, "*again,*" but his ears didn't deserve that.

Miles exhaled deliberately, his breath a soft, controlled puff against the speaker. "Okay. I've got two more patients. By the time you get here, I'll be done. Tell Abby about Finn. He might talk to her."

Her phone buzzed again.

Abby: *Finn's gone dark.*

Esme's breath hitched. *No. Gods below, no.*

Seren's words from yesterday slithered back into her mind. *We aren't done yet.*

She'd assumed Seren meant more talking about how to solve the problem. Not what she feared might be happening...

They all had their talents, but out of all of them, Gwyn was the most broadly powerful. She didn't want to believe that Seren was hurting, *killing* Gwyn, maybe even Finn right now. *She wouldn't.*

But... wouldn't she? More than twenty years of working together hadn't saved Jacob from Seren's manipulative scheme. Esme had foolishly allowed herself to be betrayed *again*.

A few messages later and Abby was in on the plan.

Tension cinched tighter as Esme prepared everything they might need to walk into a dangerous situation. She packed Miles' tactical gear, changed into her monster-hunting outfit, and grabbed a change of clothing for Abby in case what she had in her car wouldn't work. Bottles of water and snacks went into the car next.

What if Gwyn was next on the chopping block and Finn was helping Seren do it? Or what if Finn was trying to stop her himself? Maybe that was why he'd stolen her dagger. It was still imbued with all of Leon's stolen magic, so it would pack a significant punch.

Esme stared at her text conversation with Abby, gut going ice cold. She hadn't dared to name it before. Betrayal had been a ghost in the room, but now it was clawing at the walls of her mind. Even with the dagger, they had no chance against Seren if it came down to it—and they all knew it.

Less than an hour later, the sun starting to sink in the sky over the city, Esme pulled up outside the hospital. Miles climbed into the front, tic half-askew. Abby slid into the back seat, wearing her usual outrageously patterned scrubs, face pale and tired.

No one said anything as Esme pulled out of the passenger loading area.

Then Miles, his eyes darting toward her, confessed, "Okay, so... I *might* have a tracker on Gwyn's phone."

Esme snapped her gaze toward him. "I'm sorry. You what?"

"I did it months ago," he said quickly, hands raised. "I don't have to explain our recent past! You don't just stop tracking that. Also, I kind of forgot about it until a few minutes ago."

Abby groaned. "*Men*. It'll never end between them."

"Hey," Esme muttered, "I take it as a good sign that you forgot it existed."

Abby perked up slightly at that. "True. Now I'm thankful for your persistent paranoia."

Miles tapped his phone, then frowned. "He's east of the city. Fuck…"

"What?" Esme frowned, stomach already doing somersaults.

"He's in a Brotherhood warehouse."

The three of them stared off into the distance for a long moment. The growing unease was like a colony of ants crawling over them, ready to devour them bite by bite.

Abby's worried voice drifted from the back seat. "Which kind?"

Esme asked, voice too sharp, "Is there a *good* kind for him to disappear into?"

"Damnit, Morgana, if you weren't driving…" Abby growled.

Uh-oh, the harpy was coming out.

"Ugh, sorry, Esme, shouldn't have used the middle name."

When Esme glanced back to reassure her it was fine, she saw that Abby's face was ashen, her features drawn and tight, her lips pressed into a thin white line. She understood. If it were Miles in that warehouse, she'd be physically ill with anxiety too.

"It's a malevolent holding one," Miles answered.

Esme's blood turned to ice. "There's more than one warehouse for that?" she hissed.

Until Seren had revealed the truth of it, Esme had always assumed that the Corded Brotherhood had executed the monsters they caught. Not caged them. Not hoarded them like fucking collectibles.

But that wasn't the worst part. The worst part was Gwyn's dot, pulsing right in the middle of it on Miles' phone screen.

"I don't like this," Abby said finally.

"Yeah," Esme muttered, driving faster now. "Neither do I."

They would find him. And Esme would rip out Seren's damn heart for this.

CHAPTER FORTY-FOUR

CAN'T BE TOO EASY

Abby

Miles' car glided over the wet road, its heater purring to stave off the unseasonal cold that seemed to have seeped into Abby's mood. At least they didn't have to endure the bumpy ride in Esme's rattling hatchback since it was in a scrapheap by now. Its shocks were worn out and every pothole would have squeaked the soundtrack for their journey.

Doctor Smartypants had been right once again. Comfort mattered when you were driving into hell.

The unexpected cold front pummeled the Puget Sound with a deluge of rain and powerful gusts of wind, causing trees to sway wildly. Rain turned the windshield into an angry toddler's fingerpainting.

Abby gripped the seatbelt like it was the only thing keeping her from falling apart. Douglas fir and western hemlock trees loomed like wet sentinels in the headlights, their dripping branches shivering in the wind.

As they entered the Cascade foothills, the road became increasingly winding, the car leaning into each turn. Abby's stomach lurched with every curve. Instead of the typical nauseating wave of fear, she felt a disquieting unease, a deep, unsettling feeling that something inside her was rebelling.

She pressed her forehead to the window, welcoming the glass's chill to stabilize her vertigo. Gwyn was gone, taken by the evil sorceress who'd murder him for the sake of a world that was indifferent to his existence.

The rain finally let up, and Miles glanced at the GPS on his phone. "Another mile. Bear right at the next forest service road. The warehouse is a little further up."

Dreadful anticipation thrummed in Abby's veins. What would she find in the warehouse? She would sense it if Gwyn wasn't okay, therefore Gwyn *must* be fine. Right?

Her mind was spinning. All of her efforts were focused on keeping her lunch down.

A muffled *crack*, something between thunder and an explosion, rattled the car all the way down to Abby's bones. Esme slammed the brakes, fishtailing until the car squealed sideways to a stop.

"Out!" Miles barked before the tires even quit screeching. That hadn't been a natural explosion of sound.

Abby didn't move at first. She leaned forward, breath fogging the window. The scene beyond was surreal, like the world itself had birthed a nightmare made of winter and shadow. She knew exactly what this was.

With each thudding heartbeat, a burning desire for revenge against a world that dared impede her progress vibrated through her. How could this happen when they were so close?

The air in front of the car suddenly shimmered like melting glass. Then a jagged slit ripped open the sky with a dry tearing sound. Waves of fog rolled out of the tear. Frost crept in jagged fractals across the blacktop beneath.

Something inside the fissure moved—something big. So far, it looked like nothing more than a ripple of shadow.

She fumbled for the door handle. The second her shoes hit the wet road, the chill sank through her jacket, past her skin, straight into her veins.

"Behind me," Miles ordered, already unholstering his pistol. It was dark in the shade of the evergreens on either side of the road. Only the headlights and the light pollution from the surrounding cities above the tree line illuminated the way.

Teeth bared, Esme growled in frustration. These days, Abby's friend was leaning hard into the whole cambion aspect of their personality. Well, Abby had been embracing her Fae side lately as well. So good for her.

Esme's magic sprang to life as a second rip in reality formed mere feet in front of the collapsing malevolent prison. Shadows peeled out of the rift, forming three now familiar forms. Bert, Tom, and George, all in their infernal guises, stood as shields in front of the clearing fog surrounding the collapsed malevolent prison.

This fight needed to be over five minutes ago. Why was the prison collapsing so slowly? The ache in her belly was only getting worse.

Abby abruptly lost the battle with her nervous stomach. Her body betrayed her with a violent shudder. A burning wave of bile seared her throat, then splattered onto the gravel road.

"You okay?" Miles called back, voice tight with focus. Esme retreated a few steps in Abby's direction, her gaze fixed on the lingering fog. Nothing stirred within.

This wasn't how Miles and Esme had portrayed the previous prison failures. The moment the had prison materialized, the malevolents had flown out, in a literal or figurative sense. Maybe the creature was stunned?

Her pulse begged for action. She wanted nothing more than for Miles to shoot indiscriminately into the fog. Consequences be damned. But Miles was too even-keeled for that.

"I'm fine..." she managed between heaves as Esme's palm rubbed at her back. At the worst possible moment, her body and nerves had failed her.

Miles' low voice announced, "We probably have another sixty seconds. If you need to, get back in the car—driver's seat."

Abby shivered so hard she nearly vomited all over the bracelet Gwyn had given her for her birthday. The delicate gold vine was a mirror of her Corded Brotherhood tattoo.

Get it together, O'Malley. The injustice of it all made her blood boil; this whole situation was infuriating. All she wanted to do was get to Gwyn.

Please. Please let me get to him.

But life, and the inconvenience of magic, didn't care about one woman's desires.

A sleek horn, as dark as obsidian and crusted with frost, was the first thing to take shape through the dissipating mist. Next, a loud snuffling sound, characteristic of a large, hoofed animal, echoed between the trees. Its dark head, topped with scruffy equine hair, emerged.

It was massive, ragged-furred, its body glistening with frost. The sound of cracking ice marked its shifting. Like dying embers, its eyes glowed, wary of any movement.

A karkaddan.

According to everything she had read, the creature wouldn't attack unless it thought it was being threatened. However, any human scent, sound of movement, or other sign of any presence immediately after its appearance would likely trigger its fight response.

Its eyes finally tracked their way, and the momentary peace shattered.

"Esme, left!" Miles fired twice. The shots sparked off its scaled hide.

Karkaddans looked like horses, but they were armored like Pleistocene-era rhinoceroses.

Esme's troll trio lunged to intercept the charging ungulate. Armored flesh and a mass of ichor collided with a *clap*. The massive creature rose up on its hind legs and struck out at them with its hooves.

One troll's arm snapped sideways under a hoof strike, but it didn't crack. A lack of bones helped when they were acting as ectoplasmic shields. The second troll took advantage of the opening and punched the karkaddan in the stomach. It reared back with a loud huff that was more a forceful outburst of air than a sound.

Miles popped off two more shots. With a snort and a rumble, the karkaddan took three heavy steps back, lowered its massive head, and charged at the assembled trolls, dark horn a blur.

Together, the three trolls barely held it back. One of them toppled over, but Esme was able to right it quickly. Her conjurations, even with their bulk, wouldn't hold up to the damage they were suffering for long.

Abby stumbled back a step. Sick and panicked, she knew she was a liability.

"Abby, behind the car!" Miles ordered. Esme grabbed her shoulder, trying to shove her back.

But the anxiety she'd been fighting, the dread that had kept her so small her whole life, dropped from her body like a stone falling into a bottomless well. A strange, welcome calmness washed over her. She wasn't fearless, but for Gwyn, she'd be damn close.

Abby disobeyed.

She stepped forward instead of back. Static danced across her skin and flowed along her veins outward from the center of her magic. As it moved, the gold vine bracelet seemed to burn against her wrist with a reminder of everything she could lose.

The monster turned toward her, its breath fogging around its muzzle. It charged.

With her hands raised in fury, Abby let out a scream that ripped from her sore throat, guttural, entirely nonsensical, and nearly inhuman.

Her grief, her desperation, her need for Gwyn... exploded outward in a wave of—blessedly—directed magic.

"Not today, not now!" she shouted, a small woman roaring into the storm of life.

And the karkaddan jerked to a halt like it had reached the end of its invisible chains.

The malevolent shied back. Snorting again, horn lowered, it retreated three unsteady steps away.

She poured even more power into it until the air around her seemed to hum with energy. She willed it to stop, to lie down.

Miles lowered his gun and turned his head, gawking at her in stunned silence. Even Esme's trolls froze in their progress forward.

Abby's knees almost gave out.

"You've got more rounds left," Abby gritted out between breaths meant to calm the bile that threatened to rise again. "So end this. Now."

To maintain her control, Abby couldn't look away, even if she wanted to. Her control over her new power, her new strength, was getting better every day thanks to Finn, but it wasn't perfect yet.

Miles strode forward without a word, each step unhurried, predator-calm. He stopped close enough that the karkaddan's ragged breath dampened his sleeve. He leveled the gun, eyes locked on the creature's ember eyes. Then pulled the trigger once, twice, into its eye until the monster's skull cracked like a watermelon.

Blood misted the early evening air. The malevolent creature collapsed in a heap at his feet, and Miles didn't so much as flinch. Its last breath rattled out of its chest as it lay still.

Esme's trolls silently moved toward the karkaddan. While her warm, steady hand returned to Abby's back.

"You don't have to say anything," Esme murmured. "Tell me what you need. If it were Miles, I'd be tearing down the whole damned forest too."

"You're already helping," Abby answered. "I need to get to him."

Esme nodded.

One troll limped as it dragged the corpse by its hind leg. The other two heaved in rhythm, their bodies smeared with muddy dust and ichor as its weight thudded against the gravel. Once the beast was off the road and into the shadowy tree line, Esme flicked her wrist, and all three conjurations dissipated into curls of disappearing smoke.

Esme and Miles exchanged a look that Abby didn't care to decipher. A hush followed, broken only by Abby's ragged breathing and the soft click of Miles ejecting his spent magazine. He reloaded without looking at her.

"Let's go," he ordered.

Abby didn't hesitate. She yanked open the car's back door and climbed inside. Abby sagged into the back seat.

Miles slid behind the wheel while Esme jumped in and slammed the door. The car's quiet hum rose as he nudged it back onto the narrow road. Esme's eyes flicked to Abby in the rearview, but she didn't speak.

Gwyn's face flickered behind Abby's eyes. He wasn't dead, not yet. Her heartbeat agreed.

"Warehouse in five," Miles warned. "I don't know what we're walking into. Just... don't get yourself killed. Gwyn wouldn't want that..."

Abby pressed her forehead to the cold window again, ready to jump out of the car without hesitation.

The car nosed around a final bend. Another benefit of driving Miles' car was that the electric engine was nearly silent in their approach. Through the building fog, a hulking silhouette of corrugated steel and wood emerged. Miles parked the car next to a wide loading dock half-swallowed by blackberry brambles. A single overhead light near the front entrance flickered, casting yellow patches on the wet ground.

He glanced back at Abby. There was the slightest softening in his eyes. "Ready?"

Esme cracked her knuckles. Her pupils seemed to flood out into her eyes as she allowed the infernal in. Abby dug in her purse for a mint, anything to settle her nerves and take some of the focus away from what might be happening only twenty feet away.

Her voice was stronger than her fear. "Let's get him back."

Miles looked back at them with all the seriousness of a military officer. "All we have is the element of surprise. That's *it*. We can't go in guns blazing because we don't know what we're walking into. We can't pull an 'Esme' by letting the trolls barge in for us since the warehouse is warded to be opened only by a Brother's hand."

"Don't like this already," Esme grumbled.

That meant either Abby or Miles would have to position themself directly in the doorway for them to even enter at all.

"Obviously I'm doing it." With a downright withering stare and a tightening of his jaw, Miles sent Abby a withering "don't argue with me" look.

She threw her hands up in the air. Who was she to argue? He was the one with experience at this sort of thing. All she wanted was to be through that damn door! "You shield. Esme can have her trolls ready. And I can have a calming blast ready. Easy, *let's go*."

Was she being pushy? Yes.

Did her friends care? No.

Esme and Miles were right beside her as she stepped out of the car.

The air around the warehouse was thick with a malevolent miasma that pressed down on her like a frozen, sodden blanket. From the feel of it, one would think the air should stink of rotten flesh, but the air was clean and fresh, smelling of rain.

With each step she took toward the completely normal-looking door, the slick gravel shifted under Abby's shoes. Her magic buzzed beneath her skin, warning her, but of what...

Miles stopped, one hand on the door handle, the other raised in a sign to halt. As the three of them came to a standstill, he whispered, "Ready? I will silence our approach."

Esme was already summoning her trolls as Abby sensed Miles create a shield in front of himself.

Ten seconds later, Miles was opening the door.

No magic came flying their way.

Half the lights were on inside. It was deadly silent except for one familiar voice. Frozen in place, Miles blocked the doorway with his broad shoulders. For Miles to react like that, without Esme or Abby sensing a surge of magic to bind him in place, they couldn't be in immediate danger.

Abby's impatience ran away with her. She pushed Miles aside and felt the wards on the building pulse as she entered.

Abby was instantly overwhelmed by the powerful magic in the space. It pressed in on her from all sides; even her next breath felt saturated in magic. Visibly, at least, the warehouse was mostly empty, save for a large open space at its center where three people were gathered.

Finn stood closest to the door, nonchalantly leaning on a support beam, looking careworn, while Seren kneeled on the floor several feet away. The circle of something that looked like salt that surrounded her made it appear as though she were performing a ritual.

Esme and Miles fanned out beside Abby, real and conjured weapons lowered but ready, trolls flanking them. Neither moved to stop her. Abby could feel their tension thrumming toward her like a wire, but she couldn't take her eyes off what was in front of her.

There he was. Gwyn was alive, as real as he'd ever been, breathing, and *whole*.

He looked the same—tall, strong, stupidly handsome in that infuriatingly comforting way—but a subtle shift in his posture, a stillness in his stance, betrayed that something was amiss. His shoulders were set like he was bracing for something that would hurt.

Gwyn stood feet outside the salt circle. Her heart was hammering all the way up her neck at the sight.

She wanted to run to him, to shake him until he came back to himself, but her feet wouldn't move. She was stone, a statue carved by the storm of magic pressing in on all sides.

Gwyn

Gwyn hadn't moved since the circle had been completed. To anyone watching, he might have seemed a willing accomplice. While inside, he fought against every muscle straining to bolt for the door.

Seren stood in the center of a salt circle. Sprinkles of her blood lined its edges. Her serpent coiled tightly around her throat, unmoving, as if dead already.

Barbaric.

"Does salt truly enhance magical channeling?" Gwyn asked, attempting a distraction from his own bloody purpose. "And these runes. I've heard of the practice, but I thought it was far more ancient than ourselves."

"Yes to both," she answered simply.

"I thought *I* was here to channel the magic. Why do we also need the salt?"

Seren turned around, pausing her preparations. "Insurance."

Finn leaned against a support beam, rolling a golden coin between his fingers. His usual smirk was gone, replaced with tight lips and a lowered brow.

"I still think this is feckin' madness," Finn muttered half to himself, half to the cruel fate laid out for them.

Seren paid no heed to his grumbles. She slipped off her coat. The serpent relaxed across her shoulders. Not wanting to disturb the ritualistic ring she'd laid out, Seren floated the dagger from the nearby table toward herself.

It felt wrong to see the dagger there. It held memories that Gwyn wished he could eliminate from Abigail's mind. She still woke up with nightmares sometimes, reassuring him it was "just another one of Leon's memories" dragging her down. Gwyn could only imagine the blood and gore, the screams and the struggle, the horrors she'd subjected herself to in protecting them from him.

Finn raised one brow. "Since mister doom and gloom over there hasn't asked, *I will*. Just what are we supposed to do with your bloody corpse, Morgana? Put it in the boot of your car? Bury you in the sliver of land behind the buildin'?"

Seren cleared her throat. "We've talked about this, leprechaun! Though, I suppose you are correct. I haven't mentioned that I will basically... How would Esme put it... *poof* away. So you needn't get your hands dirty with my corpse." She spat the last word out through gritted teeth.

"Are you certain this is the only way?" Gwyn asked Seren one last time.

The intensity in her eyes softened, replaced by an expression of understanding and empathy. More human than before. "No," she admitted. "Certainty is for people with time. We don't have any. A prison failed less than fifteen minutes ago less than a mile away. I slowed its emergence. That will be your problem when I'm gone."

So they'd have to help with a sacrifice, then immediately deal with a malevolent. Wonderful.

Barely managing to keep his composure, Gwyn finally asked the question that had been bothering him since she'd kidnapped him from his apartment, "Why me?"

"Because you're strong enough to hate me for it and do it anyway," she replied. "Plus, there's the whole 'you made a deal with a god' thing, with all the potential consequences and divine repercussions that entails."

Their eyes briefly locked in a battle of wills. Seren kneeled and pressed a palm briefly to the earth. Magic flared around her in a pulsating glow of black and silver, alive with inner light.

"I am ready," she said. Morgan le Fay's voice was steady. Her eyes were dry.

But to Gwyn, she didn't seem prepared. In her eyes, he saw a haunted look that spoke of a world on the brink of collapse, in her posture the weight of fear and impending loss. Only a shared discontent of their current circumstances bound them together—neither wanted to be there.

"No!" The shout came from the doorway.

Abigail.

Abby

Abby's lungs ached. She'd been holding her breath through the entire exchange, waiting for someone to move, for Gwyn to look at her, for the world to make sense again. But Esme's dagger wasn't raised above Gwyn's chest. *Seren* held it above her own.

Abby's stomach turned.

Gwyn wasn't being sacrificed.

He was... Gods, what was he doing?

"*No.*" Abby's voice, raw and strained, tore through the quiet in a desperate cry born of her refusal to face the completed project Seren had so clearly started.

Gwyn's head jerked toward her. The look in his eyes nearly brought her to her knees.

Esme's dagger slipped from Seren's hands. It clattered to the concrete floor with a sharp ringing sound.

Relief. Abby felt so much relief. But also rage, worry, and betrayal.

But from Gwyn, she sensed only guilt.

A torrent of emotions crashed over her, each a searing wave, but underneath, a cold clarity of understanding settled. That look on his face, plus what Esme had said about the malevolents... if she'd been in his place, she might have done the same.

He was an accomplice. Gwyn was *helping* Seren die.

The half step forward Abby took next was her last. They were already too late. Really, they'd never had a chance. Because the dark storm of Seren's magic had them bound and utterly powerless.

CHAPTER FORTY-FIVE

THE FINAL SACRIFICE

Esme

A storm raged in Seren's eyes—F6 on a five-point scale, if Esme were being poetic.

Not two seconds after Abby's voice rang out in the quiet, the world exploded in black. They were scooped up like broken dolls in the shadowy tentacles of Seren's magic.

"You are not supposed to be here," Seren growled.

The venom in her voice made Esme realize that she'd never seen Seren truly angry before. It was so glaringly clear now that she had misinterpreted her mere irritation as something more. This was... wrath. Her full-blown fury had her magic shifting so wildly across the room that Esme would be choking on it if she could.

But Esme's mouth was covered by the tentacles, silencing any screamed reply she wanted to make. She struggled against the conjured bindings with her whole body, thrashing, trying to kick and punch.

She reached for her magic, as blunt and brutal as her temper, but it had vanished, leaving only a silence that screamed. She pushed against the void, demanded it rip, tear, and destroy, but it only yawned back, mocking her.

No spark, no upwelling of furious infernal power, *nothing*. The loss was visceral, like losing a limb she hadn't known she had.

This isn't right. This can't be how it ends.

She should be doing something—anything—but even her rage was locked behind bars of impotence.

Miles. A quick glance revealed Miles and Abby in a similar predicament, their hands and feet bound tightly, noses free for easy breathing.

Thank all the gods Seren hasn't completely lost her mind.

Esme's conjurations had vanished with her abilities. Though she couldn't see it unless the light hit it the right way, she suspected Miles' shield had dropped as well. The air was so thick with ambient magic that it was hard to tell by feeling alone if Miles or Abby was working on anything.

It took an embarrassingly short time for Esme to give up. Miles had been right when he'd warned them they didn't have a chance...

Only Finn and Gwyn were left unbound. Esme's first instinct was to name them traitors, but their expressions indicated they weren't enthusiastic participants in whatever was going on either.

"Seren! Drop 'em!" Finn snapped, taking a step toward her.

"You know I'd never hurt them, leprechaun," Seren said as she rose from her spot in the circle, calm despite the maelstrom she'd unleashed.

"You're the only one who's certain of that." Finn's voice dropped to a low growl Esme had never heard before. "Ya tend to have a one-track mind when it comes to yer goals."

Finn's face matched his rage, turning a fiery red. Gwyn's eyes darted nervously between Abby, held by the tentacles of Seren's magic, and Seren herself. He was just as shocked by their appearance in the warehouse as Finn and Seren, yet Abby's stare had briefly paralyzed him.

"This has to happen." Seren's voice was a roar. "They weren't supposed to be here—"

"And yet they are," Finn cut her off, tone dangerously quiet. He was planning something. She knew that look...

Gwyn finally peeled his eyes off Abby. The same cold, menacing, utterly unwavering stare he'd set on Miles during that fateful meeting a year before when they'd been sent to hunt Cerys fell over his face.

This is what he looks like when he's terrified, Esme realized. Gods below, had they truly walked into what she feared?

"Enough," Gwyn interrupted, stepping toward the circle. His voice was calm, but the tension in his posture betrayed him. "We should finish this. Let them go, and they'll return home."

Seren didn't move. "I can't risk it."

But something shifted in the magic, a change in the pulse underlying it all. It was small, deliberate, and out of time with the rest of the room's tension. It reminded her of velvet-soled shoes creeping.

She barely noticed it, but she'd been around Finn long enough to sense when he was shifting the perception of those around him. Seren was too distracted by considering what to do with them to realize that the devious Fae was up to something sneaky.

One second Esme felt it; the next, Finn was pushing Seren out of the circle. The ritual, because this couldn't have been anything but a ritual, clearly wasn't finished yet. Seren had been about to sacrifice herself with Esme's dagger. She'd talked about restoring the balance of magic. She'd said it demanded lives, but Esme hadn't ever considered that Seren had been planning on laying down her own.

So naïve.

But Finn had seen it coming, and he was stealing the place Seren had prepared for herself. He'd mist walked across the room and barreled into her with magic-amplified force.

Finn was grinning as he did it, but not like the trickster he always played. This was real, and the implications of what he had just done were terrifying.

"Finn, no—" Esme tried to shout. Only a strangled gasp, barely louder than a breath, escaped her lips as she pushed air past the conjured gag.

"Fionn!" Gwyn's voice cracked like thunder.

Esme braced herself to move, expecting Seren's tentacles to loosen their grip the second her body hit the floor and she lost concentration.

But Seren was too good for that.

They remained tightly bound, their hands and feet secured, muzzles of magic gagging their mouths.

Finn didn't hesitate. He carefully took Seren's place in the circle, into the magic meant for someone else. His hand shot forward, plucking the dropped dagger from the ground.

Blade in hand, he turned and faced them all. "I need y'all to listen!"

Silence gripped the room; even Seren gasped. Finn's gaze darted between them: Abby restrained, Miles resisting, Gwyn motionless, Esme paralyzed by what was unfolding.

Then Finn made a strange, looping gesture with his hand. The magic shifted again. This time it was like all of the power in the room was leaning toward him. A single flare of light burst forth from the runes written on the ground, then they went quiet.

"Fionn—" Seren whispered, voice cracking. Her upward motion ceased, and she fell back onto the concrete floor, looking for all the world like she'd just been stabbed in the back by her best friend.

"It's done," he cut her off.

Seren didn't glance up at him, only nodded. What the hell was going on? Why hadn't Seren plucked him from the circle with one of her tentacles like she'd done so easily with each of them?

"You're not supposed to be here, dove," Finn said sadly, his voice barely above a whisper as he turned to Abby. "But you're strong like your ma, your brother... and I can't undo what I've started."

Seren's sharp gaze pierced him with a silent accusation.

"You're not dying tonight, Morgan," he said gently, like he was talking to an old friend. "I won't let ya."

"Why?" Emotion made Seren's voice as fragile as a child's. How could a woman as grand as Seren shrink down to something so small?

"Ya never had a chance. You've only lived as a sacrifice. *Twice*. It's not fair. And yeah—life's not fair, I know."

Finn took another breath as they watched, unable to do anything. "But I got to live. More than two centuries of doin' what

I liked. Making a mess. Breakin' hearts. Drinkin' good whiskey with my bestie. And in the end…"

His eyes found Abby and Gwyn, then Esme, then Miles, still held back by the magic.

"…I had *family*."

For a fleeting moment, Seren's youthful features were etched with a heartbreaking vulnerability, her eyes wide and shimmering with unshed tears.

"I lived more in one year with them than I did in a hundred before it." He graced them with a genuine, full-hearted smile. "If I can give you a future—then I'm takin' the deal. I'm doin' this for my family."

A silence fell, as thick and quiet as a blanket of new snow after the tempest of the blizzard had passed.

Esme understood now. Ignorance had been bliss.

This was walking straight into a nightmare.

"*Not you, Finn. No.*" The scream tore silently through her. He was going to do it. He was going to take Seren's place.

Finn sucked in another breath and looked at Abby again. "Just… take care of 'em all, dove? I'm sorry for this. Forgive me, okay?" Finn asked with a broken chuckle.

Bound, Abby only nodded as she fell to pieces, held up entirely by Seren's magic. She'd come to the same cruel realization.

Then Finn turned back to a stunned Seren.

"Make it worth something." His voice dropped low. "I got the magic. I already know you're willin' to give the rest. Gwyn, transfer it. You were reborn for it, boy. That and takin' care of my family…"

Esme's heart froze as the full picture became clear. Finn was offering his life and his magic, the essence of who he was. Seren's sacrifice was supposed to complete the spell while Finn's spark would anchor it. While Gwyn would be the conduit. He was the only one who could guide the magic between life and death. For this, between sacrifice and salvation for them all.

Now Finn was set on reversing his and Seren's roles.

Somewhere between Finn's newfound protective zeal for his family and Seren's cryptic warnings about more needing to be done, this plan had begun to develop. And maybe if Esme had been less concerned with where Seren was leading her... she would've seen this coming.

Seren shifted, almost as if she was about to do something to stop this insanity. But her broken gaze told Esme that she'd see it done no matter what. Even if she had to pour herself into it as well.

Finn's voice rang out, soft and fond. "I got to be a member of the B-team. Let me be the hero this time."

Finn glanced at the dagger in his hand and didn't hesitate. The same hands that had once shoved a half-eaten chocolate chip cookie into Esme's mouth because "you're scary when hungry" cut off their vision of him. But she knew what horror was happening behind that illusory veil of compassion.

Seren finally made her move. Their conjured bindings evaporated instantly.

The bond Esme had shared with Finn—the pranks, the arguments, the teasing... She remembered the first time he'd fooled her into a game of tricks and mischief. He'd fallen off her dresser, laughing so hard he was crying at the face she'd given him after calling him "super creepy." Gods, he always made her laugh, even when she wanted to kill him.

All the ups and down, the laughter and shared sadness, condensed into the single, grotesque second when a drop of something red hit the salt circle below the illusion.

Esme almost moved. She almost reached for him. But her magic felt too wild, too out of control to help save a dying man. Like Finn had said, she was a "batterin' ram." She would only hurt more than she saved.

But Miles was already moving, sprinting, trying to make it there in time.

The sound that came out of Abby was half a word, half a scream of agony. Gwyn growled. Seren's mouth parted, but no words came.

But there was a flare of light. The siphoning blade was already doing its work, pulling from him. For creatures whose very essence was made of magic, like leprechauns, having their magic drained was especially dangerous.

Miles lunged, hands flaring with golden light.

But another traitorous inky tendril shot up and stopped him before his feet could so much as touch the salt line.

He was breathing hard. The look of defeat on Miles' face broke Esme's heart for a second time in as many seconds.

Finn, gods, no. Finn. They'd just lost Jacob to a selfless sacrifice. They couldn't lose Finn too.

"You always were a hero," Abby choked out between sobs. Esme finally saw that she had collapsed onto the ground.

The sound that tore from Abby after that was the raw, wordless cry of a creature with no language left for pain. Her hands clawed at her own thighs, as if she could rip out the agony and fling it at the circle.

Gwyn flinched like he'd heard that sound from her before. Maybe he had; maybe he had in the dark when Abby relived the emotional torture she'd endured in saving them all from Leon.

Seren didn't move, but Esme could see the storm breaking behind those impossibly old eyes. It was like she'd just watched her entire life shatter to pieces in front of her. If this was the ending she'd been planning for more than a thousand years, maybe she had.

Seren finally whispered, "We cannot undo his choice. We must honor it and not allow him to suffer." Her voice cracked. "I will share in his sacrifice to ensure its success."

Esme couldn't breathe. She couldn't look away. Miles slammed his fists against the tentacles, weeping openly.

Then something in Seren broke, and a tear that gleamed like crystal flowed down her cheek.

Seren, Morgan le Fay, the woman who had faced down demigods and kings, staggered forward. The tears in her eyes weren't only grief but also rage—at fate, at Finn's stubbornness, at the cruel joke of a world that would let him love them enough to do this.

With a heavy breath, Seren stepped carefully into the circle. Like a conductor performing her final masterpiece, Seren was trembling when her hands lifted. The air sang as magic, miraculously visible and shining, flowed out of her like mist from ice, pouring into the runes at her feet. The wards flared with a rhythm of something that Esme instinctively knew was held deep within the earth.

Esme's breath caught. Seren was giving so much of herself that Esme could feel it quivering in the air around them.

Then Gwyn, his hands shaking, stepped into the circle as well. His face was red and tear-stained, but his eyes never strayed from Finn. The air around him seemed to darken as he crouched. Cold rolled off him in waves, a midnight tide rising to claim the edge of Finn's life.

Esme still couldn't see Finn. But she saw the shadows that directed the light, which poured from the illusion around Finn to flood the circle in warm golden-white arcs. Flaring brighter, Seren's magic joined with Finn's. The runes underfoot erupted in light once again.

Then, all at once, like a star going supernova, the bright magic surged upward in a blinding flash. Esme thought she saw the two threads twine together in the heart of that light—a trickster's fire and a sorceress's shadows—before Gwyn bound them as one.

For just an instant, through the flare of light, Esme swore she heard his familiar, impossible laughter. Grief must have made her imagine it. Yet deep in her chest, she felt a tug, a final whisper of the trickster's magic before it disappeared.

Power arced through the room. But to Esme, it was a lightning storm made of memory and grief. The magic sang a note so pure it vibrated in Esme's teeth, in the hollow of her lungs, down to the marrow of her bones. The warehouse walls vibrated, not from impact, but from the magical weight of a sacrifice so complete it righted the balance of magic's scales.

Esme dropped to her knees without realizing it. She'd somehow conjured claws, like Oatmeal's, like the shadowcat Finn had taught her to create.

Esme curled her claws deep into the concrete. Trying to hold on, maybe. Or simply venting the helpless desperation she felt.

When she looked up, Finn had completely disappeared like he'd never been there at all. Only Seren and Gwyn remained in the circle. Still crouched, Gwyn teetered to the side and finally crumpled.

Beside him, Seren collapsed, utterly spent, her face pale and lips bloodless. The price she'd paid had taken a heavy toll on her trembling body. She had given more than Esme thought any one person could. And yet it was Finn who was gone, not her.

Esme had spent her life rebelling. But this was a fight she couldn't win, a loss no amount of fury could undo. Finn had won their long-running game of tricks and mischief in the worst way that mattered: by making his death a *gift*.

Esme would never forget the moment Fionn, Finn, leprechaun, rogue, and heart of their mad little found family, chose to die. Not because he had to, but because he wanted someone else to live.

Finn had unlocked who she was in a way no one else had. He'd taught her not to fear her emotions but to harness them, that they made her part of who she was.

Jacob had fostered her independence and never spurned her shortcomings.

Both had given up everything for the people they loved, for the future.

After two sacrifices made not out of obligation but choice—Esme understood the terrible power of love unbound by fear. Jacob had laid the foundation. Finn had sealed it in fire and blood.

Some battles weren't meant to be won with fists or force, but with the quiet, unbearable weight of devotion. Some were only won by loving enough; others by loving enough to let go.

CHAPTER FORTY-SIX

A TITAN'S FUNERAL

Miles

Miles half expected the clouds to rumble their grief for Jacob, for the sky to split open and throw lightning in a final salute. But the sky held back, gray and too gentle. Maybe the sky was also fighting to hold itself together, to not fall apart. Maybe the rain held off out of respect.

To those closest to him, Jacob's funeral *mattered* in a way that the crowds gathered for it could never understand. His funeral wasn't a funeral in any intimate sense of the word. Not for Miles. Not for Esme. Not for the people who had actually lost the man who had seemed bigger than life.

It was politics in its stiffest, most international form, with members of the Assembly flying in from cities across the world. Their pristine black coats whispered of status and restraint. Even their condolences were curated. They were more policy than sympathy, with every phrase smoothed to perfection.

He should have expected nothing less than a global production for Jacob Spencer—merchant magnate, Bastion, and the closest thing Seattle's magical community had to a patriarch. Seren moved among the crowd like a queen, with her grief tucked beneath a veneer of regal composure.

Miles stood rigidly beside Esme near the front, half listening to a speech about Jacob's legacy. She'd barely spoken since they'd arrived, but she wore her engagement ring proudly. Considering all that had happened... that was no small thing.

The speaker rambled on about how Jacob had "shaped magical infrastructure" and "fostered cross-continental alliances." All of that was true. But the speaker didn't know Jacob's sharp intelligence. They didn't know about the quiet legacy he'd left behind. About his dry wit and fierce protectiveness. They didn't know that he'd died to protect *them*.

Miles could hear Jacob's voice in the back of his mind. Dry and amused, he would subtly mock the eulogy's pomp with a single raised brow. It was a good thing his staff had been destroyed. Several people had mentioned that it would have been fitting for Jacob to be buried with it. They meant well, but they didn't know that it had symbolized his mistakes to him.

His final resting place deserved to be unburdened by his past; a clean slate was the least they could do after such bravery.

When Josiah stood to deliver his speech, Esme didn't cry quietly. She sobbed. Her grief surged again, and like a river, it became harder to stop than to unleash. He didn't know what hurt more—her sobs or the fact that he couldn't do anything to stop them.

Beside Esme, Abby buried her silent, tearful sobs into Gwyn's trembling shoulders. Something caught in Miles' throat at the sight of Gwyn's tears. Seeing someone that strong break—how could it *not* undo him?

He had pledged an oath to protect the people surrounding him. But how could he protect someone like Jacob from death, or someone like Finn from his own choices?

Miles looked away, focusing on the eulogy, on the way the light caught the silver in Jacob's portrait beside the casket. He focused on the smooth texture of Esme's hand as a stabilizing force against his own roiling emotions.

Jacob would have hated this. Though Jacob would have gone through every step of the day with his head held high. The thought comforted Miles. Jacob had loathed pomp almost as much as he'd loathed tea gone cold.

Miles didn't cry in public. Not usually. But something in him cracked when Esme leaned against him mid-eulogy and whispered, "He would've liked Josiah's speech and bitched about the rest."

He laughed. It was soft, a breath more than a sound. And then the tears came quietly, mostly hidden, but exactly the release he'd needed.

The service ended, and the crowd dispersed in hushed clusters. They left the cemetery under a slate-gray sky. The car ride to the reception was hushed, filled with Jacob's absence and the echoes of a life lived remarkably.

The hotel lobby smelled like roses, lilies, candle wax, and good British food. Seren waited outside the hall, her posture ramrod straight, her expression unsettlingly calm. Her stillness unsettled him. It was the kind that followed major upheavals like earthquakes or tsunamis when survivors had accepted the death toll but hadn't yet figured out how to keep living.

Miles didn't approach her right away. Yet his eyes didn't leave hers as he let Esme and the others file into the room for the reception. For a couple of breaths, he stood silently beside Seren, observing her pointedly ignore him before he spoke.

"So, you'll be going back to Paris?" he asked eventually.

Seren lowered her gaze to her perfectly polished black snakeskin pumps. "No."

"Good." He folded his hands, one flesh, one metal, behind his back. "Because I've got questions. Starting with what you're going to do now."

Her demure makeup, the understated jewelry, all of it only emphasized how tightly she was wound beneath them. The haunted look in her eyes, how withdrawn she'd been, told Miles—from his own personal experience—that she was battling survivor's guilt. Except she was barely managing to stay in the fight.

It was times like these when compassion was inconvenient. He wanted a clear-cut view of his feelings about her. But loss was the universal minimizer—even the mightiest weren't immune to it.

Seren turned her head and finally met his gaze. It was surreal, sometimes, seeing the woman behind the legend, the woman who looked so much like his fiancée but had no blood relation.

"I don't know yet," was all that she said.

"Shitty answer," he said quietly. He studied her profile, noting the tightness around her eyes and the way her fingers flexed at her sides. "That's not good enough. You owe Jacob, Finn, more than this. Esme too. Yourself most of all."

Seren's mouth quirked into something that wasn't quite a smile. "Excuse me?"

"I said, it's not good enough." Miles leaned closer, keeping his voice low. "You don't get to stand here, in the wreckage of everything Jacob tried to hold together, and shrug. Not after what you pulled at the meeting, plus the bloody ritual. Since then, you've completely disappeared."

He didn't hide the edge in his voice.

She straightened her spine. "I was recovering."

"Recover faster," he snapped. He caught himself and softened. "You came back because you feel guilty. That's not a reason to stay."

Seren flinched, then her voice turned to ice. "You think I'm here out of obligation?"

"Aren't you?" Miles asked. "Guilt makes people do all kinds of noble shite. But it doesn't rebuild communities, Seren. It doesn't heal people. So... Are you here because it hurts to leave, or because it matters if you stay?"

For a long moment, she didn't answer. Finally, she sighed. "I want to stay... If they'll have me."

The *they* part of that sentence probably meant Esme more than anyone else, but he wouldn't comment on it. Miles nodded once, neutral. He didn't let her off the hook yet. "You think they won't?"

"I told the closed board months ago I didn't want power. Now that Jacob's gone..." She trailed off. Her jaw clenched. "They'll want me to take the reins. At least until they can name one of their own."

"What you just said sounds less like a heartfelt desire and more like a chore you feel obligated to complete."

Her next breath was too sharp to be steady. Seren looked away, into the distance beyond the wooden doors. "Damn it all... Their sacrifices can't be wasted! I want to stay because this city, these people, deserve stability. I can unify the community. The fractured lines between groups, the infighting, the distrust"—her voice grew tighter—"if I can fix even part of that, I have to try."

Seren's voice gentled. "Transferring magic into fortifying the prisons seems to have weakened me. That lack has made some things... clearer. I still have power, but I now understand the necessity of teamwork."

Though she didn't seem thrilled about her setback, her swift realization that collaboration was the best way forward was encouraging.

"That's a better answer," he said finally. "People will follow you. Especially if you show up with open hands instead of fire blazing in one palm. That's not weakness; that's growth."

He'd harbored doubts about Nudd's silence regarding her all this time. But now he understood that, all along, Seren had always been the greatest danger to herself.

She inclined her head. "And what if I do that? What if I stay, lead, try to repair what's broken... Is that enough for you?"

His eyebrows rose. "For me?"

"You have an important position here," Seren said, like it explained everything. "And you're one of the only people in this city who doesn't fear me or need me."

And I'm Esme's fiancé, he thought, filling in the gap she so clearly wasn't ready to say aloud.

He thought about that for a moment. "I support what you're doing—politically and practically. It's right."

Seren exhaled, suddenly fascinated by her manicure. Miles frowned and crossed his arms. Silence could often say more than words.

He waited until she seemed ready to walk away.

"Don't make the assumption that this is going to be easy."

Seren stiffened.

"We know what you were trying to do, but that doesn't mean it doesn't fucking hurt." He let the anger simmer in his voice, just enough to see her flinch. She needed to suffer a bit for all the things she'd done. She deserved the sting, if not the scar. But she wasn't beyond redemption.

With a sigh, Miles relented. "Stick around long enough and Esme will adopt you like her newest stray. Just... prepare to be bitten first. Repeatedly."

Seren exhaled a huff of air that almost passed for a nervous laugh.

A grin split Miles' face. It was nice to smile, even if it was because he was making Morgan le Fay sweat. "Show up. Keep trying. Esme always cracks when she sees the good in people."

That earned him a real smile in response. "In that respect, she takes after Jacob."

"She does," he said. And gods, it hurt. He swallowed the burn behind his eyes and looked away for a moment.

"For what it's worth... Welcome home, Seren." Miles gave one definitive nod. "Now let's get inside before Esme decides to hunt us down for avoiding her."

They walked in together, two figures drawn in the wake of mourning but determined to move forward. They'd never move past the grief of the people they'd lost, but they could move through it together.

There would still be malevolents to hunt. Seren had said that the magic imprisoning them was not foolproof. While a small number might still break out, the rate of escapes would significantly decrease. His skills were still needed, but he might, at last, be able to share a life with Esme free from the recurring terror of losing her to another monster.

Nudd was still there in the back of his mind. But something about his presence felt more content, less restless, and more willing to fade into the background.

He had a fiancée to hold, people to protect, and—for the first time in too long—a life to finally, truly live.

CHAPTER FORTY-SEVEN

AN IRISH GOODBYE

Abby

Abby hesitated, hand resting on the carved wood of the arched front door set into the mossy base of a tree. She could feel the echo of his laughter in the air, remember his smile.

Esme pressed a gentle hand to her back. "You okay?"

"No," Abby said honestly. "But we're here."

Ready now, she swung the door open to reveal a house that shouldn't have fit into the space allotted to it. Cob walls, whitewashed and smooth, curved upward into heavy wooden beams. The interior was part rustic charm, part magpie's hoard. He even had a teetering stack of very stolen casino chips on a small side table. Everything smelled faintly of clove and peat smoke.

Finn's house was exactly as he'd left it—like he might step around the corner with a bottle of whiskey and enough glasses for everyone to enjoy a sip any second. Except the fireplace was cold and dark. That felt wrong. A leprechaun with the powers of an ifrit wouldn't have a stone-cold hearth.

Gwyn stepped ahead of her without a word. He crouched beside the stones and pulled two cut logs into the space. A smooth stream of fire leaped from his palm, and flames roared to life, casting the room in flickering gold.

Finn's fire hadn't needed fuel. Just like Finn hadn't needed a reason to help them. His obligations hadn't required him to become their friend. It hadn't required him to protect them, to bring so much delight into their lives. He'd done all of it for the sheer, unadulterated joy of it all.

They stood in silence for a while, watching the soft golden light drench the interior in memories of happy times. The mood shifted when the front door creaked again. Colin and Will arrived, dragging the chaos of the living in with them.

Colin took in the room with a wary eye.

Will let out a low whistle. "Damn. This place is like... a fairy tale cabin had a baby with a pawn shop."

It was their first time being here.

Abby gave a soft snort. "That's... weirdly accurate."

Esme pulled them farther inside. Only she and Abby managed to squeeze into Finn's undersized chairs. Everyone else sprawled awkwardly wherever they could. Will and Colin sat on Finn's bed while Gwyn and Miles sat on the floor.

Colin blinked at a particularly offensive golden statue of a winking goat. "You said it was going to be story time about dear old grandpa and *more*, which was very suspicious, by the way. So, what's up?"

Abby and Gwyn shared a look. It was time they knew the truth—all of it.

"We *definitely* need beverages for this," Esme said, hopping up from her chair to raid Finn's stores.

They told Colin and Will everything, from the beginning. About Miles' magic and his halo. How Gwyn had come to the United States hoping to get revenge on his father. The truth behind Leon's and Sylas' demise. As gently and concisely as possible about their reincarnations. They explained how the magic holding the malevolent prisons together had been failing. About the sacrifices that now ensured everyone's safety.

Colin just stared at her. "Wait. Back up. My sister is who now?"

"Creiddylad," Abby said, trying not to wince. "I mean, technically. But I'm still me. Just with extra baggage and trauma."

Colin blinked again. "Okay. And Gwyn is.... *was...?*"

"A psychopomp," Esme offered helpfully, "and sort of Miles' spirit's son. But they're more like disagreeable brothers now."

Will asked, "Miles is some ancient Welsh king and Esme is a friggin' demon warrior princess?"

"Don't forget that Seren is Morgan le actual-fucking-Fay," Esme added with a wink.

"Sure, *sure,* that tracks," Will said, nodding like someone who'd finally solved a riddle. "I knew y'all were hiding something. Too much drama. Too many near-death experiences. That's not normal friendship chaos. That's, like, some epic fantasy nonsense. Voodoo gods and magical trauma included."

"Voodoo?" Miles muttered.

"I'm speaking metaphorically, Doctor Smartypants," Will shot back. "Just sayin'. Your head glows and you throw up shields. I've read comics. Y'all are the 'chosen one' squad."

Abby laughed, and something inside her cracked. The painful release let in a rush of air, and she could breathe for the first time in months.

"And we're the sidekicks." A crooked grin stretched across Will's face as he reached a hand over to mess up Colin's blond hair.

Esme snorted into her whiskey. Miles pinched the bridge of his nose, but Abby saw the smile tugging at his lips.

It was nice to have more people to share the secret with, people who accepted and loved her regardless of her insane backstory.

"To Finn," Gwyn said, finally breaking his silence as he raised his glass. Gwyn giving a toast was so unusual that everyone leaned in to hear it. "He represented the best of us." His voice was quiet, but it didn't need to be loud. The grief in it filled the room.

Everyone joined in. The fire cracked louder, a sudden spark dancing toward the ceiling. For just a moment, Abby thought she heard a laugh in it. With how bizarre their lives had become, maybe it hadn't been her imagination.

"To Finn," they chorused, glasses raised. Abby lifted hers, too, but took a mere sip.

Esme's eyes narrowed, but Abby resolutely ignored the scrutiny.

They shared stories of Finn's escapades, the sounds of their laughter filling the room, until Abby noticed a single folded sheet of paper, almost hidden amongst the other items on Finn's desk. She walked to it, as if pulled there by a string. She snatched it up, fingers trembling.

It was addressed in his distinct scribble. She turned to the others. "He left us a letter."

She'd suspected he'd been planning his grand finale, but seeing this was proof.

She opened it, heart hammering, and began to read, "'If you're reading this, I'm dead. What a tragedy, eh? Don't mope. Throw a party. Drink the good whiskey (under the floorboards, because SOME PEOPLE can't be trusted).'"

Will gave a choked laugh, and Esme began tapping the floorboards to locate the bottle. Abby kept reading, "'Abigail, congratulations, lass. You've been glowin' like a pixie in love for weeks. If it's a boy, name him after me?'"

"I knew it!" Esme shrieked, standing up so fast the whiskey she hadn't put down in her search sloshed. The hug crushed the air from Abby's lungs.

Miles was next, his arms wrapping around them both, his prosthetic hand warm against her back. "Should've known when you cried at that puppy video."

Colin's jaw dropped. "Abby, you're...?"

"Pregnant," Abby admitted, laughing through the tears now welling up. "The imp apparently figured it out before I did."

Will whooped, slapping Colin's shoulder. "Told you they've been extra mushy!"

Gwyn was beaming, his usual grimness dissolving into purest, radiant pride. It made her heart hurt just looking at him. When she'd told him, he'd cried, clutching her belly, whispering promises to the unborn child as if it could already understand.

Esme tackled him next, then Miles, then Colin, who grumbled but hugged back fiercely, and even Will, who pretended to enjoy the hug far too much.

She hadn't even known how badly she'd wanted to share this. But now, seeing the joy on their faces, the way Gwyn lit up, it hit her like a wave: this baby already had a huge family.

When the chaos settled, Abby wiped her eyes, cleared her throat, and kept reading, "'Gwyn, you lucky bastard. Take care of my family or I'll haunt you for real.'"

Will snorted. "Please haunt me. That ghost would be a riot."

"'Esme, teach the kid to pick locks and keep being the best friend you've always been.'"

Esme sniffled loudly. "Gods damnit, Finn."

"'Miles, don't let all the babes you lot are going to produce grow up too proper. Keep 'em safe. Colin, I'm proud of the man you've become. I see a true leader in my grandson emerging.'"

Colin covered his mouth with his hand, blinking fast.

"'Will, you're truly a good lad. Take care of my grandson. He can have the wrong kind of stick up his arse sometimes. Give him some of your cheer when he needs it.'"

Will wiped his eyes. "Rude but also accurate."

"'About Jacob. He did what he thought was best, just like me. Forgive him for it, and please, please, forgive me too.'"

Abby's voice faltered, but she kept going because he'd love a dramatic production of his final letter.

"'Live big, all of you. Be brave enough to be fools and kind enough to be the heroes I know you are. That's what I did, and it worked out pretty damn well for me.'"

When she finished, the room was silent. No one said a word because they were too busy crying.

With trembling fingers, Abby carefully folded the note, its crisp paper whispering softly as she laid it reverently back on the desk.

The fire crackled, warm and golden. And, for a moment, it felt like Finn was there, toasting along with them.

Gwyn

In his cramped studio apartment, Gwyn's bed felt smaller than ever tonight, filled with the warmth he'd always thought would forever be denied him. Abby was nestled against him, her bright hair spilling across his collarbone. At the foot of the bed sprawled Cerys, more than two hundred pounds of gwyllgi muscle, snoring contentedly and taking up half the bed.

Gwyn lay with one arm draped protectively over Abby's middle, fingers brushing the slight swell of new life that still seemed impossible to him. He'd woken up in an unfamiliar world, stripped of his divinity and memory, driven only by a burning, bitter desire to hunt down his supposed betrayer. At first, he had moved through the modern world like a feral thing, clinging to old grudges, despising the ignorance of mages who had forgotten the ruthlessness power had once demanded. He'd survived on loaded dice and an ironclad promise to himself that he would find Nudd and exact the justice that centuries in darkness had denied him.

Yet fate had tangled him in lives he'd never meant to touch. Abby's understanding and love had shattered all of his barriers, Esme's warmth had slipped past his armor before he'd realized it, and Miles—infuriating, reckless and yet honorable Miles—had forced him to see not a jailer but a man carrying a burden as heavy as his own. Battles fought side by side, secrets confessed in the hush of exhaustion, and the revelation of Llefelys' treachery had chipped away at the vengeance and distrust he'd kept for far too long within his heart.

In place of retribution and fury, Gwyn now chose protection and truth. His solitude had been replaced by trust, at first hesitant, now something he'd stake his life on.

As he lay beside Abby or traded barbed words with Miles that no longer tasted of poison, he knew he was no longer the hunter who had risen from his grave. He was Gwyn Newman now, a man who could love and be loved in return, who had found freedom not in revenge but in surrendering to the simple, dangerous mercy of *belonging*. His past would always haunt him. He still had to face down what being a necromancer in the modern world meant. But he didn't have to do it alone.

Now he would burn the world to keep safe the woman in his arms, their child, and his new friends, too. He was breathless, in disbelief at being allowed to hold something so tender, to be in love, to have a brother in Miles, a sister in Esme.

Gwyn had spent more than a millennium clinging to a cold future of revenge. Now, he kneeled at the feet of something far rarer—*peace*.

"Cariad," he murmured, voice rough with the weight of truths he'd locked behind pride for too long. "I've... been seeing that doctor you suggested."

She stirred, lifting her head slightly. Yet he pressed on before his courage failed him. "He believes the medicine you mentioned might work to stabilize my moods."

He gave a huff of dry laughter. "I still do not understand *mood disorders*. But I wish to try. For you. For them." His hand traced the tiny curve of her belly with a gentle reverence, then he leaned down, his lips brushing her hairline softly.

Abby's answering sigh warmed his neck. "Thank you. Truly. We'll take it one day at a time, okay? No need to solve everything right now. We still have to tell Miles and Esme about your halo. Think we should celebrate like you used to back in the day?"

"*'Back in the day.'* You make me sound elderly."

She let out a delighted giggle at his frown. "I mean... we have no idea how old you are. You might be!"

"We can tell them soon," he breathed, contentment stirring in his chest where the rancid cold had once lived. "Though I do not relish the prospect of Miles urging me to submit to testing on that front. Probably by Seren. What are they going to do? Bring in a pile of corpses for me to animate?"

"Been there, done that," Abby affirmed. "You're the best, you know that?" She surprised him with a kiss on the nose, and he pulled her in close again to feel her warmth.

He let the quiet stretch for a moment, punctuated only by Cerys' soft wheeze. "Speaking of becoming the man you deserve..." He hesitated, then pushed on. "We should find a bigger place to live."

Abby's low chuckle resonated through his ribs. "Yeah... well, Finn thought of that, too. The imp left me a brand-new stock portfolio and bank account. How he even got all that money into a bank.... I don't know. He left a note about it in my closet of all places..."

She laughed again, then abruptly turned serious. "Finn must have been planning his sacrifice for weeks. He did the same for Colin, apparently. It's... more than enough for a house. For our 'growing family,' as he put it."

That trickster. Finn's cunning, even after death, had created a safer, easier future for them. He pondered the number of Finn's last days dedicated to this, prioritizing their protection over enjoying what little was left of his time on earth. Gwyn's throat tightened. "If you'll have me, cariad... I'd like to live there with you. Properly. To be a father and partner worthy of you both."

She playfully nudged him, feigning annoyance. "Gwyn, I want you stuck with me forever, you daft man."

A wry laugh escaped him. "Well, I ensured that with my bargain with Arawn, didn't I?"

She adjusted until her eyes met his in the dim light. "Apparently, I chose the same fate. But I'd do it again. A thousand times if it meant this." She traced the side of his jaw with her fingertip. "Do you think Arawn's finished meddling? Or do we get to be boring mortals until we die of old age?"

Gwyn blew out a breath, brushing her temple with his lips. "I do not know, love. I wonder—should we..." His tongue stumbled over all he'd never imagined saying. "I have so little to give. My hunting means little now that the malevolents will be fewer. I can barely navigate a grocery store. Jacob left me a 'nest egg'—he called it that—so we won't starve. Maybe the Assembly has work for a... a *relic* like me..."

He recognized his discourse was rambling when he truly wanted to know one thing. "Cariad... will you marry me?"

Abby stiffened. She was quiet too long. His chest ached with dread. Had he misread her again? Had he asked too soon?

He couldn't breathe. Every second of her silence was agony.

She let out a low, dramatic groan. He had erred in asking her so soon. He should have waited... His heart plummeted into his gut like it was falling off a cliff into the bottomless ocean.

Pulling back, he saw her frown and felt the icy grip of panic constrict his chest.

She burst out laughing, a joyous sound that echoed through the room, her eyes shining with mischief and love. Cerys perked up, saw no food or enemies around, then abruptly went back to dozing.

"This... this is exactly like your love confession! We really need to rehearse these big moments, Gwyn. Where are the flowery words? The poetry? The tears?"

How could he have missed the hints of her leprechaun heritage for all these months? It didn't matter. He loved everything about her.

Gwyn opened his mouth to speak, but the words were silenced by a tender kiss. First a teasing brush of lips, then a kiss that stole his breath away, deepening until neither could breathe. When she pulled back, a dazzling grin illuminated her face. "The answer is 'yes,' you impossible man. But you're redoing that proposal. Properly with flowers, a speech, the works. Understood?"

Gwyn sank his forehead to hers, a low, bright laugh rumbling in his chest. A profound sense of fulfillment, a feeling he'd never known in his two lives, settled deep into his bones. "As you wish, my heart. Anything, as you wish."

Her gentle chuckle made his heart soar all over again.

Chapter Forty-Eight

ONE LAST PARTY

Esme

The Sanctuary of Spirits pulsed with laughter, music, and the warm glow of fairy lights strung high in the rafters. It still smelled of spilled beer and bittersweet memories, but tonight, everything felt *just right*.

Those leaving the reception all seemed lighter than when they'd first come in. Even Maureen had left with laughter on her lips, singing off-key with Eddie on her arm. Once, she'd barely managed a kind word for Esme. Tonight, she'd toasted her without a trace of venom. If that wasn't magic, Esme didn't know what was.

Katia had exited with Beatrice in tow, off to make their own magic. Even the perpetual curmudgeons—Carloff, Ivar, and Stefan—had left with smiles on their faces.

Now, only the wedding party remained because Esme had refused to miss a single second of her own joy. The bar was hers now—to shape, to guard, to fill with memories and magic.

It wasn't just a name. The Sanctuary of Spirits was for all the ghosts they carried, for every soul who'd ever needed a second chance, a place to belong, or just one night of peace. It would be a haven for anyone like her, human and nonhuman alike. She would guard that peace with everything she had. Anyone who needed a little magic to keep going would be welcome.

With a practiced hand, she poured hydrating mocktails behind the bar, the silk of her wedding dress brushing against the glass washer Jacob had purchased to make her happy so many months before. The number of toasts that evening would have swelled Finn's chest with pride, while the sight of so much liquor being guzzled would have caused Jacob's and Sylas' faces to frown in reluctant acceptance.

Finn had made her and Abby's wedding dresses long before he was gone. Just like the ones from the Solstice Gala, they were stunning and full of sentiment. They'd found the dresses in Finn's closet, each with their names attached and numbers they could call if they needed adjustments when the time came.

Jacob must have been thinking ahead, too. When Esme invited Maureen to the wedding, Maureen had gone digging through every drawer for the papers Jacob had left her. Hidden inside was a letter, along with two heirloom tiaras from his grandmother's collection from the 1800s.

Esme wore hers now, all gold, diamonds, and a legacy heavy enough to feel like a blessing. A crown from the past, blessing her future. Abby didn't know about hers yet. Maureen was saving that surprise for her and Gwyn's wedding in a few months.

Esme leaned against the polished oak of the bar, watching her husband carry drinks to Abby, who had planted herself in a chair hours ago. Her baby bump was front and center, and her feet were luxuriating in Will's lap. Colin was flapping a napkin dramatically in front of her face.

"Stop it." Abby laughed. "I'm not going into labor from too much cake."

"You might," Will said, massaging her calves. "There's no room left in you. You're like an overstuffed empanada about to burst. *Delicious*."

"Gross! I will melt your shoes with my hot hands," Abby growled. Then she winced and added, "If I could reach them."

Colin leaned over and kissed her cheek. "Only Will would flirt and insult you in the same sentence."

"I'm multi-talented," Will said proudly.

Miles smiled at Esme and winked. His suit jacket had been abandoned hours ago, tie long gone, his sleeves rolled up to reveal the metal of his prosthesis.

Some things would never be whole again. Safety had come at a high price. The survivors carried the marks of trauma, some seen, some unseen. They had each other to lean on, and that was no small thing.

Miles sent her a smoldering look across the bar. He was so handsome and *hers*. The perfect man to build a life with.

"Watch out, Golden Daddy," Will called from across the bar, raising his glass. "You keep lookin' at her like that, and we're gonna need a second baby shower soon."

Colin choked on his beer. "Do not call him that."

"What? It's accurate!"

Esme laughed, shooting Will a glare that held no heat. "This is all your fault, you know."

Will raised his glass. "Damn right it is. Matchmaker of the century."

"You said the next date you set me up on would be 'smokin' hot,'" she murmured.

Will smirked. "And was I wrong?"

Miles, across the bar, caught the tail end and arched an eyebrow at her. Esme just grinned.

The future, where their biggest worry would be whose turn it was to vacuum, *not* whether they'd survive another malevolent attack, was a true possibility now. She could think about buying a new car and redecorating the kitchen, maybe even think about being a mom someday.

Seren, perched elegantly on a barstool with a glass of wine, watched them all with quiet amusement. She'd traded her usual armor of black, black, black and more black for a deep purple dress, her hair loose around her shoulders. When Esme caught her eye, she raised her glass in a silent toast.

Esme smirked, strode over, and plucked the glass from Seren's hand. "Nope. No toast-and-ghost allowed. The bride demands a dance."

Seren's eyebrows shot up. "I don't—"

"*Dancing.*"

Seren laughed and finished the song with her. So far, Seren's promise of uniting the magical community was proving successful. The moment wasn't only about dancing. It was a truce, a beginning, and maybe even a welcome home.

Their relationship was healing, but it wasn't without its challenges. Esme saw signs of hope for them, and that, like having others to lean on when times got tough, was going to make the future better.

She and Seren would never be mother and daughter. But mentor and mentee, maybe even friends, were directions they were already headed in.

There had been a time when Esme hadn't thought she'd live to see old age. She'd had no greater purpose, so what had been the point in planning for tomorrow? Considering love had even felt foolish. But now? Now she had a husband, a bar, and a future.

She had something new to protect—joy.

Miles walked up and wrapped his arms around her waist, his breath warm against her ear as he pulled her close. "How's it feel?" he asked softly.

"To be married?"

"To be *done*."

Esme leaned into him. "I don't think we're done. But I think we're... steady. Like maybe we're finally allowed to rest without looking over our shoulders."

He kissed her temple. "Good. I need steady. I need you happy and thriving, Mrs. Goodwin."

"Oh, I like the sound of that, Mr. Goodwin." They'd likely kissed fifty times already that day, but the one they shared next remained just as meaningful.

They looked out over the room. Seren was clinking glasses with Will. Gwyn was leaning back and unabashedly smiling. Abby was snorting with laughter, even as she tried to get off the couch and failed, with a curse. Colin was filming the whole thing on his phone, pretending he wouldn't cry watching it later and show his niece the video years down the road.

A brush of magic tugged at the edges of Esme's awareness, so faint she almost dismissed it as her imagination. It was the smell of aged whiskey and the sound of velvet-soled shoes sneaking across squeaky floorboards.

Her chest tightened in remembered grief, reaching her even in this moment of happiness.

The door's magic buzzed, announcing the late arrival or, more likely, return of another guest. But when her gaze landed on the hidden entrance, there he was.

Still bold, still swaggering, but burning less brightly. His magic was a candle's flame instead of a roaring fire. His usual mischievous smile was there, even if he looked as though he'd lost ten pounds off his already small frame.

Esme's hand flew to her mouth, holding in a cry of disbelief, her heart hammering. Miles followed her gaze, and his eyes widened, disbelief giving way to a relieved grin.

His voice was steady, loud enough to announce himself with all the pomp of the showman he was at heart. "Big man downstairs got tired of my yappin'. Broke a few rules to make me your problem instead."

Abby's face snapped up while Colin lost his footing and fell into the chair beside hers, hard.

"Takes more than dyin' to keep me from good whiskey and cake." Finn beamed. "Promise I won't pull a trick that big on you all ever again."

Finn straightened his jacket as if he hadn't just walked out of the grave, winked at Seren, and swiped the glass of champagne straight out of her hands. He raised it in a mock toast toward the newlyweds.

"Sláinte!" He downed the contents all in one go. Then he headed straight toward Abby and Colin, who were still-gaping in disbelief just like the rest of them.

Miles leaned to whisper into Esme's ear. "Would you change anything about tonight?"

She looked around at the people who had become her world. "No," Esme said quietly, hardly believing her eyes. "Not a single thing. All we ever wanted was a chance at happiness. Now... now we have that."

They'd all lost people they love—too many people. They mourned the loss of past lives, remembered and not. But tonight wasn't about loss or grief.

Tonight was about *love*. About what remained, and what came next. There would always be darkness. But now, Esme had enough helping hands to fight it and just as many friendly ones to hold if the darkness ever came back.

The Sanctuary of Spirits was full of love—messy, earned, chosen love. And the future, bright, sprawling, and delightfully uncertain, stretched out before them.

The End

ABOUT THE AUTHOR

Fantasy author Stella Hope blends myth, romance, and non-stop action in each of her novels. Her favorite stories feature strong female protagonists, their loyal companions, and a generous sprinkle of humor.

Before embracing her passion for writing, Stella embarked on an academic journey that began with bachelor's degrees in Latin and geography. Afterwards, she pursued a graduate degree in environmental science and worked as a scientist for a few years. Stella's love for books eventually led her out of the forest and into the world of libraries, where she had the pleasure of running two public school libraries.

She lives in the PNW with her family, where she occasionally has to leave her writing cave to thwart the neighborhood bear's attempts at pilfering food from her bird feeder. When she's not writing, she's doing her best to stay away from bears, bobcats, deer, and sometimes coyotes during her trail runs and hikes. Her efforts are frequently less successful than one might suppose.

If you'd like to receive sneak previews, updates from Stella, and free content available only to subscribers, please join her mailing list at stellahopeauthor.com